Clarise
Checklist fo

1. **Revamp wardrobe.** Why do conservative when you can do vixen?
2. **Perfect my shimmy.** Letting go of inhibitions at the Gasparilla Festival calls for a bit of expert shaking of "the Robinson Treasures."
3. **Collect some beads.** They're plastic? Who cares? Everybody wants them. And just look how many a good shimmy warrants!
4. **Make a to-do list.** A private list. A personal list. A what-I'd-like-to-do-with-Ethan-if-I-only-had-the-nerve list.
5. **Corporate bonding.** That's what I'm here for, right? Bonding. Corporately. As in bonding, with Ethan. Uh-huh.

HOT PRAISE FOR
GOOD GIRLS DON'T

"A sexy read . . . Pure, fabulous fun!"
— JULIE LETO, **author of**
Dirty Little Secrets

"[A] fun tale . . . Hits the right G-note."
— HARRIET KLAUSNER, TheBestReviews.com

Turn the page for more reviews!

"Wow! This is over the top, and all the fun of a sweet *Sex and the City*! Fans of sizzling romance will have a ride on cloud nine with this one."

—MAGGIE DAVIS, author of
Hustle Sweet Love

"Kelley St. John's sexy debut, *Good Girls Don't*, delivers both heat and heart, making St. John an author to watch!"

—JULIE KENNER, author of
The Givenchy Code and *Carpe Demon*

"Original, fast-paced, sexy, and sassy . . . For all you chick-lit fans out there, heads up! There's a new kid on the block, and she totally rocks."

—RomanceDesigns.com

"One of the most entertaining romances I've read in a while. Kelley St. John brings her characters to life, and readers will find themselves immersed in the story from the first sentence on . . . This is one of those 'Don't Miss' recommend[ations], guaranteed to leave readers wanting more."

—LoveRomances.com

"*Good Girls Don't* shines, and the novel has found a place on my 'permanent keeper' shelf. Kelley St. John will take the romance world by storm!"

—TheRomanceReadersConnection.com

ALSO BY KELLEY ST. JOHN

Good Girls Don't

Real Women Don't Wear Size 2

Kelley St. John

WARNER
FOREVER

NEW YORK   BOSTON

Copyright © 2006 by Kelley St. John
Excerpt from *Good Girls Don't* copyright © 2006 by Kelley St. John
All rights reserved. No part of this book may be reproduced in any form or by any electronic or mechanical means, including information storage and retrieval systems, without permission in writing from the publisher, except by a reviewer who may quote brief passages in a review.

Warner Forever and the Warner Forever logo are trademarks of Time Warner Inc. or an affiliated company. Used under license by Hachette Book Group, which is not affiliated with Time Warner Inc.

Cover design by Diane Luger and Tamaye Perry
Book design by Giorgetta Bell McRee

Warner Books
Hachette Book Group USA
1271 Avenue of the Americas
New York, NY 10020
Visit our Web site at www.HachetteBookGroupUSA.com.

Printed in the United States of America

First Printing: September 2006

10 9 8 7 6 5 4 3 2 1

To my phenomenal agent, Caren Johnson,
who cannot be considered a "Real Woman"
since she does wear size 2!
Thanks for all of the support, Caren.
This one is for you!

Acknowledgments

- Devi Pillai, my amazing and extremely insightful editor.
- Beth de Guzman, for saying she couldn't skip *any* of the scenes in this book.
- Julie Leto, Roxanne St. Claire, Sharon Pinson and Barbara Ferrer for all things Gasparilla.

(While this book is a work of fiction, the Gasparilla Pirate Festival is an authentic celebration that takes place each year in Tampa. To learn more about this unique event, visit www.gasparillapiratefest.com.)

Real Women
Don't Wear
Size 2

Chapter 1

To holidays," Ethan Eubanks said, lifting his Starbucks cup of espresso.

"To holidays," Clarise Robinson agreed, then added, "and sales. Lots and lots of sales." She picked up her peppermint mocha, complete with whipped cream and red sprinkles, and tapped it against his mug. Then she brought the cup to her mouth, laughed, then stuck her tongue in the center of the cream and captured every sprinkle.

"Amazing how you can be such an adult at the store all day, then completely lose every ounce of maturity with a single cup of coffee," he said, smirking. His turquoise eyes surveyed her over the top of his cup, but the tiny crinkles at the corners told Clarise he thought her childish antic was cute. Fine. Let him see her as his cute best friend this afternoon; tonight, he was in for a surprise. A big surprise. She fought the urge to wince, hating when the word "big" slipped into her vocabulary, even if only in her mind. "Curvy"—that was the better word. Ethan was in for a curvy surprise. She smiled.

"Okay, what's that for?" he asked, never failing to read her signals, even if he couldn't read her mind.

"I'm just looking forward to the company Christmas party tonight. I still can't believe you reserved the ballroom at the Civic Center. Nice move, boss."

A triumphant grin spread into his cheeks. "Nice try, Robinson," he countered. "That sneaky smile of yours has nothing to do with the Civic Center and everything to do with what you're wearing to the party. Go on, admit it; you're glad you bought the dress."

She placed her cup on the table and narrowed her eyes. "That thing cost me a week's commission," she argued.

"Don't go trying to pull that on me, Ms. Robinson. I'm betting you made enough to pay for that sexy number today, didn't you? You forget I see you in action on a daily basis. Every other department head wonders how you've had top sales for the past three quarters, but you're not fooling me. I've heard those women come in and ask for you by name, and I see your sales figures, remember? Moreover, I sign your checks. In truth, I'm beginning to think Eubanks Elegant Apparel can't afford you."

She laughed at that. "Right. Can't afford to lose me, you mean. My commissions may be high, but my sales are higher, and face it, Ethan, you can't live without me." She lifted her cup again, took a big sip, and silently wondered if tonight he might actually believe the statement. Would he see her in the slinky red dress and suddenly visualize the woman beyond the top salesperson? Beyond the best friend? Would he see that the girl behaving childishly right now was actually a thirty-year-old female with needs as big as . . . well, as big as her boobs and her behind? Did he ever think of her that way?

She sipped the drink and lowered the cup. Problem was, the whipped cream still towering on the top of the liquid had ended up dotting the end of her nose and causing her best friend-slash-boss-slash-fantasy . . . to laugh.

Clarise whisked away the cream with her napkin, though if she'd been at home, she'd have captured it with her finger and popped the sweetness in her mouth. Unfortunately, she wasn't home, and double unfortunately, she'd just let him catch her in another childish moment. Oh well, it was nearly Christmas. If she was going to behave like a kid, might as well do it at the right season.

"You're cute, Clarise," he said, and took another sip.

"I know," she said, trying her best to sound cocky.

He laughed again then asked the obvious. "You do love the dress, don't you?"

"With a passion," she admitted. "I swear, when you told me to buy it, I thought you'd lost your mind. I mean, generally, a Ben di Lisi isn't intended for a woman with my"—she paused, took a deep breath of air and forced a surge of confidence—"curves."

"I'm not touching that remark since it's bogus. Like you tell our customers at the store, beautiful garments are meant for beautiful women—of all sizes. And trust me; those curves were meant to be flaunted. The customers believe it; why can't you follow your own advice?"

She sipped the spicy drink, let the warm fluid coat her throat while she rehearsed her answer in her mind before uttering the words aloud for Ethan, and whoever was close enough to their table at Starbucks, to hear. "I do play this up at work," she said, then waved a hand down her abundant body. "I work with color, texture, accessories, to emphasize the parts that I want emphasized," she said, and refused to finish with, *"and downplay the parts I don't."* However, she did add, "I just don't generally wear something as—flamboyant—as that dress."

"Exactly," he said. "And I have no complaints whatsoever with the way you dress at the store, conservative, yet classy. Plus, your makeup is always flawless, and your perfected updo gives you the final touches for conveying sophisticated elegance, exactly the image we want to reflect at the store. Shoot, I can tell the women are merely buying all of the pieces so they can achieve your look."

She beamed. "Thanks."

"But," he continued.

"But what?" she questioned, glaring at him. "Don't ruin it now; you're batting a thousand, and I'm feeling pretty good."

One sandy brow lifted. "But you're always covered from head to toe, and in all honesty, if you're going to preach curve flaunting to our customers, you should actually flaunt some yourself, at least once a year." He grinned sneakily, knowing he'd hit a nerve.

Clarise swallowed. "Oh, I have no problem flaunting curves. It just isn't professional to go around showing a bunch of skin during business hours. Besides, it isn't how much you show; it's in the way you present yourself, with attitude and confidence. *That's* what I tell our customers."

"And the right clothes?" Ethan asked, naturally tying this conversation back to Eubanks Elegant Apparel.

"And the right clothes," she agreed.

"Hey, I was pulling your chain, and it appears I did a damn good job," he said, touching a finger to her cheek, which, Clarise could tell by the stinging, was obviously red.

"Look, they put out those cranberry bliss bars you love.

I'll go get us some." He stood and walked toward the food counter, while Clarise watched him move. Lord, he looked good when he walked away. Then again, he looked good when he walked toward her too. Six-foot-plus of tall, sandy-haired, muscled male in a tailored suit and confidence galore was a mighty fine thing to see.

"Pulling my chain," she said to herself. "I knew that." But did he know that the reason it was so easy for him to pull her chain was because of how thoroughly he did pull her chain? As in, revving up her sexual awareness to a fever-high pitch without laying a single finger on her? And what was up with that, anyway? They were friends, plain and simple. So why did Ethan Eubanks find his way into each and every one of her sexual fantasies on a nightly basis? And how in the world could she keep up this friendship without his seeing that her mind, and occasionally her body, crossed over that invisible boundary that separated friends and, well, more than friends? Then again, if the red dress did the trick, maybe tonight, he would look at her in an entirely new light. An entirely new sexy, sassy and vivacious new light.

He got to the counter and turned around. "You want one or two?"

Dang, he knew her well. "You think I could squeeze into that dress if I ate two?" she asked, knowing good and well she'd have ordered two if she were on her own.

He winked. "I'm sure you'll look awesome no matter what you eat. You know that." Then he turned back around and placed the order.

"Yeah, I know that," she said, lying through her teeth.

He returned with two plates, one holding a single cranberry bliss bar, the other with two. After placing them on the table, he left to retrieve a knife, and within seconds, he'd cut the third bar in half and divided it between the two dishes. "One is never quite enough for me," he said.

She grinned. "Me either."

"Okay, so give me the scoop. Who are you going with tonight? I heard a rumor that you and Riley were hooking up," he said. "That true?"

Clarise nearly choked on the first bite. Her eyes watered, but she lifted her cup and managed to get the warm liquid working its way down her throat along with the lodged chunk of cranberry dessert. "Jake Riley?" she questioned. "And me?"

He shrugged. "Maybe I misunderstood, but I don't think so. He probably never got the nerve to ask."

Yeah, right. Jake Riley was the Men's Department head and hot as all get out. While he was friendly toward Clarise, she'd never sensed anything beyond friendship. Then she thought back to this morning, when an elderly gentleman customer had wandered into the Women's Department and asked her opinion on a tie for his black tuxedo. Seems he was taking his wife to a Christmas party and wanted to dazzle her with a new tie. Clarise suggested a pink Tommy Hilfiger with shiny silver pinstripes. It was elegant and classy, and would play beautifully off of the man's wavy white hair and jet-black tuxedo. He had been so impressed with her recommendation that he'd taken Clarise back with him to the Men's Department and asked her to pick out an entire wardrobe that would "Wow" his wife. She did, then she allowed Jake Riley to ring up the sale. It was his department, after all, and she wasn't trying to steal a commission that should have been his. Jake had thanked her, and then he'd smiled, a smile that made Clarise's insides quiver for a second. It'd been warm, and genuine . . . and sexy. Had it been more than a friendly smile?

"Hello," Ethan said, snapping his fingers in front of her face. "Do I take it something *has* happened with Riley?"

Clarise swallowed, then casually waved off the question. "No, of course not. We work together, and we're friends. If he mentioned something about taking me to the party, it was probably only because of that, and in any case, he didn't ask. Besides, I told Jake earlier this week that Rachel, Jesilyn and I had decided to make it a girls' night out. They're meeting me at my place, and we're all riding together."

He shook his head. "Those two are going to get you in trouble eventually, Clarise, and—" He hesitated.

"And?" she questioned.

He grinned broadly. "And I'm betting you'll love every minute of it, whenever you do decide to let yourself go and have fun." He popped a large chunk of cranberry bliss bar in his mouth, swallowed, then raised a crumb-coated finger as he spoke. "You really should consider going to Gasparilla for the corporate bonding getaway this time around."

She'd been wondering when he'd start hitting her up to go on the annual company trip. She'd declined last year. Actually, she'd chickened out yet again and let her younger sister, Babette, take her place, but she'd already decided that this January's trip would find her alongside all of the other department heads in Tampa, drinking, partying, having a good time, and setting her wild side free—assuming she actually had a wild side. God, she hoped she did. Then again, how could she be Babette's sister and not have inherited a bit of her always-willing-and-ready sister's genes? "I am going to Gasparilla," she confirmed.

"Well, it's about time," he said, polishing off the last of his cranberry bars. "You won't regret it. And truthfully, I won't either. I'm looking forward to the show."

"The show?"

"Clarise Robinson, unplugged," he said.

Clarise felt a sassy response was in order, but before she had a chance to speak, a striking black-haired woman in a winter white minidress—a Marc Jacobs, Clarise noticed—stopped beside them with a good inch of tone tan thighs showing between the hem of her skirt and the top of their table. She shifted from one leg to the other, and Clarise was instantly reminded of Sharon Stone's leg switch in *Basic Instinct*. If the woman had been sitting down, they'd probably get the same view.

"Ethan," Winter White gushed in a sexy half whisper, "is that really you?"

He swallowed thickly, then stood and gave her a cordial hug. "Rose, how are you?"

"Just fabulous, darling," she said, then backed up a bit and indicated her outfit, or perhaps it was her body that she was showing off. Both were quite appealing, and the woman knew it. Clarise bit the inside of her cheek and mentally dared Ethan to forget proper introductions. Thank God, he heeded her silent warning.

"Rose, this is Clarise Robinson, my friend and the best department head Eubanks Apparel has ever had. Clarise, this is Rose Tate. She's studying law at Cumberland."

And she's been in your bed, Clarise silently added, noting the way Ms. Tate was practically drooling over Ethan, who didn't seem to notice. Chalk one up for the friend at the table. Clarise smiled. "Nice to meet you, Rose."

Rose tore her attention from Ethan to the table, where two plates and two coffees obviously left her out of the current equation. She looked at Clarise and gave her one of those fake smiles that Babette classified as an I'd-love-to-slap-you-but-I-can't-right-now smile. As far as Clarise knew, she'd never been on the receiving end of one of those smiles. She couldn't wait to tell Babette.

Rose stood frozen for an awkward minute, then turned back to Ethan. "Well, it was good seeing you," she said.

"You too," he managed, but didn't sound nearly as enthusiastic.

"You should call me sometime," she said, then let her smile creep up a little farther and batted long black eyelashes.

Clarise didn't know who was gawking at Ethan more— Rose, or herself—while awaiting his reply. To her immense pleasure, he appeared very uncomfortable and didn't quite know how to respond to the woman's blatant invitation. Clarise, being a true friend, naturally decided to help him out. "Well, it was really nice meeting you, Rose," she said rather loudly.

Rose, snapping back to reality, mumbled a "You too," then delivered one more overly flirty smile to Ethan and, blessedly, walked away.

Ethan dropped back in his seat with apparent relief, picked up his cup and downed the remainder of his espresso.

"Another love casualty?" Clarise teased.

"You know, I think you enjoy talking about my relationship troubles entirely too much," he said. "I actually thought this coffee chat we would attempt to focus on you."

"And then, along came a rose," Clarise said, taking another bite of her cranberry bar. "What'd you do to her?"

"Nothing, we just didn't connect."

"Beyond physically, you mean," Clarise said, knowing Ethan's track record with relationships. Every girl he dated wanted to have his babies. Problem was he kept dating women who simply didn't understand him. They didn't know anything about his business, nothing about his background and nothing about how he and his twin, Jeff, had spent their lives trying to overcome living in Preston Eubanks's notable shadow. They wouldn't understand what an accomplishment it was that both of them had succeeded on their own, elevating Eubanks Elegant Apparel to one of the most distinguished retail clothing chains in the Southeast. Moreover, most of the women never spent enough time with Ethan to realize he was more than an intelligent businessman and good in bed. (Clarise was guessing, of course, on the good in bed part. Guessing . . . and hoping to find out. Someday.) But in any case, how could these women know that he was witty and charming, if they merely tried to get in his bed? Clarise knew all about his wit and his charm, and she hadn't once tried to get in his bed. Dreamed about it, yes. Actually tried to do it? No. Not yet, anyway. And she'd have to be blind not to notice that each and every one of Ethan's former flames had that long, lean thing going. Did he ever consider the shorter, curvier and, consequently, friendlier version?

She felt the blush rise to her cheeks and dropped her face for another bite while she reined in her emotions. Then she decided to lighten the conversation, which was easy to do, given the name of his semi old flame. "So, was this the year of the flower, or what? I didn't even know about Rose, but I do remember the other ones. She makes four of the garden variety, right?"

He glared at her, picked up her cranberry bliss bar and took a bite, then dropped it back on her plate. "There were only three."

"Rose, Iris, Daisy and Verbena," Clarise chirped, clicking off fingers as she recited the names. "Sounds like four to me." Then she licked a bit of icing off the first finger.

"Trust me, I'm trying to forget Verbena."

Clarise laughed. "One of these days, a woman is going to knock you off your feet, and you're not going to know how to handle it."

"God, I hope so," he said. "I'm telling you, this dating business is for the birds. I have no idea why Jeff likes it so much."

"Because your brother is perfectly content with bed-hopping. Some people are," she said, without adding that her sister was definitely one of those people. Babette loved men, period. She wasn't overly promiscuous—or at least Clarise hoped not—but she did admit to truly enjoying a man who knew his way around a woman's body. Of course, Clarise would also enjoy a guy who knew his way around her body, given she should find one who wanted as much body as she had to offer. Oh, and if he looked like Ethan, acted like Ethan, and heck, *was* Ethan, that'd be fine too.

She stood from the table. "I've got to go get ready. Babette is helping me with my hair before Jesilyn and Rachel come over, and I promised Granny Gert I'd pick her up a new hot and steamy romance novel before I head home."

"Don't tell me. Babette went to cosmetology school too," he said sarcastically, totally ignoring the comment about Granny Gert and her need for a steamy sex book. He was used to her zany grandmother's feisty requests.

Clarise waved a dismissive hand. "No, that's one of the few career choices she hasn't made . . . yet. The current degree of choice is Computer Information Systems. She graduates tomorrow, in fact; maybe she'll actually get a job this time. In any case, I've got to get Granny's book and head home. I'll see you tonight," she said, then started to leave but paused at the exit. "You didn't say who you're bringing to the party," she said, trying not to sound *too* interested. "Any flower I know?"

He snorted. "I'm going stag, thank you very much."

"Well, will wonders never cease?" she called, as she left the coffee shop. Then she sauntered into the brisk coolness of Birmingham, Alabama, in December and thanked heaven above for company Christmas parties, red dresses that (she hoped) made abundantly proportioned women look sexy and Ethan Eubanks going stag.

"Personally, I'd recommend throwing it over your head, spraying it with some of this gel freeze and leaving it all wild and crazy. You know, that just-rolled-out-of-bed look that's so hot now," Babette said, standing behind Clarise and running her hands haphazardly through her sister's straight brown hair. "You could wear it like Jennifer Garner on the *Elektra* poster. It's the perfect color and length."

Clarise looked at her reflection in the bathroom mirror, considered Babette's suggestion and declined. "Sorry, sis. I've never worn a dress like this one—ever—and now that I am, I want to do it right. And a gown that fabulous

deserves an updo." Plus, Ethan had called her look "sophisticated elegance." There was no way she wanted to change
that opinion. She lifted her eyes to the side of the mirror,
where she could see the to-die-for Ben di Lisi hanging on
the top of the armoire in her bedroom. "If you don't have
time to do it up for me, I can get Granny Gert to give it a
shot. Plus, Jesilyn and Rachel will be here soon; they could
probably help—" Clarise started, but Babette shook her head.

"It isn't a time thing," she said. "I mean, I've got a date
tonight, but he isn't picking me up for another two hours.
I just thought your hair would look really fabulous down.
You always have it pulled up for work; don't you think
you'd really catch them off guard if you wore it wickedly
wild?" Babette tossed her blond spirals as she spoke, as if
emphasizing the sexiness associated with long, untamed
curls.

Clarise watched her sister's sassy head swing in action.
"You're right. That's a good look, and I'll give it a shot
when I go to Gasparilla next month, but tonight, I want an
updo, and you said you'd give me one."

Babette unbuttoned her red leather blazer, left the bathroom and tossed it on Clarise's bed. She returned wearing
the black silk chemise she'd had on underneath the jacket,
a faded pair of holey jeans and red stiletto boots. Babette's
wardrobe would never be found in Eubanks Elegant
Apparel, but Clarise had to admit that her sister had style.
"Yep, I promised you an updo," she said, "so we'd better
get started." She grinned. "This reminds me of high school
and getting ready for the dances."

Clarise swallowed. In high school, they'd had a lot of
fun getting Babette ready for the dances and proms. The
two of them would giggle through the event day, when

Clarise would steadily do her sister's hair and makeup, then Babette would head to the dance, typically with an older guy from Clarise's class. Clarise, on the other hand, claimed that she didn't enjoy the dances—but both of the girls knew better. She wanted to go, would have loved to go, in fact, but she was never asked. Not too many high school boys were interested in a girl as "healthy" as Clarise. But times had changed. Now it was Babette getting Clarise all decked out for the big event, and Clarise was getting ready to strut her stuff in front of her friends and coworkers . . . and Ethan. She took another look in the mirror. Brown eyes looked back; they weren't spectacular in color, but they were big and almond-shaped. Her hair was straight and also basic brown, but it could be played up with a handful of mousse, a lot of bobby pins, and Babette's talent with a curling iron. Makeup was a breeze; Clarise had always been good at accentuating her eyes and mouth, which, according to Granny Gert, were her best features— next to the Robinson Treasures, aka big boobs, and the Robinson Rump.

"You're going to be gorgeous," Babette said, licking her finger and gingerly tapping the curling iron to check the heat. She was taller than Clarise, and she was skinny, something she'd acquired from their mother's side of the family. Clarise, on the other hand, had gotten the Robinson Treasures that refused to be hidden. They sure enough wouldn't be hiding in that red dress; she just hoped they stayed contained. And on that thought, she laughed out loud.

"What?" Babette asked, spritzing Clarise's hair with gel, then wrapping a section around the hot iron.

"I'm wondering if I'll be able to control these in that

thin fabric," Clarise said, indicating her chest. Her blue satin robe gaped in the front, and at least two inches of cleavage and breast overpowered the open V.

Babette grabbed another chunk of hair, wrapped it on the curling iron and snorted. "If you flash the company, be sure to call me and let me know. I've never pictured you as the flashing type and would love to hear the details when you set those babies free."

Clarise grinned at her sister. "Well, I don't plan on flashing any of them tonight, but if I go to Gasparilla next month, I hear flashing is a surefire way to get plenty of beads." And, if she's lucky, Ethan's attention.

Babette's mouth crooked to the side, but she continued curling hair as she spoke. "You know, Clarise, that corporate bonding thing really isn't all it's cracked up to be."

Clarise's brows drew together. "What do you mean?"

"I mean that I didn't mind going last year when you decided not to make the trip, but it really wasn't all that great. And the people down there are wild, you know. They really do take off their tops and show everything for a few plastic beads—no joke. In fact, the whole place is full of bare chests, lots of alcohol, wild parties, you name it, and I'm not quite sure that it's, you know, your kind of thing."

Clarise blinked. Babette had been trying to talk her into "setting her wild side free" for years, as had Ethan. Now her sister was trying to talk her out of it? At least Ethan had still encouraged her to go. But as much as she cared for Babette, she wasn't going to let her sister, or anybody else, talk her out of the trip this time. She was thirty years old and it was high time she at least tried to locate her wild side. She'd start by testing the waters tonight with the Ben de Lisi, then let it go completely next month at

Gasparilla. "It may not be my kind of thing," she admitted, "but I'm going to give it a try."

"We can talk about it some more as it gets closer," Babette said sweetly. Too sweetly. Obviously, she thought she could talk Clarise out of going, but she couldn't. However, Clarise wasn't going to argue the point tonight, not when she was getting ready to let Ethan glimpse her sexy side. If it worked, maybe Gasparilla would involve the removal of her top, and everything else, with Ethan. She could tell Babette about the vow she made on her birthday, merely weeks ago, that she wasn't going to let that old fear of rejection keep her from going for what she wanted— and what she wanted was Ethan, as more than a friend and more than a boss. Tonight, she planned on the red dress setting that in motion. She wanted him to see her as a female rather than merely a female friend. If she accomplished that goal, then at Gasparilla, in the wildness of Tampa at the infamous Pirate Festival, who knew what might happen?

"Yeah," Clarise said, as sweetly as Babette, "we can talk about it later."

Babette finished the last curl, so that Clarise looked like a brunette Shirley Temple in the mirror. "Okay, let's make these curls shine. Here," Babette said, scooting Clarise's lighted makeup mirror across the counter, "you don't have a lot of time to waste, so you'd better make the most of it." In the next thirty minutes, Babette positioned every curl perfectly in place on Clarise's crown and accented each with a rhinestone-embellished bobby pin, while Clarise applied makeup. When they'd finished, Clarise's straight hair was a fountain of curls on top of her head, with two long tendrils hanging in front of each ear and tiny spiral strands tickling her nape. "Perfect," Babette said, admiring her handiwork. "Okay, I'm going to put some coffee on and go get Granny Gert. You're good to put the dress on by yourself, right?"

Clarise slowly nodded. Her stomach was beginning to get a bit squeamish from nerves, and she didn't want to risk moving too quickly.

Babette cocked her head to the side. "Don't worry. You're going to get his attention."

"Whose attention?" Clarise asked, her stomach clamping down tight and making her feel even worse.

"Whoever is it you're going after," Babette said, then winked. "Did you actually believe I wouldn't know you were going to all of this trouble to impress a man? And he must be really something too, huh?"

"Yeah," Clarise breathed.

"Not ready to tell me who it is?" Babette continued. "I bet it's one of those hunky department heads, isn't it?"

"You're right," Clarise said, then added, "I'm not ready to tell you."

Babette laughed. "Well, if you're going to get to the party on time and see him—whoever *he* is—you'd better get your dress on." She pointed to a sheet of paper taped to Clarise's bathroom mirror. "At least that's what the list says."

Clarise grabbed a pen from the counter and checked the items on today's to-do list. She'd always been a list person, loved setting goals and feeling that major sense of accomplishment when she checked them off one by one. Today's list had been fairly simple: 1) work, 2) coffee with Ethan, 3) buy book for Granny Gert, 4) Babette—hair, 5) Rachel and Jesilyn—girls' night out. Thank goodness she hadn't embellished the list to include flirting with

Ethan over coffee and taunting him in a red dress, but those two were most definitely on today's list, if only in Clarise's mind.

"I'll be back in a few minutes. Granny Gert is going to love this," Babette said.

Clarise moved to the bedroom, dropped her robe on the bed, then slipped into the luxury of flaming red satin. The dress was made for her, if she did say so herself, its gentle pleats following her curves and accentuating a shape she hadn't realized existed. There wasn't anything fluffy to her body in this dress. Everything was in its place, and everything looked really, really good. She couldn't contain her smile, and was still grinning giddily in the mirror when Granny Gert barged in, followed by Babette, Jesilyn and Rachel.

The three younger women made the same sound, a cross between a balloon losing air and an "ahhh," while Granny Gert slapped her hands together and giggled so exuberantly that her Robinson Treasures bounced along with the action. "Yes, child," she said. "Oh, yes!"

"What do you think of the back?" Clarise asked, turning so they could see the sexy dip of fabric that pooled at the indention where her spine curved into her behind.

"Oh, Clarise, it's perfect! Do we sell it at the store?" Jesilyn asked, wedging past the others to touch the red fabric.

"No, we don't," she said, then added in a whisper, "it's a Ben di Lisi original."

"Get out," Rachel said, her head bobbing and sending her long blond curls waving against her shoulders. "Well, trust me, that one was made for you. Every set of male eyes will be on you, Clarise. Shoot, maybe I should go home and put on something more revealing, so they'll remember to at least talk to me."

Clarise clucked her tongue. "As if. You look gorgeous. Both of you do," she said, indicating Rachel's navy velvet gown with a split showing the majority of her right leg, and Jesilyn's beaded strapless pantsuit, shimmering silver with matching heels.

"Yes, you're all stunning," Granny Gert said, "but Clarise, I'm going to be honest here. I can't say that you've ever looked more . . . hot."

Babette wrapped an arm around her grandmother and squeezed her. "Yep, Granny, you're right. She does look hot."

Rachel was still laughing over Granny Gert's remark as she steered her car out of Clarise's apartment complex and headed down I-59 toward the Civic Center. "I can't imagine my grandmother telling me that I look hot," she said, "but she's right, Clarise. You do. I bet Jake will think so too."

"Jake?" Clarise asked, perplexed.

"He's been dropping hints that he's interested in getting to know you better," Jesilyn enlightened. "Didn't we tell you?"

"No. No, you didn't," Clarise said, suddenly recalling Ethan's comments from this afternoon. Jake Riley? Interested in her?

"Well, I'm betting he lets you know on his own tonight, particularly when he's drooling over you in that dress," Rachel continued.

Clarise swallowed. Jake Riley was hot; that was for sure. But he wasn't the one she wanted drooling over her. Then again, if she looked good enough to make Jake drool, did that mean she looked good enough to make Ethan drool too? Yeah, she'd bet that was exactly what it meant. All she could think was . . . she couldn't wait. And that's exactly what she was thinking when the car started sounding like a popcorn machine, and the steering wheel started to shake.

Chapter 2

Ethan, you should probably make your announcements. The party has been going for a good two hours, and some of the attendees who have little ones are probably going to start heading home," Lillian Eubanks said. Preston Eubanks, standing a short distance away, agreed with his wife's advice. "Your mother is right. Some of the Panache folks have early-morning flights too and will undoubtedly be returning to their hotel soon. You've got an early flight too, don't you?"

Ethan nodded, scanned the room once more, but saw no sign of Clarise. He'd looked forward to announcing the potential acquisition all day, but he'd been even more eager to announce the winner of the first Eubanks Pacemaker Award. Without Clarise's presence, however, what was the point? And where was she, anyway? She wasn't the typical female, arriving fashionably late in order to make a statement. Clarise was more the "fifteen minutes prior is proper etiquette" type of woman, which was one of the things he liked most about his friend. He could always count on her to make the company look good. But tonight, he wanted to honor her achievements, and she was nowhere to be seen. Plus, he had intentionally refrained from mentioning the Panache deal during their coffee chat this afternoon. He'd wanted her to be as surprised, and impressed, as the rest of Eubanks employees tonight when he made the formal announcement. But—another scan of the ballroom—she wasn't here. And neither were Jesilyn and Rachel, his department heads for accessories and women's eveningwear. Obviously, this was a big night for the company. Where were they?

"I'll get things started," Preston said, placing his empty wineglass on a passing waiter's tray, then leaving his wife and Ethan to move toward the stage.

Totally accustomed to speaking in front of a crowd, Preston Eubanks provided background on the company, discussed the longevity of the original Birmingham location, then followed up with the successes of the newer Atlanta store. He ended with, "Yes, Eubanks Elegant Apparel has definitely had a stellar showing this year, but the future is going to be even brighter. I'm going to ask my son, Ethan, to let you in on the future plans for the company."

Ethan took the stage and decided to go ahead with the speech he'd planned, even though Clarise still hadn't shown. However, he did reverse the order, starting with the Panache news and saving the other announcement for later, just in case she made an appearance. "As my father noted, Eubanks Elegant Apparel has had a phenomenal year. In fact, the company has grown by leaps and bounds; however, we realize that you can only grow so much with two stores. Therefore," he said, as he saw several arm-punching pay-attention-to-this gestures ripple around the room, "we're looking at the possibility of acquiring more locations for business. Sixteen additional locations, in fact." He waited a moment for the soft rumble of whispers that accompanied this news. "You may have noticed we have quite a few visitors with us this evening. In addition to the spouses of our employees, we also have several members of the board of directors for Panache Clothing Stores, a chain I'm sure you'll recognize from its presence across the Southeast. Over the next four weeks, I'll personally visit each of the Panache locations, then I'll meet with Panache executives regarding an acquisition that would provide a smooth transition for these facilities from Panache to Eubanks." The smiles spreading through the audience warmed Ethan's heart. This had been his goal—to turn Eubanks Elegant Apparel into a national chain. True, acquiring the Panache chain would only give prominence to their presence across the Southeast, but it was a big step toward the final goal, and he couldn't be more thrilled. He inadvertently scanned the audience again. If he'd have known Clarise wouldn't make it for the announcement tonight, he'd have told her this afternoon. He had no doubt she'd be as excited—well, nearly as excited—as he was about his dream finally seeing fruition. Plus, he really wanted her to be present for the following announcement. Unfortunately, though, he still hadn't seen her in the crowd.

"As you've probably guessed," he continued, "the new acquisition will provide opportunity for current Eubanks employees to transfer to the new locations, ranging as far north as Myrtle Beach to as far south as Miami. If you're interested in relocating, please see my father, Preston Eubanks, during the next four weeks, while he's overseeing the Birmingham store in my absence. He'll take requests on a first come, first serve basis, and we'll do our best to fill open positions, particularly department head positions, with current Eubanks employees." Another flurry of smiles, nods and arm punches washed over the audience, and Ethan performed another perfunctory scan to see if Clarise had arrived. If she was there, he sure couldn't see her. He inwardly sighed and saw no reason to stall his last announcement.

"As I said, we've had a great year, and we're wise enough to know the reason why—exceptional employees. At Eubanks, we sell the best, but we also hire the best, and I'd like to thank all of you for doing your part to make our company look good. Tonight, in fact, we'd like to honor a Eubanks employee who has excelled not only in sales, but also in providing customer satisfaction." Ethan lifted the gold engraved plaque from its hiding place in the podium and turned it toward the crowd. "We're calling this award the Pacemaker Award, since the recipient essentially sets the pace, the high standard, for others to emulate. Tomorrow evening, at the Atlanta store's holiday party, my brother will present a Pacemaker Award to one of his employees, but tonight, I'm honoring our first recipient, a woman who never fails to provide a smile and helpful advice to her customers, always surpasses her goals in sales and has the unparalleled fashion sense that Eubanks patrons expect from our department heads." Ethan paused. He'd really wanted to give her the award in person rather than merely announcing it to her peers, so he scanned the room once more . . . and nearly dropped the heavy award when he noticed the vision in red standing near the back of the ballroom.

His voice stilled in his throat. Clarise stood, a white-gloved hand at her neck while she waited for him to continue speaking. He had searched the room a few times, but for the life of him, he didn't recall taking his gaze all the way to the back. How long had she been standing there? And if she'd been there, looking like *that,* wouldn't he have noticed?

Her hair was up, but not in the professional twist she wore to work each day; it was full of curls, several of which had escaped captivity to tumble down and brush the pale flesh of her shoulders. And speaking of flesh . . . there was a surplus of shapeliness showcased above the red fabric attempting to contain her breasts. Ethan's mouth was suddenly very dry. The dress looked as perfect on her as he'd promised her it would. He'd wanted her to feel beautiful; he'd suspected that she'd never experienced what his mother described as an "all eyes on me" kind of moment, but she had to be experiencing one now, because every pair of eyes in the room had followed Ethan's gaze and were currently focused on his best friend, and, incidentally, the most gorgeous woman in the place.

Clarise's eyes widened momentarily, then she blushed. Even from his vantage point on the stage, he could see the tinge of pink on her cheeks. Ethan smiled. He'd wanted to honor her with the award, but he was giving her more, and he couldn't be more pleased. Clarise Robinson was finally getting the attention she deserved, both professionally and physically.

"As I said," he continued, feeling an extra surge of pride in his decision regarding the first Pacemaker recipient, "this person has the unparalleled fashion sense that Eubanks patrons expect from our department heads, as I'm sure you'll agree by her choice of holiday attire. I'm honored to present the first Pacemaker Award to Clarise Robinson, department head for Women's Clothing and top salesperson for Eubanks over the past three quarters." He held up the plaque and nodded at her, "Clarise?"

Her throat pulsed as she swallowed, then she smiled and started slowly toward the front of the room. The applause for her accomplishment died down about the time she reached the steps to the stage, and she lifted her skirt enough to keep from tripping on the red fabric. It was at that moment that Ethan noticed two additional details: 1) the long black streak down the right side of her dress, and 2) Clarise wasn't wearing shoes. Her bare feet tiptoed up the steps, then the red-tipped toes disappeared when she dropped her skirt back into place, looked at Ethan, and silently mouthed, "You'll never believe it."

He fought the urge to laugh. Obviously there was a reason behind her late arrival, and he couldn't wait to hear it. If he was going to be in town next Friday, he'd bet they would discuss it during their next coffee chat; however, he wasn't, so he'd make sure to ask her about the shoes, and the smudge, tonight.

She stepped closer, and he saw the third noticeable detail to her appearance—a long, dark bruise down one side of her nose. Ethan swallowed. Had she been in an accident? Was that it? And why hadn't he thought of that before? He could have at least tried to call her cell phone and make sure she was okay when she didn't arrive on time, but no, he'd merely stood around schmoozing with his father and the Panache executives while he wondered where she was.

Not caring that they were on complete display, front and center on the stage, he reached out to touch the bruise when she neared. Was she hurt? Clarise stopped moving, then her big dark eyes lifted to his in confusion, and her throat pulsed again with a thick swallow.

"Are you okay?" he whispered, but his concerned voice magnified ten times through the microphone clipped to his lapel. His finger softly moved along the bruise, and he gasped when . . . it moved. Removing his finger, he was shocked to see it wasn't a bruise at all; it was dirt. A swift tidal wave of relief washed over him.

She blinked at him then focused on his finger, the tip coated in black, and she laughed. "Oh, dear. We had a flat tire on the way in, and I thought I got all of the grime off. Guess I missed a spot or two."

"You changed a tire?" he asked, his voice once again echoing through the ballroom. Several employees began to laugh as well.

"I helped," she corrected, "and I'm afraid I got a little dirty in the process."

Ethan suddenly remembered the multitude of Eubanks employees and Panache executives watching this exchange. He turned toward the crowd and improvised. "We can add resourceful to that list of qualities exemplified by our first Pacemaker recipient. Clarise Robinson," he said, lifting the award from the podium, "Congratulations."

"Thank you," she said, and smiled toward the group. "It's an honor to work for Eubanks Elegant Apparel, and I'm not surprised to hear the company is growing by leaps and bounds. And now, I'm going to attempt to add cleanliness to the traits Ethan listed for the Pacemaker by washing the tire dirt from my nose." The crowd applauded and laughed, while Clarise turned back to Ethan, whispered another, "Thanks," then gracefully exited the stage.

Ethan wrapped up his speech by telling everyone to

enjoy the remainder of the party, then he left the stage and searched for Clarise. He found her exiting the women's restroom. "What happened to your shoes?" he asked.

"I left them with the coat clerk," she said, grinning. "I was so caught up in trying to help with the tire that I didn't notice we'd pulled over on a muddy shoulder. The shoes are ruined, and I borrowed them from Babette." She gave him a one-shouldered shrug. "Guess I'll owe my sister a new pair of shoes. And I dirtied up the Ben de Lisi too," she said, indicating the dark streak down the side. "I'd really wanted to look good tonight," she said on a sigh.

He moved his hand to cup her chin, then tilted her face so those big brown eyes were staring straight into his. That pink tinge filtered up her cheeks, as she whispered, "What?"

"Have I ever lied to you, Clarise?"

She ran her top teeth over her lower lip in an adorable nervous gesture. "Not that I recall," she said hesitantly.

"Then trust me when I tell you that you *do* look good tonight. Better than that, you're stunning."

As often as they'd had heart-to-hearts over coffee on Fridays, he'd never seen Clarise where she appeared speechless, until now. Maybe telling her she was stunning wasn't exactly included in a typical friendship bill of sale, but right now he wasn't exactly feeling mere friendship. Ethan couldn't deny that he'd been disappointed when she'd been late, and worried when he thought she'd been hurt. Moreover when he realized that she was okay, he'd been immensely relieved. Was that how he should feel toward any friend? Desire to touch her and to verify that she was indeed unharmed? Ethan swallowed hard. He wanted to touch her again.

"Ethan," she finally whispered.

"Yeah?" he asked.

"So, you're heading out tomorrow?" Jake Riley's voice boomed as he approached the two of them. Ethan smelled the alcohol on Jake's breath and assumed Riley had helped himself one too many times to the open bar. Ethan hoped the head of his Men's Department hadn't done anything to embarrass the company in front of the Panache executives. "Yes, I'm leaving in the morning."

"You'll be back for the corporate bonding trip, though, right?" Jake asked.

"I'm planning on it," Ethan said, frustrated that Clarise hadn't been able to finish . . . whatever she'd been about to say. It had started with his name. Where would it have ended?

She smiled politely at Jake and took a small step back from the two men. "I'm going to find Rachel and Jesilyn," she said. "Jesi wasn't feeling well and thought she might want to leave early."

"You just got here," Jake said, drawing his brows together in an exaggerated frown. "If you want to stay, I'll take you home."

"Or I could," Ethan countered, not willing to let Jake Riley behind the wheel while he was obviously inebriated, and also not willing to let Jake Riley take Clarise home, inebriated or not.

"I'll ride with them," Clarise said. She turned to Ethan. "I guess I'll see you when you get back from the Panache visits? What, in a month?"

"Should be about a month," he said. "But, like I told Jake, I do plan to attend the corporate bonding trip. You're planning to go this time, right?"

"Yes," she said, to which Jake responded, "Wonderful, Clarise. You'll love Gasparilla. I'm glad you're coming." His voice sounded a bit more sober, and Ethan wondered whether that was such a good thing. Jake was obviously flirting with Clarise, whether she realized it or not, and although Ethan would swear he didn't have a jealous bone in his body regarding Clarise—they were just friends, after all—he sure was feeling *something*.

"I'm sure I will," she said. "And thanks for helping us with the tire, Jake." Then she turned and walked away, leaving the two men watching that sexy sliver of red fabric sway gently against her extreme lower back.

"I need coffee," Jake said. "Because I've got the strongest urge to run after her and tell her everything I'm thinking right now, and that wouldn't be good, would it?"

Ethan's jaw tensed. "No, it wouldn't," he managed. Then he remembered her parting remark. "You helped them with the tire?"

"Well, hell, Clarise already had the thing off by the time I came along and saw Rachel's car on the side of the road. She's pretty good with a tire iron. Then again, the view wasn't so bad either, her bent over in that dress and breathing all hard and heavy while she worked at taking off that wheel. I almost didn't want to stop her, and instead just stand there and gawk." He grinned. "But I was a gentleman and told her to let me take over."

"That was big of you, Jake," Ethan said, fighting the heat creeping through his veins. Four weeks he'd be traipsing across the South to examine the Panache stores. How long would it take Jake Riley to put the moves on Clarise? Not that damn long. And Jake was a known player, breaking more than his share of female hearts, many of whom were Eubanks employees. Ethan would damn well kill him if he hurt Clarise.

"She's so prim and proper at the store that I'd never have picked her for one who didn't mind getting her hands dirty, but she sure got them dirty all right. I was impressed with the three of them, though. When they realized Clarise's perfect manicure was botched because of working on the tire, Rachel slid her white gloves off and gave them to her. Problem solved. You've got to admire a woman who is resourceful, like you said."

"Yeah," Ethan said, definitely admiring. "Yeah, you do."

Chapter 3

Four weeks had passed since the company Christmas party, which meant four weeks had passed since Clarise had seen Ethan . . . and the way he looked at her in the red dress. She'd spoken to him twice in the interim, on Christmas and New Year's, when he called to wish her holiday greetings, friend to friend, of course. Or at least she thought it was friend to friend. He always called her on holidays, so it shouldn't have seemed odd that he remembered to pick up the phone while he was out of town, but for some reason, it did seem odd—oddly exhilarating. She'd never gotten nervous talking to Ethan on the phone before, but then again, she'd never aggressively planned to pursue her best friend romantically before. Then again, hadn't he sounded *different* as well? As though the conversation was moving a bit awkwardly because, maybe, they didn't quite know whether something had changed at that Christmas party, when he touched her smudged nose in front of the crowd and asked if she was okay, because something had definitely changed on her end; had it changed on his end too? And would she be able to tell when she saw him tomorrow at Gasparilla?

Clarise had hoped he'd come home a day or two before the annual company trip, but his meetings with the Panache executives were running down to the wire, and he hadn't been able to slice one day off of the four-week time period, which put him arriving back in Birmingham just in time to head back out. She'd wanted to see him prior to Gasparilla and to somehow prepare him for what she planned—to show him her wild and sexy side and see if he were interested at all in looking at her that way, all wild and sexy. Lord, could she even pull *wild and sexy* off?

Yes, she could, Clarise realized, *if* she had the right clothes. While she knew in her heart that she wasn't as confident as she'd like to be regarding several aspects of life (take men, for one example, and her body, for another), Clarise had a surplus of confidence when it came to fashion. She loved apparel of all types, putting odd pieces together to create a new look and helping other people do the same, and she relished the general feeling of pride that surged through her when she knew she'd hit the mark with a customer and that the woman would truly feel her best when wearing the outfit Clarise had recommended. It was a talent, and Clarise planned to nurture it and cultivate it until she reached her final, and currently, very private, goal as a fashion buyer.

There were five main classifications of clothing, as Clarise saw them: 1) business conservative, 2) business casual, 3) formal, 4) casual fun and the last classification, which Clarise could only describe as 5) sexy-as-all-get-out, undeniably sassy and to-die-for hot. Unfortunately, she had complete ensembles for every classification except the last one, and that was what she needed for Gasparilla. Consequently, that was the only classification that she couldn't purchase at Eubanks Elegant Apparel, which was the primary reason for her trip across town this afternoon. Tomorrow morning she'd board a plane for Tampa, and there was no way she'd make the trip with a suitcase of her conservative clothes. How in the world would she be comfortable flashing the masses—if she actually got the nerve to do it—in her designer blouses? The only way to let her wild side go was to look, well, wild. And the only way to look wild was to shop . . . where Babette shopped.

She glanced across the street and swallowed hard. The Body Boutique's elongated windows glowed with flaming neon, not from the lighting, but from the outfits. They were a direct contrast to the navy-and-white ensembles currently gracing the window displays at Eubanks. Gleaming bright green, sizzling magenta and blinding yellow and intensified by black lights, they commanded so much attention that traffic slowed to a crawl outside the popular store.

Clarise sat in her car and scouted the trendy shop. It wasn't nearly as classy an entrance as the one at Eubanks Elegant Apparel, but Clarise wasn't looking for classy. She needed *sassy.* No, she wouldn't have thought the vibrant colors in season, but she had to admit, they were attention grabbing.

The lanky mannequins, provocatively posed, flirted as though they weren't inanimate objects. And in Clarise's opinion, they weren't. They bristled with a lust for life, raw sensuality and plain fun—everything she wanted.

Unfortunately, she suspected that the Body Boutique's size range didn't extend to double digits. Although Babette had purchased several items from the notable store, Clarise had never set foot in the place. True, the size factor was a major obstacle, but there was also the rule that she was only allowed to wear "Eubanks Apparel" to work. Preston Eubanks, and Ethan too, for that matter, didn't believe in "advertising the competition." Not that the Body Boutique could compete with Eubanks Elegant Apparel, which only sold the finest of women's clothing. However, fine clothing wasn't what she needed. On the contrary, Clarise's plans for Gasparilla called for wild, attention-getting party clothes, like the ones displayed so prominently in Body Boutique's windows. But could she find the nerve to go inside? A year ago, she'd have said no. But that was the old Clarise, the one who wasn't planning to bare her goods at Gasparilla.

Clarise inhaled, held the breath a moment, then snarled it through her nose like a ferocious bull eyeing the target. Except her target wasn't red; it was several shades of neon. Determined, she climbed out of the car and stomped toward the building. The windows pulsed from a mad rhythm beating inside. Clarise tried to put her finger on the tune. It was extremely familiar . . .

Blondie?

She opened the door. Sure enough, "One Way or Another" belted from every wall and the ceiling. And, judging from the tremble against the soles of her shoes, the floor. Clarise closed the door, stepped forward. *One way or another, I'm gonna find ya, I'm gonna getcha, getcha, getcha, getcha.* Each tiny scrap of fabric whispered and chanted along. "I'm gonna getcha, getcha, getcha, getcha . . ."

Tie-dyed. Had everything around her converted to a tie-dyed version, or was the room spinning? What had she been thinking coming here? With this huge amount of color and small amount of fabric? This was Babette's kind of store, definitely not Clarise's. She swallowed, bit her lip and turned to retreat. She'd taken the bull by the horns, and he had promptly speared her.

"Hi! I'm Shannon—Shannon Bainbridge! Welcome to Body Boutique!"

Clarise loosened her death grip on the door handle and swiveled toward the chirpy sound. An ebony-haired all-of-one-hundred-pounds-soaking-wet pixie grinned back. Yep, this confirmed it. She'd willingly stepped into her own personal hell, and everyone else was tiny. Super. "Hi," Clarise managed, in spite of her sudden urge to hurl.

"Are you looking for something special?" too-perky-for-her-own-good asked.

"I was just leaving."

The door burst forward and nearly slammed Clarise in the nose. She backed up and four teenage girls, ditto for tiny and perky, entered.

"Can you help us?" one asked. Evidently realizing Clarise couldn't possibly work at a place like this, she directed the question toward Shannon. Go figure.

Blue glitter shadow circled the teen's eyes and three round stones sparkled from her silver brow ring. "We've got a party tonight and need a megahot look," she explained, smacking her gum—bright blue neon gum—between words.

"I've got a customer right now." Shannon gave Clarise another excited grin. "But Jadelle will be happy to help."

At that, another pixie appeared from behind a rack of clothes. She was blond and clad in a multicolored dress that could have totally served as shrink-wrap.

"Come on," Jadelle said. "We've got some great new things!"

Cheerleaders. They all had to be cheerleaders, the way they pulsed each word as though chanting a fight song. The herd of teens followed their new leader to the back room, while Clarise was thrown headfirst back to high school. Specifically, the locker room. How many times had she watched the popular crowd come in chatting and giggling while they stripped down to bras and panties? Then they'd continue the gossip session, talking about boys and movies and boys and school and boys . . . while they wiggled their perfect little bodies into their perfect little gym uniforms. Shorts and a T-shirt. What could be so bad about that? Nothing, if your body actually fit into youth-sized apparel, but if your Robinson Treasures demanded adult proportions, larger adult proportions at that, everything about that blasted fourth period was horrifying.

Clarise still cringed at the memory. P.E. A high school requirement? Whose bright idea was that? And plain shorts with a plain T-shirt? She couldn't even use color and accessories to play up her assets. Every year she prayed for a government law letting brainy, pleasantly plump teens forego school-induced sweat and take another English course. And she wouldn't even think about the days around her time of the month. If she'd thought things couldn't get worse than wearing standard school-issued shorts and a T-shirt in P.E., she'd been mistaken. Oh no, a day wearing shorts and a T-shirt while retaining enough water to fill Lake Martin—that was worse.

Clarise despised being late for any of her classes; nevertheless, she received more than her share of tardy slips for that one, because of her hide time. Each day, she'd stall in the locker room while the other girls primped. Then, when they finally left, she hustled into one of the two stalls and quickly change into her P.E. clothes. T-shirt, size adult large, and shorts, ditto for large. Sure, it'd taken less time simply to strip in the center of the big gray room. What if someone forgot something and came back? What if they walked in and saw her? *All* of her? She couldn't— wouldn't—take that chance. So, on many a day, when Mrs. Phillips blew her whistle to begin class, Clarise was missing in action. Then the tardy slip came home, and her mother signed it without question. Granny Gert had been more vocal, saying Clarise should be proud of her glory and flaunt it in front of all those "little squirts that lacked aplenty in the treasure department." But Clarise didn't see anything about her excess cargo as glorious. Torturous was more like it, particularly when everyone looked at her tiny wisp of a sister, merely two years younger, and won- dered what was wrong with the gene pool.

"So, what are we looking for today? Got a special trip coming up? A cruise? Hot date?" Shannon asked, stealing Clarise's attention from her miserable past.

She blinked, then eyed the female in front of her. Ebony spikes stuck out in all directions, with two pointed sections lining each jaw. Earrings ran around the entire shells of both ears, with silver elves suspended from the lowest circles. Funny, she'd never pictured elves in hell.

Perky's fluorescent green sweater, tighter than a swim- suit, appeared to have been slashed through the middle, exposing abs of a gymnast and a diamond belly ring. Low- rise black jeans completed the ensemble . . . since there were no shoes on her tiny feet—feet that were probably size six, from Clarise's guess, and nowhere near her size nine skis. Several rings sparkled from Shannon's toes, as did brilliant blue polish on each nail.

She looked like a rainbow had thrown up all over her. Oddly enough, Clarise liked the look. She envied a person so willing to play with her appearance and have fun at the risk of criticism. While Clarise knew sophisticated fashion, this girl was fashionably exuberant, letting her carefree, funky spirit shine through in her choice of clothing.

Clarise couldn't help but wonder . . . why couldn't she be more like that? Lifting her eyes to Shannon's wide smile, outlined in dark plum, she decided this little pixie wasn't so bad. Maybe she wasn't the enemy after all. Maybe, just maybe, she could be Clarise's ally for this venture.

"I'm going on a trip," Clarise informed.

"Cool! Where to?" Shannon asked, steering Clarise to one side of the store, then flipping through a circular rack.

"Tampa, for Gasparilla. It's a festival where pirates take over the city. Have you heard of it?"

"Quit it. Really? Sure, I've heard of it. It's like Mardi Gras, but with big swords and huge boats. Oh wow, I so want to go to Tampa for Gasparilla. Are you taking your hubby? Boyfriend? Or are ya gonna find one there?" Her grin intensified.

Clarise fought the urge to laugh out loud. Part of her wanted to confess her plan to bed her friend, maybe even convince him she was the love of his life in the process. Chances are she'd never see Shannon again, so what would it hurt? Yeah, right. As if Clarise would ever confess her secrets, particularly to a girl who'd probably have no trouble at all heading down to Gasparilla and grabbing her choice of hunky pirates. Nope, Clarise would keep that little tidbit to herself.

"It's a company trip. Corporate bonding, you know."

"Ooh, I've heard of those. What company?"

Clarise swallowed. How much should she tell this girl, a stranger, about who she was? Then, as Shannon's genuine interest shone through emerald eyes, Clarise couldn't resist. She wouldn't lie. "I run the Women's Department at Eubanks Elegant Apparel, but I'm wanting a different kind of look than what our clothing conveys." Was that a decent explanation? Would Pixie understand what she was after?

"Eubanks! Wow, they're really uptown!" She tilted her spiky head. "My mom shops there, and my older sister, but you were right to come here for what you need."

"What I need?" Clarise asked. She hadn't provided any specifics.

"You're not looking to impress the guy with your business fashion, right? You're looking to get him in bed," Shannon said matter-of-factly, apparently unaware of the shock value in her remark.

Clarise whipped her head around and quickly realized that—thankfully—no one was within earshot, then she swallowed and attempted to force some of the excess blood to leave her face. "Yeah, that's what I'm looking for," she said.

"You go, girl," Shannon said, nodding. "And with your awesome curves, you won't have any trouble finding *exactly* what you're looking for at the pirate festival."

Clarise couldn't stop her smile. Shannon was quickly crossing over into the new-and-very-best-friend category.

"Come on, I've got the perfect look for you," Shannon said, excitement pulsing through every word. She grabbed Clarise's hand and yanked her farther into the kaleidoscope store. An assorted collection of leather, beads and knotted string slid down Shannon's arm to tickle Clarise's wrist. Was there anything about this tiny person that didn't scream fun? She headed directly for a rack of seminormal colors, not the fluorescent hues out front, but vivid just the same. "It's a new line the owner is trying out, based on my recommendation. I absolutely love this designer's work. The problem is, most of our customers can't wear them," Shannon said.

Excitement raced through Clarise's veins. Finally, something the two of them could clearly connect on—discussing a new clothing line. Granted, it wasn't like any line Clarise had viewed before, but it did have a fun and flirty manifestation that begged to be touched—and worn. "Why can't your customers wear them?" she asked, fingering a lime green sweater dress. The soft texture caressed her palm, made her itch to try it on, but she didn't dare. Clarise never tried on clothing in department stores, even at Eubanks. That was something she did in private, not in a dressing room where an attendant popped her head in and asked if she was "doing okay." How could anyone "do okay" if there was always the potential for another human to see you naked? In fact, in her own department, she made sure never to invade a Eubanks customer's privacy.

"The figures. They just don't have them," Shannon explained.

"Figures?" Clarise moved her attention to a black leather miniskirt.

"Curves. These babies are made for curvy women." She waved her fingertips across several colorful sleeves on the rack. "I can't wear them, and I'd love to, but not everyone is blessed like you," she continued.

"Blessed?" Clarise blinked. She jerked her head around in a full surveillance move. Was Granny Gert hiding in the store, feeding Shannon lines of bull to convince her granddaughter the Robinson Treasures were the jewels she'd claimed?

"Of course. I can't wait to see this on you. Oh man, those guys in Tampa are gonna absolutely die." She held the green dress against Clarise and tilted her head to the side. "Really brings out the natural highlights in your hair. And your eyes, oh yeah, this shade complements mocha perfectly."

Mocha? Clarise classified them as brown, same color as her hair. Natural highlights? Talk about willing to go the distance for a sale.

"I could never wear that," Clarise said, shaking her head for emphasis. *Uh-uh. No way.*

"Sure you can. Matter of fact, I haven't had another soul in here who could, except you. You've simply gotta try it on."

"I don't try things on," Clarise explained. "I take them home, then if they don't work, which they usually don't, I bring them back."

"You're not going to let me see how good it looks?" Shannon's green eyes did a little pop thing, where the iris seemed to increase in size and made her look like Yoda.

Do or do not. There is no try.

Dang, talk about pressure, but new best friend or not, Shannon, and Yoda, were going beyond Clarise's limits. And unless the force was with this pixie—as in the force to physically haul Clarise into a dressing room and squeeze her unwilling body into these scraps of fabric—this request wouldn't be granted. "Sorry, but nope. Never. No way. No how."

Shannon laughed so hard she snorted. Her abs tightened with the action, showcasing an impressive six-pack and taking her right out of Yoda mode.

"Okay. But once you get a good view of your body in this dress, you'll change your mind."

"Don't count on it, and I'm not certain I'm going to buy it. Are you sure there's enough fabric here to cover all this?" She pointed down, but didn't bother looking at what she saw in the mirror every day. "What's the largest size?"

"You don't want the biggest one; that'd be huge. Tell you what, if you insist on waiting until you go home to try it on, I'll measure you so we get the right size from the get-go."

"Measure me?" Clarise asked incredulously. "As in stretch a tape measure around and actually log the dimensions?" An image flashed from a recent Discovery Channel show, where two beefy men tried to stretch their arms around a redwood tree and failed to meet in the middle. "You sure that's really necessary?"

Grinning, Shannon dug her tiny hand into her front pocket—quite a feat, since the pants could've been painted on—and withdrew a green tape measure. "Absolutely necessary. If you don't get the right size, it won't work."

"Terrific," Clarise said, rolling her eyes. "This is just what I need to pump up my ego for the trip."

"How's it going?" Jadelle, her eyes as excited as Shannon's, approached the two of them. She nodded approvingly toward the rack of clothes. "Oh, she's perfect for those!"

Great. Everyone was in agreement except Clarise, whose

uncertainty with the assessment was palpable. "Are you sure? We're talking about little bitty clothes and a not so little bitty body."

"Definitely. Come on, Jadelle, help me get her measurements," Shannon said.

There it went again, that image of the tree.

"Don't you have some other customers you need to help?" Clarise asked, wondering if there was anyone in the place who wasn't about to find out how hideously large the Robinson Treasures were. Surely there were some additional salespeople in the back who wanted to gawk at the woman who dared believe she could fit a watermelon through a keyhole.

"Took care of 'em," Jadelle informed.

Clarise sucked her belly in, then gave up the fight and let it go. Heck, if she was actually going to fork out the money to pay for this stuff, she might as well get something that fit. Preferably while breathing.

"We need a pen and paper," Shannon said, which Jadelle quickly supplied.

Wonderful. Not only would these two know the full extent of her bounty, but anyone who happened to sneak a peak at their notes would get a belly laugh too. Oh joy.

"Arms out," Shannon announced.

Clarise closed her eyes and obeyed. She did want new clothes, after all, different from her conservative work wardrobe. Fun clothes. Sexy clothes. And if anyone could help her find them, she'd bet it was the woman currently circling her boobs with a tape measure. Lord, Clarise hoped the thing was long enough to cover the territory.

Chapter 4

Clarise hadn't anticipated having her body sized up by two overzealous pixies. But here she was, squinting through the equivalent of two elves measuring Santa.

"Wow!" Jadelle exclaimed, forcing Clarise to pry one hesitant eye open. The sassy blonde held up the paper.

Clarise gawked at the dimension, as though staring at it would make it shrink, like she hadn't tried that before. Staring at it, harnessing it, meditating over it. Didn't matter, her treasures were determined to "shine" as Granny Gert put it. If they shone any brighter, everyone in the state of Alabama would need blinders.

She shrugged. "Nothing I can do about it, though. Even when I diet, they stay intact. And when I gain weight, guess where it goes?"

"Cool. Don't guess you'd be willing to share?" Shannon asked, plum-ringed lips grinning.

"You aren't serious," Clarise said.

They ignored her statement and moved to her waist. Then, while her gaze darted around the room and she prayed no one else would join this odd little party, they notated the circumference of her caboose. Clarise wanted to die, right here, right now. She closed her eyes and waited, then she forced them open to view the dainty women madly gathering garments from the rack.

"Perfect," Shannon said. "Oh my goodness, this is incredible. What do you think, Jade?"

"Oh yeah. And just think how this will show off her boobs!" She held up a tube top.

A tube top? "You've *got* to be kidding." Clarise attempted to wedge her way back into the conversation, which was only fair, since she was the topic of discussion.

"Kidding? No way," Jadelle said. "We've needed someone voluptuous for this line, but we haven't had anyone built for the part. If we had a decent mannequin, one that wasn't so sticklike, we could advertise some of these in the window. Don't guess you'd consider letting us take some photos of you in these clothes, would you?"

Clarise swallowed. Was this happening? *She* was the perfect model for the trendy fashions filling both sets of toned and tanned arms? "I don't think so."

"When will you try them on?" Shannon asked.

"Tonight, I guess."

"You're going to love them," Jadelle gushed. "You'll have to pry the men off with a stick. What are you doing down there, anyway? Just parades, or balls too?"

The room was taking on that tie-dyed spin thing again. Pry men off with a stick? Clarise Robinson? Surely not.

"So?" Jadelle prompted.

"So—what?"

"Parades only, or balls too?" she giddily chirped.

"Just parades, I think. The company is footing the bill, and I haven't heard anything mentioned about balls."

"I've heard you have to get your invitations to those things years in advance," Shannon said. "I've got an aunt who lives in Indian Rocks Beach. She goes to the parades, but she's never made it to a ball. Hey, are you doing anything else besides the adult parades? They have kiddie parades too, and then there are the street parties. If you're doing any of them, you'll need some more casual clothes too."

"I don't think we have an actual agenda," Clarise said, frowning. She hadn't heard anything definite about the trip, in fact, other than a group lunch Saturday afternoon when the pirates would invade downtown Tampa and make the mayor surrender the keys to the city. She supposed the remainder of their time would be spent hanging out with the other department heads . . . or, perhaps, having sex. Her frown slid easily into a smile. "I suppose I should be prepared for—anything."

"Got it," Shannon said. "Grab a pair of the hourglass jeans, Jadelle."

"I don't do jeans. Can't work this into any of them." Clarise patted her hips. "But thanks for considering it as a possibility."

They laughed. Laughed! "You *didn't* do jeans," Shannon corrected. "But you've never tried a pair of these."

"What are those?" Clarise asked, eyeing the dark blue denim. Eubanks Elegant Apparel didn't even carry jeans.

"Hourglass jeans," Shannon continued. "They're cut to curve around the woman who has perfect dimensions."

Clarise flinched. There she went again, using the p-word.

"You logged my dimensions, so you're bound to know they're far less than—"

"You really don't see it, do you?" Jadelle said, propping her garment-clad arms on her hips and shaking her head in obvious disbelief. "You're what every guy dreams of, that Marilyn Monroe, Jayne Mansfield thing that's so hard to find nowadays with everybody determined to fit in a size two. You're the real deal, and you need to play it up."

"Exactly," Shannon chimed in. "And we're gonna help ya do it."

They sounded sincere. Extremely sincere. What if, wonder of wonders, Granny Gert hadn't been feeding her a load of bull all these years? Were there men who actually liked full figures? Very full figures? And was Ethan Eubanks one of them?

"You're starting to believe it, aren't ya?" Shannon said, lifting arched black brows in speculation. "Tell us the truth. You've never really given it a try, have you?"

"Well, my boss did talk me into wearing a fitted red dress to the company Christmas party," Clarise confessed.

"And?" Jadelle asked.

Clarise remembered the way everyone had turned when she entered, gawked at her as though she were from another planet. For a fraction of a second, she thought they were appalled at her curves pushing against the slinky fabric. But then she saw the way Ethan looked at her—then Jake. Had she looked, as Ethan said, *stunning?* And if she had, could she pull it off again?

"Well?" Shannon queried.

"My boss did tell me," Clarise said.

"Tell you what?" Jadelle asked.

"What'd he say?" Shannon continued, wiggling thin, arched brows.

"He said I looked stunning."

"There now, you see?" Jadelle said, finishing off the pile of clothes she'd gathered with a hot pink sweater. "There's a man you should listen to. Obviously, he knows women."

"Oh yeah, he knows women," Clarise agreed.

"And he liked what he saw, just like every guy at the Pirate Festival will like what he sees. By the way, most of these will let you show as much, or as little, as you want," Shannon said, a soft giggle underlying her words.

Clarise couldn't control her responding blush.

"Shannon, you're getting too personal. Isn't she?" Jadelle asked. "Of course, if you wanna tell us whether you plan to really get into the Gasparilla spirit, we'll never tell."

"I haven't made up my mind." But, if they were telling her the truth, and there were men out there interested in a body like hers, why not show it off a bit? Particularly if Ethan was looking.

"What would you do, Shannon? Shirt on or off?" Jadelle asked.

"Shoot, who'd want to look at these?" Shannon said. She dropped her bounty of clothing in a chair and cupped her perky breasts, pointing prominently beneath her thin top.

"You're joking," Clarise accused.

"Hey, not everyone can get as lucky as you," Shannon countered.

"Lucky? I'd kill to have your tiny figure." Clarise surveyed her new friend, whose waiflike features reminded her so much of Babette's miniscule frame. "It's perfect."

"Not in my book. I want shape. You should see me in a swimsuit. I'm totally straight. Skinny as a beanpole, that's what my mama says. I don't even have an indention at the waist, so I look like a boy, seriously. I have to buy the high-cut bikinis so I can fake having hips, and that is such a pain."

"I know what you mean," Jadelle agreed. She placed her things in a second chair. "It'd be really cool to finally see somebody try these on. I wish you'd change your mind, Clarise. Come on. I can't tell you how many times I've dreamed of wearing these clothes."

"Ohmigod, me too!" Shannon chimed in. "I mean, can you imagine actually having cleavage, without a water bra?"

"A real jiggle. Lord, I'd kill for that!" Jadelle added.

Clarise gaped. Could these skinny women believe they didn't have the ideal physique? Moreover, did they actually think that Clarise, curvy as she was, had achieved perfection?

"Can you help me, please? I need these jeans in a two," one of the cheerleader gang asked as she neared the trio.

"Be right back," Jadelle said to Clarise, then she disappeared through the racks of clothing.

"You okay?" Shannon asked, her brow ring lifting a notch as her eyes widened in concern.

A size two. Clarise frowned, then turned to Shannon. "Do you really think my figure is appealing to men? I mean, honestly, do you?" She knew she looked good in her work clothes. The picture-perfect model of sophistication. However, at Gasparilla, the clothes would be much more revealing, and if her dreams came true, the clothes would eventually come off. And if they did, would Ethan like what he saw?

Plum-lined lips spread into Shannon's cheeks. "Definitely. Eubanks may cater to the upscale gang, but we've got the sexy market hands down. You just haven't had the right clothing to maximize your assets. These will take care of that." She patted her stack.

Clarise looked at the colorful heap with longing. She had always understood the power wielded by phenomenal clothes, but could clothes do all that?

"You want to try them on, don't ya?"

Heaven help her, she did. She looked around the store, practically vacated, except for the teen scene perusing the stacks of jeans in the back with Jadelle.

"We've got a private viewing area, you know," Shannon tempted.

"How private?"

"Your own dressing room, then a little side space with a wall-to-wall mirror and a platform. Wanna give it a go?"

Best friend or not, Clarise would normally shout a resounding no, but today, the day she was planning a trip to Tampa to fulfill her Ethan Eubanks fantasies, and the day her new friends had made her wonder if she might be semisexy after all . . .

"All right. Why not?"

Shannon clapped her hands together like a kid who'd been granted candy in the checkout line. "Cool!"

"What?" Jadelle asked, hurrying back. "They're doing fine on their own in the jeans. What'd I miss?"

"She's going to try them on!" Shannon cheered.

"You go, girl!" Jadelle exclaimed, tweaking Clarise's arm with a friendly pinch. It hurt, but Clarise managed not to flinch.

"So, ya gonna let us see?" Shannon asked.

Clarise's chest tightened, throat went dry. Tomorrow, she'd be letting everyone in Tampa see—her clothes and, if she kept her nerve, the Robinson Treasures. Might as well get in a bit of practice around friends. Practice with the clothing part, Clarise silently proclaimed. She might be willing to attempt a flash, but she wasn't ready to go full frontal, or top frontal, with a couple of pixies. Brand-new best friends or not, that pushed the limit. Tomorrow, she'd show her magnitude to complete strangers, but that was tomorrow. One day at a time.

"Just the two of you," she instructed, her eyes landing on the teenagers.

"Deal!" they both squealed.

"Only a few things though. I don't have a lot of time," Clarise said. In fact, she only had two hours before her fashion-merchandising class started at the college.

"Got it," Shannon said. "You head on back to the changing area, right through there," she motioned down a yellow-and-orange hallway, the walls painted as though flames licked them from the floor. "We'll pick our favorites."

Before Clarise could second-guess her decision, Jadelle gently, but not too gently, shoved her down the hall. "Oooh, this is gonna be so much fun," she said, as Clarise made her way to the room. Three of the walls were red; the other mirrored. You'd think the red walls would be more shocking. But of all the colors and hues and textures that had captured her attention since she stepped into the boutique, nothing stunned her more than the image in that mirror.

She'd dressed normally this morning. Simple, mature upswept hair, sophisticated clothes, subdued makeup. The picture-perfect image of a business professional, but that wasn't the picture before her now. She looked excited and anxious, ready to have sex. Did everyone look at her and know what she planned to do at Gasparilla? Would Ethan see her and instantly know too? "What will Ethan think?" she whispered to her reflection.

"Ethan?" Shannon asked, having followed her into the dressing room.

"My boss."

"You mentioned him before," she said.

"Uh-huh," Clarise mumbled, still uncertain whether she wanted everyone, particularly Ethan, knowing her thoughts.

"Something going on there?" Jadelle asked, hanging her selected clothes on the red and orange hooks lining the walls and shooting a knowing look toward Shannon. "Where does he register on the hunk-o-meter?"

"Off the chart," Clarise answered before thinking.

"Well, I bet when he sees you, he'll think about it," Shannon said.

"Think about it?" Clarise asked numbly. Could she really attempt to seduce her friend? Because that's what she was planning, wasn't it? Could she convince him to look at her *that* way?

"Sex," Jadelle supplied, and the lump in Clarise's throat moved up a bit. Have mercy, she didn't want to hurl. "If he sees you looking confidently sexy, he'll think about it all right."

Wait a minute. Clarise's heart pumped up the volume. *Had* Ethan thought about it? He had given her one of those crooked sexy grins after he saw her in the red dress at the Christmas party. But had his sexy grin been because he thought she looked appealing? Or absurd? Then again, Jake Riley had given her the same look that night and, subsequently, hadn't stopped hinting that they should "get together sometime." He hadn't officially asked her out, but he had definitely made a few references to them "having some fun" at Gasparilla. However, there were two problems with getting together with Jake: 1) She knew his track record for reeling women in, bedding them well, then breaking their hearts, and 2) Clarise didn't want Jake; she wanted Ethan.

"Well?" Shannon asked.

"Well what?"

"Are you having sex with your boss?" Jadelle asked.

"No," Clarise quickly supplied.

"Wanting to?" Shannon continued.

Wanting to? Was she kidding? More like dying to. Dreaming to.

Jadelle giggled. "Okay, you don't have to answer. We know that look."

Clarise's cheeks burned as the blood sizzled up her neck. "I really need to get started trying these on," she said, eager to change the subject. Plus, she didn't have a surplus of time; she only had an hour left to get to class.

"We're gonna give you some privacy," Shannon said. "But you will let us see you in the outfits, right?"

She nodded, not wanting to talk anymore. So far, they not only knew her measurements but also that she fantasized about her boss. What else would she share? Her weight? Over her dead body.

The door clicked loudly as they left. Like the door on a jail cell. She swallowed. There wasn't anything she could do about what Ethan had thought. What had he thought? Pushing the question out of her head, at least for now, she removed the lime green sweater dress from the hanger. The color was unique, the fabric soft and clingy. Would it be too much to ask for the thing to fit?

Within two minutes, her work clothes, a cotton blouse,

sophisticated skirt, scarf belt, panty hose and flats, were in a crumpled pile on the dressing room floor. She held the new dress to her cheek and enjoyed the feel of the cloth on her skin, then she decided to bite the bullet and try the sucker on.

"No time like the present," she said, sliding it over her head. It smoothed over her curves, pressed against her flesh. Clarise bit her lower lip, held her breath and inched her eyes open to view the mirror. How bad could it be? "Oh. My."

She heard Shannon outside the door. "Jadelle, she's got something on!"

"Wait for me!" Jadelle called, her bare feet slapping the floor as she rushed down the hall.

"You coming out?" Shannon asked, her voice echoing through the tiny crack in the door. "Or you want us to come in?"

"You can come in," Clarise said, twisting the lock.

Both bounded inside. "I knew it!" Shannon squealed.

"Man, I need a boob job," Jadelle added.

"I can't believe that's me," Clarise admitted, gawking at the image in the mirror. Ethan had told her, and Clarise agreed that she conveyed class at work. But in this dress, she could honestly say she conveyed sass.

"Like my preacher always says: 'Believe it, beloved.'" Shannon giggled. "You better be ready to fight them off, and I'm not kidding. You look incredible."

Clarise stared, unable to speak. The green *did* pick up natural highlights in her hair, like Shannon predicted, and she hadn't even realized there were highlights to be picked up. Then she took in her figure, and the way the dress hugged it like a custom-fitted glove, holding her breasts high and firm and showcasing a waist that didn't look nearly as big as she'd believed. And her hips—they didn't seem overly excessive at all. As a matter of fact, they looked . . . good. Curvy. Feminine.

"You're ready for a red carpet premiere," Jadelle said. "First-rate, all the way."

"Do you think I'll do okay?" Clarise decided not to clarify by asking their opinion on whether she could entice Ethan Eubanks, her friend and her boss, for wild sex and a possible marriage proposal.

"Better than okay. One look at you in that dress, and those men will go wild."

Men going wild. Her pulse skittered. "Guess I should try on the other pieces too."

"Yeah, but trust me, they're gonna be perfect," Shannon said. "Absolutely perfect."

Clarise grinned. The p-word again, and suddenly, it sounded pretty darn good. She continued through the clothes, selected specifically with her full figure in mind. The results were phenomenal, beyond her wildest dreams. With each formfitting shirt, stretchy dress, or curve-enhancing pair of jeans, her confidence grew. Thanks to Shannon and Jadelle, she looked the part, like a single woman ready to take on the wild and wicked ways of Tampa at Gasparilla, eager to seduce the man of her dreams— and have a heck of a lot of fun doing it. The pixies were giving Clarise the same type of first-rate advice that she gave her Eubanks customers, except Clarise helped women look and feel elegant, Shannon and Jadelle helped her look and feel—hot.

Leaving the dressing room, Clarise walked down the flame-embellished hall a new woman, one who wasn't afraid of getting burned. She was beautiful, not a cute little waif or pixie, but beautiful just the same. Bold and busty and beautiful, ready to set her fire free, let it flame, let it engulf, let it go. Smiling, she approached the cash register and beamed at the two women on the other side.

"We've had so much fun with you," Shannon said, her voice almost sad that it was over, but still managing a tinge of excitement at what they'd accomplished.

"You're gonna have a ball with this jump-start to your new wardrobe," Jadelle added.

"And the new wardrobe will jump-start the new you," Shannon added, bagging the goods.

"Yeah," Clarise said, imagining a new world, where she didn't shy from new experiences, where she saw what she wanted and went for it, where she . . . lived. "A new me."

Chapter 5

Professor Higgenbottam, Clarise's fashion-merchandising instructor, had the flu, as noted in the materials left in the bin beside the classroom door. While Clarise looked forward to the Thursday night class, and to achieving her goal as a fashion buyer, she didn't mind that the class wasn't meeting this week. She needed all the time she could get to prepare, especially after Rachel had loaned her the video that would presumably teach her the proper technique of semistripping at Gasparilla.

With her arms overflowing in black and purple bags from Body Boutique, Clarise hurried from her car to her duplex, fumbled with the key and shuffled the packages to her living room. Then she did a second mad dash to her trunk, snatched up the pink-and-white-striped bags from her last stop, jogged up the sidewalk and scooted back inside. Blessedly, there hadn't been a single neighbor in the illuminated parking lot. Normally she relished the bright-as-day lights her apartment manager installed that made 10:00 P.M. resemble noon; tonight, however, she would have treasured the darkness that would have completely hidden her wares.

Truthfully, Clarise didn't care if anyone viewed the famously known bags associated with Body Boutique's trendy attire; however, the second batch of loot, the ones with the equally well-known pastel striping and satin black handles—that was another story entirely. After her class was canceled, she'd driven to the shopping malls in Trussville, thirty minutes away, to purchase her last-minute needs at the sassiest lingerie shop in town. Clarise hadn't wanted to spend the extra time making the trip across town, but the chances of running into an old high school or college friend, or worse, one of Granny Gert's canasta buddies, were much less probable outside the Birmingham city limits. She could only imagine what they'd say if they saw her sporting armfuls of bustiers and teddies.

Normally, she'd have purchased her new intimates online and had them delivered to her door in a brown, unmarked box. But while she'd toyed with the idea of how far to go at Gasparilla for three weeks, she had only decided to bare all in Tampa on Tuesday afternoon. Not enough time for delivery.

Clarise sure hoped she had what she needed. She had merely grabbed everything sexy she could find in her size, which she classified as "big" and "bigger." But, after her afternoon at Body Boutique, she didn't see that as such a terrible thing.

Peeking in the bags, she eyed the strap of a black garter belt. No doubt the encouraging comments from her two new friends had persuaded Clarise to venture even further out of her comfort zone. Had she gone too far? Another peek, and she glimpsed fishnet stockings. She smiled. Nope, not too far at all. If she were going for it, she was going the whole way, and with the surplus of slinky items in her bags, she had enough to go the whole way a few times. She'd even bought some cotton candy dust, since Ethan liked sweets as much as she did.

What was another pound if it headed to the right location? If indeed Shannon and Jadelle had been right in their opinion, which Clarise wanted to believe. Desperately. Was starting to believe, in fact. What if she was voluptuous and hadn't even realized it?

"That you, child?" Her grandmother's voice echoed from the bedroom.

After all the trouble Clarise had gone through to keep the majority of Birmingham from seeing her last-minute purchases, you'd think she would panic at the thought of Granny Gert's getting an eyeful of her new things, but Gertrude Robinson wasn't the typical grandparent. As a matter of fact, Clarise considered her grandmother to be her best friend, the one who understood her better than anyone else. And the one who'd totally approve of the flaming red merry widow with peekaboo cups.

"It's me," Clarise affirmed, placing her bags on the coffee table and tucking the borrowed video in her purse. While she was willing to show Granny the sexy garments she planned to wear, she wasn't at all willing to let her watch while Clarise practiced stripping. Knowing Granny Gert, she'd probably want to give Clarise tips, and that would definitely fall into the TMI, or too much information, category.

Clarise rented both sides of the duplex, this side for her, the other for Granny Gert, who actually wasn't invasive of Clarise's apartment. She'd called this morning to see if she could bring over a few items for her grand-daughter's "adventure," as she called it.

"I got you a street map of Tampa with the parade routes highlighted," she called from the bedroom. "Don't miss the invasion; it's incredible. Last time I saw it was in '88, but I'm sure it's still the cat's meow. The costumes and the floats will leave you speechless."

"I can't wait."

"How was class?" Granny called. "You're home early, aren't ya?"

"My instructor was sick, so we didn't meet," Clarise answered.

"That's too bad," her grandmother said. "I know how much you like going."

Clarise smiled. Granny Gert knew her so well. Most people would cringe at spending three hours in a class-room after a workday, but Clarise looked forward to those long Thursday nights, knowing each and every class brought her one small step closer to her goal. "At least I'll be back from Tampa in time for next week's class."

"By the way, I put everything in your suitcase, along with my personal shopping list and some cash to make the purchases, but if you're having too much fun to pick up the things on my wish list, don't worry about it." Granny Gert stepped from the bedroom and started down the hall toward the front of the apartment.

Clarise took in her grandmother's traditional daily attire, which was anything but traditional. A hot pink silk dress, its top clinging to her enormous chest like a mud wrap, was paired with a skirt that flowed like liquid around her legs and brushed the tops of floral tapestry heels. She looked the picture of summer, which was to be expected for

Gertrude Robinson, in spite of the calendar proclaiming January as the month of choice. Hot-natured, that's what she called it, and Clarise had obviously inherited the trait; she didn't have a jacket to her name. And she suspected she had also inherited more than a smidgen of Granny's feistiness, though she'd never really given it the chance to surface. Time would tell.

She grinned. Looking at her grandmother was like looking in a mirror . . . with an extra forty-two years tacked on, but time had been kind to Granny Gert. True, she'd gone through a slump five years ago, after Grandpa Henry passed. He'd been her true love and enjoyed life nearly as much as she, but he wanted his "spitfire" to move on. He'd told her so, before he died, and now she had, accepting Clarise's offer of a place to stay, close enough for her granddaughter to help her if she ever needed it, but a place of her own to allow the independence she craved. From Clarise's point of view, it was a good situation for everyone. If only her father approved of her efforts to nurture her grandmother's free spirit, then everything would be super. Unfortunately, Granny Gert's disposition had skipped a generation, leaving him out in the cold. Thank goodness Clarise's mother had enough liveliness and positive attitude for a small army. The two of them were living proof that opposites attract.

"Have mercy, child. You look like you just rolled out of bed." Gertrude Robinson proclaimed, her pink-glossed lips stretching into her porcelain cheeks as she smiled. "Looks like you better tell me about your day. If you have enough energy left, that is."

"Energy?"

With her heels barely clicking on Clarise's hardwood

floor, Granny Gert glided down the hall, crossed the tiny living room and stood in front of Clarise. Then she placed her index finger beneath her granddaughter's chin and tilted her face from one side to the other. "It's all right if you don't want to talk about it, sweetie. But I'm curious—it's that good-looking boss of yours, right? The one you spend your Friday nights with?"

Clarise blinked. What was she talking about? "We have coffee, Granny, on Friday afternoons, not evenings." She situated her shopping bags. "And what about Ethan?"

Another shiny, knowing grin flashed, and Clarise saw a hint of her blurred reflection via her grandmother's lips.

"Ethan. Yes, that's the one. I knew it, you know. I suspected last year at that company picnic, when you let me tag along. I could see it happening between you two, but I figured it wouldn't take this long. Usually a spark starts a fire a bit quicker, or it used to, back in the day when your grandpa Henry came courting me. God rest his soul."

Any way Clarise looked at it, Gertrude Robinson was still in "the day." "What did you suspect?" she asked.

"Grandmothers are keen to these things, you know," Granny said, chuckling softly. "It's in our nature." She draped an arm around Clarise and guided her to the couch. "I've been waiting for this to happen, so I hope you'll indulge me in a bit of how it got started. Not the, er, overly interesting details, just the basics."

"The basics?"

"Or not," she said, shrugging. "It's up to you, dear. I'm pleased either way. So, is he going too?"

Clarise was suddenly tempted to believe her father's claim that Granny Gert lived in another world. He'd said as much when he deemed her ready for the retirement village. Clarise had nothing against the place, but her grand-mother had way too much spunk to be trapped in a complex where the main activities were bingo and shuffleboard; that was more her father's speed. Her mother and Granny Gert were much too alive to be stifled. But Clarise had to admit, right now, her grandmother seemed to be having a conversation that definitely didn't involve the here and now.

"Going too?" Clarise asked.

"On the trip. Goodness child, it's been a long time since I've had a romp in the hay, but I sure enough remember what I looked like after. Though, as much as my dear Henry and I liked variety, we never had a good time in his office. I honestly don't believe we could've pulled it off. Guess you're not as noisy as I was." She giggled girlishly. "Lordy, I bet that's more than you wanted to know."

Clarise blinked. "You think I did *that*? Today? At the office? With Ethan?"

"Oh, honey, it's okay if you don't want to talk about it." She patted Clarise's knee, then ended with a gentle squeeze that made Clarise jump. "I totally understand, and I admire your ability to keep it all in. Me, I always had to tell somebody. Made it a little more fun, in my opinion. That guess-what-we-did kind of thing. I talked to your great-aunt Sybil, God rest her soul. She was deter-mined she and your great-uncle Clyde would one-up the two of us eventually, but I swear, your grandpa Henry and I weren't gonna be outdone by anyone. I mentioned we liked variety, didn't I?"

Clarise wasn't sure she needed to hear any more about her grandparents' variety. "I worked today. Nothing else. I promise." Not that she would have declined a bit of variety, as Granny called it, with Ethan. Heck, the way she got worked up over merely talking to him, she could only imagine what sex would do, but even though she crawled on top of his luscious body nightly in her dreams, the real deal hadn't happened. Yet. At Gasparilla, however, if dreams came true . . .

Her grandmother tilted her head and considered her words. "Seriously? You haven't been, you know, getting cozy with your boss today?"

"Not my boss, or anyone else. I believe I'd remember if I had. Plus, Ethan wasn't at work today; he's been out of town working on a big deal to purchase additional stores."

"Well then, child, you sure didn't take your normal considerations with your appearance this morning, did you? Guess you were excited about the trip, hmm?"

"I spent the afternoon trying on new clothes at the Body Boutique, before wrapping up with a lingerie binge in Trussville after my class was canceled. I guess I dressed rather quickly. I look rough?" she questioned.

Granny tilted her head, evidently trying to decide what to say, then she shrugged, and blurted, "You look like you've had great sex."

Clarise laughed. "Well, I haven't."

"It'll happen, child," Granny consoled.

"I hope you're right," Clarise said, then silently added, *"and I hope it happens with Ethan."*

Granny Gert's giggle sounded almost teenish. "Okay," she said, "enough sex talk, since neither of us has had any lately. Tell me about your afternoon. You said you tried your new things on at the store. That's not your nature, so you might as well tell me what happened. And, by the way, it's about time you opened up and saw everything for what it's worth."

"What it's worth?"

"Your figure. You really do have one that deserves flaunting, sweetie."

"Actually, the two girls who helped me out at Body Boutique probably picked some things you'll like."

"Really? Well, by all means, let's have a look, and don't you dare hold out on me with the lingerie items. It's been a while since I've bought anything new, and I'd love to see what's considered *in*." She clapped her hands together. "You have time to model?"

Clarise laughed. "I don't think so. I haven't finished packing." And she still needed to practice stripping. "How about I lay them out in the bedroom for your opinion?"

"Eh," she said, shrugging off her disappointment, "I guess it'll have to do. Go on and start laying them out, and I'll finish cooking."

"You cooked?" Clarise asked, her stomach tingling in anticipation.

"Shoot, you're leaving tomorrow morning for Gasparilla, and I bet none of those folks down there have a clue how to fix good ol' turnip greens and corn bread, not to mention pintos."

"You shouldn't have done that," Clarise said, but she was inwardly celebrating. Her grandmother was the best cook she knew, and she loved doting on Clarise. Lord knows, Clarise didn't mind letting her.

"Uh-uh," Granny said, waving a mauve-tipped finger. "Don't you start now. I love cooking for you. Made you a chocolate pie too."

"With meringue?" Clarise's mouth watered.

"As if it'd be a Gertrude Robinson blue-ribbon-winning chocolate pie without meringue," Granny said, clucking her tongue as she headed toward the kitchen.

Laughing, Clarise scooped up her bags and hauled them to the bedroom. She wouldn't be able to carry all of her new things to Tampa, so a quick perusal from Granny Gert might be exactly what she needed to help her decide what to bring. Draping the items around the bed, she listened to Granny Gert's heels softly clicking down the hall. "Okay, let's have a look," Granny said, rounding the doorway of Clarise's bedroom and shuffling toward the bed. Moving both palms to her cheeks, she gasped. "Oh, wow. They're beautiful."

"The clothes or the lingerie?"

"All of it." She circled the bed, picking up the fabrics and rearranging the items so that each piece of clothing was topped with a wisp of lingerie. Then she slapped her palms together and nodded approvingly. "Yep, that's how I'd do it."

"How you'd do what?"

"Wear the unmentionables. See, you want to wear this red one with the tube top," she said, fingering the filmy lace of the merry widow.

"Why's that?" Clarise asked, ever intrigued by her grandmother's infinite wisdom and amazed that it evidently included a knowledge of intimate apparel.

"Because it's easy to pull down. One swipe and you've got everything right out in the open where it's supposed to be, right? Then you can flip it back up in a jiff, if ya want."

Clarise shook her head. "I get your point."

"Or points," Granny said, winking.

"You're terrible," Clarise said, her smile so broad it hurt her cheeks.

"So your father says," Granny quipped, with a flippant shrug. "You can tell I lose sleep over it."

"Well, I love you for it."

"Exactly. So, is there a lucky fellow, say, your boss, for example, who'll be on the receiving end of this show of sexy duds? He's been the dream guy, hasn't he?"

When Clarise didn't answer, Granny added, "Child, like I said, I saw it last year. The thing you haven't seen, however, is that spark flying from the other direction."

Oh to dream. "You imagined that, Granny," Clarise said, but she did wonder if Ethan had thought about more than friendship.

Another shrug, then Granny Gert lifted the fishnet stockings. "Oh, I had a pair of these. Wait a minute, I still do. In my second panty drawer."

How many grandmothers kept two drawers for their *drawers?* Clarise grinned. She gave Granny Gert twenty minutes tops before she went searching for her own pair of slinky hose, and an hour at best before she slid them on.

"I didn't imagine anything, young lady," Granny said, transitioning quickly into the original conversation. "So, is he going along?"

"I told you before, we're just friends. And yes, he's going on the trip. I don't know if he's getting back in town tonight or tomorrow, but he told me he'd be back in time to head to Tampa and that he'd see me there."

"Uh-huh," she mumbled. "Oh, wow, this is gorgeous. It's going to really play up your hair and eyes." She fingered the green dress.

"It does, though I didn't believe it until the girls at the

shop pointed it out and made me try it on," Clarise admitted.

"I gotta send those gals a thank-you note. They know their stuff, and so do I. Your boss *has* noticed, whether you realize it or not. I saw him looking at you, and I know that look."

"That was last year at a company picnic. He was looking at all of his employees."

"Not the same way," Granny countered.

"I don't think so, but you're entitled to your opinion," Clarise said, refusing to admit her hopes aloud. It was one thing to think it, quite another to verbalize it. *Were* there sparks on Ethan's end?

"Well, if you're not planning to fulfill those fantasies with your boss, why buy all these?" Then, before Clarise could answer, she continued, "Oh!" She turned and plopped down on the bed. "Okay. Well." She quirked pink lips to the side. "I know I joke about sex, child, but I really don't approve of you going down there to, well, do that with a stranger. I just assumed you were trying to entice your boss."

"I am," Clarise blurted, before her brain could signal to her mouth to choose her words wisely.

Granny Gert beamed triumphantly, and her rosy cheeks plumped up to push her eyes into tiny crinkles. "I knew it. You will be careful?"

"Yes, ma'am," Clarise said, her own cheeks on fire.

Granny didn't miss a beat. "You've got protection?"

Boy, did this conversation ever take a strange turn. "I do."

"Tell me something, child."

"What?" Clarise asked, bracing. What else was there to tell?

"He's the real deal?"

"Ethan?"

Her grandmother nodded.

"Truthfully, I'm not sure he's interested, not in anything more than friendship."

"Yes, dear," Granny said. "He's interested. You'll see. You know, I can tell those saleswomen steered you right. You're going to be absolutely gorgeous for Gasparilla. Everyone's gonna see how exquisite you are. Though I always knew it," she said, as the phone rang. "Drat. I was supposed to tell you to call your sister. She's been calling every hour on the hour since this afternoon."

"What's up?" Clarise asked, reaching toward the phone beside her bed.

"Don't know. She said she had to talk to you before you leave town. Sounded urgent, but then again, everything's urgent to Babette, isn't it? Tell you what, let me answer it so I can apologize for forgetting to tell you. Lord knows I don't want to tick that pistol off."

Clarise laughed, snatched the phone and surveyed the caller ID display. "It says unknown number," she said, then shrugged and handed the phone to her grandmother.

"Hello? Oh, yes, this is her place, but this is Gertrude." Her eyes widened, then her cheeks blushed with even more pink. "Oh, of course. Yes, I can do that. Sure, I'd be happy to." Her mouth curved slightly, and Clarise wondered who was on the other end. It obviously wasn't her sister.

"Yes," Granny said enthusiastically. "Yes, that's fine." She hung up and kept smiling.

"Who was it?" Clarise asked, puzzled.

"Wasn't Babette," Granny Gert said, then added, "Just one of those survey calls."

"Survey calls?" Clarise questioned.

"Telemarketer, you know. Do you like this? Do you buy that? Do you want a free weekend trip to Orlando? That kind of thing."

Clarise's eyes squinted as she scrutinized her grandmother, who, unless Clarise had totally lost her ability to read Gertrude Robinson's mannerisms, was at the most lying, and at the least, fibbing. Granny Gert swore there was a difference, though Clarise had yet to figure out what it was.

"Well," Granny said, rising from the bed and brushing her hands down her skirt, "I need to go. And you need to call your sister, and you need to eat, and of course, you need to pack," she rattled, kissing Clarise briefly on the cheek, then heading out the bedroom door. "I'm going on home now. I'm suddenly feeling tired," she said.

Clarise had no idea what was going on with her, but she knew better than to question Granny's motives. Once the woman had her mind made up, that was all she wrote on the subject. "Okay," she said, as Granny Gert's heels clicked softly down the hall.

"Call me from Tampa!" Granny yelled before the front door slammed.

Ethan snapped his cell phone shut and continued his drive across town. He was exhausted from the past four weeks of nonstop traveling, then to top things off, today's flight had been delayed for two hours due to rough weather in Myrtle Beach, but he couldn't go home yet. He had to see Clarise.

During his month of hotel hopping, he'd had plenty of time to consider the possibilities—and the ramifications— to taking whatever passed between them at the Christmas party to the next level. Hell, he didn't know or understand exactly what happened, but he'd be lying if he said he didn't realize that something had, and he'd also be lying if he didn't acknowledge that acting on that *something* might very well cost him his top salesperson . . . and his closest friend. Thank goodness, the salesperson part didn't bother him nearly as much as the friend one, which proved he hadn't totally become a hard ass businessman. But he was a businessman—a thinker and a planner—and he'd been blessed to have plenty of thinking and planning to do during the last month for the Panache acquisition. If he hadn't, he'd have probably overthought and overplanned what to do about this situation with Clarise. As it was, he'd decided the best thing to do was to simply talk to her and make sure they were okay in both the friendship and working arenas, then resume their previous platonic relationship as if he hadn't thought about having sex with her when he saw her in that red dress.

His grip tightened on the steering wheel. She didn't know where his thoughts had headed that night, and he sure as hell wasn't going to tell her, but after being on the road for a solid month, he still wanted to see her before he went home. What did that say? That he really had entertained the notion of intimacy with his friend, or that he wanted to prove that he could overcome the desire to sleep with her? Because sleeping with Clarise would botch everything— or at least it could—and he wasn't willing to risk it. He cared about her, *knew* her, more than any of the women he'd dated throughout the past few years, and he believed it was because they had kept it at the friendship level. Ethan wasn't a fool; he knew that no matter how hard he tried, he couldn't commit. Was it because, as his brother had hinted, he was married to the business? Maybe. But he was bound and determined that Eubanks Elegant Apparel would become the premiere fine clothing store for the nation, and that wouldn't happen if his focus wasn't on the company 24/7. Hell, he'd spent Christmas and New Year's on the road; didn't that say where his heart was? However, he had called Clarise on both occasions, because she was his friend. Surely that was why he felt compelled to call her—to hear her voice—on those special days.

Ethan groaned aloud. Twenty more minutes until he reached her apartment complex. He'd only been there once before. She'd been sick and hadn't been able to make it to work, but she had wanted to review some clothing samples from home, so Ethan volunteered to bring them. That time, he'd barely crossed the threshold, since she was determined to keep him from "catching anything." She'd looked so cute in an oversized pink T-shirt and gray sweats, with furry gray slippers in the shape of smiling mice on her feet. Ethan swallowed. Was it normal that he remembered every detail of what she'd been wearing that day? Sure it was. He dealt in the clothing industry; therefore, he noticed clothes. But he hadn't merely noticed her clothes; he'd noticed Clarise, away from her working persona. She'd been at home and comfortable, and that was different than the Clarise he saw every day. Even their Friday coffee chats happened directly after work, so she was still pretty much in business mode. But that day, she was merely Clarise, his friend, who was sick, and he'd wanted to say to hell with "catching anything," waltz inside and take over caring for her. However, she'd shooed him out the door in nothing flat and assured him that her "Granny Gert" would take care of things. Ethan had left, but he'd also phoned her several times over that three-day period to make sure that her grandmother was in fact taking care of his friend. Naturally, she was, and naturally, Ethan attributed his desire to check on her to friendship, because that was all it was, a friend caring about a friend.

He took a deep breath, blew it out and exited the interstate near her apartment complex. Hopefully, Clarise's grandmother had followed through with her promise to tell the guard at the gate to let him in. She'd sure sounded strange on the phone, but then again, from what he remembered of meeting Gertrude Robinson last year at the corporate picnic, she was an eccentric, fun-loving lady who probably would come across as outlandish during any conversation, on the telephone or not.

He'd expected Clarise to answer when he phoned her apartment, but she'd often told him that her grandmother happened to spend a good deal of time visiting Clarise's side of the duplex. Besides, it was probably best that Gertrude Robinson picked up the phone; if Clarise had answered, he might have simply informed her over the phone that he wasn't going to Gasparilla, and he should tell her in person. One, because he suspected she was only going because he'd coaxed her into it over numerous coffee chats, and two, because he wanted to see if that electricity that zinged between them at the Christmas party, at least on his end, could be harnessed.

Chapter 6

Clarise snapped the lid on the Tupperware bowl that held the remainder of Granny Gert's pintos, opened the fridge and slid it inside, next to the bowl of leftover turnip greens and a large silver square of foil-wrapped corn bread. She hadn't been able to eat more than a few bites, mainly because she couldn't get her mind off her upcoming trip . . . and Ethan. Her phone rang, and she checked the caller ID to see yet another "unknown number." Knowing that Babette's info would display her name, Clarise let it ring, then listened to the loud click when the caller hung up on the answering machine. "Telemarketer," she said, turning off the kitchen light and moving into her living room to find her purse and fish out the how-to-strip video. She still needed to call her sister, but first things first—she also needed to learn how to remove her top seductively. After popping the video in the VCR portion of her entertainment center, she shoved the coffee table out of the way and prepared to watch, learn and practice.

She'd planned to give it a try immediately, but found herself sitting on the sofa throughout the entire shebang, merely viewing the woman on the balcony as she tempted the men below with her impressive bosom. After the video ended, Clarise grabbed the remote control from its perch on the arm of the sofa, snatched a notebook from the top of the coffee table, and pressed REWIND. Then she watched the display again and took notes, annotating plenty of details. Hey, she was a planner, and this technique definitely called for careful planning. Figuring the third time was the charm, she pressed REWIND once more and stood. And when the woman once again began undressing for the crowd, so did Clarise.

The stripping section of the video was extremely short, so within a matter of seconds, Clarise had swayed her hips, pulled her blouse out of her skirt (in a sexy manner, she hoped) and unbuttoned the top three buttons. With what she believed was a sultry smile, she slid the last button through the hole and let her blouse fall open. She thought about what she was doing and nearly laughed out loud; this certainly wasn't the way she spent her usual Thursday evenings, but then again, this wasn't a usual week. Typically, she'd already have her weekend activities mapped out, courtesy of the *TV Guide* and her *Dining for One* cookbook, but not this weekend. *This* weekend, she'd bare her soul, and everything else, in Tampa. And if she was going to put all of—she glanced down and flinched—*this* out there, she sure wanted to get it right.

Encouraged by the chants and cheers of the partying crowd on the video, she quickly released the front closure of her bra before she had a chance to change her mind. The Robinson Treasures, as Granny Gert called them, sprang free.

She turned her attention back to the Pirate Fest video,

where a tall, drop-dead-gorgeous Adonis in full pirate garb stood in the center of the crowd with one hand cradling his drink and the other pressed to his heart. Would Ethan dress like a pirate at Gasparilla? Probably not, but right now, Clarise mentally put his face on the pirate hunk's body, for inspiration. Have mercy, she'd need a whole lot of what Granny Gert called "gumption" if she was going to pull this off.

A puff of cool air entered the room when the heating unit in her duplex whirred to life. The Robinson Treasures tingled as the breeze quickly converted from frigid to toasty. She swallowed. January in Birmingham didn't lend itself to the necessary warmth for baring your body at a downtown parade. However, Rachel and Jesilyn had promised that Tampa would provide plenty of heat . . . from the climate as well as the partying crowd.

"Come on, darlin'. You're killing us," Adonis drawled, his Southern accent even stronger than his alcohol. Clarise examined the hand against his chest. Wide palms, long fingers. She ran her top teeth over her lower lip and wondered if it were true what they said about men with big hands. Ethan had big hands. Nice. Big. Hands. Clarise had noticed, a few times. When he displayed clothing samples from new product lines at the weekly staff meetings, she forced herself to concentrate on the exquisite quality of the garments rather than those captivating hands. How was she supposed to watch those long fingers reverently touch a Hermès scarf without wondering what it would feel like to have them caressing her skin? And as head of the Women's Department, Clarise really needed to pay attention to the details, which she did, as long as she kept her mind off those hands.

"Aren't ya gonna show us something?" that sexy Southern accent continued from the guy on the television screen. He flashed a megawatt smile and made her belly flutter. That was her cue. Clarise knew he'd ask, and she was ready. She snatched a glance at her notes, then sucked in her breath and waited for his next instruction. It would come in exactly forty-eight seconds. She'd timed it. One thousand one . . . one thousand two . . .

Exhaling thickly, she focused on his baby blue eyes. She loved blue eyes, always had, probably because her own were so dang dark she couldn't tell where the iris began and the pupil ended. Not an ounce of color, nothing attention grabbing at all, which was just as well, since she spent most of her time trying to hide the remainder of her abundant body. But not anymore. After thirty years of perfecting her wallflower image, she had a chance to set herself free, let all her insecurities and inhibitions disappear and show the world, or at least most of Tampa, the real Clarise Robinson, the one she dreamed of each night, a girl who would drink and dance and party and have fun, bare her body and be proud of its bounty. And have monkey sex with Ethan Eubanks before Pirate Fest ended.

She licked her lips. Swallowed hard. Her ready-for-anything sister, Babette, would have no trouble baring her body to the masses at Gasparilla. She'd done it last year, in fact, when she'd taken Clarise's place. But then again, Babette's body was worthy of a Pirate Fest showing; Clarise's, on the other hand, was more conducive for a Fat Fest showing. She frowned, a little, then remembered Granny Gert's motto: *"Curves are where it's at, Clarise."* Taking a deep breath, she boosted her confidence once more. She did have curves, lots of them, and tomorrow she would flaunt her surplus and get what she wanted . . . Ethan. Hopefully.

Not realizing that she only had one man in mind for her wild adventure in Tampa, Jesilyn and Rachel had suggested Clarise cozy up to one of the gorgeous guys from work during the trip. All of the department heads were going, since Ethan footed the bill for each of them to attend the annual corporate bonding excursion. No doubt, each was planning to get hot and heated with someone at Gasparilla. When those modern-day pirates invade the city, like Jose Gasparilla's pirates did so long ago, the guys from Eubanks Elegant Apparel would undoubtedly want to perform an invasion too, invading a woman's bed. Surely, Ethan was planning on the same thing. Would he think about having a bit of no-holds-barred, wild and frantic sex with "best buddy" Clarise? She blew her bangs out of her eyes while her shoulders dropped a notch. Who was she kidding? Wild, frantic sex? Shoot, she'd settle for mild, lukewarm. Or any activity that involved Ethan Eubanks pressed against her. As long as it'd been, that'd be all she needed to work into a lather.

No, she silently commanded, straightening her back and lifting her chest. She refused to settle for tepid. She wanted hot, boiling, exhilarating sex, and that's what she'd get. Toe-curling, eye-glazing, heart-stopping sex, better than she'd ever had. Clarise winced. Better than she'd ever had wasn't saying much. Shoot, sex with the lights on would extend her current bedroom repertoire. She needed a better goal, or several better goals.

She glanced at her blue notebook, perched on the coffee table. For the past few days, she'd studied the Pirate Fest brochures, the parade schedules and practically all of

the Internet sites advertising the event. While she'd outlined the must-see parades, she hadn't acknowledged the
activities she most wanted to accomplish during her trip,
not on paper, anyway. Flipping past the pages of parade
routes, Clarise grabbed a pen. She'd always been a list
person, loved setting goals and feeling that major sense of
accomplishment when she checked them off one by one.
Why should her "Topless in Tampa" adventure be any different? After all, she knew what she wanted. Sex with the
lights on, for starters. She wrote it down, smiled. Finally,
a real goal, but that wasn't nearly enough, and if she was
going to do this, she wasn't going halfway.

Grinning, she scribbled *sex outside.* Sex. Outside. Her
nipples puckered at the mere thought. But she didn't want
just outside. With her pulse racing, she amended her list
to include different kinds of outside—in the grass, for sure,
and on a beach; those beach scenes in romance novels
sounded *hot.* Water sloshing around her legs while she
and her lover tore into each other like animals in heat.
Yep, she'd try that. Tampa had plenty of beach to offer.

She bit her lip. There was one more kind of outside sex
she wanted more than the others. Before she lost her nerve,
she wrote it down. *Under-the-bleachers sex.* Clarise listened to those locker room conversations throughout her
teen years. When she heard them talk about bleacher sex,
that had been the most intriguing thing she had ever heard.
She definitely wanted bleacher sex.

Yeah, all of those for outside sex. That'd work. And
lots of inside sex too. Standing up looked rather nice in
the movies, and shower sex. How could she forget her
shower sex fantasy? She'd want to get in a bit of shower
action. Hot water, hot bodies. Well, *his* body would be hot.

Maybe, if he'd had enough of those hurricane drinks everyone was holding in the video, he'd believe hers was too. She added the last two to her list.

Clarise giggled, then moved her hands to her chest when the action made her unbound treasures bounce. Could she let go enough to have kinky sex with Ethan? Was he even into the whole wild and frantic sex thing? That topic had never come up during their Friday coffee chats. Then again, what guy wasn't into wild and frantic sex? However, what she needed to learn was whether Ethan was into . . . her. And what if, at Pirate Fest, he realized that he was? Then Clarise could be like Julia Roberts in *Pretty Woman* finding her Richard Gere for wild and kinky sex and ending up with a lifetime of love. Of course, Julia wasn't pleasantly plump. Then again, Clarise wasn't a prostitute either. Who knows? Ethan could see her as more than a friend on this trip. Maybe when Clarise found the nerve to let herself go and pursue her wildest fantasies, he would see there was more to her than meets the eye. She imagined Ethan, whispering in her ear, telling her that he wanted her more than anything in the world. Ethan, having fanatic sex with her for five sizzling days, then professing his undying love. Granny Gert always said if you're gonna dream, you might as well dream big. Then again, everything about Granny factored as abundantly proportioned, dreams, bosom and behind included.

The blond hunk stared at her via the screen as though willing her to grant his next request. *Go on, blue eyes, ask.* And, since forty-eight seconds had passed, he did. "Shimmy for them, darlin'," he said, removing a strand of gold beads from his neck and dangling the glittering loop from one of those beautifully long fingers. "Come on. Give us a little shake."

Clarise flashed a siren smile, trying her best to imitate the one the woman tossed him on the video. Then she leaned forward and flicked her shoulders back and forth, sending Granny Gert's heritage swinging like heavy water balloons in front of the screen.

The knock on the door caught her midshimmy, and she abruptly stopped moving. Well, most of her did. Boom One and Boom Two still had a whole lotta shakin' going on. She whirled to snatch the remote from the couch, then slapped at the control to stop the tape. However, in her haste to get rid of the evidence, she hit the VOLUME button instead. Within half a second, blonde and friends screamed their approval at the hooters on display.

"Yeah, baby, show us what you got!" one yelled.

"Have mercy!" blue eyes added.

"Ohmigod," Clarise whimpered, grabbing a fistful of bra and shirt with one hand, while the other frantically punched the POWER button on the television. How much could you hear through her apartment door anyway? And why had she never thought to check? "Granny?" she called, hoping it was Granny Gert on the other side but knowing good and well that her grandmother had a key and would have done one of those knocking-as-she's-entering kind of things.

"No, Clarise. It's me. Didn't your grandmother tell you I was coming over? I talked to her when I called earlier, and she cleared it with the guard at the gate," Ethan called loudly from the other side of the door. "Are you okay in there?"

Murder—the first word that came to mind. She'd kill

her grandmother. No, not literally, but somehow, someday, she would get Granny back for this one. And wasn't this just great? While she was playing exhibitionist with the blond hunk on the screen, the real deal was perched outside her door. The most gorgeous sandy-haired, turquoise-eyed male she'd ever seen, who happened to be her boss and her closest friend, was merely feet away, listening. Or was he? What had Ethan heard? She attempted to control her heart rate.

"Clarise?" Ethan repeated.

Hadn't he said that he wouldn't see her until Friday, when they got to Gasparilla? Did he realize how he had surprised her by coming back early? Or how big a surprise it was? As in, a *surprise* heart attack for Clarise? She was usually pretty good at hiding things from Ethan. They'd grown close, but she still kept her secrets guarded. Not many secrets, mind you, only two. One, her real career goal. And two, the fact that he made her head swim and her heart tremble. Heat crept up her body, starting with her bulging boobs, then worked its way up her throat to settle in her cheeks. "I'm—fine, and no, Granny didn't tell me."

"I need to speak with you about the trip," he said, that sexy, raspy voice making her nipples salute.

"Sure." She yanked the megacups of her bra together and fastened the closure without taking time to situate the two mounds in their holsters. As a result, righty had a hefty portion plumped over the top and lefty had some side action happening, with a paunch of flesh poking her armpit.

"Do you need me to come back?" he asked, with more than a hint of curiosity in his tone.

"No," she gasped. Lord, would he be able to tell that she'd been practicing her stripping techniques for Gasparilla?

She scanned the room, her eyes lighting on the coffee table, haphazardly shoved against one wall. She leaned over, grabbed the edge and yanked it back in place. Thank goodness she'd already hauled all of her new clothes and unmentionables back to the bedroom. Funny thing was, Ethan would probably chalk all of this up to progress. He'd been trying to get her to come out of her shell for the past three years. If he only knew, she'd do more than that. By tomorrow, she'd come out of her top. Then, if she did it right, she'd be coming period, with the lights on, or outside, or on the grass, or all of the above. Whatever Ethan wanted . . . if he wanted. Have mercy, she hoped he did. But why was he here tonight? And did this mean she should jump-start her plan to seduce him and start a day early? She swallowed hard. Nope. Her mind had prepared for tomorrow, and she simply hadn't worked up the courage to "go for it" tonight. She needed to get to Tampa, to the wildness of Gasparilla, before she truly tried to pursue her dream. In fact, perhaps one of those tall drinks like the one the guy had been holding in the video would help ease her into seduction mode, because goodness knows right now her pulse was so jittery that she couldn't seduce him if she tried. If she'd known he was coming, she'd have at least cleaned up her apartment. Was it her imagination, or did it still smell like turnip greens and pintos?

She fumbled her way with the buttons, then jabbed the ends of her blouse into the top of her skirt, all the while thanking God and heaven above for elastic waistbands. Then she snatched her red scarf off the couch and quickly tied it at her waist as elegantly as possible, given her shaky fingers. Making certain the television was off, she took a deep breath, unlocked the door and opened it. Dang if his eyes weren't bluer than she remembered, and double-dang if he didn't look even better than last night's dream. Clarise swallowed. She would *not* think about that now, wouldn't picture the way she'd envisioned him tearing her clothes from her body in a frantic effort to touch her, hold her, get inside her. She focused on those waves of sandy hair, thick brows, strong jaw, totally kissable mouth, broad shoulders . . . heavens, what was she doing? Blushing, that's what, and from the brilliant grin on that gorgeous face, he'd noticed. "You wanted to talk about the trip?"

"Yes. Can I come in?" he asked.

Man, she'd missed his voice. "Sure," she said, trying to disguise how hard she was breathing from the panic attack his knock had initiated. She stepped aside, then nearly jumped when he gave her a brief hug before entering.

"Good to see you, Clarise," he said, while she inhaled the tantalizing smell of spicy cologne and pure Ethan as he slowly broke from the embrace and entered her apartment.

"You too," she said, trying to remember how this worked—breathing, that is. In and out, in and out, yeah, that's it. "Your trip went well, I guess?" she finally asked.

"It was great," he said, sitting casually on the sofa as if he belonged here, and in her heart, she believed he did. "The Panache deal should go through tomorrow, and we'll be an eighteen-store corporation," he said, his excitement evident in the words. But before he told her more about the deal, he pointed to the television, where a neon green arrow glowed from the VCR portion. "Were you watching a movie?"

No way. The tape was still rolling, even though the screen was off, and he could see that blinking arrow, dadgummit. "Yeah," she said, hurrying across the room, then stretching a finger toward the machine and punching the STOP button. A surge of relief flooded through her when the tattletale arrow disappeared. "Would you like something to drink?" she asked, trying her best to change the subject. "A Coke, maybe?"

"Sure," he said.

"In the can or over ice?" she asked, ever the hospitable hostess for her friend, her boss and her every fantasy.

"The can is fine." Then, while she withdrew two cans from the fridge, he turned the subject right back to that blasted tape. "Sounded like a Gasparilla parade. Trying to get an idea of what's in store?" he asked, accepting his Coke from Clarise.

Her skin tingled when her fingertips brushed his hand, and she sat abruptly on the other end of the couch to try to camouflage her wobbly knees. They'd been having their coffee chats for nearly three years, and she'd controlled herself; what had happened that made a brush of his fingers do this? But she knew; he'd looked at her, really looked at her, that night at the Christmas party, and, being the planner that she was, she hadn't stopped calculating the possibilities of that look ever since. She fought the impulse to shiver—if a simple touch did this, what the heck would a kiss do? She could hardly wait to find out. Maybe by tomorrow night, she'd know, if she could ever get the nerve to tell him she wanted more than mere friendship, and if he felt the same. So many ifs, so little time. One more day.

"There's nothing like it, seeing that big Jose Gasparilla ship sail into Tampa with hundreds of the city's most prominent men dressed as pirates set to take over the place.

Then you've got the parades and the parties," he added, then cleared his throat. "I thought I should warn you about some of the—activities—down there. The women are— hell, Clarise, I don't know how to describe it other than— wild." His mouth crooked to the side. Then he took a long drink, as if he had to do something with those enticing lips to keep from outright laughing at her attempt to blend with the wild women of Tampa. Was that it? Or was it something else that made him look uncomfortable with the statement?

Well, whatever the reason, Clarise wanted to spout some smart remark about how she could be sexy if she wanted— how she could make him want her, if she wanted—but she couldn't concentrate on anything beyond watching his neck pulse with each swallow.

Ethan lowered the can and looked at her thoughtfully. "Not that I think you should pass on the trip. I'm glad you're going, but you've never been around anything quite like Tampa during Gasparilla. I want you to be prepared."

Clarise didn't mind him giving her a few pointers. Actually, she'd have been surprised if he didn't try to prepare her, in a friend-to-friend kind of deal. In fact, that lack of preparedness was the real reason she'd asked Rachel to loan her the Gasparilla tape. Ethan was right; Tampa during Gasparilla was more than Clarise had expected. More colorful. More exciting. More naked.

"I'm ready," she said, and couldn't keep her smile from bursting free.

He laughed heartily, and the luxurious sound rippled down her skin like hot shower water, touching her every- where. "I have no doubt you're ready, but is Tampa ready for you? Clarise Robinson, letting her hair down?" He tipped his head to the side, lifted his Coke, then paused. "I remember a time when you said you'd never be caught dead at one of those parades."

"That was last year, and I had a case of cold feet. This year is—different."

"Different how?" he asked, his curiosity still evident. His eyes examined her with that same intensity she'd witnessed at the Christmas party, as though he was looking at her for the first time . . . and liking what he saw. Was he? "Different how, Clarise?" he repeated, his voice lower, sexier.

She swallowed thickly. She'd always had a hard time hiding things from this man. Truthfully, the big 3-0 had been a major factor in the decision to bare the Robinson Treasures at Gasparilla, but the truth was that she needed a wild setting to try to set her rowdy side free—and to try to take this relationship with Ethan to the next level. She turned away and glanced at a watercolor, a beach scene, on one of her walls. She'd meant to keep him from viewing her face, but she'd only managed to recall her *sex on the beach* addition to her list. Their friendship had developed so steadily over the past three years that Ethan could typically look at Clarise and know her every thought, dream and desire. Matter of fact, it amazed her that he hadn't instinctively recognized her obvious attraction, but he hadn't, and she thanked heaven above for that small miracle. So, right now, did he know that when she looked at that painting, she visualized the two of them, naked and writhing, hot and heated, wet and ready on that sand?

Dismayed at where her thoughts had once again headed, she swiveled around to glare at the object of her every fantasy. Didn't he realize how difficult this conversation was?

And was he trying to talk her out of going to Tampa? Didn't he want her there? Because it would be extremely difficult to have wild and crazy beach sex with him if she were still in Alabama. "You told me repeatedly I should take this trip, and now that I've decided to go, you're trying to talk me out of it. I'm old enough to have some fun, and I'm going to," she added, her frustration at having been caught midstrip wedging its way into the words. Then again, was she frustrated that Ethan had caught her, or that he evidently hadn't realized the one she really wanted to strip for . . . was him?

He took another drink and scooted closer to her on the sofa. "I'm glad you decided to go." The corner of his mouth dipped down, and he shrugged. "I just hate it I'm going to miss the show."

"The show?" she asked, confused. "What show?"

"Clarise Robinson, unplugged. I've got to tell you, I'm jealous."

"Jealous?" she asked, her vocabulary taking a momentary nosedive while he moved even closer.

"Of all the guys in Tampa. I've been waiting to see you let that airtight guard down for years. Now you decide to set the wild side free, and I'm stuck in Birmingham with a major acquisitions meeting. I'm not going to make the trip this year, Clarise, and hell yeah, I'm jealous."

"You're—not going?" she asked, her heart rate skidding to a near stop, from that fast and giddy thump-thump-thump to a slow, thick ka-dunk, ka-dunk. This was *not* happening. Ethan wasn't going to Gasparilla? "This is the corporate bonding trip," she said, trying to sound informative, rather than argumentative, because right now, she wanted to argue; in fact, she wanted to hit something. He wasn't going? "How can we bond, if the owner doesn't show?" she continued. "You're joking, right?" She playfully shoved his arm, partly because she wanted this to seem like a friendly conversation, but mostly because she really did want to hit something. Problem was, the rock-solid biceps stopped the momentum of her palm and started the momentum of her uterus. Clarise forced a chuckle through the sexual tension that apparently existed only on her side of the fence. If he felt anything, he'd be going on this trip, or telling her to stay home. Wouldn't he? She should have been smart enough to realize that he hadn't looked at her sexually at that Christmas party. Obviously, she'd been seeing what she wanted to see rather than reality. Here she had thought the two of them were gearing up for a wild interlude in Tampa, and he wasn't even planning to take the trip! Clarise swallowed past the urge to cry. She really wanted him to leave, friend or not.

"Like I said earlier, the Panache deal is going down tomorrow. I have no idea how long it will take, or if there will be loose ends to tie up after all of the legal matters are settled, but it's probably not a good idea for me to leave town. But it's still corporate bonding. With all of the department heads scheduled to attend, I'm sure you'll all have plenty of opportunity to bond, with or without the boss." He grinned, but it looked forced. Could he tell how disappointed she was? Yeah, he could; but he still wasn't going. Clarise wanted to hit something, again, and at the moment, that something was him. Couldn't he tell how good they'd be together? Didn't he want to find out?

"And I really am jealous," he said, and he sounded . . . regretful?

Was he regretting that he wasn't going, or was he regretting that he'd told her to go? Or was she, as usual, merely drowning in wishful thinking? What had he said about being jealous? She couldn't remember in her I-can't-believe-he's-not-going fog. "Jealous?" she questioned.

"Of the men who'll be on the receiving end of your shimmy. By the way, I heard the guy's command from the video. Did you give him what he wanted?"

Her blush came fast and furious, making her cheeks burn. She wasn't about to answer his question. She was semimad at him right now and definitely not in the mood to shimmy for him. He was sending her to wild and wicked Tampa on her own, wasn't he? And didn't that say that he was wishing her well with some other guy, as in some-guy-other-than-him? Her disappointment washed over her, but she wasn't about to let him see it. Instead, she stood and moved toward the television, then pushed the EJECT button on the VCR. *Making it in Gasparilla* popped out.

"So, are you going to let me see that shimmy? Come on, show me what you've got."

Another trickle of heat burned her chest. Heck, she'd planned to show him plenty, but it was probably more than he wanted to see, twenty or thirty pounds more, she suspected. She grabbed the video and looked up. His expression had altered from teasing buddy to compassionate friend. Did he realize how much this was hurting her?

"Clarise. I'm not serious." He placed his Coke on the table and stood, then crossed the room. She gripped the video like a lifeline, while she waited to see just how close he'd come. Ethan stopped merely a foot away, leaned casually against the wooden cabinet enclosing the television unit. "I wouldn't do you that way. You can save your secret shimmy for the guys in Tampa. It was a joke."

She blinked. Nodded. "Right, I knew that."

"But I am," he swallowed, "pleased that you've decided to have some fun. And—"

"And?" she whispered.

"And I really do wish I could go down there and see you at your first Pirate Fest. You deserve to have a good time. You deserve, well, everything you want, Clarise."

As disappointed as she was, she couldn't deny that his sincerity touched her heart. He really was her friend, and he did care about her and want the best for her. Unfortunately, he didn't seem to see that the best thing for her was him. She shifted from one foot to the other and backed away from the too-close-for-comfort situation. They were friends, good friends, and she should be happy with that. Shoot, maybe if she went to Gasparilla, she'd actually meet somebody who would be as enamored with her as she was with Ethan. It could happen, couldn't it? But, then again, she didn't want anyone else. Even Jake Riley, hottie that he was, hadn't tempted her with his "we'll get together down there" suggestion. She wanted Ethan. Too bad he apparently didn't want her.

She took her eyes from his and spotted the notebook, merely inches from his drink on the table. Oh no. Had he noticed what she'd written on the pages? Surely not. Ethan would have mentioned it—rather, he'd have teased her relentlessly about her sex fantasies—if he had. He followed her gaze. With a brief surge of panic, she stretched toward the table and casually—God, she hoped it looked casual—slapped the notebook shut. "I wish you could go too," she said, then quickly added, "since I know how much you enjoy Gasparilla and all."

"Maybe next year," he said, and again, she thought she

heard regret in his tone, or was that merely what she hoped she heard? His brows knitted slightly as he focused on the notebook. "When does your flight leave?"

"Tomorrow morning." Needing something to hold on to, she pulled the notebook and video to her chest.

He moved his gaze from the notebook to her eyes. "Better leave your apartment early. Friday morning traffic can be rough."

Clarise smiled. He was such a good friend and a terrific boss. Still, she couldn't fight that nagging little itch to know what it'd have been like to have something more with Ethan. Maybe she'd get over that and actually visualize herself with someone else eventually, though it probably wouldn't happen by tomorrow. In any case, she was going to Gasparilla. She wouldn't back out again this year, Ethan or not. "I'll leave early," she confirmed. "I shouldn't have any trouble making the flight on time. I'm almost done packing." Sure, she'd planned on this being her chance with Ethan, but she wasn't going to stay home. Even if she merely went down and had a good time with Rachel and Jesilyn, she was going to Gasparilla. She might not be getting the guy she wanted, but she was still determined to come out of her shell, or at least her top. All of those provocative clothes in her bedroom were not going to waste, even if she didn't have a sexy guy to model them for. True, he'd busted her bubble tonight, but she'd made up her mind to move forward, and she wasn't going to stop.

"Well," he said, his voice low and, oddly enough, sounding somewhat shy, "I mainly wanted to tell you about the Panache deal and remind you to be careful at Gasparilla." His mouth did that slow shift to the side that made her want to lick the corner of it. Clarise blinked past the impulse. "I should probably head out so you can finish packing," he said. "That way you won't forget anything you need."

Clarise nodded. Before this little meeting with Ethan, she'd believed her major necessity for the trip was an industrial-sized box of condoms that was already packed beneath a lining of clothes in her suitcase. Now that he was staying in Birmingham, those were undoubtedly wasting room in her bag.

"Don't worry about the store while you're gone," he said. "I'm sure you've got Abby set to run the Women's Department just fine in your absence."

"Yeah," she said, then, as if her mind knew the personal portion of this conversation had ended, it jumped into business. "I made sure she knows about the new shipment on Saturday."

"Fine," he said, all businesslike, then his face sobered even more. "I'm curious. Do you plan to take someone along to Gasparilla?"

"Take someone along?" she asked. Who would she take? Babette was currently visiting their folks in Florida and was leaving tomorrow on a cruise that would celebrate, yet again, her December graduation from college. Clarise wondered if her sister would ever stop celebrating and start working. Probably not. Then there was Granny Gert, who would come to Tampa in a heartbeat and strip down to her enormous brassiere and equally enormous panties, regardless of whether gold beads were involved, if someone like blue eyes tossed her a come-hither smile.

"Tampa tends to be an interesting place for couples to visit," Ethan explained. "I didn't know if you had hooked up with anyone while I've been gone."

Oh. Well. She should've figured that one out, but leave

it to Clarise to hear "bring someone along" and immediately think of her whacked-out family. "I'm not bringing anyone along," she said, "but I do plan to have fun." She did, though she'd truly hoped to have it with him.

"Obviously." He nodded toward the television. "I'm betting you'll have the best shimmy there."

An urge to touch him, hold him, just once before she left, pulsed through her, and she didn't resist. She'd had such high hopes, and they were falling apart, but she wanted to be in Ethan's embrace, even if only in the guise of friendship. "Thanks." She wrapped her arms around him. The video and notebook slapped against his broad back with a loud *smack,* but Clarise barely noticed. She was too lost in her close proximity to Ethan to care. This close, she identified his scent as something similar to sea salt and soap, and she inhaled it thoroughly, but then reality teased her senses, and she realized he'd tensed against her attack. So she backed up. Quick. Sure, they were friends, but she'd never been a "hugger," not this type of hugger anyway. They'd do that brief barely-a-hug greeting when they hadn't seen each other in a while, like they'd done tonight when he entered her apartment, but typically they smiled their hellos. Maybe if she'd started out hugging him as boss or friend, this kind of thing could have been a regular occurrence. How she wished she'd hugged him after her first interview.

"You're welcome," he said, his voice thick and awkward.

What had she done? Clarise forced an uneasy snigger. "Sorry. Carried away, I guess."

"No problem." He ran a hand, with long fingers, she noticed, through his hair. The short blond and brown waves rippled with the touch and made her wonder how they would feel running between *her* fingers. Then she noticed a tinge of color on his cheeks, and he smiled.

Her thighs clenched, a typical response to an Ethan Eubanks smile. Man, she had to get over this thing for her friend. *Friend.*

"Clarise?"

She looked directly into those blue-green eyes and instantly remembered all of those afternoon coffees, the two of them laughing and chatting and learning more and more about each other—as friends. "Yeah?"

"Be careful while you're gone," he said, depicting genuine concern and reminding her that he was truly a friend first and a boss second. He inhaled, as though he was going to say more, then he slowly exhaled. Hoping to hear the rest, Clarise waited a heartbeat before responding. When he didn't continue, she playfully poked him in the chest. "I'm a big girl, Ethan." She indicated the curves emphasizing that fact. "I'll be fine."

"I know." He moved to the door, put his hand on the knob. "Have fun, Clarise," he instructed, then he opened the door and walked away.

Clarise watched the door snap closed with a light click, then she sighed. Maybe it was the preparations for stripping in Tampa that had caused her to cross over that invisible boundary that existed between friends. The line that says friendship is here; more than friends is there. She'd planned to cross it blatantly at Gasparilla, but she hadn't anticipated starting that huge leap tonight. However, she had, and Ethan, being a true gentleman, graciously ignored her momentary lapse in good judgment and even told her to have a good time.

Clarise glanced at the notebook clutched tightly in her

hand. She'd had such plans, such high hopes, for accomplishing the items on her list with Ethan. More than that, she'd had a secret ambition to accomplish more—actually to win his heart while they got to know each other intimately in Tampa. But it wouldn't happen now. He was staying home, and she was going to Gasparilla to have a good time. Her fingers curled around the edges of the notebook. A good time, without Ethan—that's what she'd have, and hopefully, if she kept saying it, her heart would start believing it was possible.

Her phone rang again, and this time, her parents' number in Florida displayed on the screen. Undoubtedly, Babette was spending the night there before her cruise in the morning. Clarise picked up the phone and listened to her sister describe Gasparilla, the wild parties and the men. Little did she know, Clarise didn't care one iota about the men. Sure, she wanted to meet Mr. Right. Unfortunately, though, she was fairly certain she already had, and he wasn't making the trip.

Chapter 7

Ethan Eubanks leaned back in his chair, clasped his hands behind his head and propped his feet on his desk. His standard problem-solving position, but he wasn't sure whether it'd serve the purpose this time. What had happened last night? He'd meant to test the waters between the two of them, try to determine if he could control that crazy sexual impulse that had sucker punched him at the Christmas party. Then he'd planned to tell Clarise he wasn't making the trip to Tampa and warn her of the dangers of getting too free at Gasparilla. Even after viewing that tell-all video, she still had no clue at all of the madness; Tampa at Gasparilla was something that simply had to be experienced rather than seen. There were no descriptions powerful enough to convey the excitement, the energy and the wildness that transformed the sexual allure of the city to a fever pitch. Sexual allure. Hell, that sure described what he'd felt for Clarise, yet again, last night. The sensation had hit him like two fists to the chest when he heard that video playing and knew what she was doing on the other side of that door. He'd never thought of Clarise *that* way before. Ethan grimaced, knowing that wasn't true. Closing his eyes, he visualized the Christmas party, and the powerful surge of desire that pulsed through him when she entered wearing that dress.

And hadn't her apparel choice for that night been his fault? She'd never have ordered the sexy, red Ben di Lisi original, so similar to Kate Winslet's Oscar masterpiece, if Ethan hadn't encouraged her to wear something special. Special? Hell, he nearly popped his jaw out of socket. Sure, he'd known she was curvy under her conservative work attire, but he hadn't realized how impressive she really was. Damn impressive, by any man's standards, definitely by Ethan's.

Matter of fact, if she kept wearing outfits like that and started getting the attention she deserved from the opposite sex, she'd be wined, dined and snatched away. Goodbye, good friend. A jealous husband wouldn't approve of their Friday afternoon coffees, where Ethan talked about his latest relationship fiasco, and Clarise talked about family and work. Now, with utter clarity, Ethan realized that she'd always spent the majority of her time focused on running the Women's Department like a well-oiled machine, and when she hadn't been at work, or thinking about work, she was taking care of her unconventional grandmother or her brazen sister. Evidently, there was no time left over for a social life, or none that she cared to mention during their coffee times, when Ethan seemed to ramble on and on about why each and every woman in his life didn't quite fit the bill, and Clarise continued to inform him that he "simply hadn't met the right one."

But now she was preparing to come out of her shell and live, and it was bothering him much more than he'd have dreamed. Ethan cherished the odd fulfillment she'd provided him, giving him a relationship he hadn't thought existed. Friendship, and nothing more than friendship, with a female. Who'd have thought? But at the Christmas party, he'd entertained thoughts of more. However, he didn't want to ruin what he shared with Clarise, his friend—and a company employee, no less—by caving to temptation. "It's never wise to mix business and pleasure."—Preston Eubanks's favorite office policy. Ethan had never had a problem with his father's directive, until recently, with Clarise. But he *had* kept his infatuation under strict lock and key since that party. Then again, keeping it controlled was much easier when he was in another state. Keeping it controlled while in the same room with her, he realized, was another story entirely. She looked so adorable last night, particularly when he let on that he knew she was practicing her shimmy, but he still thought he had contained his desire. He wished her well, and was leaving her apartment. Then she wrapped her arms around him, pressed those curves against him . . . and totally caused that itch of desire to transform to a full-blown stinging need.

Ethan inhaled thickly; let it out. Good thing he wasn't making the trip, and he'd just keep telling himself that. He didn't need to blow the friendship, or the working relationship, and having sex with Clarise would potentially ruin both, wouldn't it? He recalled last year's corporate bonding trip, which had turned out to be a less-than-pleasurable experience. If he went this year, it might end up on the opposite end of the spectrum, very pleasurable, with Clarise. And that wouldn't do. What if she decided to set that wild side free with him? Her rich brown eyes had widened when she backed away from that impromptu hug.

What was going through her mind? Was it anything near what he'd been thinking? And did she also realize how something like that could potentially ruin not only their business relationship but also their friendship?

Yes, definitely a good thing he wasn't making the trip. Clarise would go to Tampa, perfect her shimmy, then set her wild side free with some lucky guy, a guy who would experience the sweetheart Ethan had grown to love—as a friend—as well as the sexy siren he suspected lurked beneath that doe-eyed exterior.

The phone buzzed, and he punched the speaker button. "Eubanks." The raspy, rattling cough that echoed through the line signaled the onset of a Preston Eubanks interrogation. Ethan pushed thoughts of Clarise aside, for now, and prepared for his father's questions.

"Son, do I hear a bit of tension in your voice? Everything's still set for the acquisition to go through, right?" Preston Eubanks asked. His words, clipped and calculated, bellowed through the speaker. Leave it to his father to hear the tension in his voice and assume it was business-related. Probably a good thing, since discussing sexual tension with Preston Eubanks would never be on Ethan's list of things to accomplish during this lifetime. "You said there were no problems with the acquisition. You said everything was progressing right on schedule," his father reminded, pausing to venture into his smoker's cough. He cleared his throat. "That is what you said," he finished.

"And you said you trusted me to seal this deal on my own." Ethan matched his father's clipped tone, syllable for syllable. He grinned, nearly able to hear his brother cheering for Ethan's confidence in dealing with the almighty Preston Eubanks. And as if on cue . . .

"Hah! Told you he was on top of it, Dad," Jeff's voice echoed through the phone.

"Jefferson, watch yourself," Preston instructed.

"But you're watching me so well," Jeff countered, his laughter barely hidden beneath the words.

"Why can't you be more like your brother?" Preston continued, the focus of his frustration momentarily shifting from one son to the other. "Ethan stays on top of his business game."

"As do I," Jeff said smugly. "In fact, Ethan, why don't you remind him again who came out on top in last quarter's earnings?"

"Oh, that's enough," Preston intervened, before Ethan could answer that Jeff's Atlanta store had in fact emerged the victor last quarter. "I'm not talking money. I'm talking attitude, business savvy. And less—"

"Women?" Jeff queried, and Ethan visualized his brother's cocky smirk and placed a hand to his mouth. No way did Preston need to hear laughter from this end of the line.

"I was going to say partying, but women too. Your brother has the sense of mind to put the business dealings first and his physical needs second."

"I guess that's because hc's so much older and wiser," Jeff said, causing Ethan's grin to broaden beneath his palm. Ethan was eight minutes older than his twin.

Preston's grumble reverberated through the speaker. "Tell me, Ethan, things are still set for signing on the dotted line this morning, right? Just tell me that's true."

"All attorneys are slated to arrive in three hours, at 11:00 A.M. sharp, along with the president of Panache. By noon, all sixteen Panache stores throughout the Southeast should be the newest acquired properties of Eubanks Elegant Apparel." He listened to his father's sigh through the line.

"Good work, son."

"Thanks," Ethan said, expecting Jeff's input. His brother didn't disappoint.

"And what about those fourth quarter earnings for your Atlanta-based son?" Jeff prompted.

Preston Eubanks gave him a resigned, "Good work, son."

"Thanks," Jeff said smugly.

"I'm going to take your mother out for breakfast," Preston informed. "Keep me posted on the progress down there, Ethan."

"Will do."

"Don't hang up, Ethan. I need to talk to you," Jeff said, as the sound of a door closing echoed through the line. Then the phone clicked when Jeff disengaged the speaker.

"You still there?" Jeff asked.

Ethan picked up the phone, disabling his own speaker. "Yeah, what's up?"

"He's driving me crazy. They've only been here a day, and it seems like a year. Plus, having the folks hanging out at my place won't do much for my social life, not to mention having him scrutinize every single decision I make in the office. Hell, every time I head for my desk, he's already sitting in the chair."

Ethan opened the computer file containing the Panache contract information. "You do realize that the fact that his permanent residence is Birmingham puts me dealing with this type of thing a bit more often, and consequently, doesn't leave me much in the way of sympathy." He grinned, knowing Jeff would rise to the bait.

"Save it, brother, you're the good son. He's never second-guessed your business savvy, and you know it. Even if he's in the same town, he's not analyzing your every move. Damn, it's been two years since that thing with Donna. You'd think he'd see that I've changed."

"I'd love to say Dad will eventually forget the trauma he experienced from walking in on you and your assistant, but somehow, I'm doubting it'll happen. Maybe if you'd calm down on the partying for a while, that'd change his opinion." Ethan brought up the e-mails from Panache's attorney for review.

"Exactly what I was thinking, which is why I'm coming to Birmingham for a while."

Ethan turned his attention away from the information on the screen. "What?"

"I thought I'd help you run things there during this merger."

"And this would help your image with Dad—how?" Ethan asked, realizing his brother always had a master plan, and not fathoming how leaving his Atlanta store to come "help" Ethan with the merger would impress their scrupulous father.

"It was always easier to focus on business in Birmingham. Dad knows I didn't really get into the party scene until I hit hot-lanta. So, I figure I'll come back to my business roots, show the infamous Preston Eubanks that I've still got what it takes to really run things professionally, and then . . ."

"And then?" Ethan asked. "Go on. What's the real agenda here?"

"And then, I'll prove to him that I'm the best person to oversee the new stores in Florida."

Everything clicked into place, and Ethan wasn't surprised at Jeff's characteristic, but somewhat illogical, reasoning. "You're wanting to live on the beach."

"Well, yeah, there's that," Jeff acknowledged.

"He's planning to keep the Panache executives in place for each of those stores, you know," Ethan reminded.

"But he'll need someone to oversee those executives. A Eubanks, preferably, don't you think? It'd really be better to have someone in the family watching over things."

"From a beach house."

"But of course."

Ethan shook his head. His brother tended to keep one thing at the top of his agenda—himself. Now, naturally, proved no exception. "Still don't see how coming to Birmingham will help. Your profit margin has steadily increased an average of twenty percent for the past three quarters. Seems like you could bank on that fact alone to convince Dad you're the right man for the job."

"One week," Jeff said. "Dad's already trying to run this ship, so I'm going to see if he's willing to put his skills to the test with a little wager. He's never been able to turn down a friendly bet."

Ethan grinned. Whether Preston Eubanks realized it or not, his "younger" son definitely knew what made him tick. There was no way their father would back down from a challenge, particularly one issued by Jeff. "What's the wager?"

"He'll run things here; I'll run things there. At the end of a week, we'll see who has the bigger profit. If he wins, I'll stay in Atlanta and stop partying."

"Stop?" Ethan challenged.

"Okay, slow down."

Ethan laughed. "And if you win, you're beach bound."

"You got it, and I need to win using the Birmingham store, since—no offense—but your store doesn't have near the traffic potential as mine. That way, when I win, he can't argue that it was merely due to location. What do you think?"

"I think he'll go for it," Ethan said honestly. "But there's no way I'll hand over the reins until the merger is set in stone."

"I'm not coming until after your meeting today. Besides, isn't it time for your corporate bonding? Gasparilla, right? That's why this is all so perfect. You'll be in Tampa—I'm assuming you're leaving after the meeting, right? And your department heads will be gone on the trip, which gives me one less asset to work with. Dad will love having me at a disadvantage, and it'll make my win even sweeter. I've got it all worked out, and, naturally, I can't lose, so go handle the bonding, brother, and let me run the ship there."

The corporate bonding trip. Ethan had already determined it wouldn't be wise for him to witness firsthand Clarise's version of *Girls Gone Wild,* but he'd be lying if he said he didn't want to. He'd used the acquisition as a warranted excuse to keep him away from her when she let herself go, and to keep him from acting on the urge to have her; but if the merger was taken care of, and if Jeff was around to handle any minor problems that could arise in the days following the deal . . .

"Or were you even planning to go?" Jeff continued. "I mean, after what happened with Red last year, I wouldn't blame you if you decided to hang out at home. You could go somewhere else for a little R and R, while I run the business. When's the last time you had a vacation?"

Ethan collapsed the contract window on the screen. No need attempting to review it while having this conversation with Jeff. "Her name wasn't Red, and you really don't know what happened."

"I know that Dad thinks I'm the womanizer, but that sexy redhead was one pissed female when she stormed into your office last year and gave me a verbal ass-kicking that would rival any sailor's. Hell, couldn't you mention you have a twin before you do a girl bad? My cheek still burns from those claws. I don't suppose she's still on the company payroll, is she? She won't be attending this year's bonding trip?"

Ethan refrained from telling Jeff that "Red" wasn't on the payroll last year either. He really didn't want to think about any of it again. That was one secret he planned to take to the grave. "She's not going."

"Good. Then I'm assuming you're heading down after the meeting?"

"I hadn't planned on it," Ethan said honestly. Panache had three days to back out of the contract, signed or not, and he didn't think it was wise to leave town. But then again, they'd hashed every potential problem out, and he really couldn't see anything major going wrong. Jeff could presumably handle any questions or small matters that could arise in the days after the contract was signed, plus, there was Clarise, in Tampa, getting wild and crazy . . .

"Oh," Jeff said, then paused. "Correct me if I'm wrong, but isn't corporate bonding—a major company expense, I might add—something you instigated to bring your department heads and you closer together? Then again, I've never seen the justification in it, myself, but to each his own. Anyway, it seems they aren't getting any closer to you if you're hanging out in Birmingham while the gang's in Tampa."

Ethan remained silent. The fiasco last year with the woman Jeff called "Red" had dampened his spirits in regard to the trip, and the potential for ruining his relationship with Clarise had emphasized his decision to stay home. But Jeff was right; corporate bonding typically required someone "corporate" along for the excursion.

"Well, tell me this," Jeff continued, not waiting for Ethan to answer. "Are you willing to take a much-needed vacation while I prove to our father that I can whip his ass, business-style?"

Good solid reasoning told Ethan he shouldn't head south to see his friend get in touch with her sexy side, but he wasn't so certain he felt like listening to reason. "If Dad agrees to your little wager, and if the acquisition goes smoothly this morning, then yeah, I'll leave." Ethan didn't say where he'd go. The friend in him wanted Clarise to set her dynamism free, because he wanted her to be happy. The man in him, however, wanted her to let go for another reason entirely. A sexy woman was a terrible thing to waste. And the man in him also couldn't quite grasp the image of that particular sexy woman . . . with someone else.

"I'll talk to Dad as soon as they get back. He'll bite; he won't be able to pass up the chance to beat me at his game. Then you wrap up the deal, and I'll be there in the afternoon to begin a Eubanks versus Eubanks showdown. I'm already packed, you know." He laughed. "And then you can fly to—wherever—for a much-needed vacation."

"Sounds like a plan," Ethan said. "I'll see you this afternoon, if you talk Dad into this crazy scheme."

"Oh ye of little faith," Jeff said. "I'll be in Birmingham in a few hours, count on it." He disconnected.

Ethan was as sure that Preston Eubanks wouldn't back down from the challenge as he was that he knew where he'd be heading this afternoon. He replayed the scene from last night. When Clarise opened the door, she'd looked flustered. *Different.* Her hair wasn't up in its traditional bun. Thank God. Even when she wore the sexy red number at the Christmas party, she'd worn her hair up; therefore, he'd had no clue of its length, of the way it shimmered. Until last night, when it fell in long, chocolate waves around her shoulders. It wasn't a bad look.

Her face had been different too. Flushed, he realized, almost as if she were embarrassed by his presence. Would she even be able to open up and let herself go with Ethan? Or was their friendship a barrier too powerful for her to set her inhibitions free? Ethan knew it wasn't a smart move to test their relationship, but he also knew he wouldn't be able to see her again without knowing whether this thing was one-sided, or whether Clarise might, in fact, be the woman he'd been looking for all along. True, he had a lousy track record with commitment, but what if, as she'd insinuated during their coffee chats, he simply hadn't met the right one. What would it be like to be a woman's friend first, and lover second? And did she even think of him that way? By tonight, he decided with a smile, he'd find out.

Chapter 8

Babette rolled her window down to experience the full effect of her arrival at the Port Canaveral docks, while her mother and Aunt Madge talked about her as though she weren't a twenty-eight-year-old adult. Moreover, like she wasn't in the backseat listening.

"Janie, I can't fathom why the child doesn't gain weight," Aunt Madge chirped, continuing her typical why-is-Babette-so-different montage, which began this morning, when she'd first greeted Babette with an extremely blunt *"How ya doing, child, and where are your boobs?"*

Babette glanced downward. Most females would require a bra with the thin lace-trimmed tank, but not Babette. So what if her nipples protruded from beneath the pale pink satin? She wanted the points to stick out—without the nipples, there was no shape happening at all.

"She has a high metabolism," her mother explained, looking in the rearview mirror and winking at Babette. "Like me."

"Thanks," Babette said, though in truth, she'd much rather have inherited the generous curves that came from the Robinson side of the family instead of the Paris Hiltonesque thinness that left all of her clothes hanging on her tall, lanky frame. Eventually, she'd correct that problem, whenever she got the funds together to cover a boob job. Unfortunately, her part-time positions throughout her extensive college career hadn't done much more than pay the mandatory bills, and while she could've used her graduation money to get the "job" done, she'd chosen to cruise the western Caribbean with her new toy instead. And speaking of her new toy . . . she turned and carefully unzipped its padded leather case, then withdrew the beauty.

"Well, if you ask me," Madge continued, "the girl should take advantage of all that free food on the cruise. You hear me, Babette?"

How could I not? Babette thought, lifting the expensive camera reverently toward the window and focusing on the large cruise ship that would provide her with a week filled with sunshine and relaxation—and plenty of opportunity for picturesque photographs. She clicked the first photo, then smiled at the feeling of excitement that pulsed through her fingertip. "Yes, Aunt Madge, I hear you," she said. "And the two of you really didn't have to drive me all the way down here. I could have left my car at the docks."

"Nonsense," Janie Robinson said, turning the wheel to enter the loading area. "There's no need in you paying those parking fees when we live just around the corner."

"Fort Lauderdale isn't just around the corner," Babette declared. In fact, they left her parents' home approximately three hours ago, three excruciatingly long hours, thanks to Aunt Madge's endless chattering.

She aimed the camera toward a dark-skinned man, his

hand shielding his eyes as he took in the grandeur of the enormous ship. Babette liked the shadow covering the top portion of his face, as well as the way his mouth seemed more intense because of the contrast where the shadow stopped. She snapped the photo, but was dismayed that one of her untamable blond curls had chosen that precise moment to whip in front of the lens and distort the image. Thank goodness she'd brought a surplus of colored scrunchies to use on the trip. This would definitely be a predominantly ponytail week if she planned to get decent photos, and she did. More than decent—she wanted breathtaking.

"Well, not around the corner, but you know what I mean," her mother continued.

"Yes, I do," Babette said, trying to control the urge to curse at the ruined photo opportunity. That would have been a good shot for her eventual portfolio, or she thought it would. She really needed a photography degree. Anyway, the chance for that image was gone, since the man had started up the ramp to board the boat.

Babette smiled inwardly. Wasn't that going to be the fun part about photography? Having to grab hold of the moment and capture it quickly, before it evaporated? And once she perfected the technique, via a photography degree, of course, wouldn't that be an amazing feeling? To know you could decide which moments to capture, to ensure they last a lifetime via a photograph? Oh yeah, she should've considered photography years ago. This was finally going to give her everything she ever wanted . . . total control.

"So what are you planning to do on the boat?" Madge asked.

Babette opened her mouth to answer, but her mother beat her to the punch.

"She's going to take five days to relax and have a good time before she starts working. Right, dear?"

Babette's smile was forced, and she prayed her mother didn't notice. "Yes, that's right."

"You're actually going to work this time?" Madge asked, twisting in the seat and lifting her penciled brows so high they disappeared beneath her platinum bangs. "Really?"

The urge to growl caused Babette to clear her throat, but she kept the defensive response in check. Now was so not the time to start an argument with Aunt Madge. She was nearly to the boat. If she could only last a little longer without blowing up, maybe—just maybe—Madge could keep from comparing her to Clarise. "The family" always saw Babette's sister as capable of anything, worthy of accomplishing every goal she pursued. Why couldn't they see Babette in the same light? Then again, she was twenty-eight years old and had never worked day one of a full-time job, and her part-time record was eight weeks. Okay, seven weeks and two days, but who was counting?

"No more eternal college student?" Madge asked.

Babette laughed and silently wondered if it sounded sincere. "I graduated, remember?"

"Yes, I do remember—all three times," Madge said. "And I won't totally complain, since I bought a new dress for each occasion. What were those degrees, again? Math was the first one, wasn't it?"

"Accounting," Babette corrected, trying not to wince as they started back into Madge's second-favorite Babette topic, lack of career ambition.

"Right. Accounting," Madge said, nodding . . . and frowning.

"Madge," Janie warned.

"I'm simply trying to keep it all straight," Madge defended. "Okay, so we have Accounting. Then what was next?"

"Business Administration," Janie answered. She gave Babette another motherly glance via the mirror. "Isn't that right, dear?"

"Yes," Babette said, her hands holding the camera in her lap, primarily to keep them busy so she wouldn't consider placing both of them over Madge's mouth. Tightly. Dare she tell them?

"Then what was this last one?" Madge asked. "The one in December? Computer Science, wasn't it?"

"Computer Information Systems," Babette corrected. "It's the business side of Computer Science."

"She has three job offers already, Madge," Janie said with pride, as she pulled into one of the covered areas designated for dropping off cruise passengers. "Maybe this trip will give you the time you need to decide which one to take, sweetie," she added, parking the car.

"Maybe," Babette said, though she'd in fact already turned down all three. There was no need to tell them that the idea of sitting at a desk all day long keying in computer programs made her want to hurl. She wasn't sure why she ever started that degree. Well, yeah, she was; the job would've paid well, very well, but she wanted more out of life than that. In fact, she wanted to show life, capture it, control it . . . via pictures. Her hand caressed the expensive camera.

"Well, I figured you were trying to get a degree in every

letter," Madge said, chuckling loudly, and sounding very roosterish, in Babette's opinion. "You've already got A, B and C covered. Accounting, Business Administration and Computer Science." She laughed more.

Babette didn't. "It's Computer Information Systems."

"Right," Madge said, climbing out of the car. Her dress, a very loud conglomeration of oversized yellow flowers and red tropical birds on blinding turquoise, whipped around her large legs in the seaside breeze. She quickly hauled Babette's bags from the trunk and chatted with the family in the next parking space. "Where are you guys from?" she asked, while Janie pulled Babette to the other side of their car.

"Honey, don't let her bother you. You're taking your time to find your way in life, and there's nothing wrong with that."

"Thanks," Babette said, and meant it. Her mother and Clarise still believed in her, unlike the majority of the family. She shot a death stare at Aunt Madge, but the woman was too busy nosing around in the other family's business to care.

A car pulled into the space next to Babette and Janie, and a curvy woman climbed out. She wore a hot pink sundress accented with flaming orange trim. Her bejeweled sandals matched exactly, as did her orange straw purse with a large pink flower. She looked at Babette and smiled happily. Babette returned the gesture. She couldn't help it, even with her current dismay with Aunt Madge. The shapely woman made Babette feel good . . . and reminded her of Clarise. Why couldn't Clarise try wearing an outfit like that every now and then? Why didn't Clarise smile happily every now and then? And why didn't Babette totally despise her sister, when everyone else totally loved her? Because, Babette silently reasoned, she loved Clarise and wanted her happy. Sure, she was jealous of her sister's ease in getting along with . . . other humans. Babette bit back her laughter. But the truth of the matter was that Babette didn't like smiling and acting as though everything was hunky-dory when it wasn't. If she was unhappy, she wanted the world to know it and fix it, so there. And Clarise had even mentioned she wished that she had as much "gumption," their wild grandmother's term for spunk, as Babette. Well, Babette might not have been blessed with Granny Gert's curvaceous frame, but she had gumption aplenty.

"Now, I know you're a grown woman and all, but I'm still a little apprehensive about you going on this cruise by yourself," her mother continued.

"It's what I wanted," Babette said truthfully. Sun, wind, a big ship . . . and lots of opportunities for great photos.

"I know, but I worry about both of you—you heading off on a cruise by yourself and your sister heading to Tampa for Gasparilla. I want you both to be careful."

"I'll be careful. It isn't the first time I've traveled on my own," Babette reminded. She'd been taking her "sanity trips," as she called them, ever since she graduated from high school. "And Clarise will be fine too. I talked to her last night. I've done the Gasparilla thing, remember? So I told her what to expect and what to watch out for."

Janie Robinson swallowed. "She's so trusting, though."

"She'll be fine, Mom," Babette reassured.

Janie nodded, but her throat pulsed with another hard swallow, and Babette suspected she was fighting a major bout of motherly tears.

"I mean it, now, don't worry," Babette continued. She

hated to see her mother cry. Hell, she hated to see anyone cry, though she'd never admit it. "I'll have a great time on the boat, and Clarise will do fine at Gasparilla." Babette had verified that several of the sweethearts from Eubanks Elegant Apparel would be along to take care of her sister. Jesilyn and Rachel would never let anything happen to Clarise. As a matter of fact, there was only one person that Babette had been concerned about, and thankfully, Clarise had verified that he wouldn't be making the trip, which was a good thing. A very good thing.

Ethan knew he should mentally be going over figures, jotting down his questions and generally conducting basic meeting preparations. The Panache executives and their attorneys would arrive any minute ready to begin the deal that would jump-start Eubanks Elegant Apparel's national presence. His mind should have been in the zone, focused, ready to determine whether each i was dotted, each T crossed. But right now, he was extremely thankful that Sam Wyland, his business attorney, was a master in contract negotiations, because Ethan's thoughts were clearly in another state. Florida, to be precise.

He assumed Clarise's morning flight would have put her there by now. What was she doing? Strolling down a sandy beach while the breeze from the bay kissed her face? Swaying her curvaceous body to the beat of a jazz band? Cheering the street performers as they defied the laws of physics with their amazing feats? And why did it fascinate him so much to imagine the possibilities? Hadn't he seen Clarise practically every weekday for the past three years? Spent every Friday afternoon with her, enjoying endless cups of caffeine and casual conversation? Teased her constantly about her ever-present guard and hoped she'd eventually let it down for someone? He should've slept peacefully last night knowing his encouragement had prompted her to live a little, but she'd never looked at him the way she had last night, and she'd damn never kept him up all night thinking about it.

He couldn't count the number of Friday afternoons he'd kidded her about needing to get ready for her "hot date." It'd been a running joke between them. They'd talk about his relationship woes, she'd skip the subject of her relationships entirely . . . then they'd part and go their separate ways with Ethan heading to his date where, typically, another woman tried to figure out why he refused to commit and Clarise heading to visit her eccentric grandmother, or straighten out her sister's latest fiasco.

But Ethan knew she hadn't foregone men completely. He'd actually seen her out a couple of times with a tall, thin guy who appeared mesmerized by Clarise's every move. At the time, Ethan had been happy for her to have someone who was giving her the attention she deserved, but now, with the possibility of the guys in Tampa doing the same, Ethan's jaw clenched.

He frowned, tunneled his fingers through his hair and concentrated on what she planned to do. He'd encouraged her to go to Tampa and show the world Clarise Robinson, unplugged. In no minced words, he'd instructed her to have a good time, but any way he looked at it, the potential for her to get hurt in that pursuit was enormous, more than Ethan cared to risk. And, as he'd tossed and turned throughout last night wondering exactly how far she'd go to let her hair down, Ethan couldn't deny there were two reasons for his concern. One, that some sorry excuse for a human being would take advantage of his friend, and two, that a man, any man, would be touching Clarise. Period. Of the two, the second one packed the bigger punch because it shocked him to his core. After all this time trying to convince her to let go of her inhibitions and take an occasional walk on the wild side, you'd think he would be celebrating her attempt to do just that. However, celebrating was anything but what he was doing now. Brooding was a more accurate depiction. Why? Sure, he'd beat the hell out of anyone who made Clarise do anything she didn't want to. That was only natural, wasn't it? She was a friend, and any decent man went to battle for a friend done wrong. It was simply the nature of the testosterone beast. But he'd be lying if he said the only reason he was jetting to Tampa in a matter of hours was to provide her with physical protection. There was something else going on here, possibly something he hadn't even realized existed until last night. Suddenly, the idea of Clarise being with a man didn't fit the bill as one of their lighthearted, chummy Friday afternoon topics. Oh no, it brought on an entirely new emotion, one that Ethan hadn't experienced for longer than he cared to admit, and he still hadn't fathomed exactly why the green monster had reared its ugly head now. But it had, with a roaring vengeance.

Sure, Clarise had always impressed him with her sweetness, her shyness, and more than that, with her friendship. But last night, she'd provided a glimpse of another layer in the multifaceted composition of Clarise Robinson. A layer that made her want to perfect her shimmy before heading to Tampa. Sure, he'd been trying to get her to take the company trip for three years, but he really hadn't ever expected her to go. That wasn't the Clarise he knew. Which made him wonder . . .

What else did Clarise Robinson hide beneath the muted façade? And why, when he'd practically bared his soul to her during those Friday afternoon coffees, did he feel he'd barely scratched the surface of who she really was? What she cared about? Her goals? Her dreams? Her desires? *Desires*. The thing that had haunted him throughout his sleepless night. Clarise had downplayed her desires throughout their friendship, and last night's glimpse of that part of her definitely fueled the sexual interest in Ethan that had been sparked at the Christmas party. How could it not? But he wasn't traipsing down to Tampa because he wanted to find out more about this sexually interesting Clarise. He was traipsing to Tampa to find out what else his friend had been hiding and to make sure no bozo hurt her while she attempted to bring those secret desires to fruition.

He viewed the e-ticket itinerary he'd printed merely minutes ago. At five this afternoon, his flight would arrive in Tampa. An hour later, give or take, he'd be in the heart of Gasparilla madness, the preinvasion parades and parties. And, if all went as he planned, he'd personally witness a caterpillar's conversion to a butterfly, then he'd personally destroy anyone who tried to clip her wings. His throat went parchment dry. Hell, he couldn't wait. Ethan still hadn't decided whether to announce his presence from the get-go. What exactly should he say? He straightened in his chair. The truth was usually the best option. "Clarise, I believe you're thinking about finally letting go at Gasparilla this weekend, and in all honesty, I'm not sure that'd be a wise move, particularly if the guy you're letting go with isn't me."

Like that would fly. How was he supposed to renege on everything he'd told her during the past three years? She was doing what he'd suggested, dammit, which should feel gratifying. Trouble was, he felt like hell. And he wondered what on earth he'd been thinking during all of those conversations or what he was thinking now, because Ethan couldn't deny he was feeling something for his friend, something that crossed that friendship line by, oh, at least a country mile, and he had no business thinking it at all.

He couldn't remember when he got less sleep than last night, tossing and turning, and unable to get her off his mind. More precisely, he couldn't get the feeling of her curvy body against his off his mind. As a matter of fact, his sheet had looked like a tent the majority of the night courtesy of Clarise Robinson. His friend. And did that have anything to do with this odd surge of protectiveness? Jealousy? That he knew her in a relationship outside of sex? Was this how it felt to notice the woman first and then the body?

Thankfully, his father had accepted Jeff's challenge, and Ethan's brother would arrive in Birmingham in a matter of hours. With Jeff running things here, Ethan would have no reservations at all heading to Tampa for Gasparilla. He lifted the itinerary again. After the nightmare in Tampa last year—one of the few things in his life he hadn't shared with Clarise, and for good reason—he'd been almost pleased when this morning's acquisition had interfered, but now he couldn't wait for the meeting to be over so he could get on that plane. Every minute wasted was a minute when someone else could be on the receiving end of Clarise's sexy shimmy.

Ethan frowned. He'd told Clarise to find someone, many times, but who was he kidding? Yeah, he wanted her to set her inhibitions free in Gasparilla, let her hair down and discover her wild, sexy side, but he wanted it to happen . . . with him.

Chapter 9

The preparade crowd on Bayshore Boulevard filled the sidewalk and spilled into the lively shops. Regardless of the January date, Tampa was hot and humid, with scents of alcohol, spicy cuisine and the salty Gulf tickling the air. Upbeat music belted out from balconies and street corners and coaxed excited partyers to dance with the captivating beat. The "corporate bonding" Ethan had encouraged wasn't happening, with the entire group splitting up and heading their separate ways almost immediately upon arriving in Tampa this morning. The Children's and Teens' Departments heads decided to grab a cab and go to the kiddie parades, so they could check out the wardrobes of the youth at Gasparilla. Jesilyn, ever the perky, friendly female, had met a guy on the plane who was going to a beach wedding at an esteemed bed-and-breakfast inn. After merely visiting with him throughout the duration of the flight, she had an honest-to-goodness date to an honest-to-goodness wedding at the inn. Rachel and Miles Watkins, Formal Wear connoisseur and the guy Rachel called "sweet eye candy," didn't even unpack before they headed toward the beach for a "nice long walk on the sand," though Clarise thought they looked more like they were heading for a nice long round of outdoor sex. Sex on the beach, just like her fantasy. Super. She'd assured all of them that she wanted to be on her own for her first night at Gasparilla, which was the truth. Goodness knows she couldn't let herself go in front of her friends. Ride a plane with them, yes. Bare her boobs with them, no.

Clarise wedged her way through the clusters of people and attempted to maintain her smile when a hand groped beneath her black leather miniskirt instead of slapping the offending varmint like she wanted. She'd spent the entire day preparing for tonight's parade, which would begin in about fifteen minutes, and she looked damn good, if she did say so herself. The brown strapless top was the perfect complement to her skirt, as Jadelle had promised.

"It brings out the depth of your eyes and the richness of your hair," Shannon had added.

Clarise didn't know about the eyes or hair, but it sure brought out her Robinson Treasures, and the fishnet stockings perfected her attempt at wild and wicked, she hoped. Of course, the three-inch heels she'd selected for the occasion were about to drive her crazy, particularly when they kept getting stuck in the street grates, but Clarise resolved the problem was a minute sacrifice for looking sexy. Judging by the sly comments and roving eyes, not to mention roaming hands, her earnest attempt at looking vixenish had worked.

She hadn't known how to carry money, credit cards and lipstick while wearing so little. There were no pockets in her skirt and certainly no room to spare in her top, but the thin-strapped, tiny purse she'd bought this afternoon at one of the festival booths seemed an exact fit for tonight's skimpy attire. Following the instructions the Tampa Police Department had provided, she wore the purse draped over her head so the strap crossed directly through the valley between her boobs. According to the police, women shouldn't carry purses to the parades, but if they absolutely had to, the bag would be harder to snatch if it were carried in this manner. Personally, Clarise thought the technique made her look like she'd donned a pageant sash for the event. With the way she was dressed, the caption should read "Miss Most Likely To . . . "

She swallowed past a hysterical giggle. If her college buddies could see her now, they'd have to revamp their bookworm, seminerd appraisal. And if her old high school classmates could, they'd surely reevaluate their goody-goody assessment of the valedictorian. And speaking of high school kids, a boy who couldn't have been more than sixteen wiggled his brows suggestively as she passed. "Ba-da-bing," he pronounced, boldly eyeing her boobs.

Clarise did a quick check to make sure the things were still in hiding. From the drool on his pathetic excuse for a goatee, she wouldn't have been surprised if the Robinson Jewels were in full view. Nope, still encased in brown fabric, although there was a bit of nipple action going on. She'd worn one of her new purchases, the flaming red merry widow, beneath her formfitting ensemble, mainly because she couldn't wait to wear the darn thing and because she wanted to have on something supersexy to bolster her courage when she dropped her top.

Thank goodness all of her buddies had vacated the premises. She'd have a hard time keeping her nerve to go through with this if she knew her fellow department heads were watching the show. Fortunately, not one of the gorgeous hunks from the store had hung around the area of their condominium. They'd left the resort area entirely, in fact. And although Jake Riley had asked her if she wanted to "come along," Clarise had said no, repeatedly—which didn't put her any closer to fulfilling her fantasies, but oddly enough, she couldn't see herself "baring and sharing" with Jake. Or anyone else, for that matter, except Ethan, and unfortunately—or fortunately, depending on how she looked at it—he was six hundred miles away. Not exactly in viewing range of her upcoming shimmy. *If* she ever got the nerve to drop the brown tube top and show off the red merry widow.

She glanced downward again to check her . . . key points and realized the problem with the undergarment was twofold. One, a lack of support, which made her boobs hover a tad lower than usual. Granted, gravity hadn't taken full force yet, though at thirty, it shouldn't. And two, lack of coverage, with the thin lace providing a nonexistent barrier to keep her overly anxious nipples in their place. Plus, the purse strap running a path through the channel drew even more attention to the mountains on both sides, like a tiny stream traversing two boulders.

Clarise had to turn the opposite direction to get away from the hormone-happy teen's glazed-over daze. Dang, she'd had her share of teenage boys giving her the once-over in high school, in spite of the oversized tops she wore, but she'd never in her life seen any of them with that tongue-hanging-out thing going on. It shouldn't flatter her so much, particularly now that she was older, but amazingly, it did. She only hoped her outfit had the same effect on older males—at least ten years older. She wasn't in the mood to get arrested for jailbait.

As she finagled her way through the crowd, her purse strap slid back and forth and made her nipples even happier to be here. It'd have been nice to forego the accessory altogether, but she needed something for her condo key, if nothing else. And in addition to the basic necessities, Clarise had the single sheet of potential fantasies tucked inside the tiny handbag. She'd ripped it out of her notebook and decided to bring it along. Why, she didn't know, since Ethan hadn't bothered to make the trip, but even so, it was there, in her purse, and reminding her of the fantasy. Besides, she could realize that someone else rocked her world, right? It could happen. Then again, Jake Riley, potential rock-her-world guy, had asked her to accompany him to the beach, and she'd turned him down. Didn't her heart realize that Ethan Eubanks was a lost cause, and she should move on? Evidently not, but maybe, during the next few days, she'd convince it to at least consider the possibility.

Clarise sighed. If she were truly going to enjoy the excitement and experience the nuances of Gasparilla, she needed to loosen up, attempt to capture the wildness around her and let it set her inhibitions free. Maybe for Jake Riley. He'd had a "look" when he asked her to go sightseeing earlier. Had his intention been to see her sights? And why had saying yes seemed so hard? Wasn't that what she wanted? Some gorgeous hottie seeing her as hot too? Yes, it was. But she simply had to get accustomed to the thought of getting naked with a guy that, well, wasn't Ethan. She breathed in deeply and inhaled the blended scent of spicy food and alcohol. It was a very alluring smell.

"I can do this," she whispered, as she smiled at a street vendor, then continued to move through the congested crowd. Another hand fondled her behind at some point, and she fought the impulse to scream. She turned quickly, but of course had no idea who'd copped a feel, and every unaccompanied man behind her smiled guiltily. Super. Clarise picked up her pace and moved away from the groping huddle. Her heart pittered so quickly in her chest, she was surprised her boobs didn't jump out of hiding merely from the vibration. She swallowed hard, blinked a few times to make her eyes adjust to all of the neon, then swallowed again in an effort to clear her ears of the throbbing from all of the noise. It'd help if she were a little more comfortable in her surroundings. In spite of her daring clothes, she still felt like a nun in a brothel.

Spotting a daiquiri booth, she edged her way through the crowd in that direction. Wasn't drinking part of the fun? Naturally, she needed to experience one drink, or two. She'd never tried the slushlike beverage, but she'd heard they were deliciously fruity and undeniably addictive. She decided one wouldn't do any harm; she wouldn't drink too much, merely enough to put her more at ease with her surroundings.

"I'll have a strawberry daiquiri," a woman called from her perch at the elongated bar.

"Sure thing, gorgeous," the bartender said, moving to one of the contraptions behind him.

The woman grabbed a pirate hat off the man at the next stool and placed it on her head. "I'm plundering," she announced to the man.

"Me too," he returned, then leaned forward and kissed

her until the woman on his opposite side yanked him away.

"We're leaving," she declared.

The lady at the bar smiled and watched them leave through the crowded exit. "Works for me," she said. "I'm keeping the damn hat."

Clarise sidled up next to the woman, whose stolen hat promptly poked her in the eye. "Ouch," she said, though she wasn't sure anyone could hear her over the roar of the daiquiri machines and the rumble of the crowd.

The woman had heard, however, and she turned toward Clarise and smiled. "Sorry." She wore a tight pale yellow T-shirt and no sign of a bra whatsoever. As if to emphasize the fact, she also wore a nipple ring, which pressed against the clingy fabric like a tiny speed bump on her boob.

"No problem," Clarise responded.

Speed Bump slid her cash across the black lacquer bar, her flaming pink nails stroking the bartender's fingers before releasing the bill, then she accepted the humongous drink. After taking a rather unladylike gulp of the concoction, her mouth went flat, and the eyes beneath the hat zoned in on Clarise's chest. "Damn, they look real."

Clarise swallowed past a flame of embarrassment. "Um, they are."

"Holy shit! You serious?" At her exclamation, several people within a three-foot radius, since that was as far as any voice hoped to carry in this chaos, turned and joined in the gawking.

Clarise suddenly remembered 4-H day in elementary school. One of her classmates brought his prized bull, and all the kids had taken turns gawking at the underside of the big animal, at those big, heavy balls. Not exactly the memory she'd expected to surface at Gasparilla. She shifted on her barstool. "Yeah," she managed, then cleared her throat and turned toward the bartender, who was also checking out her goods. "I'd like a daiquiri, please."

"What size?" Given the direction of his gaze, she wasn't sure if he referred to the drink she'd ordered, or the Robinson Treasures beneath her tube top. Clarise opted for the drink. "A—big one," she said, thinking she was going to need all the help she could get in order to loosen up around this crowd.

The bartender grinned, displaying straight white teeth and two deep dimples. Clarise's insides fluttered. He had tousled blond hair and an athletic build, like a baseball player. Definitely a guy who worked out, she surmised, watching his biceps flex against his orange Daiquiri Shop T-shirt as he leaned forward on the bar.

She moved her attention to his eyes. Green. Well, dadgum. For a moment there, she thought she had a winner. She really wanted blue eyes on her Mr. Right, and the bartender wasn't what she was looking for, anyway. She wasn't the "sex with a stranger" type, or she didn't think she was. If he'd had blue eyes, though, she'd have probably thought about it a little harder.

"We've got fifteen flavors," he said, leaning toward her face but stalking her boobs. This time, the image that sprang to mind was from the Discovery Channel. A tiger, crouched down, gliding through tall reeds toward an unsuspecting zebra. Clarise swallowed, and felt rather . . . striped. Nervous, she scanned the spinning apparatuses stretching down the back wall of the bar. With the clear front panels and the twirling mixtures inside, they reminded her of the washing machines in her apartment complex—without the clothes, and with lots of ice. Most of the flavors seemed fairly self-explanatory. Strawberry, pineapple, peach, mango. But the one at the end, the bright red one with three initials emblazoned on the top, caught her attention.

"What's DOA?" she asked.

"You go, girl," Speed Bump encouraged, lifting her Styrofoam cup and giving Clarise a playful nudge in the arm. "No better time than Gasparilla to throw caution to the wind; that's what I always say."

The bartender snickered. "Shelby, you should slow down. The parade hasn't even started yet."

"And I'm gonna get a helluva lot of beads, Rob," Shelby slurred, then fell off her seat. Two guys standing nearby gladly helped her back to her feet, then they happily accepted her wet kisses of appreciation. "Go for the DOA, cutie," Shelby continued. "With tits like those and that drink helping you ride the wave, you'll definitely get everything you want out of tonight's parade."

Bartender Rob simply shook his head as Shelby winked, then turned and sauntered through the crowd, heading back toward the street.

"What is DOA?" Clarise repeated.

"The strongest daiquiri we make," Rob confided. "Dead On Arrival. You needing something strong?"

Clarise jumped as someone bumped into her chair—and grabbed her right butt cheek. "Yes. Definitely something strong."

For the umpteenth time since he left Birmingham, Ethan rolled an impressive list of obscenities toward anyone who'd listen. Unfortunately, in the excitement of the parade in progress, no one listened, or cared. His flight had been delayed because of an uncommon snowstorm in Nashville. Snow, Ethan thought, as his body temperature continued to steadily rise, due to Tampa's humidity and wall-to-wall crowd. There certainly wasn't a chance of snow *here* in January. Nope, snow in Tampa would probably happen whenever it snowed in hell, which was exactly how hot Ethan perceived the temperature now. Of course, part of his body's heat could be attributed to a frustration peak the size of Everest. Between the delayed flight and the cabbie who'd gotten turned around in Ybor City—a cabbie who drives here daily, for crying out loud—and the resort manager giving Ethan's room to someone else, he was pretty damn hot, and he hadn't even seen the reason for this trip. Yet. But Clarise Robinson was somewhere in this crowd, and he was bound and determined to find her—before some other lucky ass did.

Figuring she'd stay close by the condominium resort he'd selected for the company employees, he decided to check out both sides of the street on that block. He'd been elated when he booked his own room this morning after someone had a last-minute cancellation, but when he'd shown up late, he learned they hadn't been willing to hold the thing, and now there was none to be found. Ethan wasn't sure how to handle that problem yet, but before he tackled it, he wanted to tackle an intriguing brunette friend, if he could find her. So where was she?

Working his way through the partying crowd reminded him of his college days, when he'd attended a Def Leppard concert and sat in the bump-and-grind section. Like the crowd from back then, there was hardly any way to maneuver through this Gasparilla pack, but he was unyielding and had a distinct advantage—he was bigger than the skinny college kids who made up the majority of the crowd. Of course, it took every ounce of every muscle working together to push his way through the madness. Thank God he worked out.

After a futile pass down one side of the street, he crossed between two floats and headed down the other. By the time he neared the end of that block, he'd nearly given up hope of finding Clarise in the overactive and damn imaginative crowd. How many swords were utilized in a single Gasparilla anyway? Ethan smirked. Obviously, he'd gotten too hot and too irritated if he was considering the number of swords surrounding him. How was he supposed to find one woman in this madness? And why hadn't he seen even one of his employees, people who would undoubtedly be able to tell him where to find Clarise?

Screams of excitement pulsed through the air, beads soared from the top tiers of elaborate floats and women lifted their shirts all over the place. The latter would've normally caught his attention and held it, at least momentarily, but not today. Today, he was only looking for one woman's display, and he'd rather it not be a public viewing, thank you very much. Ethan moved to the street corner and prepared to pass to the other side again when a man's eager proclamation piqued his interest, as well as the interest of every other male within earshot.

"Have mercy! It's coming off!" he bellowed.

Ethan turned toward the guy, a bearded swashbuckler, at least six-foot-five, who evidently could see the entire span of the crowd on the opposite side. With Ethan's six-two, he didn't have as abundant an advantage, but he could still follow the man's gaze to see where his attention had landed. The sight made his stomach clench. How the hell would he stop her now?

A kaleidoscope, *that* was the way Gasparilla affected her senses, like a kaleidoscope, similar to the wild tie-dyed vision she'd experienced at the Body Boutique. Yeah, that was it, with jazz music, instead of Blondie. She blinked a few times, took it all in, swiftly changing colors and shapes and patterns, pirates and beads and masks, music and dancing and fun. Clarise sucked on the straw of the monster-sized drink, but the potent red wonder was gone. "Dang," she said, frowning at the cup.

The guy next to her, well, one of the guys next to her— there were several now—laughed. "Here, babe. Let me throw that away for ya." He took the gigantic cup and freely tossed it. She hoped it went near a trash can, but she lost sight of it in midair. Heck, she didn't approve of littering. She started to tell him, but a hiccup caught her unaware and caused another low-rumbled laughter from the fellow, who stretched a hand in the air to snag a glittery strand of emerald beads.

"I want some," she said, eyeing the loop he draped around his neck. He had several now; Clarise had none. You'd think he'd offer to share. Another of her new best friends brought a beefy arm around her back and leaned close. His breath was hot and smelled like rotten fruit, or really strong alcohol. She attempted a baby step back.

"Honey, you show what you've got hidden under there, and I guarantee you'll get your share of beads."

Clarise looked down. Her top was still on? And after all that practicing at home? "Oh, right." She moved her fingers, which were quite fumbly, to the top of her chest and waited for the next float to come. The front of it resembled a mermaid, her long, flowing blond hair trailing behind her to form the body of the structure, where crew members tossed beads to chest-baring women. As if signaling her approval of the action, the mermaid's breasts also bulged forward, bare and bountiful, with big pink nipples that looked like rosebuds. Clarise decided she was practically the only woman here whose boobs hadn't seen the light of day, or night, as the case may be, and it was high time for that to change. She held her breath as the front wheels of the trailer passed, then watched a good-looking man on the top tier give her a nod of encouragement.

"You want them, darling?" he asked, dangling the most beautiful beads she'd ever seen from his fingertips.

She nodded, and fought the way it made her head spin.

"Then show me."

Clarise pulled down the front of her top and smiled.

Grinning like a thief, he immediately flung the beads her way. Whoops and hollers echoed in her ears . . . and a firm hand yanked the fabric up her chest. She dropped her newly acquired booty and lost sight of it amid all the shuffling feet on the street. Then she looked up and glared at the large palm still pressed solidly against her chest.

"You made me drop my necklace! What'd you do that for?" She continued staring at the big hand against her heart. It looked vaguely familiar.

"Yeah, man," one of her cohorts questioned, "what the hell are you doing?"

"She's with me," the lethal voice growled.

"I am?" She slid her gaze across the top of his hand, up his muscled arm, past a beautifully corded neck, and directly into the face of—Ethan Eubanks.

No, her brain reasoned. It couldn't be her friend, her boss, pressing one palm to her chest while the other pushed against the small of her back and purposefully guided her through the crowd. Could it? She shook her head to clear it, which was a monumental mistake, since it currently felt like a bowling ball on top of a golf tee, ready to roll right off.

"Ow," she mumbled, but her captor showed no sign of sympathy, and growled something incoherent. Uncertain of where they were going, Clarise stumbled along beside him and tried to decipher what had just happened. She'd dropped her top, got her beads and had her chest slapped. Why did the last part seem more exciting than the first two?

"I was hoping you'd look like him," she said honestly, as he hauled her into the lobby of her resort. "But talk about spittin' image."

"Your room number," he demanded.

She had to really concentrate on that one. What was it again? Oh yeah, she remembered. "Three-twenty-one," she said, proud of herself for accomplishing the difficult task. "Like a countdown, you know, three . . . two . . . one." She snorted with laughter.

He didn't. Instead, he paused at the front counter. "My room mix-up from earlier, remember?"

The attendant nodded, and it made his face blur. Clarise wanted to ask him to stop moving so quickly, so she could see if his eyes were blue, in case the guy at her side didn't pan out, but she couldn't get the words to move beyond her throat.

"Yes," Blur-Face answered, "and we're so sorry for the inconvenience. We're trying to find you something—"

"Don't bother. I'll be staying in three-twenty-one with Ms. Robinson. Please have my bags brought to that room."

"Yes, sir," he answered obligingly.

"He's—staying with me," Clarise said. She'd meant it to sound like a question, but she lost track of the tone midway.

"That's right," growling-man-who-looked-like-Ethan affirmed, before hauling her butt across the lobby and into the elevator.

She eyed him suspiciously, wondering how many prayers of thanksgiving she'd need to offer for having a guy who could be Ethan Eubanks's twin sharing her condominium. "Wait a minute. You're not Jeff, are ya?" God knows she wanted someone who looked like Ethan, but she didn't want to get hot and heated with his honest-to-goodness twin. Something about that image wasn't right. At all.

"Definitely not," he said.

"And you're staying with me," she said, trying her best to put it all together and having a rather difficult time of it. "I am."

That was it. Not a man of many words, her handsome stranger who looked like Ethan, but that was okay. There wasn't a thing on her fantasy list that involved a whole heck of a lot of talking, but the way he said it, and the way his jaw clenched so tight, she'd have sworn he was angry. How could that be? They'd just met, sort of, which was still a bit muddled. She really hadn't planned on doing "it" with a stranger, but here she was, headed to her room— correction, *their* room—with one. How did that happen again? Had she seen him in the crowd, realized how much he resembled her to-die-for friend and called him over?

Granted, she was tipsy, but if she'd seen this tribute to the male society, surely she'd have remembered. Then again, blasted—what if he didn't look like Ethan at all, and her mind was merely playing tricks on her, letting her have exactly what she wanted for a change? And did she really care, as long as she was fooled long enough to pretend?

She squinted, trying to focus enough to see if the image was confused. Nope, Ethan Eubanks to a tee. Drop-dead gorgeous and mega drool-worthy. Surely she noticed the resemblance and pursued this guy at some point during the parade. Unfortunately, their initial introduction must've slipped her mind, because the first thing she remembered was his hand grabbing her chest. Not a bad way to start their time together, in Clarise's opinion, and she had several additional memories to make with her handsome stranger. Starting right now.

Chapter 10

Ethan glared at the elevator doors and focused his attention on the mirrored finish, the crack in the center, the round glowing numbers, anything but the woman next to him, the one who'd gleefully yanked her top down while every male within viewing distance gleefully gawked. Dammit. And even though her breasts had remained covered, somewhat, with that flimsy red lace, it'd been such an incredible vision that he'd literally heard the entire crowd inhale. Salivate. Drool. Another low growl rumbled at the back of his throat. He wanted to put Clarise's luscious backside over his knee and spank her, and damned if that thought didn't turn him on. What did that say about his ability to maintain a relationship with a female without the aid of sex?

Female? Oh no, Clarise Robinson was more than merely any ol' female. She was intriguing and sweet and bright and fun . . . and sexy as hell. Friendship with this particular female he could handle; however, mere friendship with Clarise, or with Clarise Robinson unplugged, well, he wasn't going to make any promises.

He'd known what she planned to do, had known she

practiced the technique in her apartment last night, but knowing what she planned was entirely different than watching her in action and seeing—what every other man saw—Clarise Robinson baring her soul, and everything else, to Tampa. His jaw tightened. Of course, she hadn't gotten the chance to show more than her erotic bodice, since he'd ended her presentation before it started. But what had she wanted? What *had* she expected? Didn't she know what that getup would do to a guy's head? And not just the one located above the neck, because it didn't matter that Ethan had seen his share of bare breasts in his trek through the crowd. It didn't even matter that there were a few pairs equaling hers, nearly, in size. What mattered was . . . these belonged to Clarise.

Ethan shook his head. How Neanderthal could he get? Why didn't he just grab her by the hair and drag her down the hall? Here she was, in Tampa, attempting to have a good time and crack her way out of her seemingly airtight shell, which was what he'd been trying to get her to do for the last three years, and he shows up and stops her progress. What he did wasn't right, and he knew it; they were friends, *just* friends. Neither had ever expressed an attraction toward the other, so he shouldn't want her now, not in any way that extended the boundaries of friendship. But he did want her, and unfortunately, it had taken him three years to realize it. And now that he'd come to his senses, she had decided to sow her oats at Gasparilla. He closed his eyes, thought of sweet, careful Clarise, his friend and confidante, the woman who was so gun-shy around men, so tenderhearted around everyone else. And the one who wore sexy lingerie beneath her clothing. Only at Gasparilla? Or were all of those proper garments she wore to work hiding . . . red lace? Flashing that impressive chest, she had looked like a woman going for it and ready for "it" to happen soon. Had she really wanted to get *that* wild and crazy in Tampa? To be with someone she didn't know? Surely that wasn't something Clarise Robinson, ever cautious and timid, would want. Certainly, she'd merely wanted to have a little fun, raise a few brows at a parade. Yeah, she'd performed a semiflash, but she'd obviously had too much to drink and wasn't thinking clearly.

A surge of relief pulsed through him. Clarise wasn't the type of woman who'd indulge in carefree sex with a stranger. She was simply getting into the Gasparilla madness in order to make the most of her trip. Hell, he should commend her for her willingness to go so far, although he'd have preferred it if she wouldn't have gotten drunk in the process.

"Elevator sex."

He turned toward the vixen who'd mumbled the two evocative words. She gave him a thorough once-over, slow and lazy, as though she wanted to lick every inch of him. Right here. Right now. His penis, thoroughly pleased with this assessment, pressed against his zipper to give her a more adequate view. "What?" he asked, and mentally reminded his anatomy that she was inebriated.

She licked her lips, her pink tongue trailing a slow path across their fullness. "I forgot to include elevator sex on my list. We'll need to add it, okay?" Then, to Ethan's complete shock, she reached out and cupped his balls. "Ooh, I can't wait to see you. You're better than I dreamed. Even bigger than I expected."

His pulse throbbed in his ears, and several other places.

"Clarise, what did you drink? And how much of it did you consume?"

She ignored his questions and focused on his manhood, still straining in the pants. Then she slid her eyes up his body while running her teeth over her bottom lip. At his face, she blinked. "You really do look like him."

The elevator jerked as it stopped, and she inadvertently squeezed the surplus in her palm. Ethan sucked in a ragged breath while his cock continued beating a maddening rhythm, begging for the attention the remainder of his masculinity was getting.

"Um, excuse us, but we need to get on the elevator, if you two don't mind."

Ethan jerked his head toward the elderly couple perched outside the door. The man's charcoal brows were drawn together in obvious disgust, while the woman's mouth quirked into a sneaky, and quite curious, grin.

"Oh, my," she gasped, staring at Clarise's full hand.

Clarise giggled mischievously and released him. "Sorry," she said. "And we do have a room. We'll use it now." She stepped off the elevator and stumbled into the hall, still giggling. "But we *will* have elevator sex before the trip ends, right?" She lifted her brows and tossed a wanton smile at Ethan.

He swallowed, stepped off the elevator and made no comment.

"Where is my room, again?" Clarise asked, trailing her fingertips down the front of his shirt in a steady path toward the bulge in his pants.

Ethan caught her wrist and swiftly turned her to head down the hall. "Clarise, you're drunk."

"Just tipsy, I think," she corrected. "But I still know what I want. I just can't remember where the room is."

He steered her toward three-twenty-one, then realized he didn't have a way to get inside. "Where's your key?"

Another girlish giggle passed over her lips as she held up the tiny purse. "In here, with my list."

Ethan unzipped the bag and withdrew a plastic keycard, slid it through the slot and guided her inside. As soon as the door closed, she turned on the lights and pushed him across the room with more strength than he'd believed existed in the curvy package. "Sit down," she instructed. "If we're going to do it all, we need to get busy." Amazingly, not one of her words slurred while issuing the direct order.

"What do you—" he started, but halted when Clarise Robinson, his trusted friend and devoted employee, and consequently, the woman who'd been on his mind continually for the past twenty-four hours, began removing her clothes.

"You're even better than I imagined," she said, wiggling her hips to push the leather skirt down her legs. It dropped to the floor and she stepped out, revealing the lower half of the red lace number he'd seen earlier.

His mouth went dry. She had beautifully rounded hips, shaped like those of classic movie stars. With the skin-tight brown top hugging her breasts and an arrow of red lace accenting her womanhood, Clarise provided the sexiest picture he'd ever seen. Sure, he'd suspected she was hiding an extremely feminine body beneath her business clothes, but he hadn't been prepared for such an incredibly seductive figure, with tantalizing curves. A strip of red garter belt centered each creamy thigh and connected to black fishnet stockings. Her legs were perfect, nothing skinny or bony about them, shapely and curvy, in all the right places. She fingered the bottom edge of her top then rolled it north, over her glorious chest. As a result, her breasts pushed out farther and brought Ethan near combustion. He should stop her. He knew he should, but for the life of him, he couldn't make himself speak the words. Hell, his tongue was too busy roving his mouth in search of much-needed saliva. So he watched, with heavy anticipation and a hard-on that rivaled the Washington Monument. But before Clarise stripped completely, she encountered a problem, one that she hadn't foreseen and, because he'd been so absorbed in the show, neither had Ethan.

"Umph," she grunted, her head trapped in her top and the strap of her purse holding her arms heavenward.

Ethan blinked, watched her wiggle beneath the fabric, then smiled. Damn, she was cute. Although seeing her squirm wasn't such a bad thing, he knew she really needed help. "Just a sec," he said, crossing the room and trying to determine exactly how she'd managed to get into this predicament. He gently tugged her top down and attempted to ignore her magnificent breasts pushing against him. Which was damn near impossible. "Stay still," he directed, trying to keep an authoritative, and unaroused, firmness to his voice. He needed her to remain calm so he could figure out the mess, plus he didn't need her wiggling against him. It was all he could do to keep his dick in line as it was.

"Umm-k," mumbled from the fabric, followed by, "Hair."

He examined the thin leather strap through her brown locks. Sure enough, her hair had wrapped mercilessly around the obstruction. "Sit down and let me get a better look," Ethan said, tenderly guiding her to the bed.

She slowly backed up until the back of her legs met the bed, then she plopped down. "Sorry."

"It's okay," he said, and carefully unwound her hair. It was softer than he'd have thought, like silk between his fingers, and he envisioned Clarise running its bounty down his chest. God help him, he'd never had *that* image of Clarise before, but he sure had it now. His cock liked the thought and pushed against her side to let her know.

"Oh," she exclaimed, shifting her body to rub against the hardness.

"Yeah, well, what'd you expect?" He threw in a casual chuckle, much like the ones he often tossed her at work, or during their Friday chat sessions, but in his opinion, it sounded anything but casual.

Eventually, he freed her hair of the strap and removed the purse. Clarise promptly tugged her tube top over her head, revealing the entire mouthwatering ensemble she wore underneath. She stood slowly, stepped back from the bed. "What do you think?"

"I think you're incredible," he said honestly.

Her cheeks immediately went rosy. "But there's a lot of me to be incredible, isn't there?" Her lips quivered, big brown doe eyes questioned.

"You're perfect," he clarified. Did she honestly think she was too heavy? Had she not felt his cock announcing full approval of the body on display?

She flashed him an enormous smile, then twirled to show the rear view, as provocative as the front. However, he didn't get a chance to comment before she grabbed her head and stumbled backward toward the bed.

Ethan caught her midfall and eased her down. "Careful," he warned. "You had too much to drink."

"Yeah," she whispered. "But I'm afraid when it wears off you won't look so much like him." She snorted then placed her fingertips on the bridge of her nose as though the action hurt. "No offense."

It was the second, or was it third, reference she'd made to Ethan looking like someone else. But who? Only one way to find out. "Who do I look like?"

"My best friend. Guy best friend, I mean. Granny Gert would have to be my best friend, don't you think?"

"Your grandmother?"

"Yeah. Odd, huh, a grandmother for a best friend?"

"I think it's sweet," he said. She often mentioned Granny Gert during their Friday chats, in casual reference, typically discussing her fabulous cooking or laughing about one of her humorous antics. From meeting the woman last year, he'd determined that, like Clarise, she had an infectious laugh and a hell of a spunky sparkle in her eyes. Until now, Ethan hadn't equated her to Clarise's best friend, but it fit. Clarise didn't have the typical handful of female comrades who cried on each other's shoulders, talked about men and went out for an occasional drink. While she got along fine with Rachel and Jesilyn, her female coworkers, she didn't get into those types of surface relationships; she'd told Ethan that much. Still, she needed that female companionship every woman craves, someone to tell her secrets to. He'd wanted the male counterpart of that person to be him. Unfortunately, she'd identified someone else as her "guy best friend." And, thanks to the alcohol she'd consumed, he was about to find out whom.

"So who do I remind you of?" he asked again. "The guy best friend you mentioned?"

"My boss," she said, without batting a lash. "When I

dreamed about the guy who'd help me do everything on my list, he always looked like Ethan."

Damn, his chest shouldn't swell at that, but what normal guy wouldn't want to be Clarise Robinson's fantasy man? However, reality would be so much better. He took a deep breath. Time to fess up, but he wasn't sure she'd remember his confession, or any of this, in the morning. So, instead of announcing his identity, and her confusion with it, he decided to cover what seemed the safer topic. "Everything on your list?"

She nodded, then promptly grabbed her head again. "Hurts."

"It will until you've slept it off," Ethan informed her. "What list?" he repeated.

"In my purse. Go on, get it. That way we won't miss anything." She crawled onto the bed and curled up, her head on the pillow and her garter-clad behind in the air. It was a good thing he was her friend, and a decent man. Because even a friend, even her best guy friend, as she'd called him, would have a hard time resisting *that*. But resist he would, for Clarise, and their friendship. God help him. He took the purse and opened it. The thing was so little there wasn't room for much, but it held a single sheet of folded paper, along with a few other small items. He withdrew the sheet and opened it.

"Read it out loud," she said.

"Gasparilla bras?"

"Oh, that's what Babette told me I should try to get at the parades. I didn't catch one tonight, but I'm going to try again tomorrow. Not sure whether they have any my size, though," she added, rolling over on the bed, filling her hands with her breasts and grinning.

Ethan swallowed and mentally reminded his dick he was a decent man. He bet they didn't have her size either. "That's the only thing on your list," he said, frowning. What had he expected, anyway?

"Wrong side," she said, still smiling.

"Wrong side?"

"That's a note, not a list, and you don't care about that. You want *my* list. It's on the other side."

He turned the page, scanned the real list and swallowed again. Hard.

"Read it," she instructed. "I wish we could get started tonight, but my heads, er, head, hurts so bad I'm afraid I wouldn't remember it." She reached toward his arm, ran a fingertip down its length. "And I want to remember everything."

Ethan thought she had it right the first time, as far as he was concerned. *Heads.* Both of his were hurting, badly, especially after viewing this list. Have mercy.

"Read it," she coaxed. "I want to know what you think."

Well, since all the blood had left his brain and relocated, he wasn't thinking much, but he cleared his throat and recited, "Sex with the lights on."

"Yep, I'd planned on taking care of that one tonight, but—my head really hurts."

"Mine too."

She pushed up from the bed, balancing on her elbows and doing another impressive breast bulge. "Are you okay?" Leaning toward him, she placed the back of her hand against his cheek. "No fever."

He laughed out loud. He couldn't help it. She was smashed, completely, and still attempting to be the sweetheart he'd known for the past three years. Taking care of her friend while dressed like a centerfold.

"What's so funny?" she asked, running out her lower lip in a pout while moving the outstretched hand back to her own forehead. Then she slowly lowered to the bed.

"Not funny," Ethan corrected. "Cute. And it's you. You're very cute." He touched her cheek. "Extremely cute."

When she'd felt him up in the elevator, Ethan had decided he wasn't going to take advantage of an inebriated Clarise Robinson, no matter how much he wanted her, but a kiss wasn't exactly taking advantage, was it? He leaned over. She sucked in her breath, which pushed her breasts up to meet him. Stopping at a kiss wouldn't be easy, he realized, as he continued his quest for her mouth. But he'd started now, and she wanted it. Now. Her eyes focused on his mouth and a low, tender, feminine moan persuaded him to keep going.

She tasted sweet, like the drink that'd left her in this state, no doubt. But the flavor of Clarise Robinson ran deeper than the alcohol on her lips, much deeper than that. She was sweet and shy, wild and wicked, friend and temptress, all rolled up in one feisty package, and her kiss was indicative of it all. Her lips moved slowly against his, as though wanting to make the interaction last as long as possible. Then she timidly opened her mouth. She didn't bring her tongue to mate with his. Instead, she waited, as if testing the sensual waters to see what Ethan would do. Unable to hold back, he swept his tongue inside, licked at the sweetness of Clarise . . . and brought her desire to life.

As if striking a match, his tongue ignited a passion within her depths. He felt it, the stirring of her body beneath him, the dancing thrusts of her tongue with his, and the seductive moans of enjoyment purring from her throat. His hands roamed her sides, following her luscious curves, absorbing her flaming heat. Clarise turned her head, breaking the contact, and began a path of languid kisses across his jaw toward his ear. She nipped the lobe, then sucked it hard. "You look like him," she said, running her tongue around the shell and squirming her body against his. "Exactly like Ethan. God, he's wonderful. The kindest man I've ever known, and you're just like him. Like in my dreams."

Ethan blinked, her words pulling him from the passion. No way could he continue without telling her the truth. She deserved to know whom she was making love to. "No, Clarise," he said, his body on fire. "I *am* Ethan."

Chapter 11

Clarise rolled over and buried her head in the pillow. She did *not* want to feel the light of day, and she certainly didn't want to see it. Had her head been run over by a truck, or was she experiencing her first hangover? Then again, if it were her first hangover, that would mean last night's bizarre dream was true.

"God, please don't let it be true," she mumbled into the soft sheets. "I did not get drunk at Gasparilla and fondle my boss. Say I didn't grab Ethan's jewels in the elevator." Another cautious twist put her on her back, and she edged her way upward, slowly easing the sheet down her face as she prepared for the worst. The cotton scooted down her nose. She squinted, hoping she wouldn't see Ethan Eubanks in her condo, because if she did, it meant the fuzzy images currently blurring together in an odd swirling haze were probably reality chomping up to take a bite out of her brain. "God, say I didn't," she prayed, while her eyes adjusted to the light then zeroed in on the chair beside the bed. And the gorgeous man in it.

"You did."

In record time, considering the dizzy state of her brain, Clarise covered her face. "I am so fired." Then, keeping her head within the sheet, she lifted the white fabric and peered down her body—her naked as a jaybird body. "Ohmigod." A hint of a memory flashed, a vision of her asking Ethan to catch her while she danced around the room removing every stitch of her clothing. "Ohmigod." And then, unless she was mistaken, she'd pranced around in all her nude glory until . . .

She lowered the sheet, peeked over the top. "Tell me I didn't."

"I'd love to," he said, "but my bet's on you did."

Her eyes darted to the bathroom, then back to Ethan. "No way."

"Oh yes," he said. "Way." Then he flashed her one of those smiles that made her belly flutter, which, at the moment, wasn't such a great thing.

Clarise moved a hand to her stomach. "I'm going to die. I want to die."

"I'd say that's probably not going to happen anytime soon, no matter how much you begged me to put you out of your misery last night." With his eyes never leaving hers, and his smile remaining firmly in place, Ethan settled back in his chair, stretched his legs out and crossed them at the ankles. He had on a white pullover and black dress pants; in other words, he was fully clothed. And she, as she'd determined already, wasn't.

"It's okay," he continued. "Sometimes it's tough to hold your liquor. Happens to the best of us." His sandy brows twitched. "Man, I can't help but think about how much excitement I missed by not spiking the punch at the Christmas party."

She groaned. "Ethan, don't. Please, don't tease me now. This has to be the most humiliating thing I've ever done."

"Funny. I recall asking you once about your most embarrassing moment. If I remember right, you declined to answer, even though I'd already fessed up to the time I was locked out of the gym in nothing but a jockstrap."

As if she could've produced any coherent words while thinking about *that* image. That particular Friday chat confession had even caused a new fantasy to surface in her regular course of Ethan dreamfests. This one had him as a high school senior, locked outside in nothing but a jockstrap. Then she walked up and asked if she could help him cover his cheeks . . . and everything else. Her face burned. Now was so not the time to get turned on by an Ethan fantasy involving bare cheeks. And speaking of bare body parts . . .

She lifted the sheet again, peered down and wished her clothes would magically reappear. They didn't. "Dang. Look at me," she whispered.

"I have," he said, prompting her to poke her head above the sheet and glare.

"Ethan, I swear, you're making it worse."

One corner of his mouth quirked up. "Yeah?"

"Can't you see I'm dying here?"

"Again? Cause I could swear you declared yourself dead five times throughout the night. Oh, and by the way, I loved the wild outfit. What I saw of it before your striptease, that is."

Her eyes swept the floor and located the black leather miniskirt, and a few feet away, the brown top—then one fishnet stocking draped over the foot of the bed. Where the other had landed, heaven only knew. While her stomach rolled, she continued searching and finally spotted it near the closet door. Okay. With all of her outer clothing accounted for, Clarise looked for her intimates. There wasn't a stitch of them to be seen. Dare she ask?

"Behind you," Ethan said, before she muttered one word.

Turning, she squinted, as though it wouldn't look so bad if the image weren't in focus. Nope, still looked pretty bad, or good, if she were going for porn flick appeal. The red merry widow hung from the bedpost like a blazing flag, pronouncing the wild woman who reigned on the mattress below.

"And to think, I'd always figured you for the white cotton and practical, cross-your-heart type. Who'd have known?"

A wave of mortification washed over her as she melted into her pillow and pulled the sheet back over her throbbing head. "Oh, God, this can't get any worse."

That sexy chuckle penetrated the sheet barrier and teased her nipples into perfect points. Terrific. How was she supposed to hide a case of high beams under a mere sheet, especially a case of Clarise Robinson high beams? Like the rest of her, they were quite significant . . . and at the moment, apparently proud of it. Just super.

"Come on, Clarise. I realize our conversations have never ventured toward our preferences in undergarments, but go ahead, admit it. You've played the boxers or briefs game on me, haven't you? All women do it. So, tell me. What'd you guess, boxers or briefs?"

"Briefs," she answered, before thinking through the ramifications of the single word. Now Ethan knew she'd had beyond-friendship thoughts and that they included picturing him in his underwear. Thank God she hadn't been more specific and informed him she'd also embellished the vision to include Velcro sides. She listened for his response, waited, then curiosity got the best of her, and she slid the sheet to her neck.

He'd leaned forward, elbows on his knees and hands clasped beneath his chin, as if he were conducting a casual interview. But his eyes had darkened to navy and were anything but casual. "Any particular color?"

"Black," she whispered, recalling the hue most often covering his perfection in her dreams. At the beginning of her dreams. By the end, he was au naturelle and gloriously impressive.

"Not a bad guess."

Her stomach clenched, or maybe it was her uterus, but she winced at the intensity.

Ethan leaned closer, and the atmosphere in the room instantly shifted as quickly as his teasing grin shifted to a frown of concern. "Do you need another washcloth?"

Clarise blinked, suddenly remembering last night with vivid clarity. Doubled over the porcelain throne, hurling for all she was worth, and Ethan beside her, offering cold cloths and words of comfort. No. Way. "I don't need a washcloth. I need a do-over," she whimpered, retreating back to her sea of covers.

"A do-over?"

"Of yesterday, everything that happened yesterday, and especially everything that happened last night."

His sexy laugh should've made her feel better. It didn't. In the past twenty-four hours, she'd gotten naked, and then gotten sick, in front of her best male friend, who happened to be her *boss,* the one man she admired, and fantasized about, more than any other. And if memory served, and she feared it did, the one who'd been on the receiving end of a copped feel in the elevator. In the elevator!

"I felt you up," she croaked.

"And did a damn thorough job."

Dang, she had actually thought things couldn't get worse. "Can we discuss my resignation?" she pleaded. "I'd appreciate it if I could resign instead of getting fired, if you don't mind. Of course, I'd understand if you refuse," she added, feeling downright pathetic. How could she have let this happen?

"I have no intention of firing you, Clarise. Hell, you're the best employee I've got."

She sat up, which made her head throb. Holding it with both hands, she mumbled, "You're not going to fire me?"

His eyes moved to her chest, which was quite bare, thanks to the sheet's slide to her waist. She lifted it and tucked it beneath her armpits. "Sorry."

"Don't be."

"Right. You saw, um, everything, last night."

He didn't speak, simply nodded.

"And you're not going to fire me?"

"After learning how much you got into the spirit of the corporate bonding trip? How could I? Then again, I didn't catch you attempting to bond with anyone I recognized. That's assuming you're counting that flashing technique as a prelude to"—he cleared his throat—"bonding."

"Everyone headed in different directions," she said. "And I wasn't sure if I was quite ready for Jake." She moved her hand to her mouth, as though she could push that back in.

"Jake?" he questioned, his brows pulling together. "Were you planning to—bond—with Riley?"

She shrugged. "I wanted to," she paused, then decided to

continue, carefully, "have fun. But when he asked me to go sightseeing, and I thought he meant to do more . . . "

"You said no," he surmised.

"Didn't make sense to me either," she said disappointedly. "Except . . . "

"Except?"

She shook her head, then moved a hand to her temple when the pain seemed to vibrate all the way to the back. "Except I couldn't picture myself with Jake that way, you know."

Ethan nodded, but didn't speak.

"My head hurts," she repeated.

"That's what happens when you spend your Friday afternoons drinking rum instead of coffee. And you're quite more vocal with the rum too."

"Rum?"

"You had a daiquiri, right?" he asked.

She nodded.

"Then yeah, rum. And a strong one, at that."

"Dead on arrival," she whispered.

His grin broadened. "No wonder you prayed for death."

"Very funny." She swallowed. "Did you say I was—vocal?"

"Definitely."

Vocal? What did that mean, exactly? Lord, what had she said? Or worse, what had she done?

"Don't worry. My lips are sealed."

Oh. God.

He lifted his brows and winked. Winked! Surely she hadn't divulged her fantasies. Her very graphic, and extremely inventive, Ethan Eubanks fantasies. Or worse, surely she hadn't acted them out. And if she did, she'd never forgive herself for forgetting it.

"Of course, you'll probably need to remain sober for your remaining experience at Gasparilla. How're you going to know what it feels like to be wild and crazy if you can't remember it?"

"Right," she said. "Definitely plan on staying sober." Why wasn't he telling her what she said? What she did? Clarise looked at his eyes. Yep, Ethan had that glimmer, the one that announced he was up to something, typically a bit of mischief. And from the grin that accompanied it, she'd bet the mischief had plenty to do with last night's show, not the show at the parade, but the one in her room. "What?" she asked. "You look—"

"How do I look, Clarise?"

"Guilty."

"Of?"

"I'm not sure, but um—" she stammered.

"Yeah?"

"Did we, you know, do anything?"

"You mean you don't remember it? No fireworks? No bells? Hell, I'm losing my touch." He smiled wickedly, and her heart rate tripled involuntarily.

"Ethan, don't treat me this way. We didn't, did we?"

Laughing, he shook his head. "No, Clarise, we didn't. Give me a little credit. You were smashed."

"But you're up to something, aren't you?"

He smoothly shifted from his chair to the side of the bed, where his body heat swiftly seeped through the sheets and warmed her flesh like long, hot fingers. Clarise looked at his hands. Yep, those fingers were long, and one hand currently rested palm down on the sheet, inches from her waist, with merely a thin piece of fabric between them.

"I'm simply wanting to talk to you, Clarise. Friend to friend."

"Okay." She couldn't remember ever having a friendly conversation in the buff, or with a man on her bed, but, with Ethan, she was certainly willing to give it a go.

"Although we don't need to discuss your employment status, since there's no way in hell I'm going to lose my top salesperson, we do have something else to discuss."

"All right." Clarise took a deep breath. No problem. She'd made a mistake, and he'd decided to see it for what it was, a momentary lapse in better judgment and a mistake a dear friend could easily forgive. Holding the sheet in place, which was tougher with his weight adding to the tension, she straightened and leaned against the headboard. So Ethan had been here last night and witnessed her attempt to get wild and crazy. It wasn't a totally terrible thing. They were friends, anyway, and friends saw each other at their best and worst, right? Her brows drew together. Why *had* he been here? In Tampa, when he had stayed in Birmingham for the acquisition meeting with Panache? And more importantly, why had he been *here*—in her room? Several key factors from last night's events didn't add up. At all. "Wait a minute," she said.

"Yeah?"

"Why are you here?" And had he been here all night? Well, of course he had; she remembered that much. He'd stayed through it all, hadn't left her side. Warmth washed over her, settled in her chest, then moved lower. Ethan had taken care of her through a drunken mess. Why? *Because that's what any friend would do,* she thought. Sure, that was it, friendship at its finest. Nothing more. Certainly nothing more. Right?

"I finished up all of the loose ends with the Panache deal, then my brother came to Birmingham and offered to run the show while I attended the annual corporate bonding excursion."

"Oh." Not what her fluttering heart had hoped for, but she'd take what she could get, particularly where Ethan was concerned.

"And the reason I'm in your room is because this wonderful resort of ours gave my room to someone else before I arrived. So, if you didn't mind, I planned to ask my friend if she'd be willing to loan out the couch. Or something."

Or something. What exactly did he mean by *or something?* Because she'd be more than inclined to discuss the options.

"So you don't have your own room?" She processed this bit of knowledge, looked around. Yep, one bed and one bed only. No sofa to offer. Worked for her.

"Not anymore."

"And that's why you found me?" The memory of his strong, extremely large hand slapping over her breasts at the parade came through loud and clear.

"More or less."

"You can stay here." Like she had to give him permission. She'd beg if he wanted. And what did Ethan Eubanks's "staying here" involve? He'd already seen her naked, right? So, what was the verdict? She eyed him. He didn't look repulsed. As a matter of fact, he looked rather interested. *Please.* "But I don't have a couch." Might as well fish for info.

"The oversized chair worked last night," he informed, and her hopes dropped.

She bit her lip. Heck, she should've known he wasn't interested in a bit of bed sharing. He was simply in Tampa at Gasparilla with nowhere to stay. Of course he'd ask his buddy, who had a room he was paying for, to let him bunk in. But then again, someone who looked like Ethan, acted like Ethan, could have his pick of women at Gasparilla. He could stay with any of them for the extent of his stay, truth be told. Basically every woman Clarise had seen at the parade had been in prowl mode. They'd snatch this hunk of magnificent male in a heartbeat. But he'd asked to stay with her. Did he really mean to stay on the chair, or would he be interested in more? And what did a girl have to do to find out? Man, she wished she had more experience in this kind of thing. Babette would know what to do, no doubt. As it was, Clarise could count her sexual encounters on one hand and her partners on two fingers. Not a lot of knowledge there for handling dancing naked in front of your friend, then finding out whether he wants to play house for a few days.

She grinned and bit back a hysterical bubble of laughter creeping up her throat. So, she hadn't had anything this incredible happen in her less-than-exciting life before. Didn't mean she wasn't up for a bit of on-the-job training, courtesy of Ethan Eubanks. He could teach her any and everything she needed to know about playing one-on-one for a few days, if that's what he wanted. A tinge of something tickled the back of her brain, the realization that an interlude with her boss might not be the best thing for her long-term career goal. What would happen if he didn't want to employ someone who'd been a fling? She pushed that thought aside. Things like this didn't happen to Clarise Robinson, ever, and for all she knew, he really only needed a place to sleep. So he'd asked his friend. Then, when he'd found her plastered, he'd helped her, every time she got sick, every time she'd yelped about her aching head. A big thick lump settled in her throat.

"Are you okay?" he asked, his head tilted. "Because I have something that I believe we should discuss."

"Yeah, I'm okay." She swallowed. "What do we need to discuss?" If not her resignation.

"This list." He unfolded the paper and scanned it, while apprehension made Clarise's flesh sting.

Oh. No.

"Actually," he said, "there is a way for most of these. Oh, I added elevator sex to the end, since you asked me to last night."

Clarise stared at the sheet of paper. What had she been thinking, writing all of that down? He had her list, a list where, in her mind, he was always her partner for the events. Her neck and face were so hot they hurt. He'd *seen* her list, knew what it meant. She did another check of his expression. Nope, definitely not an I-think-you're-deranged-and-never-want-to-see-you-again look.

"I have a proposition for you."

She attempted a swallow, but it quickly escalated into a hard gulp. "Proposition?"

"I understand you want to accomplish these—goals—at Gasparilla. You said as much last night. But I believe it'd be better, safer, if you were to experience them with some-one you know."

"Someone I know?" Two things soared through her

mind. One, did he really think she would have done all of that with a stranger? And two . . . Oh. God. Yes.

"Exactly. And since I'm the reason you're here, and I'm assuming you've had some thoughts of me in that sense before, since you mentioned it last night."

Lord help her. What did she say? "Since I mentioned— what—exactly?"

"That you'd dreamed your lover would look like me." He sat forward, placed a knuckle under her chin and grinned.

His touch should've been harmless, but it shot an arrow of intense desire directly to the center of her thighs. Clarise wanted to die, right now. Fast. Slow. Painfully. Or not. Didn't matter. But she definitely, most certainly, wanted to die.

"I was quite flattered," he added, at the same moment her heart thunked over of its own accord.

"Flattered?"

"Of course."

"That I wanted my lover to be like you?" she asked, thinking she'd obviously misunderstood.

"Yeah. And I was wondering if you'd be willing to improvise your plan."

"Improvise?" she whispered.

"Let me play the part and help you fulfill the fantasies on this list. I know you wanted it to be someone you didn't know, but don't you think sleeping with a stranger is a bit risky these days?"

So, was that the reason he was offering, to protect her health? Not that she minded any reason that put Ethan having sex with her, but she'd kind of hoped . . .

"But do you want to?" she asked, unable to resist.

"Do I want to?"

"Sleep with me. Enough times to accomplish everything on that list." She timidly pointed toward the paper.

Amazingly, his smile grew wider, and his eyes smoldered, as though he were actually turned on by the idea of getting down and dirty with Cautious Clarise. With his friend.

"Would you? Want to?" she asked.

"Oh yeah."

A hot rush of liquid pooled between her legs. Sure, she knew he wasn't in love with her, or even in lust with her, but he did want to sleep with her, for some strange reason, and dang if that didn't seem good enough to her libido. She blinked. He thought she simply wanted to sleep with a stranger? However, he was willing to play stranger for her fantasy—to keep her safe. No, it wasn't the ideal scenario, where he wanted her because he loved her and couldn't live without her, but he wanted to have sex with her, so Clarise wasn't about to knock it.

"You're willing to get, you know, wild and crazy and do all those things with me? Even though, well, it's me?"

"Because it's you."

Oh no. Don't get the hopes up too high. "Because you'd rather I didn't spend all of Gasparilla sleeping with strangers?"

"That isn't why I offered."

"You offered because I want a stranger, and you don't think that's safe," she deciphered, needing to hear him actually say the words, in case her heart had any mistaken ideas about this situation.

"Listen, if it *has* to be a stranger in order for your fantasy to be fulfilled, I understand, I guess. But hell, Clarise, I wanted you to have fun. I didn't expect you to do something this . . . reckless." He moved from the bed to the chair. Then he leaned back and looked ill at ease with where this conversation had headed. But Clarise had to know what was going on and exactly what his offer entailed. Yeah, she wanted Ethan, any way she could get him, even if only for a few days. But she wanted to know where she stood up front. He had the power to take her heart and trample it, and she wanted to be prepared. Even though she suspected the minute he touched her, she'd be lost forever. Trapped in an eternal I-want-Ethan-and-no-one-else-will-do funk.

"Well, I wanted him to look like you, anyway," she said.

He relaxed again in the chair. "Like I said, I'm flattered."

"But you're not looking for anything else, right?" she asked, still needing to hear it from his lips, so she could attempt to keep her heart in line. "Just fantasy sex in Tampa, then back to normal when we get to Birmingham, right?"

"I haven't said anything about commitment," he reminded. "Or is that part of your fantasy? Were you hoping for a commitment, Clarise?"

She inhaled, blew it out slowly. "Commitment isn't on the list, is it?" She attempted to make it sound like a joke, rather than a half-lie, and thought she did a pretty decent job.

"Not on the list," he repeated, but his smile wasn't as broad this time.

Okay. She knew where they stood, and she could handle it. Fantasy sex with Ethan would be worth the fallout, even if she'd have to perform damage control on her heart when they got back to Birmingham. "All right," she said, refusing to hide her eagerness. "So when and where do we start?"

Chapter 12

Clarise giggled shamelessly while hot water pelted her skin. In all her Ethan fantasies, none of them ever involved him as her sex slave, rather *sex stranger,* for a weekend. Longer than a weekend, she countered. Four glorious days. She, and the remainder of Ethan's employees, weren't scheduled to return home until Wednesday morning. Smiling, she wondered if any of the others from work were going to have nearly as much fun as she'd have during this trip, or nearly as much sex.

She squirted a surplus of peach body wash on her loofah and squished it into a foamy lather, then she rubbed it down her neck and across the swell of her right breast. He'd fondle this breast before the day ended. Heck, he'd fondle a lot more than that, wouldn't he? Because that's what wild, crazy sex involved. Lots and lots of fondling.

Clarise had felt certain they'd get the ball rolling straightaway, having a romp in the sheets with the lights on to cross the first fantasy off her list. However, Ethan had suggested she take a hot shower to sober up while he mapped out their itinerary for the day. Their itinerary. Maybe she should offer

up a bit of advice. Let's see . . . afternoon Gasparilla invasion parade, sex on the grass, evening parade, sex standing
up, on the way back, sex in the elevator, in their room, sex
with the lights on. Another giggle pulsed up her throat.
Ethan was planning their day, and she couldn't see any way
for it to be anything but incredible.

She lathered every inch, then stepped under the stream
and closed her eyes. The water covered her like a hot liquid blanket and reminded her of every sensitive part she
wanted Ethan Eubanks to explore. She hummed an exhil-
arated sigh and hadn't finished rinsing her body when the
temperature in the room changed. A soft, cool breeze
pierced the steamy heat and brought her already overly
excited nipples to new peaks. Knowing the only reason the
temperature would change so suddenly, Clarise froze and
held her eyes shut. Was he ready for the games to begin?
Wasn't that what she wanted? And if it was, why did a swift
surge of panic wash down her curves in perfect time with
the water?

She stepped farther into the spray. The shower door was
glass, completely transparent. Right now, Ethan could see
everything. Her throat closed in, face began to sting. He'd
seen her completely nude last night and hadn't said or insinuated anything about being appalled, but still . . . this wasn't
nighttime. And she wasn't filled with daiquiri. Suddenly,
her fantasy didn't seem very appealing. She turned her back
to the bathroom door and cringed. Would the glass mag-
nify the Robinson rump? What had she been thinking?
Surely Ethan was getting more than he bargained for—
literally.

In spite of the water pulsing against the shower walls,
she heard the faint click of the bathroom door close, felt the

temperature readjust to contain the heat. Had he looked at her and changed his mind? Rejection dripped from her pores, the same feeling she'd encountered so many times growing up, when party invitations were handed out at school and Chunky Clarise came up empty-handed. Her eyes burned as tears threatened to join the shower water. She kept them pinched tight to hold her emotions in check and inadvertently dropped the loofah sponge.

The shower door creaked as it opened. Her heart pumped so fast she could hear her pulse ringing in her ears. Clarise slid one eye open, while Ethan, boldly and blissfully naked, lowered into the pulsing stream and retrieved her sponge. He rose to stand against her, his jutting, thick erection nudging her side. "You need this."

She touched the sponge, shivered as her hand met his. "You have no idea." While the water rushed over her shoulders to pulse against his chest, she eyed him brazenly. His wet hair, the color of caramel, formed seductive waves in the shower's steam. One lock slid forward on his forehead, and she timidly stretched out a finger to push it back from his face. Her inner thighs clenched at the interaction of the soft, springy texture against her skin. Following her lead, Ethan moved his fingers to her face, tenderly placed the backs of his fingertips against her temples, then slowly brushed them down her cheeks to her neck. Clarise sucked in a breath and prayed it wasn't possible to faint from too much stimulation, because Ethan was stimulating the devil out of her ready-to-be-stimulated self right now.

Tiny water droplets clung to his lashes. Never in her life would she have believed she'd have sex with Ethan Eubanks, let alone shower with her gorgeous friend. No way would she miss the chance to survey every wonderful inch, and with that thought, her gaze headed beyond the sexy cords of his neck, past the delicious sprinkle of hair on his chest, down the impressive contours of ripped abs to the place where the line of hair, the trail to happiness, in her book, led. Inch by wonderful inch.

"Wow," she whispered, and as she stared, it moved. "Oh, wow."

He placed a fingertip beneath her chin, tilted her face toward his. "You're doing wonderful things to my ego, Clarise. But I have to tell you, I was thinking the same thing." His finger slid a slow, easy path down her neck to the protruding nipple of her left breast. "Wow."

Her lip trembled at his appraisement. Yeah, the Robinson Treasures were "none too shabby" as Granny Gert said, but what about the rest of her? She momentarily pushed the doubt away and feasted on those baby blue eyes, transforming from pale crystal blue to smoldering clouds of desire. *For her?* While her brain worked feverishly to process that anomaly, he cupped both of her heavy mounds, leaned down and sucked the water from one burning tip. Then he moved to the other and clamped his mouth over the end, drawing the nipple inside while she gasped at the painful, yet blissful, torture.

Clarise's back accepted the bulk of the shower stream and shielded Ethan while he laved her breasts. The remainder of her body tingled as well, not from the pulsing strokes of water against flesh, but from the sensual sensations produced by Ethan's masterful mouth, teeth and tongue. She couldn't imagine feeling anything better, until his hands got in on the action. His arms circled her hips, and his palms and fingers began a thorough kneading of her behind.

Clarise instantly tensed. "No."

He stilled, withdrew his mouth from her breast and his hands from her cheeks. "This isn't what you want?"

"I'm—" She didn't know what to say. I'm too fluffy? That'd always been the word of choice around the Robinson household. "Fluffy," like a rabbit or a stuffed animal, not like a sexy female, which is what she wanted to be more than anything else. Her hands drifted down in an attempt to hide—everything.

Ethan followed the path of her palms, trying valiantly to conceal her womanhood and as much of her ample hips as possible. "Don't cover anything, Clarise."

"But," she stammered and hated that she sounded like a child.

He lowered farther, to his knees, so his eyes were directly in front of her hands. Then he slowly slid them out of the way. "I saw all of you last night," he reminded, while a single stream of water found its way past her side to push against his temple and trickle down his jaw. He smiled, which shifted the water's path to slide directly in front of his ear.

Clarise licked her lips. She wanted to lick the water, every drop, away. "And you still want me." She barely breathed the words and wasn't sure she could handle his response.

"Every luscious curve." To emphasize the fact, he brought his face to her right hip and sucked her heated flesh until her knees went weak. Then he pulled away and peered at her through spiked, wet lashes. Brilliant blue eyes asking for permission to continue. His mouth curved. "Shower sex was on your list."

"Thank God."

His low rumbled laugh echoed against the tiled walls.

"But we don't—we can't—"

"Can't what, Clarise?" He ran his hands around to cup her cheeks once more, but never took his eyes from hers, even though her female center was directly in front of his face.

"Protection," she muttered, absolutely sick she hadn't thought to put any in the bathroom. Nope, the whole dang box was still sealed in a bedroom drawer.

"I thought about it," Ethan said, his hands sliding against her wet flesh to caress her hips and curve to the front of her thighs. "And I decided we wouldn't need it. This time."

"Won't need it?" she hissed, unable to concentrate fully while his talented thumbs moved slowly toward her clitoris. Closer . . . closer . . .

"Your fantasies," Ethan continued, "Did they only involve different locations, or did you have different methods for sex as well?"

"M-methods?" Her mouth was dry, in spite of the shower steam.

"Positions. Activities. Were there different ones in your fantasies?"

She shook her head. Her sex fantasies had basically been that—fantasies—with a guy who looked like Ethan, acted like Ethan, and could potentially turn out to be Mr. Right to boot. She hadn't really gotten into formally identifying types of sex, other than lights on, standing up, on the grass, that kind of thing. What exactly was Ethan referring—

His tongue licked her clit.

"Oh!"

"This time is for you, Clarise."

Her eyes flew open and jerked down to see his mouth by her wet, brown curls. "But I want you inside of me."

"And I promise, you'll have me there," he said. "But not this time."

"But I've never—no one's ever—" Dang, her face was turning red; she could feel it. Sure, she'd thought about oral sex a time or two, but she'd never thought someone would be willing to go down on her, and she sure didn't know if she could handle that much attention *there.* Her sexual experiences were so few and far between that when they happened, she screamed through her orgasm as though the world ended. What would she do if Ethan Eubanks were to get her off with his mouth? Heck, they'd probably hear her yelling in Alabama. "I don't think—"

"That's right. Don't think," Ethan instructed, his brows raised and his mouth curved in a very sexy, very confident smile.

Have mercy, he knew what to do. She could tell by the way he looked at her, as though he wanted to eat her up. And suddenly, though she'd never thought it possible, she wanted exactly that. Ethan Eubanks, her boss, her friend, her fantasy. Eating. Her. Up.

"And if I am going to be the first to do this to you—" he continued.

"You are."

"Then I'm going to do it right." He placed a hand behind her calf and raised her leg, settled it on the edge of the shower stall, so she completely opened before him. She swallowed, determined to do whatever it took to help Ethan "do it right."

"You may want to hold on, Clarise." He nodded toward a wall handle, undoubtedly for washcloths, but in this case, it'd be Clarise's safeguard to melting into a lifeless heap when her body came undone at his touch.

"Okay." She grasped the handle with both hands, which put her at an angled position, and oddly enough, increased the sexual awareness of Ethan Eubanks's proximity to her core.

"Can you feel that?" he asked. Staring boldly at her intimate flesh.

"Feel what?" Was she supposed to be feeling something already? What if her body wasn't the kind of body conducive to oral sex? She'd read plenty of books, tons of articles in *Cosmo,* even gotten a pretty good picture from movies. But what was she supposed to feel before his mouth ever hit the spot?

"The water, running down your hip, to the center of your thighs and dripping a path across your tender pink clit, past your full lips, to the very essence of you," he said. "Can you feel it, Clarise?"

Until his description, she would've sworn she hadn't felt a thing, but now, she did. Every single droplet's path to that very destination, which was on fire now and begging for a sensation she'd never had before. "Yeah," she whispered. "I do."

"Feels good, doesn't it?" He took a finger and placed it on her hip, then followed the trail he'd described, across the crease of hip and thigh, through her wet curls, past her clit—which produced a sharp involuntary gasp from her chest—then to her center, where he dipped the finger inside.

"Oh!"

"You're so tight, so hot," he said appreciatively.

"Yes," she whimpered, and to Clarise's complete and utter shock, he withdrew the finger, slid it between his lips and sucked it while she watched. This wasn't a dream. Even in her most wicked Ethan Eubanks fantasy, she'd never conjured anything like this, which was proof her sexual imagination was in dire need of this. In dire need of Ethan.

"Very hot," he added, inserting the finger once more, then dragging it up her swollen lips to her clit. He ran a tiny circle around its heat, and her core clenched. Hard. Her hips jerked forward, and her hands gripped the handle until she knew she'd pull it off the wall. "Please." Ethan didn't need to be asked twice. He parted her curls with his fingers, then thoroughly stroked her clit with his tongue.

Sex had been nice, when she'd had it. She'd actually had a real orgasm a few times, but for the most part, she'd faked it. However, she had enjoyed sex enough to know she wanted it again, but not the kind she'd had before. Clarise wanted sex like in the movies, where bodies convulsed and screamed and got hot and sweaty and unraveled beneath a lover's skillful touch. She'd never had that. Until now. Lick, flick and suck. Was *that* the technique going on down there? Cause that's what she was feeling over and over and over, building and building. Lick, lick, flick, flick, suck. Lick. Suck harder. Goodness, she wasn't going to last very long at all. A current started deep inside, circling and spiraling toward Ethan's talented mouth. Her nipples were on fire, stomach dipped in and bore down on the oncoming tremor, then his fingers slid down her lips and one jutted inside. Then two. In and out. Lick and flick. In. Out. In. Out. Lick. Flick. Suck.

Clarise screamed through her release and fought to hold on to the handle. If she let go, she'd drop—and probably drown, because if she did let go, there was no getting up. Her body had shattered into a million pieces before completely melting at Ethan's touch. She wouldn't be surprised at all when this magnificent orgasm ended if she no longer existed and were a mere puddle in the base of the shower. Completely liquid and extremely hot.

He rose and pressed against her, holding her trembling body while she collapsed against his muscled frame. "You can let go now," he said, prying her fingers from the bar.

"I don't think I can."

He kissed her neck. "Clarise, you're beautiful."

She released her grip on the handle. *Beautiful?* No, she knew better, but she was too spent to argue. And amazingly enough, her insides were already clenching in anticipation of something quenching that stronger fire. The one deeper inside. "I want you," she whispered.

He smiled against her cheek. "And you'll have me. We've got several more things to cover on your list."

To hell with the list. She wanted him, and she didn't think covering the things on that list was going to quench her desire. Oh no, if having intercourse was anything like what she'd just experienced with Ethan Eubanks, one time would only fuel the flame. Heck, six times would probably just whet her appetite. She wanted him. Period. All of him. The man she'd come to respect and know and want so desperately, not just physically, but emotionally too, over the past three years. The man she'd thought was completely unattainable. A few romps in the hay weren't going to fix this hunger, and Clarise knew it now more than ever. She wanted, desperately wanted, Ethan.

She breathed a heavy, contented sigh against his chest. Telling him would ruin everything. He was simply going above and beyond the call of friendship duty to fulfill her sex fantasies, so she'd stay quiet, for now, and enjoy everything on her list. If she'd only known, that list would have been much, much longer. Long enough for an eternity. But for now, she'd take what she could get, and the next thing she'd get would have to wait until after the "bonding" luncheon. She bit her inner cheeks to keep from laughing out loud; that'd spoil the sensation of her face nuzzled against his warm, wet chest, but Clarise inwardly smiled, certain that none of Ethan's other employees were bonding quite like this.

Chapter 13

I can't believe the resort gave away Ethan's room," Jesilyn said, leading the way toward the Tampa Convention Center, the site for their luncheon.

"Yeah, he pays for all of this, and then he doesn't have a room to show for it," Rachel said, pausing to stick her nose against a jewelry store window. "Oh man, that sapphire is incredible!"

Clarise and Jesilyn peered over Rachel's shoulders to look at the ring, the exact color of Ethan's eyes when he was aroused. Clarise smiled. Until a couple of hours ago, she wouldn't have known.

Smirking, Rachel turned from the window. "Well, at least Ethan found a friend willing to let him bunk in." Then she spotted something at the next store and hurried ahead. Grabbing an oversized pirate's hat from a wire rack, she pushed it on top of her blond curls. "So," she said, looking at her reflection in the store's window, "is there any chance this arrangement could turn into more than merely bunking in?" She took off the hat and placed it back on the rack, then handed Jesilyn a bright red one. "Come on, Clarise, it's Gasparilla. Maybe you two should, you know, investigate exactly how far your 'friendship' can go."

"Friends don't sleep together," Jesilyn said, putting the hat back without trying it on. She attempted to smooth Rachel's curls, springing out in even more directions than usual. "Besides, Ethan isn't just her friend; he's her boss. Not a smart move. It's like Clarise said, she's helping him out because he needs a place to stay, simple as that."

Rachel turned back toward the window, shook her head, then fiddled with the curls until they were wild again. "Nope. I disagree. Friends definitely sleep together." She grinned, then, before Jesilyn could ask specifics, she changed the subject. "So what happens if you decide to hook up with someone while you're here, Clarise? I get the feeling Jake is planning to 'get to know you better' on this trip."

Clarise shook her head. "Miles told you that, didn't he? He heard Jake ask me to walk the beach with him yesterday and jumped to conclusions. Trust me. Jake Riley isn't interested, not beyond friendship." Or at least she didn't think he was. Sure, he'd been flirting, but Jake flirted with everyone. Then again, Jake had seemed to imply he wanted more on this trip, but she didn't want to talk about that now. It didn't matter anyway; she had her sex slave for the week all lined up, thank you very much, and his name was Ethan Eubanks. She bit back the urge to giggle. If Rachel and Jesilyn knew what she'd done this morning, they'd— well, she didn't know what they'd do, but they sure wouldn't believe it.

"Which leads back to what we were saying," Rachel said. "There's nothing wrong with friends sleeping together."

"Something you want to tell us?" Jesilyn asked accusingly.

"Me?" Rachel asked, placing a palm against her chest. She let her red-tipped fingers drum against her sternum then shrugged. "What on earth would I have to tell?" Laughing, she ran ahead to a street performer juggling several bowling pins.

"What do you think?" Jesilyn asked Clarise, while Rachel giddily tossed several dollars in the performer's hat.

"About sleeping with friends?" Clarise responded, and tried to keep her face from turning beet red.

"No," Jesilyn said. "About whether she's already slept with Miles, or whether she's merely planning on it happening before the day is over. And how awkward are things going to be at work after the two of them sleep together and then it doesn't work out? Trust me, it won't be pretty, but I doubt Rachel cares."

"You don't think they should get together?" Clarise asked, her chest clenching. "Weren't you the one who said, 'What happens in Tampa stays in Tampa'?"

"Come on," Jesilyn said, cocking one arched brow as she spoke. "You don't really believe that, do you? And I'd say they're definitely going to get together, that's a given. I just hope it doesn't ruin everything. Miles is a player, and Rachel won't like being played."

"Are you guys coming, or what?" Rachel called, motioning for them to hurry. "I'm sure everyone else is already there."

"We'd have been there a half hour ago if you hadn't stopped to window-shop," Jesilyn observed. "And I'm betting 'everyone' isn't who you're wanting to see."

Rachel winked. "Don't you remember? What happens in Tampa stays in Tampa."

"Oh yeah, they're going to get together," Jesilyn said under her breath. "I'd say it's as sure as—well, as sure as I'm going to get with Andre."

And as sure as I'm going to "get with" Ethan, Clarise thought. Would sleeping with her friend ruin everything? And did it even matter? Because there was no way she'd ever tell Ethan no, and there was no way she'd ever regret finally being with him completely. No matter what.

Saturated with partyers who'd started celebrating early at the annual invasion brunch, the Convention Center bristled with Gasparilla energy, providing an electric atmosphere for the company luncheon. Rachel, Jesilyn and Clarise entered to find a surplus of beads and an excess of partying.

"Oh wow, this is incredible!" Rachel exclaimed, her blond spirals bouncing against her back as she took it all in.

An abundantly muscled hunky pirate placed several shiny strands of red and gold beads around her neck. He leaned close and brushed a fingertip down her cheek. "A virgin to Gasparilla?" he asked.

Rachel's blue eyes blinked rapidly, and her lips curved into a silly grin. "A virgin? Me?"

Miles had been standing at the bar with Jake when the female trio entered. But after hearing the man's comment—and Rachel's response—he left without placing his order and unflinchingly stepped between Rachel and the smiling male. "We've been to Gasparilla before, but it's the first time any of us have been to the convention center for the invasion." He wrapped an arm around Rachel's waist, pulled her close and made her jump. Rachel's attention moved from the bead guy to Miles, and her grin broadened. She looked toward Clarise and Jesilyn, watching this odd display with interest, and winked.

Muscle guy didn't seem to mind his current use as jealousy bait. On the contrary, he obviously enjoyed Rachel's schoolgirl response and Miles's discomfort. "So I guess that means you're a virgin too," he said to Miles, whose face quickly tinged red. "Hardly," he growled, then he turned and looked pointedly at Rachel.

Rachel absolutely glowed, and Clarise realized she and Ethan weren't the only Eubanks employees who had seen a bit of sexual interaction during their first night at Gasparilla. And speaking of sexual triumphs, as in the guy who'd readily supplied her first experience with oral sex—make that phenomenal oral sex—this morning in the shower . . .

Clarise scanned the restaurant for Ethan. He'd left right after their shower to make sure everything was ready for the luncheon. He'd actually asked her to come along, but she'd insisted it wouldn't be smart to let the others in on the new aspect of their relationship. Everyone knew they were close, but no one knew how close they'd become as of this morning. Or rather, last night, if she counted Ethan's big hand slapping against her breasts at the parade, or the memorable moment when she boldly cupped his jewels in the elevator.

She laughed loudly, but since a jazz band was belting out an upbeat tune by the entrance, and another live band geared up onstage, no one seemed to notice. So she laughed again. It felt good to release the surge of minor hysteria that developed as a result of her major shower orgasm, so she let the laughter bubble free, continuing until thick tears trickled down her cheeks, which made her laugh even more.

"Clarise?" Jesilyn stepped away from Rachel, Miles and Jake, currently moving toward a gathering of tables in the far corner of the restaurant, and tilted her head questioningly. "Are you drunk?"

Clarise blinked away the tears and fought the impulse to start another bout of stomach-tingling laughter. *Drunk?* No, not today; last night, however, was a different story. But she wasn't complaining about the outcome of her first tangle with overindulgence. As a matter of fact, after last night, Clarise would have to say her three most favorite words were "Dead on Arrival." She laughed again, and finished off with a very unladylike snort. Thanks to that potent daiquiri, after three years of dreaming about wild sex with Ethan, today, probably in a matter of hours, she'd finally experience the whole shebang. Totally. And it would be even more amazing than the shower sex this morning. Shower sex. With Ethan. Goodness, she needed to laugh some more. She inhaled, with the full intention of saying something coherent, but then her jubilance with the situation intervened, and she cracked up again.

"You are drunk!" Jesilyn exclaimed, her big brown eyes popping wide at this realization. She quickly turned her head toward the group and sent her black hair swinging. Then she pivoted back toward Clarise, lowered her voice, which really wasn't necessary with all the party noise, and whispered, "I'm not believing it, Clarise Robinson, drunk in Tampa, and before noon."

"I'm not—" Clarise started, but Jesilyn didn't give her a chance to finish.

"Stick with me. I'll make sure no one takes advantage,"

Jesilyn instructed, in her I'm-sober-and-you're-not tone, then she paused, and added, "Unless you're wanting to lose your senses with one of these hotties. I've got to tell you, I met tons of gorgeous guys last night at that wedding." With a stern grip on Clarise's biceps, as though she thought her friend might topple over at any moment, Jesilyn slowly steered her toward the group.

"I'm not drunk, Jesi." Clarise stopped walking and swallowed through another itch to giggle. "I'm just excited to be here, experiencing all of this." *And experiencing Ethan.*

Jesilyn released her death grip, and Clarise rubbed her arms in relief. "That's right," Jesilyn said. "You never came down for any of the other bonding trips. And each year, Ethan makes sure we do something different, like the convention center luncheon. We've never been here before to see the invasion firsthand. This place is unreal, isn't it? The *Jose Gasparilla* will dock right outside, and we'll get a great view of the hot pirates storming the city. It'll be almost as incredible as the wedding last night with Andre."

"You had a good time?" Clarise asked, glad Jesilyn was no longer "protecting" her. She probably didn't weigh one-twenty, but Clarise would guess the majority was pure muscle.

"I've never seen anything so romantic in my life."

"And what about Andre?"

"Andre," Jesilyn repeated, her voice dreamy and her dimples dipping inward. "Man, he's got romance down to an art. I mean, wow! He lives here, you know, in Tampa."

Clarise listened intently. Seemed that Gasparilla had sparked all kinds of sexual energy in their small group. "Are you seeing him again?"

"We're going to one of the parades this afternoon. The

innkeeper invited all of the wedding guests to watch from the front porch," Jesilyn answered, as they quickly met up with the remainder of the Eubanks group.

Clarise couldn't help staring at Ethan as he and Robin Kennedy spoke with a tall gentleman in a Tampa Convention Center shirt. Ethan's sandy hair was more wavy than usual, probably because he hadn't taken time to dry it after their shower. *Their shower.* She sure liked the sound of that, not to mention the memory of his mouth on her . . .

"So, how about this afternoon?" Jake said, the warmth of his words feathering against her ear.

Clarise gasped. She'd been so intent on watching Ethan that she hadn't even noticed Jake approaching. "What?"

He chuckled, low and deep. "It's me, Clarise, no need to be so edgy." Pushing her hair behind her ear, he repeated, "I asked if you'd like to hit one of the parades with me. And for the record, I'm still smarting from your rejection yesterday. You won't let me down again, will you?"

A week ago, she'd have been thrilled to be on the receiving end of Jake's invitation, and the suggestive tone behind it, but that was last week. More importantly, that was before last night. And this morning. She forced a friendly laugh. "Don't even pretend that you didn't go out and find some other female to walk the beach with you, Jake."

He grinned, showing straight white teeth and a smile that would have melted her into a puddle. Last week. "No one as intriguing as you. So how about it? Want to head to a parade later?"

"I would," she said, fighting the urge to glance at Ethan as she answered. She sure didn't want to let Jake, and the remainder of the group, in on their personal activities. "But I've made plans."

Jake's look of surprise caught her off guard. She'd been so certain he was doing his typical tease Clarise thing, where he wasn't really asking her out. Sure, he might have taken her to the parade, but had he really wanted more than friendly companionship? She'd suspected yesterday's invitation to walk the beach meant something, but she wasn't sure until now. Because, like he said earlier, he looked like a guy who'd been rejected . . . by Clarise. He blinked a couple of times, hazel eyes in a forest of brown lashes, then ran his hand through his dark waves and quickly regrouped. "Change your plans. We'll have a good time." He raised his brows a notch, not much, but enough that Clarise knew she hadn't imagined the confident, cocky command, or the suggestive nature in his tone.

Jesilyn, standing slightly behind him, mouthed, "Go for it." If she only knew, Clarise *was* going for it. With Ethan.

"I really can't change them now," Clarise said, and this time, she did sneak a glance at Ethan, still standing by Robin and talking to the tall man who she assumed to be the caterer.

Jake's mouth twitched. "You hooked up with someone else? Is that it, Clarise?" He smiled at the end of the question, as though he were joking, but Jesilyn's wide eyes said Clarise wasn't the only one who heard the disappointment in Jake's tone. He cleared his throat, lowered his voice a notch, and added, "Look, everyone has a little fun down here." He indicated Ethan, who had turned toward them and smiled.

Clarise's chest tightened. That smile might have been toward all of them, but it sure seemed geared specifically for her. Have mercy, she couldn't wait for the luncheon to end. She remembered so clearly the way those turquoise eyes turned stormy navy when he was aroused, and she wanted to see them that way again, dark, stormy and dangerous.

Pointing to an item on the menu, Robin tapped Ethan's shoulder to regain his attention. His chest lifted with what appeared to be a heavy sigh, then he looked at the menu and nodded.

"Looks like I was right," Jake said to Miles, standing nearby with his arm still draped possessively around Rachel.

"Right about what?" Rachel asked, tilting her head to peer up at Miles. She was no more than five-two, so his six feet practically towered above her. Clarise looked back at Ethan. How tall was he, anyway? His mouth came to her forehead when they stood side by side, and since she was five-six, that'd put him at—what?—six-one maybe? Six-one and five-six; was that a good combination for snuggling? For more than snuggling? She breathed deeply at the image and almost didn't hear Jake's response.

"I bet Miles a hundred that the boss would appear before the trip ended," Jake said. "Especially when his dutiful store manager offered to oversee the show. You can pay me now," he said. Grumbling as he shook his head, Miles fished a few bills out of his pocket and slapped them into Jake's hand. Jake counted the twenties, nodded, then smiled like a thief when he pocketed the money.

Jesilyn turned to look at Ethan and Robin, both smiling as they spoke with the caterer. "What are you saying, Jake?"

"Just that Ethan comes down here for more than 'corporate' bonding," Jake informed, his voice lowered even more in spite of the loud music. "And as Miles and I learned last year, his favorite Gasparilla color is red." He smirked, eyeing Robin, currently holding her long strawberry hair back with one hand while she leaned over the table to snatch a roll. Her thin pink tank dress dipped with the action and flashed the top curves of her perky breasts. She looked at Jake, smiled and straightened. Then she took a bite of the roll and nodded approvingly toward Ethan and the caterer while she chewed.

"He's not seeing Robin," Clarise intervened. That had been the rumor around Christmas, but Ethan had confirmed to Clarise that the gossip was false. He'd never dated Robin. As a matter of fact, he was dating some other female at the time. Clarise couldn't recall the name, because it didn't matter. Particularly now, because now he wanted Clarise. Case closed. She frowned. Was this really just a temporary romp or could it be more? Then she took a deep breath, blew it out, and told herself to stop being a ninny. She was going to have sex with Ethan today and nothing—nothing—was going to mess with her excitement over that. Not even wondering whether the first time would also be the last.

"Robin is dating that reporter at the *Birmingham News,* guys," Rachel informed. "She and Ethan are not seeing each other; besides, Clarise would know if they were. He tells her everything."

"The boss's pet," Jake said jokingly, and Clarise chose not to comment. Then he clarified, "I didn't say he was 'seeing' her. I said that both of them are down here to have fun, and I bet they have it together." He shrugged, looked at Clarise. "I'm thinking everyone should have a little fun at the Pirate Festival. Don't you?"

"What he does is his business," Clarise said. *And what he does with me is ours.*

"That's my point," Jake said. "He's having fun, and I'm sure he plans on all of us having fun too." He stepped forward and took Clarise's hand. "We should have some," he said, then paused and tipped one corner of his mouth upward in a sexy, suggestive look that Clarise bet he practiced in the mirror, "fun, that is," he finished.

"It's time to get started." Ethan's voice dominated the room, in spite of the blaring music. Clarise turned to find him standing merely feet away and focused on the way Jake's hand covered her own. She wiggled hers free and stared at those blue eyes again, dark and stormy, but with a different turbulence than this morning. This time they were fiery, intent, and determined. Her feminine core quivered. He was boldly and powerfully male, and he was staking his claim. Heaven help her, he was hers . . . for now. As if he knew her very thoughts, he turned those turbulent eyes from her hand to her face. She thought she should say something clever, or at the bare minimum, blink; but she couldn't do either, so in preparation for conversation, she licked her lips. Those blue eyes watched her action and seemed to instantly turn from fiery to steamy. "It's time to get started," he repeated.

She managed to nod. "Yes, it is," she agreed, knowing Ethan's statement had nothing to do with the luncheon and everything to do with her fantasies.

Chapter 14

Ethan thought the luncheon would never end. In fact, he wasn't sure it had, since he handed the reins over to Robin the minute the group decided to move outside to get a close-up view of the *Jose Gasparilla* and the elaborately dressed pirates. Blessedly, Robin Kennedy was more than capable of running the show. Clarise had stated that she didn't want to draw attention to their newfound interest in one another beyond friendship, but damned if he didn't draw a hell of a lot of attention when he reacted to Riley making the moves. It was all he could do not to pummel one of his best employees—and one of Clarise's friends. Ethan wouldn't be surprised if she hadn't caught on to the way Jake looked at her in her new, sexy ensemble of a short skirt, fitted blouse and boots, but Ethan sure caught on. The guy wanted Clarise, and Jake wasn't known for his bedside manner. He was a love them, leave them and carve another notch in his bedpost kind of guy. In other words, he wasn't nearly the right man to help Clarise accomplish the items on her list. She deserved someone who would give her the sexual fulfillment she dreamed of, but who also cared about her and wouldn't hurt her in the process. A friend and a lover. Besides, she'd admitted she wanted her dream lover to look like Ethan, act like Ethan. Damned if that didn't make his chest swell, along with another part of his anatomy.

He drove the rental car down Bayshore in search of a parking space close enough to the next parade to be accessible by walking, but also near enough to his final destination point to provide the element of surprise. After the parade, he'd fulfill another of Clarise Robinson's fantasies. Granted, he hadn't planned on their first physical union to take place under the bleachers at a football stadium, but what a way to make a memory. And the fact was, he'd never had "bleacher sex," as Clarise had called it on her list. He looked at the woman in the passenger seat. Before this week, he'd have sworn he knew her better than most people, even her eccentric grandmother and rowdy sister, but she'd certainly shown him another layer of her many facets last night, then yet another this morning. He'd never wanted to please a woman more than he wanted to please Clarise, never wanted to make a woman feel more desired, because she *was* desirable, whether she realized it or not. He'd started showing her that in the shower this morning. Evidently, his attempt worked. She'd looked *different* when she arrived at the luncheon. Confident, and extremely sexy. It was a very nice look on Clarise, and Ethan felt another swell of pride knowing he'd given it to her.

She rolled her window down and pointed her face into the air, while the breeze whipped her brown ponytail around to whack against her cheek. She squinted at the silky whip's attack but giggled just the same. Damn, she was cute. Particularly now, wearing a plain white blouse, khaki skirt and tennis shoes. It wasn't her first choice of clothing when they'd gone back to the room to get ready for the parade. Oh no, her first choice was a lime green skintight sweater dress and strappy sandals, not very convenient for parades, unless you're a single woman attempting to pick up a man, which, Ethan realized, had been her goal when she'd packed. Thank goodness she brought a couple of outfits befitting the parades outside the main invasion, like the one they'd attend this afternoon, a parade geared for families. Ethan had been thrilled to see that there were a few casual ensembles in her wardrobe. Maybe she hadn't been certain that the new look would mesh well with her usually reserved yet classy style, but it did—very well, in fact. However, Ethan didn't want her under any assumptions that the sexy clothing was the only thing she had going. Regardless of his store's claim that "clothing makes the woman," Ethan knew better, particularly when it came to sensuality. It isn't the clothes that are appealing; it's the woman inside. And sensuality radiated from Clarise.

Ethan grinned. After he'd seen every intimate part of her, had tasted it in fact, she'd still been timid about dressing in front of him. Shuffled in the bathroom and donned the lime green getup, then shuffled right back when he'd reminded her they were attending the "family" parade. He admitted the green had been sexy as hell and played off those big doe eyes and silky brown hair, plus the way the sweater fabric clung to every delicious curve brought him to full attention. But the thought of bleacher sex with her in the sweet outfit, with her ponytail and tennis shoes, well, that worked too.

They stopped at the end of the parade traffic line.

Looking out his window, he inhaled humid Tampa air, filled with scents of spicy seasonings and strong alcohol. Numerous homes on the outskirts of the parade route had open garage doors and sported large gatherings of friends huddled around big tables and chowing down on plates piled high with food. Ethan concentrated on the scene and tried to take his focus off the woman merely inches away. He needed to get his aroused state under control if he planned to stand beside her during the parade and watch her go for beads. Shirts stayed on at these parades, but he still suspected Clarise Robinson could flaunt her stuff, covered or not. She embodied sexuality. Ethan wasn't sure how he'd missed it during the past three years. He'd caught a glimpse at the Christmas party, but right now, the flame was undeniable, even when she was enthralled with the carnival atmosphere surrounding their car.

Clowns with big balloons shaped like pirate ships stood on each street corner. Black-and-gold-striped booths advertising souvenirs and ice cream dotted the sidewalks. Clarise squealed like a child as she took it all in. "Ooh, they've got cotton candy," she said. "Let's make sure to get some at the parade."

"All right," he said, as though denying her any request would even enter his mind.

She turned toward him, flashed a satisfied smile, then returned to examine the scenery. Satisfied. Oh yeah, she'd been satisfied this morning, all right, courtesy of him. And she'd be satisfied again, a few times, before the day ended. But for their next encounter, he wouldn't stop with her satisfaction. She wanted Ethan inside of her, and as promised, he'd give her what she wanted. It took all he had not to pull the car down a side street and fulfill that particular request immediately, to feel those slick folds around him. She'd grabbed his fingers and clung to them like a vise when he'd slid them inside her hot center. Hell, he'd never wanted inside a woman as badly as he'd wanted inside Clarise this morning. But, although that was what he wanted, it wasn't what he needed, not if he planned to turn this fantasy thing into what he really desired, something more substantial with Clarise.

How many Friday afternoons had he told her about his latest dating fiasco, about the women who simply didn't make him feel that stirring inside, the type of excited longing that two people require to have something more? He'd never met a woman who made him forget work completely and think more of her than his next deal. It wasn't as if he hadn't wanted to feel that with a female; he simply hadn't. He'd even told Clarise that he was starting to believe he'd never find it. While a few women had claimed his interest sexually, the relationship had never gone beyond the bedroom. All physical, no emotional, which was okay, unless you were thirty-three and sincerely wanting more than mere sex. Looking for the whole package. Ethan felt the possibility of that now, with Clarise. That sense of union they'd shared last night, when she'd had too much to drink and needed help from him, her friend. Then this morning, he'd watched her sleep. He smiled, remembering the adorable way she shifted in the covers, hanging one shapely leg off the bed, then pulling it back under the sheets in retreat, before slowly sliding it back out again, as though uncertain whether she wanted to be uncovered and wild . . . or cocooned and tame. Both suited her, in Ethan's opinion. And that intoxicating combination was part of what made her exactly what he wanted.

He'd been shocked when she admitted commitment wasn't on the list. Shocked, but not deterred. Ethan would have Clarise Robinson, not just sexually, but emotionally as well, which was why he'd held back in the shower and given satisfaction to her needs, rather than his own. It'd been so easy to jump directly into hot and heavy sex with Clarise, and he'd be doing that soon enough, thanks to her detailed list. But heading into sex without the nuances of getting-to-know-you foreplay seemed a near-impossible method to convince her that they should explore the possibilities of more than a few days of the hot and heated. He couldn't deny he was putting the cart before the horse, as the saying goes. How would she see they were compatible beyond sex if they merely spent the next four days hopping from bed to bed? Or in Clarise's case, bed to shower to grass to bleachers to elevator . . .

Ethan bit back a laugh. It was a good thing he was in shape. Most men wouldn't be able to keep up with Clarise Robinson's demands without the aid of a little blue pill. But he didn't want merely to appease her fix for sexual fulfillment. He wanted her to see him as more than a thorough lover. Ethan wanted to be her friend, her lover, her confidant, her everything. Too bad he hadn't realized that when they were just friends. In any case, he'd started their one-on-one time together by keeping her from baring her God-given assets to Tampa, which, Ethan deduced, was a very good thing. The world wasn't ready for Clarise Robinson unplugged.

Another chortle attempted to make its way up his throat, but he swallowed it down. He didn't want her to hear him laughing. She was too self-conscious as it was, and he sure didn't want to feed that portion of Clarise. In fact, he planned to show her exactly how appealing she was to him, how appealing she'd be to any man, possibly for the rest of his life. But first he had to convince her he was more than her friend, more than her boss, more than a guy who'd take part in her fantasies. He wanted to be there to take care of her, always, like he had last night when she'd been sick. Holding her, comforting her, watching over her. It was natural, being with Clarise, tending her needs as if he were meant to be there, in bad times, like when she'd pleaded for death while hugging the toilet, and in spectacular times, like when she'd let herself go in the shower.

Her scream of release echoed in his mind. He'd never forget the passion behind it. The thrill at knowing *he'd* caused her to lose control. And even though he hadn't entered her, yet, their sexual level had gone beyond anywhere he'd been before with the kind of earth-shattering, mind-boggling sensation where you share a mating of your souls, and you see a person as more than a lover. You see her as your future. His future. Yeah, Ethan silently admitted, that was exactly what he was seeing. A future.

Three years. He'd wasted three years with Clarise, the complex conglomeration of trusted friend, considerate employee and bona fide siren, all rolled up into one distinctive, mesmerizing package. She'd been right there all along. The woman who could make him want her so bad it hurt, give off more sexual fire with her shower orgasm than Ethan had ever witnessed. And the woman who'd admitted she wanted sex with a lover who looked like Ethan. That meant something, didn't it? Sure it did. Whether Clarise realized it or not, she didn't want an Ethan Eubanks double. She wanted the real deal. *Him.* Not a stranger, and not some hot and spicy fling.

Hot and spicy. Damned if that didn't sum her up. She'd been so hot, so fiery tight, with all those luscious curves flexing and shivering. He'd been spellbound by every aspect of satisfying Clarise. Her ample breasts pushing against his mouth while he sucked on the fullness of her nipples. The pulsing of her feminine core as he licked her essence. Her body trembling at his touch, until she tensed in that final moment before she screamed her release. And how she screamed.

Forget it. His aroused state wasn't subsiding today, not until that hot, liquid heat he'd tasted between her legs enveloped his length. How long would this parade last, anyway?

"Throw me something, mister!" Clarise yelled as the next elaborate float, modeled after a circus theme, neared. She'd polished off a fluffy pink cone of cotton candy and was experiencing a mega sugar high, or a mega Ethan high. Either way, she felt good. Candy and doubloons sailed through the air, while kids and adults alike scrambled for the loot. Occasionally, a bagged cone of her favorite treat found its way over the side of a float.

"I love cotton candy," she said, watching a blue one hurled to the other side of the street. "Hey, that needed to come this way!" she yelled to the guy tossing the goods.

"You're enjoying this, aren't you?" Ethan asked.

"Are you kidding? It's incredible!" She heard him laughing, something he'd been doing most of the day, and it thrilled her to her toes. That laugh, that sexy rumble from his to-die-for chest, was produced for her. Oh yeah, she felt good. Real good.

In the center of the circus float, the ringmaster, complete with top hat, red coat and tails, flicked his handlebar moustache and winked at Clarise, then bent over to find something in a box near his feet.

"Oooh, he's getting me something good," she said, clutching Ethan's biceps while she waited for her next prize.

The parade was in its third hour, and so far, she'd warranted more beads than she'd thought to gain during the entire trip. Currently, they draped her neck in a heavy glittering medley of red, gold, purple and white. She loved them, in spite of the weight of her bounty pulling more on her shoulders than her Robinson Treasures. But Clarise didn't care; she felt like a kid with her favorite treat. Of course, the treat of choice was the hunk of gorgeous male standing beside her laughing at her outrageousness rather than the beads draped around her neck and the candy and doubloons filling the goodie bag he'd purchased on her behalf.

While the ringmaster continued rummaging through the box, a skinny waif of a blonde, dressed as a trapeze artist, spotted Ethan. "Oooh, baby, I've got some nice ones for you," she crooned.

The back of Clarise's neck bristled. From what she could see of the bony body in the skimpy outfit, the girl didn't have *anything* for Ethan, nothing close to what Clarise had given him this morning, when he'd had more than a mouthful of her breasts. She turned to watch Ethan's response and brushed the Robinson Jewels against him, in case he'd forgotten what he seemed to enjoy so much earlier. Sure, she'd never felt empowered by her full figure before, but the more Ethan had looked at her today, the more she remembered how he'd called her "beautiful," the more she believed it. As she watched his polite nod to the bony waif, her belief was further intensified. Ethan liked curves. Moreover, he liked curves on her.

Take that, Blondie.

For so many years, she'd felt out of place next to Babette, with her rail-thin body and sculpted cheekbones. Clarise's cheeks were pleasantly rounded, like the rest of her. Now she realized that wasn't necessarily a bad thing, particularly with the way Ethan's eyes kept assessing those curves, cheeks, breasts and behind.

He raised his hand to catch the glittering beads Skinny tossed his way, then turned to drape them around Clarise's already-covered neck. "They'll look better on you than me," he said. "What do you think?" But before Clarise could answer, a tiny voice, one that had been squealing above them throughout the entire parade, pleaded. "Oh, Daddy, I want those!"

Ethan and Clarise turned simultaneously toward the little girl, perched on the top of a six-foot homemade ladder chair. The chairs known for helping children obtain those sought-after beads lined both sides of Bayshore Boulevard like tall, wooden soldiers and placed the kids at eye level with the lowest tier of the floats. On top of this particular chair, the curly-haired redhead had her baby blue eyes on the beads Skinny had flung at Ethan, the beads currently draped around Clarise's neck.

"Please, Daddy. Mommy. I want those!" She leaned over the side of the chair and stretched a chubby little hand toward the ground and the desired beads.

Ethan had already encircled Clarise's neck with the purple strand, accented with pirate faces on every other bead. It was the prettiest necklace Clarise had received so far, and consequently, it was the one the little girl favored.

A tender smiled played with Ethan's full lips. "I'm assuming you're willing to share a strand," he said, his crystal blue eyes glittering, in spite of the dimness of the afternoon.

Clarise swallowed, nodded, and ducked her head to help him remove the beads. Removing the strand, Ethan's hand flicked beneath her ponytail, and her neck tingled. Then he stepped away from Clarise to hand the prized beads to the waiting toddler. She had a gap in her top row of teeth, and she smiled so broadly her tongue stuck through the hole. That smile touched Clarise's heart, but it was nothing compared to what Ethan's did when he looked at the beautiful little angel as though she'd hung the moon. How would he look at his own child? Like that? Yes, Clarise suspected, and more. Her heart bubbled. Ethan Eubanks, business owner, friend, lover and father. Oh yeah, she could see it. She swallowed, determined to stay in control. Yeah, that was her real dream, but right now, he was simply helping her with her list. She had to remember that, until she figured out a way to take the magic of this week back home. Somehow.

"Thanks. You made her day," the little girl's father said, shaking his head at his daughter's boldness but grinning just the same.

"No problem," Ethan said. "Her smile made mine." He wrapped an arm around Clarise and squeezed her waist. "Beautiful, isn't she?"

"Yes, she is."

The girl fumbled with the beads until she put them over her head. Then she reached both hands toward the circus float, at a standstill in front of them, in search of additional loot.

"Looks like she's ready for more," Clarise added.

"Looks like," Ethan said.

"So am I."

His fingers curled against her skin. Mouth moved to her ear. "I believe we've seen enough of this parade."

"Couldn't agree with you more." Her voice sounded raspy and hungry, even to her own ears.

"Here ya go, darlin'!" the ringmaster called, and as Clarise turned her eyes toward the top of the float, he flung an odd-shaped item over the side.

Ethan stretched a hand to catch the flimsy material, looked at it and shook his head. "This is supposed to be a family parade, but I guess your exquisite assets got the best of the ringmaster," he said, stashing the item in their bag.

"What is it?" Clarise asked. She'd removed the bulk of her necklaces and dropped them in the bag at the same moment he'd shoved the new item inside. Peering in, she squinted to see her newest prize while Ethan, chuckling, guided her through the crowd.

"Exactly what you've been wanting," he answered, then elaborated, "A Gasparilla bra, complete with a pirate's face on one cup and a sword on the other."

"Really?" She'd wanted one from the first time she'd heard the item mentioned, but she'd yet to see one, and now she had one of her very own. "Will it fit?"

Something akin to a growl sounded from Ethan as he wedged them through the back of the crowd and started down the sidewalk in the general direction of their car. "I'm anticipating finding out later. Personally."

"You're going to help me try it on?" she teased. "Because

sometimes it's hard to fit them in a bra. They don't typically cooperate, so you have to kind of lift them up and put them in the right place."

His grip on her hand tightened so much she gasped. And the thrill of having that kind of effect on Ethan Eubanks was addictive. She had to continue.

"Because if you don't situate them just so, the fabric can pinch my nipples, and that wouldn't be very good, would it? Having my nipples pinched all day, particularly when I'm trying to work? Because they're extremely sensitive, as you've probably noticed, so when they're pinched, they stand out like two beacons beneath my shirt. Not exactly the most professional appearance—"

He stopped walking and yanked her to him, dropping the sack of parade loot to the ground. Beads and candy and doubloons clattered against the asphalt as he pressed his hard erection against her belly. His mouth captured hers without restraint, his tongue thrusting in and out, in and out, in perfect rhythm with the hips moving against her.

She moaned and tried to get closer, which was impossible, since they couldn't have slid one shiny doubloon between their bodies.

Pulling away, he nipped her lower lip. "You're going to kill me, Clarise."

"I'm trying."

That low, sexy laugh rippled down her skin. "I want to take you somewhere special for this," he said, and his eyes looked smoky, though that could've been because the night sky was steadily blanketing Tampa.

"How far?" she asked, wiggling against him. She did not want to wait long, didn't think she could.

"Not far. We're nearly there. But hell, I'd planned for it to be slow, easy and sensual."

"And?"

"And I can only promise one of the three," he said, pressing another kiss against her lips. When he broke away, her eyes blinked in the dimness. His jaw was tense and set in a determined line. Then he grabbed the bag in one hand and her palm in the other and led her down the street. Within minutes, they neared a brick building, a high school, and her pulse flittered.

"Which one?" she asked, as they circled the building and headed toward the football stadium. "Of the three? Slow? Easy?"

"Sensual," he confirmed, and she held the urge to laugh. "We'll have slow and easy. I promise you, we will. But not this time."

Chapter 15

For the entire afternoon, Ethan watched her squeal for beads, shimmy like nobody's business, and cheer for her hard-earned loot. All the while fighting his hard-earned hard-on. He'd nearly decided he could make it until the end of the parade before he drove into her, then her "ready for more" comment punched him low. Right below the belt. Add the detailed instructions on how he could help put her delicious breasts in a Gasparilla bra, and he'd nearly come in his pants, like an inexperienced teen, for crying out loud. Ethan Eubanks, who'd been dubbed "marathon man" by more than one of his previous lovers, was ready to self-combust at the mere thought of Clarise's hidden pleasures. But they wouldn't be hidden long. Because he sure as hell wouldn't wait.

"Where to?" she asked, as they neared the end of the football bleachers.

He'd had no idea what the stadium would be like when he found the location of the nearest high school on the web this morning, but he'd been determined it would work. Examining the concrete walls on the ends, the thick pillars within its center, he knew for certain. *Perfect.* They crossed the solid earth and stamped over wild weeds that had grown beneath the stands. Wild and determined to burst free from their confinement, like the curvaceous woman at his side. Pulling her within the first section, he pressed her back to the pillar. Then he nipped her lower lip with his teeth and slanted his mouth over hers while she squirmed. Pushing his tongue inside, Ethan tasted chocolate and strawberry and cotton candy, her parade treats, combined with the intoxicating sweetness that was purely Clarise. He shoved his erection against her, the zipper of his pants rubbing his cock with each movement and making him even more eager to dive into her wet heat.

Clarise responded like an animal in dire need to mate, clawing at the front of his jeans until she had them unfastened and unzipped. Wasting no time at all, she grabbed the waist and pulled down. Then she encircled his erection with both hands. "Mmmmm."

Ethan was surprised he had the wherewithal to remember the condom, but he did, thank God. He withdrew a foiled packet from his pocket, moved her hands and sheathed his length. Then he grabbed the sides of her skirt and bunched it in his palms, his pulse pumping madly when his knuckles finally grazed her lush thighs.

"I can't be gentle this time, Clarise." He yanked the skirt up and slid one hand to her center and desperately hoped he would find her panties as wet as he anticipated. His fingers only met a hint of wet satin around the edge of her slick folds and fiery heat. Recognition body-slammed him. Wild indeed. "No panties," he confirmed.

She bit his neck. "Yes, panties," she corrected. "No crotch."

Damn, she'd be his undoing. Unable to wait a second longer, he shoved her against the pillar, lifted her legs to his waist and thrust inside. Clarise's molten need engulfed him, held him tight as he pushed deep, becoming as much a part of her as she was becoming a part of him. Her full breasts met his chest with each thrust, with hard, stiff nipples evident in spite of the layers between them.

"Yes, oh, yes," she urged, as he continued delving into her tight-as-a-fist center. He was so close, so damn close, but hell, he couldn't. Not until . . .

Ethan shifted her body, then reached between them, beneath the bunched fabric of her skirt at her waist and found her swollen clit. Her mouth was clamped on his throat, sucking and biting through each plunge, but she arched wildly against his hand when he found her secret spot. With sweat beading at his temples and his jaw clenched to maintain control, Ethan slowed his thrusts and concentrated on her gasps, her quick inhalations of preclimax.

"That's right, baby," he urged, burying himself within her while he caressed the tender cleft. "I want to feel you come around me, darling. Ride it, Clarise. Ride it hard. Let it go."

She spread her legs wider, pressing against his finger, while he pumped inside. "D-don't stop," she whispered. "Please."

"Never." He increased the quick strokes to her clitoris while he let his own strokes pound thoroughly into her tight heat, in perfect time with her building gasps, her thrusting breasts.

She sucked a large gulp of air, and Ethan felt her entire body tense in preparation. With one final, deep plunge, he

merged completely with Clarise, both of their bodies finding gratifying release, while he captured her scream with
his kiss.

The drive to the condo reminded Ethan of when he'd
first started dating and was taking the girl home, that anxious feeling of wondering if and when you'll see each other
again—and how far to go at her door. But in this case, he
wasn't wondering whether he'd see her again or even what
would happen when he took the girl home. Oh no, in this
case, he wondered when he'd *have* Clarise again. And how
far she was willing to go . . . in their relationship. Because,
much like in high school, Ethan Eubanks wanted to go all
the way.

She'd rolled the window down again, and the humidity
of Tampa at night wasn't much better than the daytime,
but with Clarise at his side, it seemed damn euphoric. Inhaling deeply, she angled over the console and nestled against
him. "That was incredible." She'd made the claim a few
times since they left the stadium in search of their car. And
each time, amazingly, she seemed more in awe of their
stadium sex. Of course, Ethan couldn't deny the pride at
her assessment. He knew the truth as well as she. It *was*
damn good.

"Fulfilled that fantasy?" he asked.

"I'll say."

The memory of Clarise beneath the bleachers would be
forever tattooed on his mind. Moonlight spilling through
the stadium seats illuminating her face and intensifying the
hunger in her eyes, and in her mouth, as she panted through
their mating. Her hot, wet center, open and ready in the
midst of a strip of satin. Bountiful breasts heaving and push-

ing against him with every thrust. Legs tightening around his waist to pull him close and hold him inside. He'd never forget the vision of a sweet, shy Clarise turned wild and wicked, and he'd make more of those memories with her before their time in Tampa ended. Hell, before the night was over, if he had his way. Judging by the way she snuggled against him, he'd have his way.

"No more parades tonight?" she asked.

"By the time we get back to the condo, they'll be done."

She leaned closer, kissed his neck, then nibbled his earlobe. "Then what will we do?"

He stopped at a traffic light. Crowds from the parades had cleared, and street sweeper trucks trudged their way down the parade routes to clear the enormous amount of debris. Thankfully, the removal of traffic and obstacles meant they'd be at the condominium in a matter of minutes. "What would you like to do, Clarise?"

She ran her hand up his thigh and pressed her palm against the outline of his penis against his jeans. "Well, we could hang out in our room until something comes up."

The light turned green, informing Ethan it was time to move. His cock hardened, informing the same thing. "Baby, it won't take long."

Clarise felt like skipping through the resort. Better yet, she wanted to scream to the rooftops that she'd had wild, frantic, frenzied bleacher sex with Ethan Eubanks. With Ethan Eubanks! She glanced around the lobby and outer edge of the resort's private bar, half-expecting to see some of the gang from work hanging out and enjoying the end of another night at Gasparilla, but evidently, the entire crew had already headed to bed for the night. Whether alone or with company, Clarise didn't know or care. She was accomplishing the items on her list with the guy she'd dreamed about for years, and that was all that mattered. Not one of her Ethan fantasies had involved a set of bleachers and a concrete pillar against her back. Funny, that hard beam pushing into her spine should've taken away from the enjoyment rather than intensifying it, but intensify it did, the pain against her back only making the blissful invasion of her front more potent. Damn potent, if she did say so herself. Her orgasm curled her toes until her legs cramped and her eyes watered. By glory, she couldn't wait for it to happen again, and it would, soon. By the time they reached their room. Then, watching Ethan's face as he pushed the elevator button, she suspected it might happen before they reached the third floor. Worked for her.

"Come on," he said, guiding her inside.

A couple of inebriated partyers, college fraternity boys, judging from the Greek insignias on their shirts, piled in after them.

"Hell of a Gasparilla," one of them said, his breath foul enough to pass across the elevator and make Clarise flinch.

"Sure is," she returned, trying to be polite in spite of his drunken state. Then she emitted a small yelp when Ethan's palm slid into the back of her skirt.

"Damn," the other claimed, turning to view the original elevator occupants and immediately focusing on Clarise's nipples, protruding in spite of bra and shirt. She tried to think of a response to put the pervert in his place, but before she could speak, Ethan did.

"They're taken," he informed.

Clarise snorted as the guy flashed a crooked grin and shrugged, then followed his friend off at the second floor.

"Lucky you," frat boy called as the doors closed.

"Yeah," Ethan agreed. "Lucky me."

The walls of the elevator were mirrored, so she waited until the doors closed to view his smoldering eyes in their reflection.

"Taken, are they?" she asked, unable to resist.

"Damn right." He reached in front of her and punched the STOP button before they hit the third floor.

"What are you doing?" She feigned shock but failed to sound surprised.

He pulled her against him so his hard length pressed into her back. Then he lowered his face and nudged her ponytail away with his chin. The five o'clock shadow that had transformed him from clean-cut and gorgeous to rough, rugged and dangerous scratched her tender skin. "As if you don't know," he whispered, his warm breath fanning beneath her ear.

"How long before it starts back up? Or a buzzer sounds? Or—"

His lips stopped her speech. The awkward stance only added to the appeal. Ethan's front against her back, her head angled to give him complete access to her mouth, and that hard rod pressing against her spine, announcing exactly what would happen. Soon, she hoped. He nipped her lower lip as he broke the kiss. "You did ask me to add elevator sex to your list, didn't you?"

She nodded, but the niggling fear still squirmed its way forward. "But I hadn't really thought about the possibilities of getting caught."

His smile, as usual, caused her thighs to clench. "Adds to the fun, don't you think? The potential for getting caught with your pants down," he said, turning her so she faced one of the side mirrors, "Or in your case, with your skirt up. Bend over, Clarise."

Heaven help her, she couldn't have said no if she tried. Yes, the elevator could start moving at any moment, and yes, if it did, they'd be at the third floor, where possibly, people would be ready to ride. But yes, Clarise was ready for Ethan to ride *her*. Now. A handrail hung midway across the wall. She grabbed on and closed her eyes, eager to concentrate on feeling Ethan possess her once more. The fabric of her skirt grazed her legs, and she shivered as he bunched it up above her waist.

"Now spread your legs, darling."

Clarise nodded, eager, wet and ready.

"You're so beautiful."

Cool air kissed her cheeks and the hot center that burned for Ethan's touch.

"Open your eyes, Clarise."

Once again, she followed his command.

"That's right, baby. I want you to watch."

Although she'd known exactly what she'd see, the picture in front of her caught her off guard. It was so erotic, seeing her body bent over, knowing her skirt left her womanhood completely bare to his access, and also knowing Ethan remained fully clothed.

"I want you," she said.

He slid his hand between her legs, guided one finger inside. She instantly clenched to grab on, to hold him, any part of him, within her.

"Oh yeah, you certainly do." Then he removed the finger, and Clarise wanted to cry from the withdrawal. He wouldn't stop now. He couldn't.

"Please, Ethan."

His hands moved up her sides and slid the top button of her blouse through the buttonhole. She vaguely remembered doing the same thing two days ago in her apartment; however, it hadn't been near as intoxicating to watch her own hands at the task. Watching Ethan's, however, pushed a surge of warmth to the tips of both nipples and made them strain against the fabric of her bra. Slowly and surely, one button at a time, he opened her shirt and let the sides fall.

In her recent shopping trip, she'd purchased the barely there bra, its cups cradling the lower half of her mounds and providing even more of a surplus of cleavage than usual. Ethan ran a fingertip across the lace edge and pressed gently against the swells. "Nice."

Her nipples were on fire now, begging for that touch to move a fraction lower. Then with one deft flick of his fingers, he unclasped the front closure. Her breasts spilled out freely, and he growled appreciation at the sight.

"Look at you, Clarise."

She did, and swallowed. The round tips of her breasts were a shade darker than normal, undoubtedly owing to her intense arousal. They were almost a cinnamon color, in contrast to her white skin, and her nipples were hard points hovering from within his palms, which cupped her breasts fully. "Oh, my," she whispered.

"My thoughts exactly."

Clarise watched him run his thumbs across the peaks, then pinch them while she pushed against his erection and burned to feel it inside. He released her breasts and straightened behind her. She licked her lips, so anxious, so ready.

Ethan unfastened his jeans, pushed down the zipper . . .

And the elevator buzzed to life.

"Ohmigod," she gasped, a surge of adrenaline-based

panic rushing through her. Getting caught sure hadn't been on her list. "Ohmigod."

But Ethan simply leaned over and slammed the button once more. "Guess that's how long we have before it buzzes again."

"You mean we're going to—we're *not* going to stop?" She looked up, then giggled when she realized she hadn't released her death grip from the rail, hadn't made an effort at all to cover her bare behind. What if the doors had opened? If they had, there'd for sure have been a full moon in Tampa tonight.

"Stop? Before we fulfill your fantasy? Not a chance." He shifted behind her, and she listened to the telltale rip of foil.

"You're everything I thought you'd be," she said, then wondered if that wasn't laying things out there a little bit strong. No matter; she didn't care. That's how she felt. It wasn't as though she told him she wanted to birth his children, in any case. Although she did.

His hands moved forward to cup her breasts once more, and he began a slow, thorough massage, filling his palms with the surplus, then easing forward to once again pinch her excited nipples.

"Ooooh, yes," she whispered, closing her eyes as her womanhood flexed in direct result to his sweet torture.

"Clarise?"

"Mmm-hmmm."

"Open your eyes."

For the past three years, she'd wanted to see Ethan Eubanks making love to her, and now that it was happening, she still acted as though it were a dream. She would've laughed, but upon opening her eyes, she saw nothing funny.

And everything exhilarating. His big, tan hands were a stark contrast to the full, bulging breasts.

"Watch," he instructed, taking a thumb and forefinger to each nipple and rolling them until they plumped, and her core begged for release.

"I can't wait, Ethan. I swear I can't."

His palms slid down her sides, over her bunched skirt, then to the front of her thighs. Gently he spread them wider, and he lowered his body so his erection nudged her center.

"You said I'm everything you thought I'd be, right?" he asked, while the pads of his thumbs started a maddening assault on her clitoris.

Clarise nodded, incapable of speech. His thumbs moved quicker, pulsing and pushing until she couldn't hold back anymore.

"I'm going to—I'm about to—"

"That's right, baby. Come for me. And, in case you're wondering, you aren't everything I thought you'd be either."

Her mind struggled to process his words, while her body soared to get there. Just a little more. She was so close.

She wasn't what he'd thought?

His strokes got even quicker, even more potent, and her body responded wildly. Pressure mounting, building, pushing her forward.

But what did he mean?

Ethan plunged into her with a long, deep thrust that first took her breath away, then powerfully pushed forth her blatant scream. She looked at the mirror and saw her eyes glaze as her orgasm sailed free.

"I'm—not what you thought," she managed, while he continued long, hard strokes that drove her right back to the brink. She was going to come again. She could feel it, couldn't stop it any more than she could stop her next breath. But she had to know. "Not what—you thought," she repeated, while the lurking orgasm intensified.

"No"—he pushed into her again and again, while her passion built and spiraled and churned . . . until she released a second orgasmic cry—"you're *not* what I thought, Clarise. You're more."

Chapter 16

So much for wooing her. Ethan hadn't taken it slow or easy one damn time yesterday, not under the bleachers, not in the elevator, and not the two times in bed last night. His intentions had been good, damn near noble, in his opinion. He'd planned to show her how much he cared, how sensitive he could be to her needs, but whenever he touched Clarise intimately, his own need became so powerful he could hardly get his cock out of his pants before he embedded it in her dripping heat. Yeah, *that* was the way to convince her what they have, or could have, exceeded sex. Ethan rolled over and gently pushed a single brown lock from her sleeping face. She looked so peaceful, so completely comfortable beside him in bed.

He'd never had much experience at waking up with someone. Hell, he hadn't had a lick of experience in that area. His previous relationships had been purely recreational, with everyone knowing the stakes up front. No sleepovers. Sleepovers meant commitment, and he hadn't wanted to give unwarranted hope, since he'd never found a woman who made him feel that way. But this time, he was the one hoping, and although Clarise Robinson knew he'd spend several nights in her bed, she'd been totally up front about the reason—fulfilling the fantasies on her list. Surely he could convince her to modify her list. Say, to include waking up together daily from now on rather than simply satisfying her wild itch.

She mumbled something incoherent and twisted toward him. The sheet slid down, baring her left breast, which nudged his biceps as she snuggled.

Hell. How was he supposed to spend time letting her see their potential at long-and-lasting when his dick could care less if she knew anything beyond his long-and-lasting stamina? Which had finally come back into play during their first tumble in an actual bed. It'd taken concentration beyond measure, but he'd managed to keep his cock from exploding long enough to merit a bout of shock and praise from Clarise over his endurance. Then again, they'd already had sex twice by the time they hit a mattress. That in and of itself helped him achieve his goal of staying inside her as long as humanly possible before climaxing. However, three times in a day hadn't sated his appetite for Clarise. Oh no, she'd cuddled against him during the night, her hips undulating as though she were dreaming. About him. About *them.* And sure enough, when he'd stroked the tender flesh between her legs, he'd found her drenched and ready. Again. The fourth time had been just as good as the first, and the only reason they stopped after that was pure exhaustion. Today, though, he didn't want to spend every moment trying to get inside her pants.

Yeah, right.

But he wouldn't. He wanted to get inside her heart, and that, Ethan feared, would take every ounce of willpower he possessed, particularly when she was so eager to have him inside her pants. How was he supposed to discuss his hopes and dreams of a potential future when her list kept sneaking into the conversation—and making his dick rise to the occasion? He'd spent the past three years informing her during their Friday coffee chats how he seemed to be incapable of having anything beyond the physical with women. Couldn't he have once mentioned that he did, eventually, want the suburbia bliss? Instead of the fact that he was beginning to believe it didn't exist? And now that he thought it was a possibility, with her, how was he supposed to spring it on her now that she insinuated that was exactly what she *didn't* want?

"Commitment isn't on the list," she'd said. Boy, if that wasn't life throwing him a curve. He was considering settling down, while Clarise wanted sex and no commitments. He brushed a kiss against her ear, then inhaled her feminine scent as she curled against him. He wanted her, and he needed to make today work as a way of showing her their potential future. Yeah, he had no doubt they'd tumble, a time or two, before it ended, but he wanted to talk as well, to get to know this intoxicating woman who'd become not only his friend but also his lover.

The sound of a marching band drifted up from the street below and reminded Ethan of the parade currently taking place outside their condominium. He'd listened to the street sweeper repeat its chore this morning, the chatter of businesses gearing up for the day, the crowds gathering on the sidewalk. All of the sounds distinctive to Gasparilla in Tampa. Then, while he'd showered and cleaned up, the first parade had passed. Now the second parade of the day stomped beneath their balcony, and his beautiful Clarise, undoubtedly exhausted by their evening of sexual gymnastics, slept through it all.

Ethan chuckled and snuggled against her curves. As usual, his eyes had opened at precisely 6:00 A.M., and he hadn't returned to sleep. Growing up in the Eubanks household, there were always plenty of things to do for the department store in the early morning. Meetings planned with buyers, inventories carefully navigated, employees properly motivated to sell . . . with style. The family was determined to make the place worthy of its "Elegant Apparel" name, and through years of hard work, determination and meticulously planned expansion, they had. After Ethan and Jeff became adults, Preston Eubanks concentrated even more on the bigger picture, bringing their small Southern store to national proportions. Merely two years after opening their second store in Atlanta, their profits had quadrupled, thanks to Preston's careful selection of location near the Mall of Georgia and Jeff's business sense. While Ethan and his father were the sure-and-steady kind of entrepreneurs, Jefferson Eubanks took a different approach. He was a risk-taker, plain and simple, but he was smart about the chances he took, and his store reaped the rewards of his business savvy.

Ethan smirked. He had no doubt Jeff would win his current wager with their father. His brother's penchant for outrageous forms of advertising had paid off in Atlanta; it should work as well for the Birmingham store. In truth, Ethan would have used some of Jeff's techniques already, but he'd always favored their father's approach to business—slow, steady and stable. Build a business that stands on its own, and it'll stand the test of time and change—another of Preston Eubanks's favorite philosophies.

He looked at Clarise. There hadn't been anything slow or steady about their rapid progression from best buddies to heated lovers. As a matter of fact, Ethan would have to classify this as a very "Jeff" type scenario. Risky. Savvy. And while he wanted this relationship to stand the test of time, he also wanted it to start with a bang, so to speak. With their time at Gasparilla, he believed it would. Sure, it was risky, fast-forwarding from friends to lovers in a span of days, but as his brother's risky tactics had played off in business, with amazing success and unquestionable profitability, Ethan totally planned on his relationship with Clarise having the same results. Amazing success.

She moaned in her sleep. Funny, he'd never taken her for a late sleeper. He wondered if he could adjust to waking up later and staying in bed each morning a little while longer . . . with Clarise. Even though he'd hired Robin Kennedy to ensure everything at the store ran smoothly, he still woke at the crack of dawn ready to prepare for a profitable day. He supposed it was due to his hands-on approach to the business, or perhaps he hadn't been fully ready to turn over the reins to his competent store manager, efficient or not. However, with Clarise at his side, perhaps he could get used to letting the crew run the ship. Wasn't that what owning a business and making it work was all about? Hiring a diligent group to conduct the day-to-day activities while he kept his focus on the big picture? Wouldn't that be what was necessary for the new Panache acquisition to achieve success? Looking at the big picture and delegating duties accordingly? Sure, it was. But he hadn't released the day-to-day drill because he hadn't had a reason to let go. Now he did. Clarise.

His top salesperson since she began working at the

store, Clarise had amazing insight into the fashion world, particularly the realm of the Women's Department. Even more specifically with regards to clothing for curvaceous women. Her recommendations for fabrics that accentuated, rather than downplayed, a woman's natural assets had produced a faithful bounty of affluent women who swore they'd only shop at Eubanks and only accept fashion advice from Clarise. Did she realize what an asset she was to the store? Ethan had told her repeatedly, not only in her performance reviews but also during their Friday chats, but he suspected she believed his praise to be friendship-induced. It wasn't. Sure, they were friends, but she was gifted in women's clothing and exactly the type of person Eubanks Elegant Apparel needed to oversee the women's departments in each of their stores, the new Panache stores included.

He made a mental note to speak with his father and Jeff about the asset of having a knowledgeable department head, preferably someone like Clarise, in each new store. *Someone like Clarise.* There weren't many women like her out there, no others that Ethan had found yet. And wasn't he the lucky one to have found *her*? First as a friend, and now as a lover. But unfortunately, while their friendship had grown steadily over the past three years, Ethan had no doubt that she'd always held back, hadn't opened up nearly as much as he. Shame he hadn't pushed harder to get to know the real Clarise. He'd tried continually to let her know how intriguing she was, had outright told her, in fact. But she'd taken it as a he's-saying-it-because-he's-my-friend kind of thing. He should've worked harder to convince her it was the truth, and he should've worked harder to learn more about her hopes and dreams, to strengthen their friendship bond even further. But he'd do that, starting today. Turn that friendship into something only lovers shared. Something she'd want for life. An over-the-top bond, both emotionally and physically. They'd sure built a sexual bond in the past twenty-four hours, had probably broken a few records, as well as a spring or two in the bed. But he only had three more days to prove their ties were strong enough for commitment. So today, he needed to get inside Clarise's head. And her heart.

She breathed in deeply, exhaled slowly, then wedged one big brown eye open.

"Good morning," he said, running a finger beneath her chin.

Her cheeks rose as she smiled, then she slid the sheet above her mouth. "Morning," she mumbled, both eyes open now and beautifully sleepy. A trombone sounded from the street, and she turned toward the window. "Oh no, the parade. We missed it."

"Well, yeah, we missed the first one. The second one isn't completely over, but for the most part, yeah, we missed it too."

"Oh dear. You planned on going to those, didn't you?" she asked.

"There aren't any specific plans," he corrected. "I had mentioned it would be fun to take in an early parade, but nothing is set in stone. Besides, there's another uptown parade tonight. It's a real showstopper. We'll catch that one."

"What time is it now?" she asked, squinting as her eyes adjusted to daylight.

"Half past two."

"Two? Oh my." She pushed up, and the sheet dropped

to her waist, exposing the two full mounds that had pressed against him all night. His groin tightened, and he sent a mental directive for his dick to stay in line. Predictably, it didn't listen.

Blushing, Clarise started lifting the edge of the white cotton toward her chest, but Ethan halted her hand.

"Don't cover up. I've seen you. All of you. And it's perfect."

Her lids moved to half-mast, and her lips, still kiss-swollen from their middle-of-the-night sex, curved. "No one's ever called me that before."

"Their loss." He wrapped an arm around her and pulled her face toward his.

She slapped a hand to her mouth. "Wait," she mumbled into her palm. Then she stood from the bed, grabbed Ethan's discarded shirt from the floor and wiggled into it.

"Where are you going?" he asked, watching her fingers fiddle with the hem.

"To brush my teeth," she mumbled, shrugging in the oversized shirt, which slid off one shoulder. The bottom of the fabric fell just past the apex in her legs and made her look even sexier.

He watched her scoot into the bathroom and listened to the water run, heard the bristles of the brush moving against her teeth. Last night, he'd run his tongue over those teeth and she'd shivered. An erogenous zone she hadn't known she had, as were the backs of her knees, her inner arms and her eyelids. He'd found them all last night, learned her most intimate secrets by listening to her small pants and gasps. And he'd never forget. Today, however, he'd delve deeper. Learn her mind and heart, and hopefully, in the process, learn how to gain her love.

"Didn't want to scare you with bad breath," she said sheepishly as she scurried across the wooden floor and jumped on the bed.

Ethan laughed. She looked like a little girl on Christmas morning, ready to open her first present. And from the way she drank him in, he knew exactly which gift she wanted to open first. Maybe he wouldn't start with the one-on-one conversing, not until he satisfied that hungry look in her eyes, but eventually, before the day ended, he would. Surely he would.

Deciding that eating breakfast could provide a bit of a stall tactic before the next sexual interlude, he reached to the side of the bed and lifted the tray he'd obtained earlier from room service. Her eyes moved from the tent pitched beneath the sheet to the plate filled with beignets. He'd been thrilled to learn the restaurant downstairs offered the delicious French pastries for breakfast and had assumed Clarise would love the unique treat.

"Hungry?" he asked.

She nodded. "In a couple of ways."

He couldn't fight the smile at that acknowledgment. "Why don't we try this way first, then we'll move into satisfying that other hunger."

"As long as you promise to satisfy it."

An animal. Who'd have thought? Clarise Robinson couldn't get enough, and although he still needed to move beyond the sex, eventually, he loved it, loved the way she eyed him as though she wanted to lick him from head to toe. He swallowed, wondered if that were another fantasy she hadn't mentioned. "I promise to satisfy."

She giggled, nodded toward the plate. "I've wanted to try beignets, but haven't had a chance. So is there a trick to eating them?" She reached for one of the square pastries, covered in powdered sugar, and moved it toward her lips.

"Yeah. Don't inhale," he said, but his instruction was too late.

"Why—" Clarise had still been speaking as the powdered sugar neared, and sure enough, she got a blast of white powder on the back of her throat. Dropping the beignet back to the plate, she coughed until her eyes watered, while Ethan laughed until his did the same.

"Gee, thanks for the warning," she said, swallowing past her tears.

"You have to admit, I tried."

"Not hard enough, obviously." She reached for the discarded beignet. "Dang, all the sugar fell off."

"That's what this is for." He lifted the small silver shaker perched beside the plate.

"What is it?" she asked, her brown eyes wide.

He shook more powdered sugar on the bare pastry, then held it toward Clarise. Sprinkles of white snowy powder flitted to the sheet. "Extra sugar is a must with beignets."

This time, she made it to her mouth with the pastry, chomped down and chewed, while her eyes rolled to the back of her head. "Oh man, that's so good."

Ethan swallowed, watched her throat pulse through the bites and her chest swell as the sweet substance collided with her tongue.

"Aren't you going to have some?" she asked, finishing off the first, then licking the sugar from her fingers. One finger at a time. Ethan wanted to die right then and there.

"Yeah, I'll have one." He picked up a beignet and hoped eating would help his concentration level, but while he chewed, she started on her second one with even more enthusiasm than the first.

"This is delicious!" she exclaimed. Then licked each finger again, slowly but surely, one at a time, her tender pink tongue lapping each bit of snowy white powder away.

Ethan shoved the remainder of his beignet in his mouth and swallowed. "We need to add something to your list."

Hell, he'd planned to be good. And he would, eventually, but first, he'd be damn good at it.

Clarise swallowed her last bite, ran her damp finger through the leftover sugar on the plate and plunked it in her mouth while Ethan spoke. She'd been enjoying the beignets so much she hadn't seen his eyes change color, from that crystal, translucent blue to the stormy, smoldering blue she'd witnessed last night. Her pulse quickened.

His jaw clenched. Powerfully muscled chest moved steadily in and out as he breathed, deep and strong, the same way he inhaled and exhaled yesterday, and again last night, when he wanted her. Like he wanted her now. Her thighs quivered in anticipation. She was still sore from yesterday's encounters, but she wasn't too sore. She'd never be too sore to want Ethan inside of her, and the look on his face, in his eyes, told her that's exactly where he wanted to be.

"Add something to my list?" she asked.

He lifted the tray, placed it on the nightstand beside the bed. "That's right."

"We haven't finished everything that's on the list now," she reminded. Dang, she hoped he still planned on it.

"We will."

Uh-huh.

He wore a pair of black boxer briefs and nothing else.

They clung to the tops of his thighs and outlined the kind of quadriceps she dreamed of, along with a thick, hard erection, also the kind she dreamed of.

"I love those," she said, boldly eyeing the briefs.

"I know."

"I guessed right, didn't I? Black briefs."

"Depends."

"On what?" she asked.

"On me. I wore them because of your guess."

Okay. Wow. He wore black briefs for her. Maybe now was the time to tell him about the Velcro option. Nah, not yet. Instead, she'd make sure her next dream of Ethan in black boxers was intensely accurate, which called for a thorough examination. She moved her eyes to his chest, wide and sculpted, two hardened plates of muscle with dark disks in each center. Then she licked her lips and longed to flick her tongue across those disks, like she'd done last night.

Ethan slid back on the sheets, placed a pillow on her side of the bed. "Relax, Clarise." He raised a brow and tilted his head toward the pillow.

"I don't think that's possible."

"Then don't relax," he countered, and his lip quirked to the side. It was a sexy, seductive twitch. And he knew it. "But I want you to lie down."

Her nipples hardened. "All right." She began crawling to the head of the bed, but he placed one hand on her shoulder to stop her progress.

"Not like that," he said.

"Not like what?"

"Not with your shirt—or rather, my shirt—on."

She was completely naked under his shirt, and he knew

that too, but because she wanted whatever new fantasy Ethan had in store for her, and because she wanted to feel the empowerment she'd experienced last night when she'd been nude in front of him, she shucked the shirt and boldly tossed it to the floor.

He hissed in a deep breath, and she grinned. Yeah, power was a good thing. A very good thing.

She put a lot of sexy squirm into the remainder of her crawl across the bed, but she lost track of her path when she noticed the damp spot at the top of his briefs. That telling dot of moisture from the tip of his erection. Oh yeah, he wanted her. Bad.

"On my back, or on my stomach?" she asked, leaning toward him and letting her breasts hover mere inches from his side.

He swallowed, eyes turned from blue to gray.

Clarise couldn't hold back her smile of triumph.

"You're evil," he accused.

"I'm learning to be."

"I'd say you've got it mastered, and I want you on your back, by the way." He paused for a second, nodded toward the pillow. "Now."

Clarise didn't giggle this time. She shivered. Everywhere. What did he plan on doing? And how long would it take until he got going? Another marching band bellowed past, the drums beating a wild Jamaican theme that joined the frantic beat of her heart.

"What are you adding to my list?"

He lifted the silver cylinder from the tray, brought it to her hip and grazed the cool metal against her skin. Her entire body quaked. She watched him raise the container, move it above her heart, then slowly tilt it on its side. Soft, white powder snowed down upon her skin, tingling and tickling and making each nerve ending bristle. He sprinkled her nipples thoroughly while she fought the impulse to writhe beneath the substance.

"Sugar sex," he informed. Then he grinned. "Don't move, Clarise. I want to see you covered in sweetness."

She held her breath while he coated her body in the powder. When he finished, she exhaled, slowly, so the sugar remained intact. Inclined on the pillow, she could see everything, every part of her body sprinkled with white sugar. Her breasts were white-capped mountains, her stomach a snowy valley, and between her legs—a fire hidden within a blanket of snow. But a fire Ethan would find.

Summoning up the courage to be the wild woman in her dreams, she licked her lips and tasted a hint of the sugar left from her beignets. The same taste he'd soon experience from her. "Are you wanting something sweet, Ethan?" she purred in the sexiest voice she could summon.

"That depends."

"On?"

"On whether you'll let me share."

She blinked. Heck, she thought she had this figured out, but he'd thrown her, and she didn't want to tell him she was too naïve to know what sugar sex was. Was it something everyone did while in Tampa? Because someone should've clued her in, since asking for details didn't seem quite appropriate when you're spread out on a bed thoroughly sprinkled like a first-rate dessert. It had looked fairly self-explanatory, like he'd sprinkle her with sugar, then lick it off. Wasn't that how it—

He clamped his mouth over one nipple, sucked the sugar completely off and made her back arch right off the bed.

"Oh dear, I spilled some—"

Ethan's tongue, sweet and covered in delicious powder, licked inside her mouth, mated with hers in a delicious, sugary ecstasy.

She moaned, while hot liquid pooled between her thighs. "Oh, my."

But before he responded, he attacked the second nipple, sending her off the bed once more. This time, however, she was ready. Her mouth pressed against his and her tongue thrust inside in search of more of the delicious treat. Then, while she was still soaring from the surplus of sugar against her taste buds, Ethan moved down her stomach, licking and sucking and nipping. When he reached her thighs, he sucked each one thoroughly before returning to her waiting mouth. This time, she tasted more than sugar. She tasted her desire.

"Ethan," she panted, as he passed her aching center and made his way slowly down her right leg.

Clarise thought she was doing okay, holding her own in this intense sexual onslaught, until he made his way back up and nipped her inner thigh. "Ethan, I can't wait. Don't make me."

His laugh sounded nearly sinister, as though he enjoyed torturing her, and in a way, she was glad he did, because waiting for him to thoroughly lick, suck and nibble her other leg made her core pound harder than the drums outside their window. Slowly, he worked his way closer to her center.

Clarise quivered. She needed to be touched, and he knew exactly where. "Please, Ethan."

As if he were waiting to hear her beg, he eased her thighs apart and lapped at her clit. She pushed toward the sweet invasion, and he held her there. Kneeling in front of her, he raised her hips until she couldn't be more opened. Then he licked the white powder away. Thoroughly. Completely. Totally.

Clarise's world unraveled, and Ethan Eubanks became the center, the part she refused to let go.

Chapter 17

Ethan had never cared much for the whole aspect of personal shopping. Sure, he liked finding an incredible product and offering it to the Eubanks Elegant Apparel patrons, but he left it up to the capable fashion buyers to personally select the most exquisite garments. They were his eyes and ears for the industry, and they brought the best products back for the store's selection. Ethan, his father and Jeff then personally selected the best of the best, and those items made the cut to be sold by Eubanks Elegant Apparel. He liked having the final say, and he'd thought he liked being completely out of the loop on the initial search for products. He wasn't a typical shopper, but watching Clarise peruse the whimsical booths of the street festival, tasting the samples of Cuban cuisine, oohing and ahhing over the handmade jewelry changed his tune. Maybe he didn't care about personal shopping in general, but shopping with Clarise was a hell of a lot of fun. Those big doe eyes lit up when she saw something unique, squinted in determination when she bargained the price and absolutely glittered when she acquired something she wanted. Ethan examined each reaction; all were downright adorable. Downright Clarise.

They held hands and laughed while working their way through the booths, enjoying each other's company as if they were dating . . . or had been married for years while managing to hold on to that original spark, which was exactly what he foresaw in Clarise. A woman to live with, laugh with, love with. Their morning—correction, after-noon, since she'd slept until two—had been perfect. Shar-ing beignets, then sharing each other. And now, they casually shopped for her grandmother's treats. Moving from the unique excitement of the bedroom to the nor-malcy of the street hadn't proved that much of a switch. He loved being with Clarise. Hot and heated, writhing in the sheets, or holding her hand and chatting through what locals termed the "Latin Quarter." They felt right together, in both areas.

"Oh, this is perfect." Clarise lifted a shiny silver pirate's sword from a table draped in purple velvet. "What do you think?"

"I think it'd help you hold on to the memory," he said.

She lowered it and gave him a smile that went beyond her curved lips and spread to her eyes. "What about you? Would it help you hold on to the memory?"

He cleared his throat. "I won't need anything. I'll remember every moment of my time with you."

She laughed as though he weren't serious, as though he were merely joking. He wasn't, and before the trip ended, he vowed she would realize that. Clarise motioned for the booth's attendant and paid for the sword, then she stared at it a moment before adding it to her bag. "I won't forget either," she whispered. Then she walked to the next booth and didn't look back. But Ethan was fairly certain, even without seeing those telltale eyes, that he'd heard a definite hint of regret in the simple statement. *Regret.* Regret that it had happened? Or that it would end?

"Granny Gert wants one of these too," Clarise said, draping a long red swath of fabric over one shoulder. Her expression had lightened, and she'd apparently moved on from her earlier statement.

Ethan decided not to press the issue. Yet. They'd talk about what had happened between them, what was still happening between them, before they left Tampa. And he'd ensure his future with Clarise, because he sure as hell wasn't having a future without her.

"Let me," he said, stepping forward to pay the man behind the table.

"Granny Gert's rather independent. She gave me the money to buy her things, but it's sweet of you to offer."

"Tell her I insisted," Ethan said, accepting his change. "And that I'm buying it because I enjoy the company of her granddaughter."

She gave him a timid grin and nodded. "All right." Fingering the shimmering fabric, she added, "We should think about these in accessories at the store. The scarves we have now are more sophisticated, I know, but this could turn a professional dress into an evening ensemble, don't you think? Several of the new spring arrivals in the Women's Department would benefit from a sash like this." She held the red fabric to her cheek. "It's well made too. Chiffon silk, isn't it?"

The woman behind the table grinned. "Yes, it is. My mother taught me how to weave it. We color the fabric as well with a natural dye. My mother learned the technique when she was a girl in Bangladesh."

Ethan's attention piqued. The uniqueness of the scarf—or sash, as the case might be—would definitely appeal to Eubanks customers, yet he would have missed the allure without his savvy sidekick. "Do you have a card?" he asked the woman in the booth.

"And would you be interested in selling these in large quantities for retail?" Clarise added.

"Why, yes," the woman answered, her face practically glowing with anticipation.

"I'll get back to you within two weeks," Ethan confirmed.

"Here. Take a few more," the woman said, handing him a purple one embellished with tiny gold tassels, an emerald one with a marbled tint and a pearly white one accented with a crimson rose print.

"I'll take them," Ethan said, "but not without paying for them." He fished more bills from his wallet and handed them to the smiling lady.

"That wasn't what I meant," she said, "but thanks."

"You're welcome."

"And you will hear from him soon," Clarise informed. "He keeps his promises."

The woman nodded, apparently overjoyed at the potential of selling her scarves beyond the Latin Quarter. Ethan was overjoyed too. Not only had Clarise helped him find a unique product for the store without the assistance of a fashion buyer, but he'd also heard her verify that she saw him as a man who "keeps his promises." Good. Because soon, he'd promise her the moon. He only hoped she'd take it. Wrapping his arm around her waist, he guided her through the remaining booths, while she described her unconventional grandmother.

"She loves colors. Bright, bold colors," Clarise explained, fingering a purple blouse with a bright red collar. "Most people wouldn't think this would work for a woman with a lot of"—her voice faltered, but then she grinned, and added saucily—"shape. But it's actually very flattering with curves. And the color says she isn't hiding from her God-given assets."

"Not hiding is a very good thing," Ethan said, placing a fingertip against the edge of Clarise's magenta tank top, then trailing it down her arm to her wrist.

She tilted her face toward his. "All this time, I've been helping other women show off what they had, but I haven't followed my own advice." Those big doe eyes widened, the way they had each Friday afternoon during their afternoon coffees, when she'd made a statement and awaited his response. He wouldn't let her down now. She needed to hear the truth, and he needed to give it.

"You have no reason at all to hide behind clothing and no reason to confine yourself to black and navy." Her colors of choice, he'd say, until that red dress at the Christmas party, then again this week with her "setting the wild side free" party. "And I agree that these blouses are perfect for women with lots of"—he moved the back of his fingertips to her right cheek, then slowly slid them down her neck, along her collarbone, then down her side, letting them brush the beautiful outer swell of her breast—"shape," he continued, while Clarise's eyes flitted closed and her mouth formed a soft smile.

"I love," she whispered, then those brown eyes opened, "this."

Ethan moved his hand to the small of her back and pulled her close, then tenderly kissed her. He'd thought those first two words had been leading somewhere else, but he wasn't overly disappointed. She was beginning to feel it too, that connection beyond sex, and he reveled in witnessing each step of her progress.

"Do you want that top?" the man tending the booth asked, his voice a little louder than necessary as he tried to penetrate the sensual energy zinging between Clarise and Ethan.

"Yes," she said, turning back toward the vibrant table. "I'll take it. Oh, and these too." She fingered a set of shiny purple-and-red bracelets displayed beside the blouse. "Granny Gert loves bracelets. Anything that makes her jingle when she walks," Clarise added, which made the salesman grin. She giggled in return.

Ethan loved the sound of her laugh. It was real and honest and fun. Like Clarise.

She added the items to the growing bag of goodies for her grandmother. Then they left the street vendors and headed back toward their condo.

"You and your sweetie have a fight?" The elderly woman tilted her head, and the corners of her mouth dipped down. "You seemed so happy the other night."

Clarise looked up to see a woman she vaguely remembered. Then she blinked and realized this was one half of the couple that had been standing outside the elevator that first night, when she'd been snockered and Ethan had taken her back to their room to take care of her. Then later, to fulfill the first item on her list. She held back the tears. "No, we didn't."

The woman's silver-haired counterpart then crossed the lobby to join his wife. He was carrying two cups of orange juice and handed one to the woman. Then he looked at Clarise. "You didn't sleep last night, little lady?"

Clarise twisted in the chair that had been her haven for her private "pity party," as Grandma Gertrude called it, and looked at the big grandfather clock perched in the center of the resort lobby. Five-thirty . . . in the morning. And she'd been sitting here under a ficus tree for, what, two hours? Ethan would probably wake soon and realize she'd slipped out of bed. She really should go back, but she wasn't ready to face that onslaught of emotion again. Not yet.

"What did he do to you?" the older woman continued. She pushed a branch aside to move closer, close enough to wedge her bony little hip on the edge of Clarise's seat.

Clarise had picked this shady spot, beneath the large tree, because she wanted privacy, wanted to be alone with her thoughts—something that was fairly difficult to pull off with Gasparilla taking place in the city. But she had, for a while. Since 3:00 A.M., in fact, when she left Ethan sleeping and found her way to the lobby, her personal sanctuary, to think about what he'd done and to try to figure out how to deal with it. So far, she didn't have any answers.

"Tell me, sweetie," the older woman urged. "Maybe we can help."

"I can't," Clarise said then sniffed, and a tear spilled free. What would she say, anyway? That he'd made her feel loved? That she couldn't enjoy their time together now, for her fear of it ending when they returned home? That she'd felt more desirable, more sexual, and more deserving of someone like Ethan, than she'd ever felt in her life—and that the thought of the dream ending made her cry? "I'm sorry," she whispered, "but I can't tell you."

"Here, hon," the older man said. He reached around his wife and handed Clarise the other cup of juice. "Maybe it'll make you feel better."

Clarise swallowed, sniffed again. "Thank you."

"Come on, Esther. I think she wants to be alone, dear." He gently took his wife's arm and eased her from Clarise's chair. Then he smiled at Clarise. "You and your young man remind us of our granddaughter and her new husband."

"Yes," Esther said, "and we want them—and both of you—to be as happy as we are."

"Thank you," Clarise said, her throat closing in. She lifted the cup of juice and sipped to keep from audibly sobbing. She wanted to be happy too, and she was, but she also knew it wouldn't last forever.

The couple left, presumably to visit the street vendors before the parades got started this morning. Clarise watched them leave, then sank farther into the chair beneath the tree and hoped she could calm her rattled state quickly, in time to return to their room before Ethan woke. But how would she deal with the bizarre situation? How could she tell him that she'd fallen, completely and totally, in love with the guy who was her best friend and her boss, for goodness sake? And the man who'd been willing to fulfill her sexual fantasies without the burden of commitment. Was it a burden?

"Commitment isn't on the list," she'd said. Damn, why hadn't she scribbled it somewhere on that paper? She closed her eyes and remembered yesterday, returning from the Latin Quarter and having another round of frantic, fren-

zied sex. They'd paused long enough to order room service, then sat on the balcony and enjoyed the parade as it passed outside. Several men on the top tier of the floats crooned for Clarise to display the Robinson Jewels, but she'd politely declined, knowing Ethan would have no part of it. He considered them "taken," as he'd told the guy in the elevator two nights ago. Of course, he was only referring to their being taken temporarily. Dang it. Personally, she considered them, and the rest of her, taken too. By Ethan. And not merely in Gasparilla. How was she supposed to turn off this "thing" they had going? The way he made her feel, it had to be more than mere sex, didn't it? Wasn't he feeling it too? And how, if you ever experience something like this, do you live your life without it?

Last night, the parade crew had enjoyed her shimmy enough to bestow Clarise with a healthy booty of beads, which Ethan found *extremely* useful. She shivered at the memory. Ethan, slowly undressing her and guiding her to the bed, then draping the glittering, cool beads over her naked body, covering her completely, before removing them with painstaking care, letting each round sphere glide across her flesh, while she waited, breathlessly, for Ethan Eubanks to bare her body. Then bare her soul. Because *that's* what happened last night. After the parade, and after he'd teased every sensitive nerve ending with the endless strands of Gasparilla necklaces, Ethan made love to Clarise. *Made love.* Plain and simple. Nothing about their bonding last night had been mere sex. He'd held her, caressed her, talked to her throughout their mating. They'd truly joined, not merely seeking physical satisfaction, but longing for the emotional bond between lifetime lovers. She'd felt it. What if he hadn't?

"There you are!" Rachel's voice broke through the memory with a blatant slap of reality.

Clarise dropped her cup to the floor, and the remaining orange juice spilled freely over the white marble tiles.

"Look what you made her do, Rachel," Jesilyn said. "Don't worry, Clarise. I'll go get some napkins." Within seconds, Jesilyn had cleaned the spill, and Rachel had bullied her way into the chair with Clarise.

"Scoot," she demanded, squirming her skinny bottom next to Clarise's rounded one. "And give us all the details."

Clarise swallowed. This was *not* happening. "Details?"

"About you and Ethan, silly," Rachel continued.

Jesilyn tossed the wet napkins in a nearby trash receptacle, then returned frowning at Rachel. "You don't know if there's anything to tell."

"Their phone was off the hook, Jesi," Rachel said, cocking one brow for effect. She twisted awkwardly to look at Clarise. "Isn't that right? We were trying to see if the two of you wanted to take in the parade with the gang, but we couldn't get through. The lobby clerk refused to give us your room number and only offered to keep ringing you for us, but of course, since your phone was off the hook, we never got through. I can't believe we forgot to get your room number," she added, barely pausing between words to breathe.

"It isn't any of our business," Jesilyn scolded. "Is it, Clarise?"

It wasn't, Clarise agreed silently, but she refused to be rude to her friends. She also decided to attempt to keep their room number private. That's all she needed was her friends knocking on their door in the middle of the two of them working on her list. She smiled; she couldn't help it.

"See!" Rachel said, pointing to Clarise's grin. "That has guilty written all over it."

"Oh, hush," Jesilyn said.

"The phone was off the hook, wasn't it, Clarise?" Rachel asked.

Clarise distinctly remembered Ethan smiling as he unplugged it last night, and she nodded.

Rachel smiled triumphantly. "Told you, Jesi."

"It's still none of our business," Jesilyn repeated. "Isn't that right, Clarise?"

"Actually, I really would rather keep this private," Clarise admitted.

Rachel slapped her hands against her thighs. "Well then, don't ask me to give you the details about my past three days with Miles. He's asleep now, by the way, and he should stay that way for a while, because he said he's—"

"Thoroughly exhausted," Jesilyn intervened. "Trust me. I know. She's been giving me the details for the past hour, ever since she dragged me out of bed in the middle of the night to tell me everything."

"Oh, shush, you wanted to know," Rachel said.

"Not at four in the morning, I didn't."

Clarise was thankful the subject had turned away from her weekend with Ethan. She decided to help keep it that way. "What about your guy?" she asked Jesilyn.

"Didn't work out," Jesi said matter-of-factly.

"Oh, go on, tell her the rest," Rachel instructed. Then, without giving Jesilyn time to actually do it, she barreled on, "He wanted her to Jell-O wrestle."

"What?" Clarise asked, temporarily taken out of her own bout of misery to determine what in the world was involved with Jell-O wrestling. Though she had an idea.

"Evidently he owns a club in the Latin Quarter, and he wanted a new subject for his most popular form of entertainment Saturday night," Rachel enlightened, grinning.

"I thought you were going to watch the parade at the inn," Clarise said, turning toward Jesi.

"We did, and then we headed to his club," Jesilyn answered. "Where he tried to get me to put on a bikini that wasn't much more than dental floss and flounce around in a pit filled with red Jell-O."

"With another floss-coated lady," Rachel added, nodding so hard her blond spirals bounced.

Clarise didn't know what to say, so she said the first thing that came to mind. "Ew!"

"Exactly. But I wasted no time getting out of the place."

"You wasted enough time to get red Jell-O splattered all over your new blouse," Rachel reminded.

Jesilyn looked at Clarise and shrugged. "There was a *competition* going on when we got there." Then she laughed. "Hey, at least I found out what he was really like before we slept together."

"That's Jesi," Rachel said. "Always looking for the positive." She shimmied out of the chair and clapped her hands together. "And speaking of the positive, as in the positively scrumptious guy I've got waiting in my room, I think I'll head on up. Maybe he slept enough to be ready for another go."

"You're terrible," Jesilyn said.

"And you're crazy for not going after Jake," Rachel snapped back. "He was putting the moves on her last night at the parade, but she didn't accept the challenge."

"That's the problem with him," Jesilyn said. "He wants a challenge, and once he gets what he wants, he's done. I think I can live without being uncomfortable at work every time I see him."

Rachel smirked. "I say live for the moment, and I'm about to go live another moment with Miles. I'll catch up with you two later." She turned and started to walk away, then abruptly stopped her pace. "Wait a minute," she said, quickly turning and heading back. "We nearly forgot to give Clarise her gift!"

"My gift?"

Jesilyn smiled. "You're going to love it." She opened her big leather purse, dug around inside, then withdrew a white cylinder, about the width of a sheet of paper, with a silver cap at each end.

"What is it?" Clarise asked.

"You'll see," Jesi said, removing one of the end caps, then carefully sliding a folded sheet of yellow, apparently aged paper, from the center. She handed the sheet to Rachel.

"We bought it at an antiques shop in town that specializes in notable documents," Rachel said, then cleared her throat. "Ahem. This license entitles the bearer to be a lewd and abandoned woman for a period of one year."

Jesilyn shook her head, but couldn't hold back her grin. "It's a genuine license to prostitute. Evidently, they were issued in the late 1800s. This one belonged to a woman named Bella LeDeaux."

"But now it's yours," Rachel said, handing the paper to Clarise.

Clarise blinked at the extravagant penmanship. "You bought this?"

"Don't worry. It's actually a copy of the real deal, so we didn't spend too much, but it suits your decision to take a walk on the wild side in Tampa, don't you think? Now you actually have a license to do it," Rachel said.

Clarise laughed. Rachel and Jesilyn never failed to lift her spirits. Now was no exception.

"Okay, so I'm off to practice my own lewdness on the man in my bed," Rachel said, spinning on her heel and sashaying toward the elevator.

"Take it easy on him," Jesilyn said. "Some people actually like to sleep later than 4:00 A.M."

"Hmph, we'll see." Rachel's voice trailed after her as she entered the elevator, then winked at the two of them before the doors slid closed.

"I'm not believing you bought this," Clarise said, eyeing the unique document.

"It was Rachel's idea, of course," Jesilyn said, propping her hip on the arm of Clarise's chair. "And you can spill now, by the way."

Clarise looked up at her friend. "Spill?"

"Whatever's eating at you," Jesi explained. "You can't tell me you were sitting out here by your lonesome this early in the morning with Ethan Eubanks asleep in your bed unless something was wrong. So spill."

"I didn't think I was that obvious," Clarise said. "Rachel didn't notice."

"Rachel is on a sex-induced high, so she's oblivious to most everything that doesn't involve her libido. So, what's up? Did he do something stupid?"

"No. I did."

"I'm listening," Jesi said, tucking her hair behind her ear and tilting her head toward Clarise.

"I fell in love with him, but he's just helping me do the things on my list."

Jesilyn blinked, quirked her mouth to the side and squinted while she processed the heap of information in Clarise's statement. "You're in love with him," she finally said.

"Definitely."

"And you're certain he doesn't feel the same?"

"Commitment wasn't on the list," Clarise said, feeling miserable. Wanting something to do to keep from crying, she rolled up the license and slid it into the cylinder.

"The list," Jesilyn repeated thoughtfully. "What list, exactly?"

"My list of sex fantasies," Clarise said hesitantly, but Jesilyn didn't miss the punch of the statement.

"Sex fantasies?" she asked loudly, then as Clarise sank farther into the overstuffed chair, she repeated softly, "Your sex fantasies? You have them listed?"

Clarise swallowed, nodded. "You know how much I like making goals," she said, attempting to explain, since saying the words "sex fantasy list" out loud seem to make the whole scenario seem even more bizarre. What had she been thinking? Writing all of *that* down?

"Goals?" Jesilyn asked, her tone disbelieving. "Goals for what, exactly?"

"Things I've always wanted to try. Things I wanted to do during this trip." With someone who looked like Ethan and acted like Ethan, and who, consequently, ended up *being* Ethan.

"So you made this list," Jesilyn deduced. "And I won't even ask you what was on it . . . "

"It started with sex outside," Clarise informed.

"O—kay," Jesi said. "Anyway, you made this list, then Ethan found it?"

"Actually, I gave it to him Friday night after the parade, when I was smashed."

"You were drunk," Jesilyn asked, once again very loudly, and once again, Clarise squished her behind deeper into the chair's cushion in an effort to hide from the stares of the other early risers in the lobby.

"Not that it makes any difference, but most people down here get drunk at least once during Gasparilla," Clarise said defensively.

"I know, but most people aren't I'd-rather-keep-my-brain-cells-intact Clarise Robinson either."

Clarise grinned at that. She hadn't even tasted the champagne at the Christmas party last year, but that was more because she was afraid it would make her belly puffy, and there was no room for extra puff in the red dress. Some clothing could be classified as "fat clothes," or clothes that easily disguised bloating, or a few extra holiday pounds, or a couple of glasses of champagne; that dress definitely didn't fall into the fat clothes category.

"Okay," Jesi said, scooting off the arm of the chair to sit beside Clarise. "So, you made a sex list, got drunk, shared it with Ethan and then . . . "

"Then he offered to help me accomplish everything on the list," Clarise said matter-of-factly.

"Mighty generous of him."

"He's my friend, Jesi, and he wanted to protect me. He didn't think I should go out and do all of 'that' with someone I didn't trust. And he knows I trust him."

"Like I said, mighty generous," Jesilyn repeated, grinning. "And so the two of you have been checking the items off the list, right?"

"Multiple times."

Jesilyn laughed heartily. "Holy cow. Man, if Rachel was here, she'd so want details, but I'm going to try to be big about this. So . . . you're feeling more than sex, right?"

Clarise nodded.

"And he isn't?"

"Like I said, commitment wasn't on the list, and we both agreed it shouldn't be."

"You discussed it?" Jesi asked, obviously surprised by this added bit of insight.

"More or less," Clarise answered, remembering their conversation that first morning.

"Well, I say you discuss it again," Jesi reasoned. "I'm betting if you're feeling something, then he probably is too. And what's more, I think it's way cool."

Clarise swallowed. "I thought you said sex with friends wasn't smart and that sex with the boss was a definite mistake."

"I was talking more about Rachel than you. You remember how weird everything was between Rachel and Nick Summers at work last year after the Gasparilla trip. I didn't want that happening again. He quit, remember?"

"I never knew the whole story," Clarise admitted. Since she'd given her Gasparilla trip to Babette, she'd been fairly out of the loop on what went on during last year's corporate bonding excursion, but she had heard the rumors about Rachel and Nick, even if Rachel had refused to divulge.

"Basically," Jesi explained, "she couldn't get enough of him during the trip. They were going at it like rabbits the whole time, a lot like what she's got going now with Miles, then when they got back home, she'd had enough.

Thought what happened in Tampa stayed in Tampa and didn't want any reminders."

Clarise vaguely remembered Nick trying to talk to Rachel in the employee lounge, and she even more clearly remembered her friend callously giving him the cold shoulder.

"He couldn't stand to see her every day after what they'd had, or what he thought they'd had, so he quit. And he was amazing in Men's Footwear. It's a shame Eubanks lost a good employee over a Gasparilla sexcapade."

Clarise frowned.

"Oh, shoot, I'm not talking about you," Jesilyn quickly improvised. "You and Ethan have been friends for years. Rachel never gave Nick the time of day until she ended up wanting a bed buddy at Gasparilla. Seriously, this is nothing like what you've got going." She moved her face closer to Clarise's and smiled brightly. "Besides, Rachel didn't have a sex list. You've got to get major points for originality there. That little list of yours could be the sole instigator for a very-long-lasting and uniquely inspired relationship."

Clarise managed to grin. "It isn't that little a list."

"You go, girl." Jesilyn stood, then held out her hand to pull Clarise out of her pity perch. "Seems like you should get back up to that room and keep checking off those items."

Feeling a bit more at ease with her situation, Clarise stood, and the cylinder fell to the floor.

Jesilyn picked it up and placed it in Clarise's palm. "Don't want to forget your license," she said, smiling. "Now you can do whatever you want."

"Thanks. I think I will." Minutes later, Clarise crept across the hardwood floor of their room and gently slid the cylinder into the outer pocket of her suitcase. Then she noticed her now famous folded paper on the dresser nearby. Taking a quick peek at Ethan, breathing deeply in his sleep, she reached for the folded sheet. Opening it, she read the list she'd jotted on a whim, yet the instigator that had sparked this entire magical interlude with Ethan.

Sex with the lights on. *Check.*

Sex outside. *Check.*

Standing up. *Double—no, triple—check.*

Bleacher sex. *Oh yeah.*

Shower sex. *Yes, multiple yes.*

Elevator sex had been added at the bottom of the list in Ethan's scrawling script and could now be checked. Thoroughly explored that one, they did. And then there was sugar sex, God help her, not even on the list, but worthy of being there for sure. Two items remained unaccounted for . . .

Sex on the grass and sex on a beach. Two items, and two days. Today and tomorrow were all she had left of her private heaven with Ethan. Then life would return to normal. A big, fat tear bubbled from one eye and dropped on the page, blurring "sex on the grass." Another tear followed, plopping directly beside the first. As if they knew which of her fantasies would never come to fruition, at least not with Ethan. *And if not with Ethan, then not with anyone,* Clarise silently declared. Heck, if not with Ethan, Clarise didn't want *anything* with anyone. But Ethan Eubanks was, whether he realized it or not, by all past indications, commitment-phobic. Sure, he usually had a drop-dead-gorgeous creature on his arm at company functions, but never the same one twice. Plus, he'd told Clarise firsthand that he simply hadn't found a woman who made him feel the whole till-death-do-us-part thing. He was obviously looking for perfection, and if there was one thing Clarise knew for certain, she wasn't perfection.

She quirked her mouth to the side. She believed he'd felt the connection between them. How could he not? Particularly last night. Folding the paper, she returned it to the dresser, then wiped her tears away with the back of her hand. What if he *hadn't* felt it? Silently, she crossed the room and gazed at the sleeping man on the bed. His sandy waves were tousled, and his mouth relaxed, forming an easy smile. The whiteness of the soft sheet provided a stark contrast to the tan, muscled firmness of Ethan Eubanks. Was he dreaming? And if he was, was he dreaming about her?

Running her fingers along the edge of her shirt, she slid it up and off her body, then dropped it to the floor. Then she shimmied out of the gym shorts she'd worn downstairs and quickly discarded panties and bra. If she only had two more days of feeling Ethan's body completely aligned with hers, she didn't want to miss one moment. She lifted the covers and crawled in, snuggled against him. The scent of their lovemaking lingered in the sheets and on their flesh, and she inhaled it thoroughly as he wrapped an arm around her.

Ethan brushed a tender kiss on the top of her head. "Morning," he said, his voice sleep-sexy.

"Morning."

"Time is it?"

"Seven."

His body tensed, then relaxed, and he kissed her head again, chuckling low in the back of his throat. "See what you do to me, Clarise? I never sleep until seven."

She grinned against his chest. He'd been so soundly

asleep, in fact, that he hadn't realized she'd left. "Maybe you should."

Another soft kiss moved against her hair. "Maybe I should." Then he pulled her against him and rubbed his palm up and down her spine until Clarise surrendered once more to the euphoric bliss of sleeping in the arms of the man she loved.

Chapter 18

Ethan had two reasons for the activities he'd planned for Monday. One, he needed to fulfill Clarise's sex on the beach fantasy, and two, he believed a more family-oriented setting, the kiddie parade, would lead her to see the two of them taking what they have into the real world and making it last. Thank goodness the parade was scheduled for late afternoon. He'd slept until noon. *Noon.* As far as he could remember, Ethan had never let a day pass when he wasn't up by daybreak and ready to work by eight. However, even after he'd roused momentarily early this morning, with Clarise nestled by his side, he'd returned to sleep, without one thought of the day's itinerary until she nudged him awake and said she was hungry. Hungry for food this time, since Ethan had no doubt her sexual appetite had been thoroughly satisfied.

They shared a muffaletta from an Italian sandwich shop for lunch, and he'd been totally infatuated watching Clarise get her first taste of the unique sandwich. She'd never had one of the plate-sized monstrosities before, but, unsurprising, she'd been game to try. Her eyes rolled heavenward during each bite of seasoned salami, pastrami, olive paste and cheese, and she blissfully moaned her contentment. That moan nearly caused Ethan to give up his noble plan for the day, since the sound was nearly identical to the sweet sound she produced when her climax neared. It'd been damn near intoxicating watching her chew, swallow and dig back in, as if she couldn't get enough. The same way she reacted to making love. And the same way he felt about her. He couldn't get enough.

"Look, it's starting," she said, stepping off the sidewalk and peering down the street to see the beginning of the children's parade. This parade was smaller than the main invasion parade, but just as much fun. And since it was geared to kids, Clarise had dressed appropriately. She looked like a young girl, ready to have a day filled with fun, exactly what he had planned.

Ethan didn't recall ever seeing her in jeans before, but she wore them today. And hell if they didn't showcase the luscious curves he'd been exploring all weekend . . . and wanted to explore again. If he'd been any less inclined to have her in a family setting, he'd have suggested they spend yet another day within the confines of their room, which would have totally defeated his purpose, showing Clarise they could incorporate the friendship they'd shared for years into the sexual dynamic they'd developed over the weekend. Thank goodness they left the condo in search of lunch. If they'd ordered room service again, he might not have withstood temptation.

"You ever been to this parade before, lady?" a boy who appeared to be around ten asked Clarise. He wore a Tampa Bay T-shirt and well-worn jeans. So well-worn, in fact, the fabric on both knees was missing in action. He clutched a big burgundy mesh bag, also emblazoned with the local team's logo, in one tightly fisted hand, and Ethan noticed it already held a few strands of beads.

"No, I haven't. Is there something I should know about it? Because I could really use someone to show me the ropes if you're willing," Clarise said, smiling at the kid.

Ethan grinned. Tons of children bunched around them on the sidewalk, and she was having a ball. This was the kind of woman he wanted, a girl willing to let herself go and have fun. Some of the too-pretty-to-have-their-hair-touched women he'd dated in the past would've cringed at all the shoving and pushing, and with all the kids, but Clarise Robinson was completely at ease conversing with the four-feet-and-under crowd.

"Yeah, I got something that'll help ya." The boy dug in his pocket and pulled out a pair of red plastic sunglasses, warped and scratched from the jaunt in his pants. "You'll need these."

"Why do I need—" she started, but halted when the first float paused in front of them and thoroughly bombed the crowd with candy, beads and plastic toys. *Bombed* was the appropriate word for the action. Buckets, literally, of Gasparilla treasures were flung from both sides of the apparatus, as though the crew members were attacking the crowd rather than giving them exactly what they wanted.

"Because Mom says the stuff'll put your eye out!" the kid yelled, scooping up his treasures and dumping them in his goodie bag as fast as his hands could move.

"Oh!" Clarise quickly attempted to shove the glasses on, but before they reached their destination, a parachute toy and two gold doubloons sailed against one side of her face. "Your mom's right." She pushed the glasses up her nose then scrambled with him, and all the rest of the kids, for loot. "Come on and help us," she ordered Ethan, who, blessedly, wore his sunglasses.

"Yeah," the boy urged, "Help us, mister!"

For the majority of the parade, Clarise and Ethan stayed at knee level, gathering treats for the kids, then distributing the coveted loot among all the youngsters. Ethan couldn't remember the last time he'd had more fun, or the last time anything had felt more *right*.

When the parade ended, in spite of all the candy and toys that had been hurled their way, Clarise and Ethan had nary a stick of gum in their pockets, but they had face-splitting grins. The kids were abundantly grateful for the extra candy and toys they obtained due to the couple's efforts and in the end, every child within a ten-foot radius distributed hugs to their new adult friends. As they headed back toward the rental car, Ethan's arm encircled Clarise, snuggling against him in her postparade elation.

"That was wonderful," she said, squeezing him while they walked, as if she couldn't get close enough, which was exactly how Ethan felt. He wanted her even closer, and he'd have her that way soon.

"Yes, it was."

"Seeing the parade from a kid's perspective—how neat is that? I'd say the floats here were as pretty as the ones at the grown-up parades, don't you think?"

"Actually, most of those floats are used in the adult parades," he informed. "They run them again here to get more use out of them and to let the kids enjoy them."

"They enjoyed them, all right."

"Yeah," he said, grinning. "They sure did."

Other parade goers passed them, children giggling and

exclaiming about what they'd caught. A couple of little girls, their necks draped in beads and their faces painted like clowns, ran past them. Pigtails waved at Ethan and Clarise as they chased each other down the sidewalk.

Clarise audibly sighed. "I love kids," she said, then her body tensed. It was only a slight bristle of tension, but since they were pressed against each other, Ethan felt it. Did she regret letting him in on this little tidbit, or was she wondering how he'd respond? In any case, he didn't want her to have any doubts where he stood in that respect.

"I love them too."

"Really?" Her body eased at once, and her face tilted up to peer at his. "You seemed to enjoy yourself today, but I didn't know if it were because of the parade, or if—"

"I love kids," he repeated. "They're fun."

"I'll say." She laughed, and the sound of that laugh warmed his heart. Then she stopped walking and placed a finger to the bridge of her nose, where the red plastic glasses rested. "Oh dear, his glasses." She turned to scan the crowd, but there were so many kids she had no way to spot the boy who had scrambled beside her for goods during the parade.

"I think he meant for you to keep them. Besides, you gave him a few pairs, didn't you?" Ethan had witnessed loads of cheap sunglasses flung from a beach-themed float, and he'd also seen Clarise scooping them up and happily distributing them to each child.

"I guess I did, didn't I?"

Nodding, he unlocked the car, opened the passenger's door and waited for her to climb in. Then he rounded the front and slid into the driver's seat.

"Where to now?" she asked.

"It's a surprise. Rather, it would be a surprise, for a

woman who hadn't generated a list of specific activities to be covered this weekend."

"It's still a surprise," she countered. "I'm banking on the beach instead of the grass, but I still don't know the location you have in mind, so it's definitely a surprise. And one I'm ready for, by the way."

He had no doubt of that. She was always ready. Ethan held her hand as he drove toward Indian Rocks Beach, a short drive from Tampa, but far enough away to provide the privacy they needed. Her eyes widened when he slowly steered the car toward a small parking area in the midst of several beach cottages.

"This isn't exactly vacated," she pointed out.

"It's the beach," he said. "You didn't specify which beach, or that you wanted it to be secluded. This okay with you?"

She turned in the seat, peered at the road curving along the beach property. Cars and trucks traveled sporadically down the ribbon of asphalt. Her mouth crooked in a half frown. "It's not quite dark."

"Not yet."

"And there's a good deal of traffic. Right there." She pointed toward the road. But Ethan had been here before, and although he'd never had sex on the beach, he knew of several areas completely enclosed by the tall sea grass native to the Gulf. They'd have their own private room, with sand on the floor, a blanket of starlit sky for a ceiling, and the Gulf for a wall. It'd be perfect. He parked the car and turned toward Clarise. She left her hair down today, its straight length resting on her bare shoulders. A ring of the fabric composing her top circled her biceps. The pale pink-and-white-checked cloth with puckered gathers seemed more befitting a little girl than a tempting, curvaceous woman, which made her even more tempting, in Ethan's opinion.

"Are you afraid someone will see us, Clarise?"

She ran her palms down her jeans-clad thighs and bit her lower lip. "No. Well, yeah, maybe." She shot another glance at the traffic, watched a car pass, then looked back at him, her eyes wide and fearful.

"Do you trust me?" His question caused another quick dart of her eyes toward the street, where a rattling rusty pickup now made its way down the road. But, despite her obvious apprehension, she turned back to Ethan and forced a smile.

"I'm a little nervous about this," she admitted, "but yes, I trust you."

"You weren't nervous at the football stadium," he reminded.

"It was pitch-black, and there wasn't a soul in sight," she said. "But I did list sex on the beach."

"Yes, you did."

"And I guess that involves a bit of risk, right?"

"The elevator involved risk too," he reminded.

Her face burst into a brilliant smile, and she laughed. "When that buzzer went off, I thought I was going to die right there."

He leaned forward, pressed his lips to hers, then softly sucked on her lower lip. "But you didn't want to stop, did you, Clarise?"

"No," she whispered breathily.

"And you trusted me."

"Yes." The darkness of her eyes intensified. "Completely."

He suspected she was remembering watching herself lose control in the elevator's mirror. It pleased him enormously to visibly see her reminisce and realize how turned on she was by the memory. Today's activities would undoubtedly do the same.

"I trust you, Ethan," she repeated, her tone whispery and erotic.

"Good." He knew she trusted him physically, but today he wanted to learn whether she trusted him emotionally as well. Would she trust him enough to talk to him, open up to him, without holding back? Would she share her body *and* her heart? "Then let's go for a walk."

"A walk?" Her genuine surprise made him grin. Did she actually think he would throw her on the ground for down-and-dirty sex in front of a train of spectators?

"A walk down the beach, since we have a little time before dark."

She smiled, relief sparkling in those big brown eyes.

"By the way, we *will* have sex on the beach before we return to the condo, before we return to the car, in fact, just in case you're wondering. But I swear, I won't do anything to embarrass you."

"I believe you."

"Then let's go." He withdrew a soft blanket from the backseat. "We'll need this."

They exited the car and walked down a short side street leading between the majority of beach cottages. Two couples sat at a white picnic table near the edge of the beach. They were chatting and playing cards, but paused to nod and smile at Clarise and Ethan as they passed.

"Do you think they know what we're planning?" Ethan asked.

Clarise blushed fiercely. "Lord, I hope not."

"I'm sure they know exactly what we're doing," he teased.

"They do?" she asked, looking back at them in obvious panic.

He laughed. "Yes, they know we're going for a walk on the beach. It's fairly obvious, isn't it?"

She punched him. Hard. And her laughter penetrated the warm salty air . . . and his heart.

"Leave your shoes here," he instructed, pointing out a grassy area beside the wood plank beach access. He kicked off his, then waited for her to do the same.

"What if someone takes them?" she asked.

"Then I guess we'll buy more shoes."

Laughing, she tossed her sandals, then wiggled her toes in the sand. "This feels good."

"Yeah," he agreed. "It does." Only Ethan wasn't talking about the cool sand beneath his feet. They walked hand in hand, his thumb stroking the sensitive skin inside her palm.

"Wow." She stopped and surveyed a large cruise ship, dark water swooshing against its side as it made its way through the Gulf of Mexico. The engine rumbled steadily as it moved against the current. They walked in silence, while the ship shifted lazily along the waves, and while Ethan pondered how to get Clarise to open up. He was her friend, for crying out loud, but when it came to getting her to talk about commitment, which she'd informed him wasn't on her list, he was clueless. Why? Because he didn't want to force her into sharing anything she wasn't ready to share, that was why. And because he cared about her. But dammit, he didn't want it ending when they returned to Birmingham. How could they go back to being mere

Friday afternoon coffee chatting friends, after they'd shared *this?* He only had two days before they returned home. Ethan winced, remembering last year's return from Gasparilla and the awkward incident that occurred back then. Unfortunately, he'd have to tell Clarise about it, given the other party involved, and damned if that didn't figure to be a gigantic obstacle in their path toward a long-term relationship. But he wouldn't worry about that now. One step at a time. And the most important step was getting Clarise to admit that this thing they'd started had the potential to become more. Much more.

"Look." She pointed to a long, snowy white egret sailing above their heads.

In spite of its elongated body, the bird was graceful in its approach . . . until it nearly collided with a boy's head. The teen had been riding a bicycle down the concrete path that ran between the condos and the beach, but he stopped and watched the tall bird land on the deck of a vast beach house. Shrugging, the kid reached in his backpack, snatched a newspaper, then slung it toward the back of the house. It hadn't been aimed at the bird, but the egret departed nonetheless.

"It's almost as if that bird was playing a game with him," Clarise said, still staring at the boy throwing papers toward each home sporadically placed in the midst of the condos, which claimed the majority of the beach.

"Maybe he was."

She began walking again, her hand comfortably clasping his. "I didn't even realize kids still delivered papers on bicycles. My father said he had a paper route growing up and made the deliveries on his bike, but our newspaper was always delivered by an adult in a car." She looked at him. "Do you ever see kids delivering newspapers in Birmingham?"

"Yeah, but the majority of them are sixteen or better, and they all drive."

"Too bad. There's something old-fashioned and fun about a boy on a bicycle delivering the paper."

"That's the way I did it."

"You delivered newspapers?" she questioned. "On a bicycle?"

He nodded. "I didn't always work at the department store. Dad thought it was important for his boys to earn their own keep in business before he gave us jobs working for him. I had a paper route; Jeff designed and sold model cars."

Her mouth dropped open slightly, then she laughed.

"What?" Ethan asked.

"With you being twins, I would have thought your career choices as teens would have been similar. I can't imagine two jobs that are more different."

"Hey, what can I say? I'm the traditional one. Jeff's the risk-taker."

"I've never heard of anyone designing model cars," she admitted. "Building them, yes. Designing them and reselling them, no. Why would someone want to buy a model that was already complete?"

"It was the design," Ethan explained. "I guess you could say that Jeff was a little ahead of his time, since he was playing 'pimp my ride' with those model cars. He'd give them custom paint jobs and have the engines so meticulous that you'd swear they were real." He shrugged. "That's the kind of thing he does now to make his store stand out in Atlanta. He advertises with flair, which is what he's doing this week in Birmingham. He made a bet with our father that he could outsell him, with Dad running the bigger Atlanta store and Jeff running the smaller, Birmingham one."

"He's running our store?"

Our store. Ethan liked the sound of that. "Only this week, to prove he can handle overseeing the new acquisitions in Florida."

A small gasp echoed in the breeze. "Are you going to Florida too?" The hint of disappointment in her tone told him she didn't want him leaving. Good to know, because he had no intention of doing anything of the sort. He liked Birmingham, liked the people there, particularly the one squeezing his hand a little tighter while awaiting his answer.

"I'll stay in Birmingham and have a hand in the company's big picture. There's no way I won't, since I handled all of the details with the acquisition. That's not Jeff's cup of tea. Me, on the other hand, well, that's right up my alley. I like looking into the future; he likes focusing on the here and now. But when you put the two of us together . . ."

"You've got everything covered to give Nordstrom's a run for their money," she said, and her death grip on his palm relaxed.

He grinned. "I believe my father said those very words. And Jeff and I may be night and day, but we work well together. Twins aren't usually totally alike, you know. Most siblings aren't."

"Babette and I sure aren't. She's the wild one, the risk-taker, in our scenario."

Even though he could agree, he chose not to. Yeah, her

sister was a hellion, but the past few days had told him that Babette Robinson wasn't the only one in that family with spunk. And he'd say the real "wild one" of the bunch was the one currently standing on a sandy beach at dusk, her big doe eyes blinking in the salty breeze while she waited to hear what he said when comparing her to her sister. No problem. There was no comparison. "I'd say the real wild one would have to be the one who composed a sex fantasy list and headed to Gasparilla to accomplish each wicked item on it. Has Babette ever done anything like that?"

Her cute lower lip dropped open again, then that sweet mouth curved into a grin. "Not that I know of."

"See? Lucky me, I have the unruly sister."

She punched him in the arm and leaned against him playfully. "I bet that's the first time anyone has ever called me the unruly one."

"If the shoe fits," he said, which made that gorgeous smile even brighter. "And double lucky me, since I have the gorgeous wild one in my store, every day, working as the best damn department head in the South, helping other women look and feel gorgeous too—in my store's clothes. What's not to like about that?"

Clarise swallowed hard. "Do you really think I'm the best?"

"I've told you that before," he reminded her, surprised that she hadn't already realized he'd never given her anything but the truth.

Another thick swallow made her throat pulse. "And do you really think I'm gorgeous?"

Damn, why didn't she see it? "I do, and so does any other male who happens to look your way." He decided to lighten this conversation, since she looked on the verge of tears, and he didn't want to make her cry. "And did I mention my best department head also looks really good in the shower?"

She delivered another sound punch to his arm. "You're making it sound like I slept my way into the job."

He shrugged. "Hey, whatever works."

This time, she stopped walking, put her hand behind his neck and lowered his face.

Ethan let her, of course, expecting a hot and heated kiss.

She bit his lip. "Just in case you have any glitches in your memory, Mr. Eubanks, I did *not* sleep with you until I had already obtained the status of"—she paused then grinned—"best damn department head in the South."

He pulled his bottom lip in and checked for blood. Surprisingly, he tasted none. "Actually, there aren't any glitches in my memory, Ms. Robinson, about anything that has to do with you. Your initial job interview, for example, when you stunned me into silence with your ready-for-the-runway ensemble. A silk white blouse and black skirt that you'd obviously purchased at the store. I recognized the pieces, of course, but hadn't seen them put together so well, or on a woman who wore them so nicely."

Her lip twitched slightly, as if she were trying to determine how to respond. Then she whispered, "You remember what I wore?"

Thrilled she was starting to see the big picture, Ethan nodded. He'd noticed her from that first day, and though it took him three years to see the truth, that she should be his forever, he had seen *something*. From that very first day. "Yeah, I remember. And it was the classic long strand of black pearls, knotted seductively beneath your breasts, that pulled the entire look together."

Her lip quivered. Tears spilled forward. He really hadn't wanted to make her cry, but she was sure crying now. And smiling. Which couldn't be a totally bad thing, right? She swallowed, and a small red splotch appeared at the base of her neck. "Thank you."

Was she thanking him for remembering her attire the first time they met? Or for helping her see how appealing, how desirable, she was as a woman? Either way, he was glad he'd told her the truth; from their first meeting, she'd made an impression. "You're welcome."

They started walking again, Clarise staring out over the water and Ethan reflecting on everything that had happened between the two of them since that initial job interview. He wanted more than the casual friendship they'd shared until this weekend. For the first time in his life, he wanted it all. And he wanted it with Clarise.

She turned away from him, toward the water. "When we were growing up, Babette and I didn't exactly complement each other the way you and Jeff did. She may have been younger, but I was the one who couldn't compete. Babette was the pretty one, the thin one, and she didn't try to make me feel bad about my—size—but I did anyway. Just being around her, standing next to her at family reunions and seeing people whisper about the differences. Or at school, with only two years between us, she was always right there, the perky little sister that everyone adored. It was hard not to hold that against her back then, and she didn't deserve that. She really didn't try to rub it in my face or anything." Her voice was faint, as though admitting her insecurities regarding her sister were tearing at her very soul. And Ethan, knowing more about

Babette Robinson than Clarise realized, silently wondered if the hellion hadn't played on those insecurities back then.

He cleared his throat. Now was not the time to inform Clarise that he'd seen firsthand how conniving her little sister could be. Sure, he'd have to come clean. But not now. "You're beautiful, Clarise, and you were beautiful back then too. You just didn't realize it. I only wish I'd have known you then, to tell you." He placed a finger to her cheek and tenderly brushed a tear away. "And to show you—then."

As if uncomfortable with the direction of their current conversation, she turned to view a ship sailing smoothly out to sea. Then she twisted to look at him and shoved her hands in her pockets. The action made them dip down and flashed him a sweet view of the flesh between the edge of her shirt and the waist of her jeans. "You're making me believe it now, you know."

He smiled. "Good."

The red splotch spread toward her collarbone. She inhaled deeply, and her breasts lifted the pale pink fabric of her shirt for a brief moment before she exhaled. "Why did you tell me now? About remembering what I wore that first day? All of those afternoons over coffee and you never mentioned it."

Okay. It took some time, but she was starting to see that he'd always noticed her, and evidently, it scared her. Unfortunately, it also reminded her that she wasn't like her sister. If she only knew, not being like Babette was a very, very good thing. "I simply want to know you better, Clarise."

"Why?"

"Because you're special."

"Because we're friends," she clarified. "And for today and tomorrow, we're more?"

"Yeah, because we're friends, and yeah, because right now, we're more, but also because I want to be closer to you." He took a deep breath. "I wasn't trying to make you uncomfortable; I don't want you uncomfortable around me, Clarise. I want the opposite."

She shivered. "It's so hard to believe this is real."

Ethan wrapped an arm around her. "You want to sit down?"

She nodded.

He unfolded the blanket and let it catch the gentle wind, then he lowered it to the sand. They sat on the soft cloth, a thin covering over the cool beach. Ethan pulled her closer and held her in his arms while the wind whistled through the sea grass that bordered their private haven.

Clarise sniffed loudly, then laughed. "Things like this, where a guy tells a girl he remembers the first time he ever saw her—oh, and consequently, where the same guy offers to fulfill her every sex fantasy—don't typically happen to girls like me. Girls who are . . . "

"Voluptuous?" he completed, which made her laugh even harder. "And how do you know things like this don't happen to them? Maybe every curvy, desirable female has had a guy beg to accomplish her sex wish list. Maybe, they didn't kiss and tell."

"I don't recall you begging."

"Trust me. I would have."

She grabbed his arm and squeezed. "You are rotten Ethan Eubanks."

"If it's rotten you want, you've got it." He leaned back, crooked his finger beneath her chin and tilted her face to his. The sky had darkened as late afternoon turned into early evening, but he could see her dark lashes, spiked from tears. "I'm sorry if I upset you."

"It's okay. I've just—I've never been able to talk to anyone about all of those feelings before, especially about how I've always felt inferior to Babette." She paused, then added, "Well, no one besides Granny Gert."

"I'm glad you talked to me."

She sniffed, rubbed her eyes with her fingertips, then kissed his chin. "We've only got one more day, Ethan. I don't want to waste a minute. Make love to me here."

His spirits fell then lifted in one hard swoop. *One more day.* She'd said it. Clarise didn't intend on bringing what they shared back home. Those three words, *one more day,* ripped at his heart. Almost as much as the other two words she'd stated afterward made it swell. For the first time yet, Clarise hadn't said she wanted to "have sex." And that, Ethan thought, would see him through the dilemma of proving how much they shared, because Clarise had asked him to do exactly what he planned. *Make love.*

Chapter 19

Clarise had made a tactical error. With the emotions involved in sharing her insecurities with Ethan, she'd slipped up and asked him what she really wanted. Had he noticed? *Make love to me here,* she'd said. As his long fingers tripped inside the gathered elastic edge of her blouse and slid it down her breasts, she realized Ethan was more than happy to oblige . . . with giving her sex on the beach, she reminded herself, not making love. Though her mind and, more importantly, her heart adamantly refused to recognize the difference.

The wind whistled as it pressed through the tall grass surrounding them on the sand. Did Ethan stop here on purpose? Where they were practically enclosed by the tall, swaying reeds and provided with complete privacy? As if anyone could see them now that darkness had settled over Florida. But still, Ethan had promised he wouldn't embarrass her when he fulfilled her fantasy, and, as she'd told the woman with the exquisite scarves, Ethan Eubanks kept his promises. He was protecting her once more, she realized, as her shirt bunched beneath her heavy breasts, and her arms were trapped at her sides by the capped sleeves. Ethan had also protected her Friday night, when he'd arrived just in time to keep her from baring her body, or at least her breasts, to Tampa. Sure, she'd shown the lace-encased view, but given a little more time with that potent daiquiri pulsing through her system, and she'd have taken it all off. She had no doubt. After making sure she kept the majority of her clothes on, he'd continued taking care of her when the impact of the slushy drink met her empty stomach and made her feel like she actually was Dead On Arrival.

Throughout the weekend, he'd given her the most exciting sexual experiences she'd ever hoped to have, all because he wanted to protect her from getting hurt. He hadn't wanted her wild fantasies to get her in trouble. Going above and beyond the call of friendship, for sure. Then today, once again, he'd held her and taken care of her when she finally admitted out loud that she'd resented growing up next to her feisty, sexy and tiny sister. And when she'd finally admitted the truth, Ethan had listened, without passing judgment. He gave her exactly what she needed, a friend to trust, someone who would listen and who knew her well enough to understand and someone who made her believe she didn't have to continue this crazy comparison game with Babette. He said she was beautiful, and Clarise's heart believed him.

"You're beautiful, Clarise," he said, as if he knew the very words her mind kept repeating. Slowly, he slid a palm up her belly, over the gathered fabric of her shirt, then to the center of her pink strapless bra.

She closed her eyes. His hand had crept across her stomach, and she hadn't even thought to suck it in. What's more, he hadn't seemed to notice. *He thinks I'm beautiful.*

Unhooking the clasp, he let the two sides of the bra fall open and immediately clamped his mouth over one breast, while his opposite hand gently kneaded and massaged the other. Both tips peaked and pulsed under his masterful touch, until her back arched from the blanket to get closer. He reversed sides, kneading the wet nipple while pulling the other inside his mouth. It was more than she could take. Rather, she wanted to take more. Of Ethan. Right here. Right now.

"More," she whispered, feeling an urgent need to convey the burning passion, the aching hunger. "I want more."

"Tell me what you want, Clarise."

Her hands were still trapped by the fabric, and she squirmed to free her arms. "I want to touch you."

Filmy clouds cloaked the majority of the moon, but there was enough of an illumination to see his smile.

"I want that too," he admitted. Then he gathered the fabric of her top in both hands and shimmied it up and over her breasts, freeing her head and arms from all forms of confinement. Her jeans were still in place, but she didn't care. He'd remove those too, but right now, she had to feel him, touch him, the part of him her core burned to have again.

Her blouse had barely left her body before her hands began wrestling with the button on his jeans. Dang, it was tough to concentrate when she wanted him so badly. Finally popping the metal through the buttonhole, she lowered the zipper, then nudged his jeans down, moving her hands within his briefs to . . . *yes.* He was hard. For her. Long. For her. Thick. For her. And he had that exquisite drop of moisture at the tip, a sign that he was oh-so-ready. For her.

She circled him with her palm, thrilled when the warmth

of him transferred to her skin, tingled up her arm and made her nipples ache. Even more noticeable with the sand's coolness penetrating the thin blanket, Ethan's heat cloaked her with—desire. "I want you inside of me."

"Exactly where I want to be." Unlike her, his hands didn't fumble at all with the closure on her jeans, or the zipper, or the thong panties she'd worn for the occasion, though he did pause to emit a sexy whistle when his hands met the wispy thread of pale pink lace between her thighs.

She'd never dreamed of wearing a thong before. Sexy lingerie, yes. But a thong? No way. However, she'd purchased one—or three—in her mad dash through the store in Trussville, and she'd wanted to wear this pink one, the one that matched her blouse exactly, for Ethan. Because she knew he'd like it and because the way he looked at her, and the way he continued to praise her and tell her she was beautiful, had given her the confidence she needed to pull it off. Speaking of pulling it off, Ethan was doing just that. Pulling the thong from her body. With his teeth.

"Ohmigod."

"Mmm-hmm."

After he'd stripped her completely, he ran a hand between her legs, up her thigh, then brushed the backs of his fingertips across her mound. She instantly bowed upward toward his touch. "Please."

"You're so wet," he revealed, as if she didn't know. Then he licked his fingers, and she wanted to die. If he didn't get inside her soon, very soon, she suspected she would. "Ethan—"

"Yes?" he asked, smiling as he removed a foil packet from his back pocket.

"You know."

Then he shucked his jeans and dang if he didn't look even bigger than she'd remembered.

"What is it, Clarise?" he repeated, while he stroked her clit with his thumb and let his hardness press to her side. *Her side?* She had to have him. Soon. And she was tired of being nice about it. "Please" was undoubtedly the word he expected, but Clarise wasn't asking. She was demanding.

"Now."

The sound he returned was half laugh, half growl and wholly erotic. "As the lady wants," he said, rising to kneel before her and sheathing his length with the condom.

It shouldn't have been so intoxicating, watching him roll the soft latex over his hard penis, seeing him touch himself in preparation for making love to her. But, heaven help her, it was, and her center practically quaked in anticipation. She opened her legs wider, watched him get closer, hovering over her and waiting for—*what?*

"Make love to me," she said, before her mind had a chance to stop her mouth.

Then, as he plunged inside, she prayed to God that "making love" was what he was doing.

Ethan drove back to the condo with the sweet memory of Clarise's command etched in his memory, and one main goal on his mind—finding a way to make this last. This couldn't be a fling. He wouldn't let it.

"*Make love to me.*" She'd said those words. Twice. And damned if they weren't the most perfect words in the English language. Nearly. There were three others he wanted to hear from Clarise's mouth, but that would come, as soon as he figured out how to convince this sexy lady to add commitment to her list.

"Commitment isn't on the list."

Well, if it hadn't found its way to the list yet, Ethan was going to make damn certain it got there. Fast. Preferably before they returned to Birmingham, to reality—and to the truth he still needed to tell her about last year's trip to Gasparilla. He swallowed thickly. No way would he think about that now. *That* might take her thoughts away from commitment completely, and everything else with Ethan. But hell, he hadn't done anything wrong. Had he?

"I need to call Granny Gert," she said, as they neared the condo. "She asked me to check in with her while I'm here, and I haven't called her once." She laughed softly. "I guess my mind has been on other things."

"Well, I hope so, or I've been doing something wrong."

"Trust me, you haven't done anything wrong." She stopped beside the room and glanced up at him, those big brown eyes filled with—what? Ethan couldn't tell. There was something different about this look, something he hadn't seen before. Excitement? No, not this time. Sexual hunger? Ethan didn't think so, though he totally planned on satisfying that again in the very near future. He touched a fingertip to her temple, trailed it down her cheek and gently moved her hair behind her ear. She continued looking at him, and he had it. Admiration. That's what he saw in those eyes tonight. An amazed wonder that he hadn't "done anything wrong." And everything right.

Ethan said a silent thanks that he'd been the lucky guy to experience this part of Clarise. Obviously, she hadn't had a lot of guys "doing things right." Well, that was changing now, because Ethan totally planned on continuing his pursuit of keeping this fiery, sexy woman satisfied, physically and emotionally, for as long as she'd let him.

Clarise's cheeks flushed slightly, and she turned toward their room. Was she uncomfortable letting him know that he'd fit the bill in the accomplishing sexual fantasies task? Because her affirmation hadn't done anything but make him want to do it again. And again. He slid the keycard in the door while Clarise reverted to the original subject of conversation. "Granny said she wanted to make sure I'm okay, but I'm betting she mainly wants to find out if I bought all the stuff on her list, or if she'll need to come down herself to get it."

Ethan opened the door and stepped inside. Obviously, Clarise wasn't ready to discuss her recent admission. More than likely, she also didn't want to discuss her word choice at the beach. *"Make love to me here."* So Ethan wouldn't push the issue. Yet. "Tell you what," he started. "While you call your grandmother, I'll call Jeff and see how things are going at the store."

"You haven't checked in this weekend?" Her tone of surprise hit the mark. He *hadn't* called or checked in. Yet the store survived without him; his cell phone hadn't rung once since his plane landed.

"Nope, I didn't check in." And damned if that didn't prove a few things. One, he trusted Jeff's business instinct enough to know his brother could efficiently run the show in his absence. And two, he'd enjoyed this trip with Clarise so much that he hadn't thought of business at all, beyond the luncheon with employees on Saturday. During last year's trip, he'd brought his work along and even implemented the initial concept for purchasing the Panache chain while sitting in his room and watching the parades pass by. Solo. Ethan had never been one for sex with a stranger, and he'd also never been one for sex with employees. Until this weekend. Then again, he hadn't spent *all* of last year's Gasparilla on his own.

Clarise crossed the room and withdrew her cell phone from the bedside table.

"Tell your grandmother I said hello, if she remembers me, that is."

"Oh, she remembers you."

That got his attention. "Should I ask why you seem so sure?"

She shifted from one foot to the other and looked extremely uncomfortable. Quirking her lip to the side, she finally answered. "No. You shouldn't ask."

Ethan winked. "You realize I may ask her why you're so sure she remembers me, the next time I see her."

She shrugged while she dialed. "Suit yourself." Then within minutes, she was chatting away with her grandmother and telling her all about the pirates, the parades and the city. Funny, she didn't seem to have any inclination to inform Granny Gert of her sex list.

Ethan smirked.

Clarise narrowed her eyes as though she knew exactly what he'd been thinking. She probably did. He pointed toward the balcony then headed outside to phone Jeff. Inhaling, he welcomed the warm humidity of Tampa at night. That thick heat had bathed Clarise's naked body when he'd undressed her on the beach and made a January night feel like June. Dialing Jeff's number, he considered what he'd be doing this June. The acquisition would be in full swing, Panache would undergo a fluid change to Eubanks Elegant Apparel, and he'd be with Clarise. *If* everything went the way he wanted.

"About time you called," Jeff answered.

"What?" Ethan asked. "No hello?"

"Definitely not. I've got to brag to somebody, and you know how Dad can't stand to lose. I couldn't exactly tell him how well my campaign is going."

Ethan grinned, not surprised one iota that Jeff already had an ad campaign in motion back home. The guy was amazing with marketing. "Your campaign?"

"Hell, yeah. And it's a good thing your skeleton crew knows their stuff about running the show when the key players are in Tampa. I've worked them to death, but no one is complaining."

"That's because they're on commission, and I'm betting that work is beefing up their checks."

"Damn straight," Jeff said with pride. "Half the females in Birmingham came to the store today to enter. And I'm expecting the other half tomorrow."

"To enter?" Ethan watched an elderly man, his dark skin blending into the shadow beneath a restaurant awning, unfold an aluminum chair on the opposite side of the street.

"Our contest. I ran a full-page ad in Sunday's paper."

"A full page?" The store typically ran half-page ads when they were advertising a new line, but a full page? And when the majority of Ethan's department heads were on a corporate outing in Tampa?

"Robin's fiancé helped me get it in," Jeff explained. "And by the way, it more than paid for itself today with the women who came to the store because of the contest."

"What contest?" Ethan repeated.

"The one we're running this week. It began today and runs through Friday. Customers are invited to put together a complete ensemble, everything a woman would wear to look exceptional. We're creating the look of the Exceptional Eubanks Woman."

Ethan sat in one of the black wrought-iron chairs that graced his balcony. The hard metal pressed into his back and instantly reminded him of making love to Clarise. Her fingernails had raked his skin, and he could feel the pressure of the chair against that tender flesh.

"When a woman thinks she's created the best possible outfit, she logs each piece on a contest entry form. We're asking for specific blouses, skirts, pants, shoes, accessories, everything. They're loving it," Jeff said excitedly, while Ethan tried to focus on the information rather than the memory of Clarise's nails upon his back.

"How do you decide who wins? And what do they win?"

"That's the best part. I've lined up Ella Dujardin, the fashion editor for *Sophisticated Southern,* to judge. The winner gets every item of clothing from her ensemble *and* her photo featured in the magazine. Ella thought it was an excellent idea for a local feature story and asked to spotlight the store within the article." He cleared his throat. "Guess you'll need to thank me for getting you the added exposure."

Ethan laughed. "Thanks, but I know you're just doing it to get the Florida deal."

"True, but it's helping you in the process," Jeff reminded.

"Won't argue with you there. So, how's Dad's side of this competition faring?"

"He can't compete," Jeff said flatly. Then, because he couldn't help it, he laughed. "Hell, he's doing pretty good, but I'm going to win."

"Well, we'll find out soon enough," Ethan said. "I guess

I'm supposed to stay away from the store until the contest ends?"

"Right. Don't come back before Saturday. That's all I need, Dad telling me you came home and saved the day, and thereby my attempt is null and void. Nothing is going to ruin my chance at the new deal."

"How do you know he wouldn't give it to you either way, win or lose? You want the position, and you've done a great job in Atlanta. Why wouldn't you do equally well in Florida over several stores? Seems to me Dad would have given you exactly what you wanted if you'd only asked."

"Hell, I think he would too. But it's more fun to win it."

"And to beat Preston Eubanks," Ethan said.

"Yeah, there's that," Jeff said, his competitiveness second only to their father's. "But since I don't need you home before Saturday, you could extend your Gasparilla trip if you want."

"I think we'll keep it the way it is," Ethan said, turning in the chair to peer through the window at Clarise. She was evidently still talking to her grandmother, with one hand holding the cell phone to an ear and the other gesturing wildly through each word. Currently, she slapped it against her waist and shifted her hip to that side in a move that he'd classify part Marilyn Monroe, part Bridget Jones. Damn she was cute.

"We?" Jeff asked. "I don't suppose you're talking about Red, are you?"

"Definitely not," Ethan said, reminded once again that he still hadn't had *that* conversation with Clarise. How was he supposed to tell her?

"Listen, I don't know what happened with the two of

you, but hell, I didn't even officially meet the woman, and I wanted her."

"Want-*ed?*" Ethan asked. Jeff had brought up "Red" on several occasions over the past year, and Ethan hadn't surrendered the woman's identity. No doubt, the feistiness had appealed to his brother, but if Jeff only knew, that was one fiery package that burned. Literally. Damn, she still had the potential to cause trouble—by torching his chance with Clarise.

"Fine," Jeff relented. "Yeah, I'd like to be with a woman who is so damn turbulent. There was more passion, more fury in her that day than I've ever seen in anyone—male or female. It's bizarre. The woman was stark-raving mad and ready to go for your throat."

"And that impresses you?" Ethan asked incredulously.

"Immensely."

"God help you, brother."

"Which, I suppose, means you still aren't going to divulge her real name?"

"No," Ethan said, realizing that if things were going to work out with the sexy woman chatting with Granny Gert, he would have to inform Jeff of "Red's" identity. Have mercy.

"Then tell me, if you aren't with Red again, who makes the 'we' you mentioned?"

"Clarise."

Ethan waited for Jeff's response. None came.

"Clarise Robinson," Ethan added, prompting his brother.

"Yeah, I know," Jeff said. "I'm just surprised."

If Jeff said anything derogatory about her, brother or not, he was going to hurt. "What?" Ethan dared.

"I'm surprised it took you so long," Jeff admitted. "I

mean, Dad could see it; Mom could see it; I saw it. The only one in the dark . . . was you."

Ethan blinked. What the hell? "Saw what?"

"That she's perfect for you. Sexy and smart and intelligent. We never could figure out why the two of you stopped at friendship, especially after all three of us saw you drooling over her at the Christmas party. Really, Ethan, you were pathetic. I need to teach you a thing or two about being cool around women. First you botch things with Red . . ."

"That's not the way it was."

"Whatever you say," Jeff countered. "And then you take too damn long to see what is right in front of you. But hey, I'm glad you saw the light. I swear, I'd have asked Clarise out myself if I hadn't thought you'd have killed me."

Jeff would have asked her out? "Over my dead body," Ethan said, not mincing words.

Jeff laughed. "Good. You've finally got as much spirit for a female as they've always had for you. Not bad. And if you don't mind, try not to do the same thing to Clarise that you did to Red last Gasparilla. That obviously didn't go over well."

"I'd never hurt Clarise," Ethan said emphatically.

"Good to know," Jeff said, then added, "Listen, I've got to get the store ready for tomorrow's opening. Things are going great here; don't worry about this place."

"Good to know," Ethan mimicked. Then he disconnected and sat staring across the street while he replayed his own words in his mind. *"I'd never hurt Clarise."*

The man beneath the awning pulled a large box out of the shadows. It creaked as it opened, and he withdrew an object from inside. A streetlamp caught the glimmer of a guitar, which he tenderly placed within his hands. Then he pulled at the strings and played a melancholy, sad refrain that washed above the idle chatter and sporadic noises from the street below and moved directly to Ethan's heart.

"God, don't let me hurt her."

By the time he headed back inside, Clarise was in the bathroom probably preparing to go to bed. Tomorrow would be megabusy, since she'd claimed she wanted to attend as many of the last day's parades as possible. It would be draining, for sure, and Ethan suspected she would want a night of real sleep before the marathon day, which was fine. Making love to her on the beach had been phenomenal and could sate his outrageous sexual appetite for Clarise Robinson if it had to, at least until tomorrow. He needed to let her relax, because he believed that was what she wanted, to take it easy and perhaps spend a night simply cuddling before their biggest Gasparilla day. However, that belief did a 180 when the bathroom door opened and Clarise, in a red satin bustier, thong panties and thigh-high stockings complete with garter belt—*garter belt!*—emerged. And, on further examination, Ethan's throat went from slightly parched to bone dry. God help him, red high heels.

"I hope you're not sleepy," she purred, sauntering across the room and placing her palm against his chest.

His heart pounded so hard it hurt, and he suspected it beat a frantic path against that sweet little palm. Sleepy? Was she serious? How could a guy be sleepy while looking at perfection in red high heels? "Not at all."

"Good. Because tonight, you're taking orders."

"Orders?" He sounded completely at ease with the idea, but inside he was screaming, *"Hell, yeah!"*

"Orders," Siren Clarise repeated, and pushed him toward the bed. "Now take them off."

He grinned. "What if I want you to?"

"Who's in charge here?" Her mouth quivered a bit with the question, and Ethan suspected she wasn't quite as comfortable in her authority role as she'd have liked, so he decided to make it as easy as possible on her. Obviously, this was yet another method of overcoming her previous insecurities, and he'd be damned if he didn't help her accomplish her goal.

"You're in charge," he said, swiftly pulling his shirt over his head and tossing it to the floor.

Her eyes focused on his chest, then eased downward, seeming to zero in on the narrow line of hair that etched its way between his navel and the top of his jeans. "And the pants," she added, her voice a throaty rasp. She'd forgotten to direct him to remove his shoes, but he did so anyway. If he'd wanted to tease her, he'd have pointed out the error, but he didn't want to tease. He wanted to please.

Shoes, then socks, then pants. He didn't remove his red boxer briefs, however, as he assumed she probably wanted to issue a separate order for that task. Or do it personally. Either way suited him just fine. His erection strained against the soft fabric, and he was so damn hard, so ready, that it stood firm and high above the waistband. Evidently Clarise noticed. Her eyes fixed on the hardness, and she ran her top teeth over her lower lip. The gesture was sexy as all get out.

"Anything else?" he asked, feeling she might need to be reminded of the game she was playing.

"Yes," she whispered. "Everything. You were supposed to take everything off."

"These too?" he asked, running a finger inside his shorts then snapping the waistband against his flesh.

She jumped at the whiplike sound, but quickly recovered. "Those too."

Ethan removed the briefs and stood before her completely naked and completely aroused. The red bustier she'd donned for the occasion had way too little fabric to contain her magnificent breasts. As a result, they were all but spilling out of the top and making his dick salute.

"The bed," she directed, stepping closer.

"On my back or stomach?" he asked, following her line of questioning from their first night together.

"Back."

He did as ordered, then watched as she crossed the room and reached in the dresser drawer to withdraw a small, pink jar.

Well, well, well.

"What's that?" he asked, refusing to disguise his piqued curiosity.

She returned to the bed, and Ethan saw there were actually two items in her hand. The jar and something else. Something extremely fluffy. And pink.

"You aren't the only one who had a sugar sex fantasy," she said, sitting on the edge of the bed and removing the lid from the jar.

"I'm not?"

"No." She leaned across to place the lid on the table and let her plumped up breasts hover mere inches from his mouth in the process. Ethan licked his lips. "I brought cotton candy dust, just in case."

"Just in case—what?" he asked, as she dipped the pink feather into the jar.

"In case the man who helped me fulfill my fantasies was good enough for it." She brushed the powder-coated feather up one side of his penis, while Ethan gritted his teeth to maintain his composure.

"Good enough?" he managed, while she teased his cock with the soft feather and sugary powder.

Clarise coated him completely, his cock and his balls, before placing the feather and jar on the nightstand, then she leaned her face close to view her handiwork. Damn close, but not nearly close enough.

"Good enough for what?" Ethan asked again, his eyes locked on her mouth, so near his dick.

"Good enough to eat."

Chapter 20

It'd been incredible to see how far a single jar of cotton candy dust would go. Anxious to cuddle with Ethan again, Clarise scooted across the bed in search of the glorious male she'd licked from head to toe last night, but instead of meeting firm, muscled flesh, her hand merely swept the soft textures of the quilt until encountering a sheet of paper. Clarise eased her eyes open and squinted past the morning light spilling into the room, then she focused on the clock beside the bed, displaying 6:32.

"Didn't sleep late today, did you?" she mumbled, turning her attention back to the note in her hand.

I wanted to get you something special for breakfast. I'll be back soon. Ethan
P.S. I'm taking the sticky sheets down to the maids' station on my way out.

Clarise giggled. The sheets had been unbelievably sticky after her cotton candy feast. As a matter of fact, everything had been sticky, particularly Ethan, but he'd loved it. The sugar sex he'd provided with the sprinkle can of powdered sugar hadn't been nearly as messy in the end as her performance with that magical jar of candy dust and the feather. Plus, the sex they'd had following beignets occurred in the afternoon, so they'd merely left the condo and returned to clean sheets, courtesy of maid service. Last night, on the other hand, the sheets were totally covered in the delicious treat by the time she finished devouring Ethan. So much so that they'd had to remove the sheets and sleep on one of the quilts provided in their room. She'd had nearly as much fun helping Ethan wash off in the shower as she'd had licking the sweet substance from his impressive frame. It'd taken a lot of rubbing to get the residue to release from his body. And, of course, that rubbing and touching and sliding of flesh against flesh put them in another anxious frenzy that ended with hot and heated sex in the shower. Not a bad thing at all, her idea to purchase that jar. She'd never look at a cone of her favorite treat again without thinking of Ethan's jutting erection, candy-coated and ready for her mouth.

Grinning, she climbed from the bed and headed back to the shower. Might as well clean up and get ready for the day, her last day in Tampa with Ethan, but not their last day together. If she'd doubted his feelings before, she didn't now. Though he might not have mentioned the "L" word, she'd felt it in his touch, seen it in his eyes. He shared those indescribable feelings that she had for him, whether he realized it yet or not, but in case he needed to hear it from her first, she planned to tell him. Today.

Within twenty minutes, she'd showered, dried her hair and put on her usual minimal amount of makeup. Ethan seemed to like her face natural, which made him even more perfect in her book. He liked *her,* in spite of her extra pounds and her lack of feminine finesse. She smiled giddily at her reflection in the mirror. Today, she'd tell Ethan she loved him and wanted to be with him forever. And, unless she'd totally misread the genuine passion in those crystal blue eyes, he'd tell her he loved her too.

A loud knock at the door broke her reverie. Exiting the bathroom, she grabbed her robe, wrapped it around her body and headed toward the pounding noise. Surely Ethan hadn't forgotten his key. Then again, maybe he couldn't open the door if his arms were filled with her "special" breakfast, or maybe he simply needed to be welcomed back by a curvy lady in a pink satin robe.

"Your hands are full?" she sang sexily, swinging the door open.

Jake Riley, his dark hair tousled wildly and his eyes unbelievably bloodshot, stood on the other side of the door. "I didn't believe it," he said.

Clarise nervously tugged the sides of her robe together and attempted to tighten the sash. Then she glanced down to make sure all of the important parts were covered. They were. Barely. What did he want?

"Jake?" she questioned. "You didn't believe—what?" Though she thought she knew.

"You and Ethan. You, sleeping with the boss." His breath was rank, and she suspected he'd pulled an all-night drunk. Not totally unheard of when it came to Jake, but still, she was surprised he had found the nerve to: one, locate their room, two, knock on their door, and three, question her for sleeping with Ethan. Who did he think he was, anyway? He was a coworker and a friend, simple as that. And yeah, he'd given her a semiproposition a few days ago, but she'd thought he was over the fact that she'd declined his offer. Hadn't he been putting the moves on Jesilyn? But obviously, he wasn't over the rejection, and Clarise was appalled. She suspected that if he were being completely honest, he'd have added a few words to his accusation. He'd have said, "You, sleeping with the boss, and *not* sleeping with me."

"Jake, you're my friend, but I don't see that what I do in my room is any of your business." Then, when his glare intensified, she added, "We care about each other."

He stepped toward her, filling the entrance and making it impossible for Clarise to close the door and leave him in the hall until he sobered, which, judging from the sickening smell of his breath, was going to take a while. "I can't believe it doesn't matter to you. I mean, hell, it was Gasparilla then too. Doesn't it bother you at all knowing the two of you have slept with the same guy?" He leaned forward and swayed. "He's going to dump you like he did her, you know, right after Gasparilla. This is a yearly trip for fun and games. When we get back, you're simply another notch on his bedpost, and how are you going to work with him, to even look at him, after that, Clarise?" He shook his head again and winced. "I thought you were better than this. I thought you were different."

Clarise processed his words, then asked the one question that formulated in the midst of his tirade. "What are you talking about?"

Jake's eyes widened, jaw dropped open, then hung slack.

"What?" Clarise repeated, wondering when Ethan would walk up on this odd interchange. What would he say about Jake's attempt to sabotage what they shared? She really didn't want any trouble between Jake and Ethan. From the look of things, Jake simply pulled an all-nighter and wasn't thinking clearly.

"Hell, Clarise. I thought you knew. Last year," he stammered.

"Jake, Ethan will be back any minute. I think you should leave," she said, her irritation with this situation growing by the second. "And what Ethan did last year doesn't have anything to do with what we're doing now."

A hint of a smile crooked his features into a sinister sneer. "I can't believe the bastard didn't tell you. Hell, I can't believe she didn't."

"Jake," Clarise warned, her hand cupping the edge of the door in an effort to show him his visit had ended, "I've got to go now." She eased the door toward him, but he refused to budge until he said the words that cut straight to her heart and stabbed it completely.

"Your sister. Last year, she was the one in his bed."

It took Clarise less than two minutes to get Jake Riley out of the doorway and less than two seconds to slam the door once he did. Her head throbbed so intensely she had to squint to see, throat pressed in so tightly it hurt to breathe, heart clenched in her chest, skin burned. The giddy emotions that had bathed her in the euphoria of a woman in love now took a bitter, drastic turn. She no longer felt warm and gooey inside. She felt cold. Betrayed. Fighting the impulse to fling herself on the bed and have a good, hard cry, she took a deep breath and calculated how much time she had before Ethan returned. No way did she want to see him now. Or ever.

She replayed Babette's advice from their last phone conversation. She'd warned Clarise to be careful and instructed her not to do anything she wouldn't do. Clarise cringed. Babette also asked her who would be attending the trip— specifically asking about Ethan.

The cotton candy felt sickeningly sweet in her stomach. Ethan. And Babette? No, she wouldn't think about her perfect little sister now. She didn't have the time . . . or the inclination. Ignoring her streaming tears, she crossed the room, grabbed her suitcase, whipped it open, and flung all her belongings inside. By the time she finished, sweat beaded her forehead. It wasn't due to overexertion; it was due to the sick churning in the pit of her stomach. Babette. How could she? How could he? All of those sisterly conversations throughout the past year replayed in Clarise's mind. Babette knew. She knew exactly how Clarise felt about him, didn't she? Or did she? Clarise had never spelled it out exactly, but wouldn't a sister be able to tell? And couldn't she have once mentioned she spent last Gasparilla with him?

And Ethan. How could he have kept this from her? An entire year of Friday afternoon coffee chats talking about everything under the sun—except the fact that he'd done *everything* with *her sister!* In the midst of her cryfest, Clarise sucked in a thick gulp of air and inadvertently started coughing. Great. She'd probably stop breathing and pass out if she kept this up. Her head throbbed, hands shook, stomach quivered uncontrollably. And he—correction, *they*—weren't worth it.

She got a grip on the cough attack and concentrated on channeling her despair . . . and converting it to anger. It didn't take much effort. All she had to do was focus on the facts. Ethan didn't love her. He never had. Shoot, he didn't even care enough to tell her about Babette. He'd been just fine having the skinny sister during one Gasparilla and the fat one the next.

"No," Clarise said aloud. Then she swallowed and clarified, "Hell, no. Not fat. Curvy." Because there was no way she'd dub herself as "fat" again. If there was one thing she'd learned over the past five days, it was that she was abundantly curvy. And undeniably sexy. Ethan might have hidden his past with Babette, but he hadn't hidden anything when he'd looked at her last night. He'd wanted her. Bad. Well good. She hoped he still wanted her, because he damn sure wasn't going to have her again, and she hoped that hurt the massive male ego that convinced him he could have two sisters without repercussion. Though the skinny sister may have been willing to let him get away with it, the shapely sister wasn't. No way. No*how.*

For three years, she'd shared a friendship with him, but never, ever had she told him about her resentment toward Babette, about the pain involved with the constant comparisons of the two by everyone from their high school teachers to their family members. Never had she shared that with him, or with Babette, for that matter. It had been too personal, too painful, and too close to the heart, something she'd only confide with the man who'd help her overcome those insecurities for the rest of her life. But yesterday, she *had* told him. And more than that, she'd given him everything, *everything* she had to give. Her body, her heart, her soul. He effectively took them all. Then left her empty.

Clarise's jaw clenched tight. She'd wanted to convert despair to anger. Mission accomplished. Storming from the room, she left Ethan Eubanks, and her dreams, behind.

* * *

Whistling, Ethan entered the elevator and punched the button for the third floor. Yesterday had, without a doubt, been the most phenomenal day of his life, and today promised to be even better. Clarise had thrown him for a loop last night. She confided in him about how she'd always felt about her sister and therefore let him see her vulnerable side. Moreover, she'd seemed thoroughly convinced, finally, that she had no reason at all to feel inferior to Babette Robinson. No reason whatsoever. Then Clarise asked him to make love to her on the beach, and they had. Made love. Because what they shared on that cool sand was much more than mere sex. They'd bonded completely, physically and emotionally. Then the incredible woman had shown him an even more intoxicating layer forming the multifaceted lady he loved. Cotton candy sex. Yeah, it sounded sweet, but hell. He nearly came when he saw her in the flaming red outfit. Add a jar of cotton candy dust, a feather and Clarise's talented tongue, and he hadn't lasted longer than a first-time teen, which seemed to turn her on even more. She loved having that power over him, and hell, he loved giving it to her. Besides, it had provided her with an even bigger goal—making him come twice in one cotton candy tumble. Incredible, that woman of his. Rather, that woman who'd be his, if today went the way he wanted.

Shifting the large breakfast carrier to his left hand, Ethan fished the keycard from his pocket. It'd taken him longer than he'd planned thanks to the heavy Gasparilla crowd, but he wanted Clarise to have a delicious breakfast in bed. The Belgian waffles and strawberries would provide a unique treat for them to savor as he informed her of his plans for their future. He couldn't wait to hear her say she wanted the same thing. He'd felt it in her touch, seen it in her eyes, but he wanted to hear it affirmed from that beautiful mouth. Needed to. He'd planned it perfectly. They'd confess their love over waffles and strawberries, and make a beautiful memory, one that they could tell their kids and grandchildren. That thought made his smile widen even more.

Slowly opening the door to the room, Ethan prepared to wake Clarise with breakfast . . . and his love. But the bed was empty. So much for making breakfast in bed a part of the morning that he confessed his true feelings. Ethan fought the urge to curse at the crowd of people who had filled the restaurant and slowed his progress, but he wouldn't let his frustration with tourists ruin the moment. They'd simply share breakfast on the balcony, then he'd explain how he planned to make her happy, to satisfy her every need, forever.

"Clarise?" He walked through the room then peered into the bathroom, also empty. Turning, he walked toward the balcony and pushed the curtains aside. "Honey, you out here?" He grinned at his tone, so domesticated, but the balcony, like the remainder of the room, was devoid of life. Where had she gone?

Ethan stepped back inside and noticed his note from this morning in the center of the bed. He moved toward it, wondering if she'd written something at the bottom. Placing the breakfast carrier on the bed, he lifted the page. Nothing had been added. However, a second sheet of paper, smaller than the first, was tucked beneath his original letter. Picking it up, Ethan read her note, the letters sharp and slanted, nothing at all like her usual curly script. He also noticed more—the paper had several puckered areas where the words were blurred and misshapen, as though it'd been splattered with water. Or tears.

"No."

> *How could you claim to care for me and keep something so important from me? How stupid could I be? I thought my dream had come true, but it wasn't a dream. It was a nightmare. You. Babette. You should have told me, Ethan. Since we were girls, she has had everything I ever wanted. Everything. I guess this really isn't that different, but it hurts so much more.*

Damn. He was going to tell her about what had happened; he really was. Today, after he told her that he loved her . . . and after he told her that he'd never felt anything toward her sister. With his heart heavy in his chest, he continued reading, and it went from bad to worse.

> *I don't want to see you again. I mean it. Consider this my notice—I'm leaving the store. I won't come back. I can't. I never want to see you, never want to hurt this way again.*

He wadded the note in his fist and flung it across the room with fervor, then let a stream of curses fly, not holding back one overenunciated syllable. How had she found out? And why did she have to hear it before he had a chance to tell her himself? Surely Babette didn't tell her. She didn't want Clarise to find out any more than Ethan did. But Clarise had found out, and she'd been hurt. Who told her? And what exactly did they tell? He didn't think anyone knew about that night. Anyone besides Babette Robinson, that is, but obviously, someone did.

He crossed the room and yanked open the drawers her clothing had occupied. All were bare. No more sexy lingerie. No more cotton candy dust. No more Clarise. He moved to the bathroom, then the closet. Sure enough, any presence of Clarise Robinson had been removed from the room. Her toiletries, her suitcase, her clothing. Gone. Damn. Where did she go? As if he didn't know. The Clarise he knew, the Clarise he loved, would return home, back to her shell, probably never to venture out again. Thanks to Ethan. He had to stop her, had to tell her that he'd been trying to make her dream a reality, not squash it to a pulp. But squash it he had.

Okay. *Handle the situation,* his managerial instincts directed, and in this case, handling the situation meant finding Clarise and clearing up this mess. He snagged his phone from his pocket and dialed her cellular. "Come on, Clarise."

It went straight to voice mail. He left a message, but knew she wouldn't listen to it. With no way to reach her before she got on a plane, if she hadn't boarded one already, Ethan decided to do the only thing he could. He grabbed his suitcase and began packing. Sure, he'd planned on professing his love in Tampa, but Birmingham would do. He shoved everything in his bag and decided to make one more call. Before second-guessing his decision, he dialed her home number.

"Hello. This is Clarise. I can't take your telephone call at this time, but please leave a message. I'll be happy to return your call as soon as possible."

Ethan's brows lifted. Her message was probably a lie,

when it came to him. She wouldn't return his calls. Ever. Unless . . .

What the hell.

"Clarise, this is Ethan—don't delete this message. Not yet. I love you. There. I said it. And I'm on my way to Birmingham to explain. I want you, Clarise. And I want to work this out. I'll be on the next plane." He disconnected.

Okay, so it wasn't the romantic conversation he'd envisioned over waffles and strawberries, but desperate times call for desperate measures, and he'd just told a woman he loved her, something he'd never done before, over her answering machine. He loved her, and he'd make her see the truth about the two of them, after he told her the truth about Babette. Desperate times indeed. Leaving the condo, he hailed a cab, which was a miracle in itself, given the parades were set to start in two hours. "Miracles. I'll need plenty of them today," he said, sitting in the backseat while the cabbie jerked the car to life and steered him in the direction of the airport and, hopefully, in the direction of the woman he loved.

Five hours later, thanks to the cabbie's driving like a bat out of hell and the airline's having an available seat on standby, Ethan stepped off the plane at the Birmingham airport. His bag had been too large for carry-on, so he started down the concourse toward baggage claim. While waiting for the conveyer to distribute his luggage, he withdrew his phone and dialed her apartment.

"Hello. This is Clarise . . ."

He listened to her voice and waited for the moment when he could tell her, again, that he wanted to talk, to tell her—everything. Primarily that he loved her and wanted to spend his life with her, but before her message ended, the line clicked.

"You're Ethan, aren't you? I saw your name on the caller ID."

"Yes," he answered, stepping away from the noisy conveyer system when he recognized the voice. While he'd talked to Gertrude Robinson merely a few days ago, when she agreed to grant him passage past the complex guard, he hadn't seen her since she'd stopped by to visit Clarise during the store's Christmas extravaganza. At that time, she'd been hard to miss; her flaming orange dress and heels stood out like a buoy in the sea of winter garments.

"She doesn't want to talk to you," she said, snapping his mind from the memory with her statement.

"I know, but—" Ethan started; however, Granny Gert wasn't finished.

"She's not here anyway. Said she wanted to go for a drive and think, and she said if you called to hang up. If you came by, to slam the door in your face. If you left a message, delete it. Listen, I don't know what happened, but let me tell you, I've never seen her more upset, and I don't know if I can forgive you for that, even if you did say you love her."

"Did she get my message?" Ethan asked.

"Yes and no."

"Yes and no?" he asked, moving to a vacant bench away from the airport crowd. He sat down, then stood back up and paced while he waited for Granny Gert's answer. Clarise didn't want to talk to him or see him. So much for miracles.

"Yes, she heard your voice, but no, she didn't hear your message. As soon as you started talking, she pressed the delete button and left. Slammed the door so hard my great-grandmother's picture fell off the wall, and I'll tell you right now, it's a good thing that photo wasn't messed up, cause I'd have blamed you. And whatever you did to hurt my granddaughter."

"I need to talk to her, Ms. Robinson. To explain."

"What have you got to explain?" she asked. "What did you do?"

Ethan swallowed. Clarise hadn't told Granny Gert about Babette. That didn't really surprise him. Even though Clarise was upset with her sister, she wouldn't talk down about her to their grandmother. His Clarise simply wouldn't do something like that.

His Clarise.

Gertrude Robinson huffed into the phone. "No, don't tell me," she instructed. "She said she didn't want me to know, and I'll respect that, but I really thought the two of you were meant for each other. The fact that you've ended up being a horse's behind really ticks me off."

"We are meant for each other," Ethan said. He wasn't going to argue the horse's behind comment, since right now, he felt like a jackass for not telling her about Babette sooner. But he had no doubt that he and Clarise were meant to be together. He couldn't imagine being with anyone else. Didn't want to.

"She said she didn't want to see you again and that she was quitting her job. That certainly seems odd if she's meant to be with you, don't you think?" she said, her words whipping through the phone as though she'd slap him if she could reach her hand through the line.

"I didn't mean to hurt her," Ethan said honestly.

"Yeah, well, you did. And I think you should give her the space she needs."

"I need to talk to her. Then, if she still doesn't want to see me," he started, and once again, she interrupted.

"No," she said flatly. Then she blew an exasperated breath through the line. "Tell me something. Was it the truth? Do you love her? Really?"

"Yeah, I do," Ethan said.

She waited a moment, then whistled softly. "I sure wish my dear Henry was here to help me at times like this." She took an audible breath. "You sound so sincere . . . "

"I am."

"Henry, I sure hope this is the right thing," she mumbled, then cleared her throat. "Now I'm only doing this because I think my granddaughter may feel as strongly about you, even if she seems as though she'd just as well castrate you as speak to you right now."

Ethan's groin tightened involuntarily. "Ma'am?"

"That was one of my mama's expressions. I don't use it much, but it seemed to fit."

"Oh," he said, for lack of a better word.

"Anyway," she continued, "what I'll do is test the waters for you. I'll try to put in a good word for you, whenever she decides she's ready to talk about you again, and I'll let you know when it's safe to show up. That's the best I can do," she said, in a that's-my-offer-take-it-or-leave-it tone.

"I want to see her tonight."

"No," she said. "It's too soon. Trust me, I know my granddaughter, and she needs space. You should give it to her. If you really do love her, you will. Besides, she heard you on the machine and knows you tried to call. I'll let her know you called again. That's good enough for now."

"But—"

"No," she repeated. "If you show up, it'll only make

things worse. She isn't ready to see you, Ethan, and if you're as smart as she claimed—before she was mad at you, of course—then you'll wait until she is."

Ethan groaned. This was not what he'd planned, at all, but as much as he wanted to force Clarise to see him, his gut told him that Gertrude Robinson knew what she was talking about. "All right. For now. But I'm not going to wait forever. Hell, I don't know if I can promise to wait a day."

"Well, try," she said, then added, "Goodness, she's back. Gotta go." She hung up.

Ethan slapped his phone shut and cursed Clarise's wild sister. He'd thought he had handled that awkward situation last year as well as any red-blooded male could. He hadn't wanted to hurt Clarise by telling her the truth back then, and he honestly hadn't wanted to hurt Babette either. Hell, he'd thought that whole "incident" was over and done. But here it was, costing him the woman he loved. His mind traipsed back through time, twelve months ago, to the memory of Babette Robinson, smiling provocatively while wearing a white fur coat. And nothing else.

God help him.

Chapter 21

Clarise wore the sexy, skintight green sweater dress she'd put on for Ethan on Saturday. On that morning, she changed clothes after learning they were going to one of the family-oriented parades, but not before she'd seen the way he'd eyed her in this dress. Shannon and Jadelle had steered her right on this one, for sure, and now two more of Clarise's female buddies were helping her out. This time, her accomplices were Rachel and Jesilyn, both of whom were determined to help her forget all about Ethan Eubanks via a bar full of good-looking strangers and a bottomless glass.

She supposed there was a bit of spite involved with her apparel selection. Ethan would keel over if he saw the way guys at the bar drooled over her in the formfitting dress, and right now, that's exactly what she wanted. Ethan Eubanks. Dead. So there.

Grumbling, she stomped her strappy high heels through the crowd and ordered another daiquiri. She'd told he-who-does-not-care that she'd forego strong drinks from now on, but since he didn't care, what did breaking her word matter? Goodness knows he didn't seem overly concerned about breaking her heart, so what was a broken promise on her part?

"Feeling better yet?" Rachel asked, her pink eye shadow glowing beneath the bar's black lights.

Clarise accepted the drink from the bartender and took a big sip. "I'm getting there."

"Still won't tell us what he did?" Jesilyn asked.

Clarise simply shook her head. She didn't want to get into the details, particularly since both of her friends still worked at Eubanks Elegant Apparel. She really didn't want to cause any problems there. Ethan paid them very well, and they enjoyed the income and status that came along with being department heads at the prestigious store. Clarise had enjoyed that too, until yesterday. Or rather, until today, when she officially called Jeff Eubanks and told him she wouldn't be back. Bless his heart, Jeff tried to convince her to stay and even offered her an impressive increase in commission to accomplish his goal. But she declined. No doubt Ethan hadn't informed his brother of their awkward situation. Then again, he had no reason to tell Jeff. Clarise, on the other hand, had every reason to tell her sister.

She took another big sip of daiquiri and thought of Babette. They were different, that was true, but they had always been close. So close, in fact, that Clarise had never confessed to her sister how jealous she was of Babette's physique, not to mention her gumption, the way she went after everything she wanted—and usually reached her goal. Unfortunately, Ethan had fallen into the category of "something Babette wanted," and although Clarise believed she could eventually forgive her sister, she didn't believe she could ever be with a man who'd also been with Babette.

And she didn't know whether she could ever forgive Ethan for hiding the truth. She sucked a big gulp of daiquiri through the straw, then slapped her fingertips to her forehead to combat a piercing jab of brain freeze. Great, she couldn't even enjoy being bad with a daiquiri. Even her body wanted to make sure she stayed miserable.

Moving back into the fray of the crowd, she saw Miles Watkins working his way through the thick river of partyers. When he was finally within earshot, he yelled, "Hey, Clarise! It wasn't the same at the store today without you. You sure you're not coming back?"

"I'm sure," she answered, trying to be heard above the crowd.

"Wanna talk about it?" he asked.

"No."

One side of his mouth quirked up. "Okay. Well, do you want to tell me where Rachel is? She told me that they were taking you here tonight and asked me to come, but I haven't seen her at all in this crowd."

"There you are!" Rachel said, easing beside him and pressing a soft kiss to his lips. "Glad you came."

He grinned. "I didn't know I had a choice. You said to come or else."

"That's right," she said. "And you came."

"Yeah, I did."

Clarise watched them chat and kiss, all the while remembering merely two days ago, when she and Ethan were doing the same. The past week echoed in her mind like an intriguing movie trailer, rated XXX. She leaned against the bar and closed her eyes, then let her memories take over . . .

Ethan's mouth on her private flesh, licking and sucking

and teasing until she screamed her release. Their close call in the midst of elevator sex, and the way she'd looked in that gold-tinged mirror when she came. Beneath the bleachers, with the cool concrete pillar against her back and Ethan, hot and hard, pushed into her core. The way her breasts had looked when covered with powdery sugar, the way her womanhood looked when doused with the same sweet, white substance, and the way her body shuddered through a fury of orgasms when Ethan thoroughly licked her clean. Shower sex. Oh. My. Slick suds sliding between them, hot water pulsating against their flesh, her foot propped on the shower's edge while she held on to the ceramic handle. Ethan's head between her legs. And then the beach, the soft blanket teasing her nerve endings, while she asked him to make love to her. *"Make love,"* she'd said. Not *have sex.* A dastardly faux pas on her part.

And as the last vivid image pressed forward, she opened her eyes and gulped another mouthful of daiquiri, then fought another stab of brain freeze. Had that actually been *her* Monday night? Careful Clarise? Slipping into that red naughty-as-sin outfit and ordering Ethan Eubanks to remove every stitch of clothing? Getting turned on as he followed her commands, then covering his perfect body with cotton candy dust? Clarise shivered. She'd never received or given oral sex before this weekend. It'd been intoxicating enough to be on the receiving end, but when she'd run her tongue up and down his hard length, felt that hard pulse within her mouth as she'd taken in as much as she could hold . . .

Have mercy. Her nipples hardened. She had expected to hate it, even though she wanted to give him everything, to do *that* for Ethan because he'd done so much for her, she hadn't expected to become so enthralled in tasting him, or in feeling his blatant manhood within her mouth. But she had. In fact, she'd paid tribute to every mesmerizing inch. Licked him like he was a Tootsie Pop and she wanted to determine exactly how many licks it took to get to the center. It'd been wonderful, and she'd wanted to do it again, to feel *him* come apart at *her* mouth's command.

Evidently, she'd taken that memory through to the straw, because as she sucked the thing again, she got air bubbles. No way. It was gone? How fast had she drunk the thing, anyway? And did she feel light-headed? She didn't think she felt light-headed, but what if she was drunk and too far gone to know it? This could not be good. After tossing her DOA last Friday, she'd promised herself to stay clear of the deadly daiquiris for the remainder of her life. But she hadn't gotten a DOA this time. This one was peach, which meant it was safer, right? It'd merely make her relaxed, which was what she wanted, but her head was definitely feeling light.

"Want to dance?" a deep, throaty voice whispered against her left ear. She turned to see a tall, blue-eyed man with one of the sexiest smiles she'd ever seen. Blue eyes. Sexy smile. Her skin tingled from the close proximity of the blue-eyed stranger. But he *was* a stranger, and moreover, he wasn't Ethan. The guy's eyes inadvertently slipped down to view her breasts, prominently displayed within the green stretchy fabric.

Clarise frowned. Like Ethan had declared, they were taken, as was her heart. Her lip quivered, eyes watered. "I—can't." She looked up at him. No crystal blue eyes now. They were smoldering gray, the exact color of a cloud filled to its capacity with heavy rain. Or a tornado.

"Fine," he growled, then turned and left.

"What happened?" Jesilyn asked, wedging her way through the crowd to stand beside Clarise. "I saw the hottie come over. Did he ask you to dance?"

Clarise nodded.

"Is it that bad? You can't even dance with anyone else?"

"No, I can't," Clarise said miserably. "Jesi, I want to go home."

"Sure thing. Let me make sure Miles is good to take Rachel home since I'm the chosen one."

Clarise nodded, then watched Jesilyn, tonight's chosen one, or designated driver, inform Rachel that they were leaving.

"You gonna be okay?" Rachel asked, abandoning Miles momentarily to check on her friend.

"Yeah," Clarise said. "And don't get me wrong. This was a very nice idea, but I'm not in the mood for going out right now."

"Okay. Call me tomorrow, though," Rachel instructed, before returning to Miles.

"I will."

Ethan turned off ESPN's coverage of the upcoming Super Bowl. Normally, he'd have been interested in the teams, the stats, the superlative event of the year for the male population, but his attention wasn't on football. How could he think about the game without remembering the way Clarise had come undone during their phenomenal night of bleacher sex? He swallowed thickly, closed his eyes, and could nearly hear her scream of release.

Damn. He'd had enough of this waiting. He wanted to see her, and he was going to make it happen tonight. He picked up the phone and started to dial her number, but since he'd called twice already and hadn't gotten more than her answering machine, he hung up. Regrouping, he dialed his office. As he predicted, his brother was working late, obviously taking no chances at losing the wager with their dad.

"Eubanks," Jeff said.

"Did you hear from Clarise?"

"Not since this morning, when she quit. I guess you're still not up to giving me details on how you lost our best employee during your corporate bonding session?"

"I'm going to get her back," Ethan said, listening to the clicking of computer keys as Jeff apparently continued working as he spoke. Good thing one brother could keep his mind on the family business. Ethan couldn't begin to think of the store now, not until he cleared up this mess with Clarise.

"You're going to get her back?" Jeff questioned. "Are we talking professionally, or personally?"

"Both."

His brother's low chuckle echoed through the line. "Hell, Ethan, what do you do on these trips to make women hate you so much? You supposedly find the real deal with Clarise, and then she quits. And you know I haven't forgotten last year, and that hot little redhead who tried to claw my eyes out before she realized you had a twin."

"I really don't need you bringing her up again. Not now," Ethan said.

The computer keys stopped clicking. "Is this about her? Red?"

"You could say that."

"Damn, Ethan. You took her down there too? Is that it? No wonder Clarise was pissed."

"No, I didn't take anyone else to Tampa. I was with Clarise—only Clarise. But somehow, she learned about what happened last year before I could tell her, and she left."

"You're telling me Clarise left you over a woman you were with a year ago, when you and Clarise were nothing more than friends?" He made a grunt sound into the phone. "Doesn't sound like the Clarise I met. Talk about a jealous bone. Honestly, Ethan, is that really the kind of woman you think you want for life?"

Ethan leaned back in his recliner, closed his eyes and told Jeff the truth. "Clarise had every right to get pissed. 'Red' is her sister, Babette."

It didn't take Jeff long to process that little bombshell. "No. Way. Hell, Ethan, you were with sisters?"

"It's complicated."

"I'll say it is. Did you really think Clarise wouldn't find out?"

"I thought I had a little more time before I told her. Unfortunately, someone else beat me to the punch. I left yesterday morning to get our breakfast and came back to find her gone. Evidently someone told her in the interim even though I was certain no one else knew."

"Did her sister—Babette, was it?—tell her?"

"I don't think so, but who knows? Maybe. If she did, she obviously didn't tell her everything."

"What do you mean?" Jeff asked, computer keys now silent. "What else is there to tell?"

"Plenty. But like I said, it's complicated."

"I won't argue with you there. You've got complications to the max with this one," Jeff agreed, then had the nerve to laugh into the phone.

"If you're trying to piss me off, it's working," Ethan warned.

"Well, you've got to admit, this is one for the record books."

"If I could talk to Clarise, I could explain this mess, but she won't answer the phone," Ethan said, hating his situation. He'd fallen head over heels, and Clarise didn't even want to talk to him.

"Have you tried just showing up at her apartment?" Jeff asked.

"Twice. It's a gated community, and she refused to buzz me in."

Once again, Jeff's laughter surged forward, and once again, Ethan wanted to get his hands around his brother's throat. "I mean it, Jeff. You're pushing it."

After his chuckles subsided, Jeff relented. "Okay, okay. I get it. You're having a rough time, but I might be able to help you out after all. Miles Watkins was in the employee lounge earlier and said he was going out to meet Rachel tonight. Said the girls were going to try to cheer Clarise up and asked him to come along."

Ethan sat forward in his chair. "Did he say where they were going?"

"Struts."

"And you didn't feel the need to call and tell me?" Ethan growled, as he stormed across the room and grabbed his keys.

"I didn't think—"

That was as far as Jeff got before Ethan hung up and headed out the door.

* * *

Within a half hour after leaving the bar, Jesilyn pulled into a parking space outside Clarise's apartment. "Want me to come in for a while?" she asked.

"No, I'm fine. I'm going to sleep, anyway."

"Looks like you've got company," Jesi said, nodding toward the shadow peeking out the window.

"Granny Gert. She was worried about me. Good thing I came home early, since she won't go over to her place until she knows I'm safe."

"She's a sweetie," Jesilyn said.

"Yeah, she is."

"So, you're definitely not coming back to the store? I mean, it's such a great job, and you're amazing in the Women's Department."

"I can't work with him."

"He didn't come in today," Jesilyn said, her voice barely a whisper. "I kept expecting you to ask, but I thought I'd tell you."

Clarise had wondered whether Rachel or Jesi had seen him since they'd returned from Tampa. She had wanted to ask, several times, throughout the night, but she hadn't wanted to seem as though she cared. Even though she did.

"Looks like Jeff will keep running things through this weekend, then Ethan will come back," Jesilyn continued. "By the way, I'm going to miss seeing you every day."

"We can still go out at night," Clarise reminded.

"Yeah, we can. You call me if you need me, okay?"

"I will." Clarise climbed from the car and slowly made her way to the apartment. If she wasn't drunk, she was definitely tipsy, because the sidewalk seemed to tilt with every step. Finally, she put her key in the door and entered.

"I've got to go, Madge," Granny said, her hand clasping Clarise's phone. "She's home." Granny patted Clarise's cheek and motioned toward the couch, while she closed the front door and wrapped up her conversation. "Yes, I'll call you tomorrow. Good night." She clicked off the phone, then sat beside her granddaughter. "You okay?"

Clarise had heard the same two words repeatedly throughout the night. Every other time, she lied. Now, she didn't. "No."

"Was he there? At the bar?"

"No."

"But you kept thinking about him?" Granny asked, her hip pressing against Clarise's side as she wrapped an arm around her shoulders.

"Yeah, I did. I should have stayed home."

Granny nodded. "I was afraid of that. Give it time, dear. You've had your heart busted, and a heart takes a bit of time to heal, definitely longer than a day. It's too soon, even for going out with your friends. Why don't you take a nice hot bath, then get a good night's rest? Shoot, sleep as long as you want. You don't have anywhere to go tomorrow morning, do you?"

Clarise nearly moaned. No, she didn't have anywhere to go, because she didn't have a job, but she wouldn't worry about that tonight. Tonight she wanted to follow Granny's advice to the letter. A nice hot bath and a whole lot of sleep. Hopefully, the daiquiris she drank would help that sleep come quickly and deeply. Maybe the alcohol would even keep her dreams from pressing their way through, and she wouldn't spend tonight like she'd spent last night, dreaming of making love to Ethan. If she were lucky, she wouldn't dream at all. She took her bath, climbed into bed . . . and knew that she wouldn't be that lucky.

* * *

"Have mercy, Babette, what have you done?" Aunt Madge's penciled brows shot up so high they completely disappeared behind her platinum bangs.

Babette smiled smugly as she strutted toward the awaiting car. She pointed toward the open trunk and instructed the porter to put her bags inside. Then she turned to face her aunt and her mother, both of them as slack-jawed as she'd expected. "You like it?" she asked.

"No," Aunt Madge said. "Make that hell no."

"Mom?" Babette questioned, shaking her head to let the new black bob fall into place. The hair was sleek and sexy, like Catherine Zeta-Jones's "do" in *Ocean's Twelve*. Babette loved the look; moreover, she loved the change.

"It's—nice," Janie Robinson said. She stepped forward and hugged Babette. Then she sighed. "Does this mean you have some news? Maybe that you decided which job to take?" She sounded so hopeful that Babette almost hated bursting her bubble.

"Yeah, I have news," Babette said, making sure to let her excitement pulse through each syllable. She'd known her mother would equate her new hair with a new life. That'd always been Babette's signal of something major on the horizon. She'd left middle school a blonde, entered high school a brunette. Her first year of college, she bleached it out stark white, save one stripe of hot pink in front of her left ear. Since then, she'd been auburn, chestnut, platinum, red, even a funky shade of purple for a short time. Matter of fact, she'd had nearly every color imaginable—except black. But wasn't black the color for artists? And photographers?

Her hand clenched the strap of the camera bag, while her heart thumped a happy excited rhythm. She'd gotten some amazing shots on the trip, particularly of the men and women taking part in the cruise parties. In fact, she thought she'd made a definite decision regarding the area in which she wanted to specialize—fashion photography.

"Well, we're waiting," Aunt Madge said, interrupting Babette's thoughts. "I'm guessing your news is that some-body died on the boat, hence the black." Her brows went MIA again, but Babette wasn't going to let Aunt Madge's cynicism ruin her plans, as if anyone could stop her from doing what she wanted. Ever.

"I've decided I'm not ready for a full-time job yet," Babette said, while her mother forced a wary smile and a nod. "I'm going back to school."

"You owe me fifty bucks," Madge said, showing Janie her palm.

"Hush, Madge," Janie instructed then turned back to Babette. She visibly took a deep breath, let it out slowly, and cleared her throat. "Going back to school?" she finally managed, and amazingly, still maintained her forced smile.

Babette didn't waver. "To study photography."

"Well, for the love of Pete." Madge tossed her hands in the air.

"Madge," Janie warned.

"Yeah, yeah. I know. She's finding her way and all that crap, but all the schooling in the world ain't gonna put food on the table if she doesn't work."

Janie frowned at Madge.

"Give me the keys," Madge instructed. "I may have to listen to Blackie here and her new plan of attack on life, but I sure as hell won't do it while standing out here bak-ing." She waited for Janie to fish the keys from her purse and grabbed them. "What I wouldn't give to have a real winter in Florida every now and then," she grumbled, climbing in the car.

"Honey, how do you plan to pay for more school?" her mother asked, her voice surprisingly calm.

"I'm going to get a job in a photography studio," Babette said without hesitation. When Janie looked doubtful, she added, "Or maybe I'll freelance for a newspaper, or sell photos on my own." She shrugged, but didn't frown. She was happy about this decision, and no one, not Aunt Madge, her mother, or anyone else, was going to change that.

Janie sighed, but didn't ask additional questions about money, which was just as well. If Babette had made it this long with her part-time gigs getting her by, she could make it another four years. Easy.

"The black hair," Janie said.

"Yeah?" Babette asked, bracing.

Her mother reached forward and ran her thumb and forefinger down the front of Babette's inky locks, then tucked a small section behind her ear and smiled. "It's nice, but I've always been partial to your natural color."

"Red?" Babette asked.

"It's the exact same color as my mother's was," Janie reminded. "But—"

"But?"

"But like I said, the black is nice too."

Babette smiled. Her mother had never judged her unpredictability, had never told her she should be more like Clarise, the smart daughter with her original hair color . . . and a steady job. Janie Robinson understood how two girls with the same genes could be so different and even encouraged both of them to pursue their very different goals. Clarise's goal would soon be within reach. She'd informed

Babette that she only had one more semester before she obtained her degree. Babette was proud that Clarise was finally getting what she wanted. Though they were different as night and day, they cared about each other. Because of that, Babette knew Clarise would support her decision to go for the degree in photography.

"Everything's loaded," the porter said. He closed the lid on the trunk.

Babette tipped him and climbed into the car, where Aunt Madge was talking nonstop on her cell phone.

"Well," Madge said, "if you ask me, she should keep it up. The guy hurt her, so he's history. Enough said. Where is she now, anyway?"

Janie backed the car up, but shot a look at Madge and whispered, "Let me talk to her when you're finished."

"Mom," Madge said, "Janie wants to talk to ya." She handed the phone to Babette's mother. "Don't worry. He hasn't seen her yet," Madge told Janie.

"Who?" Babette asked, while her mother took the phone.

"Hello, Gert," Janie said. She nodded and did a few "uh-hmmms" into the phone, then asked, "Well, is she doing okay?" She waited again, nodded then frowned. "No, she hasn't called here. Guess she didn't want to talk about it, but I appreciate your letting us know. And thanks for being there for her, Gert."

"She need to talk to me again?" Madge asked loudly.

Janie shook her head, then disconnected. "She said she had to finish getting dinner ready. Said she wanted to cook Clarise her favorite tonight."

"What happened to Clarise?" Babette asked, knowing a favorite meal from Granny Gert meant Clarise was either sick—or upset.

"She had her heart trampled," Madge answered. She turned in the seat and pointed a finger at Babette. "I tell you one thing, if I was in Birmingham right now, I'd have that guy's balls on a platter."

"Madge!" Janie scolded.

"Oh, all right. Well, I'd make him pay," Madge declared. "In a way that was very . . . inventive."

"Who hurt her?" Babette asked. She hadn't even known Clarise was seeing someone, and she'd talked to her right before the cruise. Surely Clarise would have mentioned if she'd met a guy.

"That damn boss of hers," Madge said, while Babette's world tilted off-kilter. "What's his name again?"

"Ethan," Janie supplied.

"Ethan—Ethan Eubanks?" Babette shrieked, then did her best to maintain her composure when Madge looked at her questioningly.

"You know him?" her aunt asked.

"I've met him," Babette said, wondering just how red her face was, since it was burning like she'd eaten five-alarm chili.

"Well, next time you see him, you can let him know that her aunt is planning to personally fix him so that he sings soprano—permanently."

"Lord, Madge," Janie said. "Please."

"Oh, all right, but Clarise is tender. She's sweet," Madge argued. She shot a quick glance toward Babette. It lasted only a second or two, but it was long enough for Babette to see that her aunt, and probably everyone else in the family, was still comparing her to Clarise. She sure wished they'd get over it. But more than that, she wished the guy who'd evidently broken her sister's heart wasn't Ethan

Eubanks. Of all the men in the world, why did it have to be him?

"The thing is," Janie explained to Madge, "Gert believes Clarise is in love with him and that they'll work this out."

"In love with him?" Babette asked, her voice a little louder than she planned.

"From what Gertrude said," Janie continued, "they took their relationship beyond friendship during the company trip, but then something happened that caused Clarise to leave him down there."

The company trip. Babette felt sick. "In Tampa?" she asked.

"Yeah," Madge said. "That Pirate Festival thing. I tell you what, I'd like to take a sword to that guy, specifically his—"

"Honestly, Madge," Janie said. She continued to reprimand her sister-in-law, but Babette didn't listen. She was too busy concentrating on the implications of Clarise's getting with Ethan, and Clarise's getting upset with Ethan. Upset enough to leave him in Tampa.

Clarise knew.

"I need to get an earlier flight back," Babette blurted, then added, "I need to get back to Birmingham in case she needs to talk."

"That's a good idea, dear," Janie said, smiling at Babette via the rearview mirror. "I'm sure she'd like having you to talk to."

"Yeah," Babette said. *Or to strangle.*

Chapter 22

By the time Ethan entered his office Thursday afternoon, he'd been two days with less than six hours sleep, couldn't remember the last time he'd eaten and had a hangover the size of Mount Rushmore, thanks to his trip to the bar last night, a trip where Clarise Robinson never materialized since she'd vacated the premises long before he arrived.

Jeff looked up from banging the keys on Ethan's computer and grimaced. "You look like you were hit by a truck."

"I feel worse."

"And you came to the office?" Jeff asked.

Ethan dropped in a chair and snarled. "Looks that way, doesn't it?"

Jeff stood. "Wait here." He left the office while Ethan focused on making the room stop spinning. Within two minutes, his brother returned with an oversized mug. He shoved it toward Ethan's nose. "Drink it."

"I've had coffee."

"Not enough, evidently. Here," Jeff repeated. "Miles told me you came to the bar, and she'd already left. Oh, by the way, don't get any smart ideas thinking I'm going to get your coffee on a regular basis."

"I know you too well for that," Ethan said, taking the mug.

"And Miles also said you then decided to stick around and drown yourself in Jägermeister."

"Right again," Ethan said, raising the cup to Jeff, then sipping the bitter concoction that could have doubled as motor oil. "Hell, this is terrible."

"Thanks. I made it this morning, around eight."

Ethan squinted at his watch. "It's four in the afternoon."

"Yep," Jeff said, imitating Ethan's tone. "The coffee was cold, but I nuked it for you."

"Gee, thanks."

"Go on, drink it. You need something stout," Jeff instructed.

"Jägermeister is pretty damn stout."

"Obviously, but this is what you need, particularly if you're going to try to see her again."

Ethan gulped another bitter swallow and squinted through the horrid taste. "You know where she is?"

"No, but Rachel and Jesilyn should be able to tell you. That is why you came to the store, isn't it? To see them and get the scoop?"

Ethan shrugged. "I couldn't think of anywhere else to go. I tried calling her again, but I got her grandmother. Again."

Jeff laughed. "Well, after you drink that, you should be up to questioning her friends. If she isn't planning to go out with them tonight, they should at least know where she'll be."

Ethan sat the cup on the desk. "I've had enough of your

coffee, if this crap can be classified as coffee. I'm going out on the floor and talk to Rachel and Jesilyn."

"Fine, but you might want to stop by a mirror first. You look like shit. And the shirt is hideous, by the way."

Ethan glanced down. When did he get this shirt? And where? "Hell."

Jeff smirked. "My bet is that Miles had something to do with your new clothing purchase, though I'm sure he didn't think you'd wear it all day."

The shirt was pink, pale pink, with seven words in bold black font . . .

Don't Laugh. This is Your Girlfriend's Shirt.

"It's a good thing he's already had his progress report for last quarter," Ethan said.

"My thoughts exactly," Jeff said, grinning. "You gonna change?"

"Damn right," Ethan said. He stood up, gathered his bearings, then moved toward the closet in his office and quickly located a clean white dress shirt and slacks.

"Nice choice," Jeff said. "Pink really isn't your color."

Ethan glared at him.

"I'd say it's a good thing you have a personal shower here," Jeff said, pointing toward the bathroom door. "This would be a great time to take advantage of that too."

Ethan didn't say a word. He was so used to his typical role of being the logical brother that Jeff's sound suggestions threw him for a loop. Besides, he did need a shower, particularly before he found Clarise, convinced her that he'd done nothing wrong and proclaimed his love. All before the day ended. If he had to climb that damn eight-foot concrete wall around her apartment to get to her, so be it. No way was he spending another restless night knowing she was in the same city and wouldn't bother returning his calls. Enough was enough.

"Is that for me, or her?" Jeff asked, as Ethan neared the adjoining room, where a hot shower, fresh clothes and a toothbrush awaited.

"What?" Ethan asked.

"That look, the one that says you're going to get what you want, like it or not. Me or her?" Jeff asked.

"Both." Ethan slammed the door as he entered the next room.

After he'd showered in the hottest water he could stand, shaved and dressed, he emerged a new man.

"Where's the pink shirt?" Jeff asked.

"I'm burning it as soon as possible."

Jeff leaned back, clasped his fingers behind his head and grinned. "Gotta admit, I'm still surprised you walked through the store wearing it."

"I didn't, thank God. I parked out back."

"Good. I'd have to hurt you if you scared my customers away with your postdrunk attire."

"*Your* customers?" Ethan asked.

"Hey, they're mine this week."

"One week, and one week only," Ethan announced. "And that's because I was nice enough to help you out."

"It's because you wanted some time off with Clarise, and don't try to pretend any different."

Ethan smiled, feeling much better after the steamy shower. He had wanted time to explore the possibilities with Clarise, and explore they had. Unfortunately, it hadn't ended the way he wanted, but as far as Ethan was concerned, it hadn't "ended" yet. And it wouldn't, not if he could help it.

"Let me know what Rachel and Jesi say," Jeff said. "And by the way, I found out who told Clarise about Red."

Ethan's grin quickly faded. "Who?"

"Riley. Evidently, he'd gotten intimate with a few bottles of tequila and decided to stake his claim on Clarise. Guess he figured to do that, he had to get you out of the way."

Riley. "Jake?" Ethan asked. "He didn't know about what happened with Babette."

Jeff shrugged. "I'm simply repeating what Miles told me."

"What did he say? Exactly."

"Apparently, Miles and Jake saw her leaving your room last year around dawn, but they decided to keep the matter to themselves since they didn't want to hurt Clarise. But Jake obviously decided someone should tell Clarise the truth." Jeff held up his palms. "Hey, you never know what a guy will do when he's had too much of the bottle. I've heard some wear pink T-shirts."

Ethan glared. "I'm going to talk to Jesilyn and Rachel," he repeated, then added, "And Jake."

"He didn't come to work."

"Smart move," Ethan said, leaving the office.

Jeff returned to viewing yesterday's sales figures on his computer screen but didn't get beyond the first line before he heard the office door open. "Change your mind?" he asked, swiveling in the chair and expecting to see his brother.

"Yes and no," Preston Eubanks said, marching into the office as if he owned it. Then again, he did. "Yes, I changed my mind about the Florida position," Preston said. "And no, I didn't change my mind about your playboy status. Do you realize how many calls come into that office from

Atlanta socialites wanting to take *you* out? When did women get so bold?"

"When were they not?" Jeff turned the chair so he could view his father head-on, then he put his elbows on the desk and steepled his fingers beneath his chin. "You're home early."

Preston huffed grumpily and took a seat across from his son. "And not a moment too soon, if that man I saw storming from your office was my other son."

Jeff smirked. "He was."

"Well, what the hell did you do to him?"

"I didn't do anything," Jeff defended himself, grinning. "Clarise Robinson, however, has completely knocked his picture-perfect world on its ass."

"You mean off its axis, don't you?" Preston said, his weathered cheeks crinkling as he held back a grin.

"I said what I meant." Jeff leaned forward. "So, tell me why you're here before our contest ends, who you left running my store, and what decision you made about the Florida deal."

"We're done discussing your brother and Robinson?" Preston asked.

"Just figured we'd cover my tribulations first, then when Ethan gets back, I'll let you move on to his."

Preston set his smile free. "Damn, we're so alike, it scares me."

"So I've been told. Now give me the scoop."

"I'm home early because your mother realized that when Ethan returned from his trip, both of her boys would be in Birmingham. Therefore, she wanted to come home and do the whole family thing. Dinner is on Sunday at noon, and she's expecting both of you there."

"I know better than to miss it," Jeff said, making a mental date with his mother's pot roast for Sunday. "And who did you leave running my store?"

"Avery Miller. I reasoned that I should let him get used to the job, since I'm planning on his running the show there full-time, once you move to Florida." He quirked a brow and waited for his son's response.

"You didn't even wait to see who won," Jeff stated, somewhat disappointed that he wouldn't officially win the bet.

"Didn't really matter. I was going to ask you to oversee the Panache stores anyway, told Ethan about it a couple of weeks back, when he finalized the acquisition details. He doesn't want to leave Birmingham, so this will be perfect. He'll stay on top of the overall corporate structure, keep us focused on the future, and you'll oversee each of our acquisitions along the way, starting with the Southeast, then moving on to our national plan. I assume that works for you."

"Hell yeah, it works. But why did you accept the bet if you knew you were going to give me the deal anyway?"

"Ethan said he'd been trying to get you to come down and set up a new marketing plan for the Birmingham store, but he couldn't get you away from Atlanta long enough to pull it off."

Jeff shifted in his seat. "Nice try, Dad, but our little contest was my idea, remember?"

Chuckling, Preston Eubanks stood and moved to the window, then peered out at the neighboring buildings. "That's what we let you think, son."

Shocked, Jeff opened his mouth to argue his point, but halted when the office door flung open and a whirlwind of red and black—red leather minidress, black stiletto boots and jet-black hair—barreled in.

"What did you tell her?" she demanded. Her dark eyes glared at him as though he were evil personified, then they widened as she noticed Jeff's father by the window.

"Oh, don't let me stop you," Preston said. "This sounds extremely interesting."

"She thinks I'm Ethan," Jeff said. "Again." He turned to the woman. "You realize this constant bout of mistaken identity could easily slam a guy's ego."

She snarled at him like a Doberman. "You're Jeff?"

"Yeah, and you're Babette," he said. "By the way, I liked you better as a redhead. It suited the personality." Ignoring her dropped jaw, he started introductions. "Preston Eubanks, this is Babette Robinson. Babette Robinson, meet my father."

"Pleasure," Preston said, extending a hand.

She shook it, briefly. "I apologize for barging in," she said, a hint of humiliation in her formerly heated tone. "But I really need to talk to your son. Your *other* son."

Obviously bemused, Preston grinned. "This one isn't good enough for you?"

"Dad, trust me. You don't want to tick her off." His hand moved to his cheek, where she'd clawed him last year when she'd mistaken him for Ethan.

"If I remember right, I told you I was sorry for that"—she paused, then added—"misunderstanding."

"Yeah, you did," Jeff said. "Right after you attacked me."

Preston's chuckle reverberated through the suddenly quiet room.

"I need to speak to your brother," she hissed through clenched teeth.

"He'll be back momentarily," Jeff said, in no rush to honor her request. He was having fun sparring with the younger Robinson, and truthfully, he hadn't seen this much spunk in a woman since, well, the last time he'd seen Red. Her black eyes sharpened, shooting daggers straight through him, and Jeff decided making Babette Robinson wait, for anything, probably wasn't a wise move for self-preservation. "Listen," he said, "if you want to know what he told your sister, I can tell you. He didn't say a word."

Preston's bushy silver brows inched upward. Babette noticed. "I'm Clarise Robinson's younger sister," she explained.

"Ahh," Preston said, nodding, "I see the resemblance."

Once again, Babette's jaw dropped, but she didn't comment. She looked as though she were trying to figure out if Preston Eubanks was trying to pull her chain. Jeff glanced at his dad and knew without a doubt that he wasn't. Obviously, Preston saw the similarities in the two sisters—the same energy, the same excited and vivacious zest for life—or that's what Jeff assumed. Jeff sure saw the resemblance, even if Babette seemed unaware of the mesmerizing appeal of Robinson women, the sweet sexy one who worked for Eubanks Elegant Apparel *and* the spicy sexy one who stood before him ready to pounce.

Her mouth dipped down on one side, and she pivoted toward Jeff. "He didn't tell her anything?"

"That's right."

"So she doesn't know," Babette muttered, then glanced toward Preston.

"I believe I'll take a walk through the store," Preston said. "See how things are going with your latest advertising endeavors."

Jeff nodded, while she shifted from one foot to the other.

"Nice to meet you, Babette," Preston said before leaving. "I'm sure I'll see you again." As soon as the door closed, she geared up for another round.

"The reason she left him in Tampa had nothing to do with me?" she clarified. "Is that what you're saying? He didn't tell her?" With her red-glossed lips half-open, like a model striking a pose, she waited for his answer. Her eyes were wide with unhidden interest, cheeks flushed from anger. Jeff had the sudden, crazy urge to kiss her. Good thing he also had the vivid recollection of her nails clawing his cheek.

"He didn't tell her," Jeff repeated. "Someone else did."

She blinked, mouth snapped shut and eyes squinted in apparent disbelief, then she folded her arms and shifted her hips again. It was a damn sexy move, particularly with the knee-high stiletto boots she'd paired with the leather mini. Jeff had a brief impulse to ask her if she wanted to enter the store's best ensemble contest, but then thought better of the inclination. She wasn't here for Eubanks Apparel; she was here for answers, and he was being cruel withholding what she wanted. He cleared his throat. She might have attacked him last year, but Jeff had never been one to treat a lady wrong.

"Apparently, a couple of our employees saw you leaving Ethan's room last year. One of them has the hots for your sister and had a problem with her getting cozy with Ethan. So he decided to tell her that the two of you . . . "

"Oh, no," she gasped. Her eyes widened again, but this time it wasn't anger. She was upset. Babette turned and moved slowly to the chair. "Clarise must have thought," she continued, sitting down and dropping her head to her hands.

Her shiny black curtain of hair tilted forward to totally hide her face, but she couldn't hide the tear that landed on her skirt.

Jeff moved to the corner of Ethan's office that housed a watercooler and retrieved a pointed paper cup. The fixture sloshed loudly, while Babette Robinson sobbed softly. Damn, he hated to see, or hear, a woman cry. "Drink this," he said, holding the cup beneath her hidden face.

"Thanks." She sniffed, then looked up at him with eyes smudged terribly by watery mascara.

He withdrew a handkerchief. "You may want to use this."

She nodded and dabbed it daintily beneath her eyes, then stared at the black mess on the cotton.

"Don't worry about it," he said, propping his hip against the desk. "Have you talked to Clarise?"

"No. I just got back in town and wanted to find out what he'd told her first," she said, then shrugged. "Actually, now that I think about it, I wish Ethan had been the one to tell her. I should've told her last year, but I really didn't think she'd ever have to know." She shook her head. "God help me if Granny Gert finds out."

Jeff didn't know what to say to that. The tough little spitfire that had clawed him last year, then barreled in ready to repeat the feat a few minutes ago, seemed to be concerned about her grandmother finding out that she was a grown woman who'd slept with a guy at Gasparilla?

"I've got to find Clarise and tell her the truth," she said.

"Not without me you don't," Ethan said. He still looked rough around the edges from his bout with the bottle last night, but his features softened when he obviously noticed Babette's tear-stained cheeks. "I need to talk to her too."

She cleared her throat softly, as though dreading this

conversation, and looked away from Ethan as she spoke. "She doesn't know what really happened, does she?"

Ethan shook his head, while Jeff wondered what really had happened between the two of them.

"Why didn't you tell her?" Babette asked.

"Believe me, I've tried. She won't buzz me in her apartment, and she has your pit bull grandmother guarding the phone."

Babette's laughter perpetrated the tension in the room and accentuated Jeff's infatuation with the feisty Robinson sister. "Granny Gert is going to kill me over this," she repeated, then abruptly stopped laughing.

"Clarise won't tell her," Ethan said. "She's not like that."

Babette tilted her head and formed a slight smile. "You love her."

"I'd rather talk to your sister about that first."

"God, I hope she forgives me," Babette said. "I guess you're going with me to talk to her?"

Ethan nodded.

She stood, pushed her hand in the pocket of her skirt and caused it to dip down. Ever observant, Jeff caught a glimpse of tan flesh above its edge. She withdrew a car key . . . and caught him looking. Her eyes met his, and Jeff braced for a smart-ass remark. It didn't come. Instead, she lifted one brow and gave him a half smile. Well, hell. Once this "situation" was over, he was definitely going to give Red a call.

"We can take my car," Ethan said. "I'm assuming you'll be able to get us past the guard outside her apartment, and the grandmother inside."

Babette smiled. "I could, but Clarise isn't there." At

Ethan's downfallen expression, she added, "But I know where she is, and we'll take my car. It's probably faster."

"I doubt that," Ethan said.

"Don't," she instructed, and the feisty gleam in those black eyes returned.

When they left the office, Jeff joined in. For one thing, he liked the way Babette moved as she walked. For another, he wanted to see her fast car.

Preston Eubanks met them near the store's entrance. "Ms. Robinson, is that your—vehicle—parked outside?" he asked, his tone unreadable.

"I was in a hurry," she explained. "I'm leaving now."

Preston nodded, and Jeff became even more anxious to see what *vehicle* his father referred to. He didn't have to leave the store to find out. Babette had parked her car in the middle of the sidewalk directly in front of the entrance. Customers frowned at the multicolored CRX, but thankfully were willing to walk around it to enter. From the look of the uprooted azalea bushes, Babette hadn't been in the mood to navigate for obstacles as she sought Ethan Eubanks.

"I was in a hurry," she repeated.

"I'm going to refrain from commenting," Ethan said, gawking at the tire tracks in his previously well-tended landscaping.

"Good," Babette said. "Now get in."

"We can take my car," Ethan repeated, indicating the black Beemer in the side lot.

"If you want me to move mine out of the way," Babette countered, "then you'll let me take it."

Jeff admired her, issuing an I-dare-you glare toward his brother—and his father.

"Take it," Preston urged, watching from the store's doorway and attempting to welcome curious customers who were captivated by the hunk of junk in front of Eubanks Elegant Apparel.

Jeff walked to the driver's side and reached for the handle. "The door does open, doesn't it? Or do you just slide in like the Dukes?"

"Try it and see," she said.

He did. Amazingly, it opened, and a flurry of photographs hit the pavement by his feet.

"Oh no." Babette dropped to the ground and started carefully scooping the glossy pictures from the sidewalk to her arms. Jeff stooped down to help and quickly noticed the quality of the black-and-white images on the eight-by-tens.

"These are incredible," he said, holding one up and tilting it in the light. "Who is the designer?"

Babette glanced at the photo, a woman in a sexy halter dress descending a flight of stairs. "I don't know."

"What about the photographer? Who took these?" Jeff asked, reaching for the next photograph. It featured a couple dancing exuberantly on a gleaming wooden deck. A full moon reflected beneath their feet and placed them in an iridescent spotlight.

"I did," she said.

"Outstanding," Preston Eubanks observed, peering over Babette's shoulder at the photos now collected in their hands.

She opened her mouth, looked at Jeff questioningly then smiled. "Thanks."

"You realize it doesn't matter how damn fast this thing is if you never get it going," Ethan growled.

"Right." Babette took the photographs from Jeff, but paused a moment when her fingers brushed his. "We need to hurry." She placed the pictures in a folder on the backseat and climbed in. Then she cranked the car, backed up and peeled out.

"There's a lot of fire in that woman," Preston said from behind him. "She's got spunk."

"That's one word for it," Jeff said, watching the car speed away. "Complete opposite from her sister."

"Funny, that's what everyone used to say about you and Ethan," Preston observed, nodding at a customer walking toward the store. While Jeff pondered a response, Preston continued, "You know, there's something else that woman has too."

"What's that?"

"Talent."

"Talent?" Jeff questioned.

"I've been thinking . . . in order for Eubanks Elegant Apparel to really make our presence known in the industry, we'll need our own catalog. I'd want it to be superb, of course, with outstanding photographs."

"I'll see if she's interested."

"I rather thought you would," Preston said, issuing a cough that sounded suspiciously similar to his laugh and failing to hide his smirk. "And while you're seeing if she's interested, find out if she wants the job too."

"Where did you get this thing?" Ethan asked, indicating the vehicle that was currently trying its best to go from zero to a hundred before they exited the parking lot, thanks to the wild woman behind the wheel. What had he been thinking agreeing to let her drive?

"I'm kind of in a hurry to see my sister," Babette informed, using a hand-over-hand maneuver to peel onto the street at a ninety-degree angle and toss Ethan's shoulder against his door in the process.

"You can't be more anxious to see her than I am. But hell, I'd like to get there in one piece." His head still reeled from last night's tangle with Jägermeister, and this woman's driving "skills" weren't helping. Not to mention the fact that his stomach was in knots at the thought of seeing Clarise—and having her turn him down. The past two nights had been near unbearable, a powerful hunger to touch her again, hear her voice, hold her in his arms. Ethan thought of those big brown eyes widening when she realized how desirable she was and how the mere beginnings of her smile brought him to a near-combustible state of arousal, and not merely because of her sexual appeal, but because—she was Clarise. His Clarise. He hoped.

"I bought it from a junkyard." Babette took his attention off his apprehension when she screeched to a halt at a red light. "Perpetual college students don't have a lot of spare cash."

Ethan decided to try to keep his mind off of the looming interaction with the woman he loved. With Babette's driving, and the state of her "vehicle," he had plenty of other items to consider in the interim. Such as staying alive. As she punched the gas once more, he analyzed the car, which had provided a stark contrast to the storefront of Eubanks Elegant Apparel. The body on the driver's side was pale purple. From what he could tell of the passenger's side, it was pure Bondo. The hood was shiny royal blue with a hot pink swirling flame that looked like something off *Pimp My Ride*.

Babette cranked the window down, and cold air immediately whipped in. "Sorry," she said, "but this will help me stay alert to think clearly when I see Clarise. Strange, it didn't seem that cold when we were standing in front of the store. Anyway, I didn't sleep at all last night, and I sure don't want to botch this."

Ethan chose not to point out that he hadn't slept in *two* nights, or that it didn't seem that cold outside the store because they weren't doing 110 miles per hour on I-59.

"I never meant to hurt Clarise," she continued. "Sometimes I say things that don't come out right, but I really do love my sister. I just tend to act first and think later." Before Ethan could speak, she added, "And I don't need any comments about it from you. It's difficult enough trying to see you after what you did."

"After what *I* did?" Ethan shot, unwilling to hold his tongue on this particular matter. Babette Robinson's ability to act first and think later had damn nearly cost him a chance with the woman he loved. In fact, depending on how Clarise reacted when she heard the truth, Babette still could have done him in with her impulsiveness. No way was he taking the blame on this one. "What *I* did?" he repeated.

"Listen, we don't need to argue about this now," she instructed, as though she hadn't been the one to open this can of worms. "Let me tell you about the car." Then she barreled into another discussion without so much as apologizing for her insinuation that last year's fiasco was Ethan's fault.

He held back on the urge to throttle her. *"Marry the girl, marry her family."* Wasn't that the old saying? He shot a glance at Babette, driving like Jeff Gordon and talking ninety-to-nothing in the process, and not one of those words accepted any blame for last year. Then he thought of Granny Gert, playing watchdog over Clarise's phone and even her answering machine, since she'd informed him she'd deleted his messages. Marrying this family would be interesting, Ethan realized. A swift surge of excitement pulsed through his chest. Marrying Clarise—and her family—was something he wanted very much, interesting or not. God, he hoped the woman in the driver's seat didn't say the wrong thing when they got wherever they were going.

Babette didn't even break her stride in solo conversation. "The teenager in the apartment next to mine is a vo-tech student," she rattled on. "I let him and his classmates practice on Sylvia"—she patted the dash—"that's what I call her. Problem is, giving them that kind of free rein means I have no say in how she looks, so she's eclectic, wouldn't you say?" she asked, as though Ethan could get a word in. Damn, how long till they got to Clarise? Babette took the next exit by storm, rushing through the yellow light at the base of the ramp.

"But they also work on engines," she continued. "And by the way, we're nearly at Lowery. Hope she's okay, and I hope you're ready for this. Goodness knows I'm not. Two minutes until we're there," she concluded, pushing the gas pedal to the floor.

"Lowery State? The college?" Ethan yelled over the frigid wind rushing around his ears.

"You want to see Clarise, right?" she screamed. She glanced at Ethan as they entered the campus. "Oh Lord," she said, whipping into a parking space in front of a big brick building.

"What?" he asked.

"She didn't want you to know about her classes, did she?" Then Babette looked up and gasped. "Oh, no."

Ethan followed her line of sight—and saw Clarise. She'd evidently been walking toward the building's entrance and had stopped to view the car screeching into the parking area. Her hair was twisted up in some fashionable knot; it was the same style she always wore to work. Funny, he'd never looked at it back then and immediately thought of nuzzling her neck. He did now. He'd also never noticed how intriguing she looked in the long black leather coat that was her winter staple. He did now. He'd also never seen the look of disappointment, and then quickly of disgust, that turned her features from a combination of sweet and sexy to a definite expression of ready to kill.

"Oh no," Babette repeated. "I should have thought of how this would look."

Chapter 23

Clarise knew the owner of the rumbling muffler before she turned to verify that her sister's car was making its way on campus. She squinted to see Babette, whose window was down and whose hair was—black? She sighed. Wild and sassy and feisty Babette. No wonder Ethan, like most men, had been captivated by her charm. A hint of sunlight filtered through the cloudy sky, and Clarise saw the car more clearly and noticed that Babette wasn't the only passenger.

"Oh my," she whispered. She'd known this confrontation would come, had even suspected it would happen today, but still, seeing Ethan in the car with Babette had a strange effect on her senses. A strange, green effect, and she so wanted to be done with her petty jealousy of her sister. But here it was, rearing its ugly head again. Clarise stopped and stared at them as Babette whirled into a parking space. Then she watched her sister jump out and run up the sidewalk, her stiletto boots clicking wildly and her very black hair bobbing frantically.

Ethan's door opened, and he also climbed out of the car.

White dress shirt. Black slacks. A damn fine handsome man, and a man she thought would be hers. He looked at Clarise and gave her a rueful smile. Then he followed in Babette's wake, but at a much slower, much more controlled, and incredibly sexy pace.

"Clarise, it wasn't his fault!" Babette blurted. She placed a hand to her chest, her red leather-covered chest, and pounded at her heart. "It wasn't," she repeated breathlessly. "He didn't do anything wrong."

"I know," Clarise said, while Ethan made his way up the sidewalk, then stopped between the two sisters. He wasn't standing close enough for her to feel his body heat, or so Clarise thought, but she sure was feeling something, and looking at his questioning blue eyes didn't help it go away. No. She couldn't—wouldn't—get lost in those captivating eyes now. She looked at Babette.

"You know?" her sister asked.

"Yes," Clarise said, taking a deep breath and gaining the composure she'd need to tell them the rest. "It wasn't your fault, Ethan," she said, stealing a quick glance at the man she had loved. Who was she kidding? The man she *still loved.*

"You know what happened?" Ethan asked.

Clarise nodded, then forced her attention away from that face, those eyes, that mouth. Standing this close was way too tempting, particularly when she'd made up her mind.

"Who told you?" Babette asked. She folded her arms beneath her chest, which was covered in a short-waisted red leather jacket with a silver zipper up the center and made her look extremely sexy. It was an outfit Clarise could never pull off, thanks to her Robinson Treasures.

"Jake," Clarise said simply. "And I wanted to talk to both

of you individually, but this way is better. I'll only have to say it once. There was absolutely nothing wrong with the two of you sleeping together last year—"

"Wait a minute," Ethan started, but Clarise put up her hand.

"Let me finish," she said, and the two of them exchanged odd glances.

"Okay," Babette said. "Go ahead, we're listening."

Clarise wished Babette's linking of herself with Ethan in that statement didn't sting so much, but even so, she'd tell them the truth. "Babette, you probably didn't even realize that I felt, you know, that way about Ethan."

"I didn't," Babette verified.

Clarise swallowed, nodded. Man, this was tough. "And Ethan, you and I were merely friends, so naturally, you could have been with Babette, or anyone else, at that time if you wanted."

"Clarise, we—"

"Please, Ethan, let me go on. This is hard enough as it is." He resignedly nodded.

"But I've got to tell you that these past few days were more to me than a chance to check items off my sex list."

"You have a sex list?" Babette interjected. "Get out!"

"Babette," Clarise warned.

"Sorry," Babette said, grinning.

Grinning! Clarise's mind reverted to their childhood days, when the two girls had heated disagreements and dang nearly pulled each other's hair out by the roots. Literally. Then she also recalled how quickly after those fights that they would hug and make up and go back to normal, like they would do today, when all of this craziness subsided. And when Ethan Eubanks was out of her life for good.

"Stop smiling," Clarise cautioned her sister. "I can still get a good grip on your hair if need be, whether it's short and black, or long and red."

Babette's dark eyes popped open, and she smiled more broadly. "Yes, ma'am."

Clarise glared. Babette's smile disappeared.

"Clarise, I love you." Ethan's statement caused her heart to still in her chest. She'd planned this out so well, what she would say, what she would do, how she would feel. And Ethan pronouncing his love in the middle of it hadn't been factored in. At all.

"What?" she asked.

"I love you. I was planning to tell you Tuesday morning in bed over breakfast, but I'm not going to miss another opportunity to let you know. I love you. With all of my heart, I swear I do."

"Awwww," Babette crooned, which earned her another glare from Clarise. "Well, it's sweet," she defended.

"Ethan," Clarise said, her insides quivering from emotion. He loved her? Really, truly loved her? But how could she forget . . .

"Yes," he said, stepping closer and consequently, making her thighs clench in anticipation. Have mercy.

"I love you too," she admitted, and watched his face transform into a brilliant smile. "But," she quickly added, "I can't have a relationship with someone who slept with my sister. I know both of you were perfectly free to do *that* together, but I won't be able to be with you without thinking about it. I know I won't. And I, well, I'm not willing to have a relationship like that." Her lip quivered, throat clenched, eyes began to water.

"He saw me naked," Babette said, while Ethan's mouth fell open.

"I really don't want details," Clarise said, and she meant it.

"No," Babette continued. "He saw me naked—and he didn't care."

Clarise blinked. "What do you mean?"

"It was a misunderstanding," Ethan said, but Babette shook her head.

"No, Ethan, it wasn't, and it's about time I owned up to what I did. I swear, though, I didn't know you had a thing for him, or I'd never have tried to get him to sleep with me. As it was, though, he wasn't interested. Jake saw me leave Ethan's room, but it wasn't because he slept with me. It was because he kicked me out."

"I wouldn't put it like that," Ethan said. "As I recall, I suggested you'd enjoy yourself more in your own room."

"And I hated him for that," Babette said. "It was the first, and only, refusal I've ever received. It rather hurt." She let her lower lip pucker, but got no sympathy from Clarise, or Ethan.

"You didn't sleep together?" Clarise asked, baffled.

"I went to his room in a fur coat and nothing else," Babette said, as though this was a regular run-of-the-mill occurrence in her daily life. "Dropped that baby to the floor and stood there in all my glory, and he asked me to leave. Trust me, it wasn't one of the finer moments in my life."

Clarise looked at Ethan. Ethan looked at Clarise and moved even closer. Close enough to kiss.

"I'm going to go check out the new sound system the boys installed in my car," Babette said, turning and clicking away, while a couple of male college students whistled from the parking lot. Babette tossed her hair, then called back, "I bet they wouldn't send me away." She then sashayed toward her car, her hips swaying as though the sidewalk was a Paris runway, and she was the star attraction.

"You turned her down?" Clarise asked.

"Doesn't look as though it hurt her confidence any," he said, while Babette whistled back at her new admirers.

"No, it doesn't," Clarise agreed. "But it may very well help mine."

Ethan smiled easily. "How's that?"

"Why did you turn her down?"

"She wasn't the Robinson sister I wanted," he said.

"Uh-uh. You and I were no more than friends then, and you know it," Clarise said, moving toward him and placing a finger against his chest. She felt the strong, steady thud of his heart, and her breathing quickened.

"Okay," he admitted. "That's true. We might have only been friends then, but I knew enough to know that I didn't want to ruin that friendship by sleeping with your sister. Your friendship meant a lot to me, Clarise. It still does, but your love means even more." He winked. "You said you loved me."

"You said you loved me first," she said sassily.

"Exactly." He cupped her face within his palms and slowly lowered his lips to hers.

Clarise closed her eyes and accepted the warmth, the excitement, the intoxication of Ethan's kiss.

"Hey, Clarise, you're going to be late," a guy called from the doorway to the building behind them.

Ethan groaned reluctantly as he pulled away. "Late?" he asked.

"For my class," she whispered, her knees still wobbly

from his close proximity, and from the realization that her dream was coming true.

"What class?"

"Ever wondered why I never wanted to go for coffee on Thursdays?" she asked.

"You said you spent Thursdays with Granny Gert," he reminded.

"I do, after my fashion-merchandising class."

"Fashion merchandising?" he asked, grinning.

"I want to be a fashion buyer," she said, then added, "Actually, I want to be the chief fashion buyer for the Women's Department of a store that specializes in supreme quality garments, or that's what I put as my career objective on my résumé."

Ethan's grin disintegrated. "You're sending out résumés? To other department stores?"

She held her smile in check. "Is that a problem?"

"Hell yeah."

"Why is that?" she asked, eager to hear his answer.

"Because there's no way I'm going to let someone steal my best department head away, particularly if she plans to take on the role of my best fashion buyer."

Clarise winced as Babette pumped up the volume on the sound system in her car. Toby Keith's "I Ain't As Good As I Once Was" blared through the parking lot.

"That should be her theme song," Clarise said, but she couldn't help but laugh when she saw Babette head-banging her way through the country tune.

"Did you hear what I said, Clarise?"

"Yeah, but I've worked too hard at getting this degree to have the job handed to me. I want to earn it."

"And you will, at our store. Don't you dare send that résumé out."

"That sounds like a threat, Mr. Eubanks," she teased.

"It's a promise, Ms. Robinson, and while we're talking about promises, I've still got to keep mine." His blue eyes practically smoldered, and Clarise knew where this conversation was headed, directly to desire. She couldn't wait.

"What promise is that?" she asked.

"To fulfill every item on your sex list. We've still got one more to go."

Clarise's heart thumped out a happy beat, and her feminine core yearned to feel him, deep inside, once again. "One more to go?" she asked, feigning ignorance.

"Sex on the grass," Ethan said. "And I will keep my promise, as long as we can improvise the fantasy."

"Improvise?"

"Definitely," he said, looking extremely cocky and abundantly sexy.

"Improvise how?" she asked, while he slipped his hand inside her coat, then ran it up her side, to softly stroke the outer side of her breast. Clarise moaned softly, then whispered again, "Improvise how?"

Ethan brought his mouth to her forehead and kissed her briefly. "Sex," he whispered, then placed another kiss on the bridge of her nose. "On the grass," he continued, placing his lips to each eyelid, then one cheek, and then the other. While Clarise melted.

"Ummm-hmmm," she mumbled.

His mouth moved to her neck, hands moved over her body within the shield of her coat. Clarise's mind raced to the memory of the shower, and his talented mouth. Her nipples burned for that mouth, as did every other heated part of her body. "Sex—on the grass," she whispered breathily.

His path of kisses ended at her left ear, and he sucked the tender lobe. "Sex. On the grass," he repeated, the warmth of his words fanning her ear. "On our honeymoon."

Epilogue

Although each bridesmaid's dress was unique in design, they were all the exact same shade. Red. Bright red. It wasn't a traditional bridesmaid color, but then again, Ethan's bride wasn't known for traditional purchases. As the chief fashion buyer for Eubanks Elegant Apparel, the fastest-growing premier clothing retailer of the decade, she had to stay cutting-edge to remain ahead of the competition. And Clarise Robinson, soon to be Clarise Eubanks, was renowned for keeping their company ahead of the game. Though she'd merely started in the fashion-merchandising field after obtaining her degree last year, she had wasted no time at all accomplishing her goal, or rather *goals*. Clarise had an entire list of them that she enjoyed checking off periodically. She was known for lists, this bride of his, and even had one for the honeymoon night.

Ethan had been surprised this morning to awake and find her honeymoon "to-do list" taped to his mirror. He'd been even more surprised when he realized Clarise's idea of "to do" equated to things "to do" with Ethan. Most of the items they had done before, minus sex on the grass, which they vowed to first try on their honeymoon. But the last item was the one that made him laugh out loud. His bride, she claimed that she wasn't the feistiest of the Robinson sisters, but Ethan begged to differ.

He listened to the first notes of the wedding march, saw his bride exit the cabana and begin her walk, barefoot, through the sand. They'd decided to marry in Tampa. It had seemed the natural location, given their history, but the last item on Clarise's list wouldn't require hot sand or water or wind. It'd require a hell of a lot of what Clarise's Granny Gert called "gumption." On Ethan's part.

A persistent clicking took his mind off her list and caused him to change his direction of focus to the maid of honor. "Babette," he whispered, while trying to maintain his smile for the crowd. "Not now."

His future sister-in-law snarled at him, then continued clicking rapidly. "I will never get this shot again," she hissed back. "And I'm taking it."

"Give up," Jeff, Ethan's best man, mumbled in his ear. "She won't listen, and she damn sure doesn't care about your opinion."

Ethan could have asked if Jeff and Babette had a fight, but there was no need. The two were always fighting with gusto, then making up, with even more gusto. Evidently, the system worked for the two of them; they'd been together, on and off, for a year. It started when Babette developed the initial design of the company catalog. Jeff thought the black-and-white images lacked the sass of color; Preston had vetoed, saying they depicted class. The critics agreed with Preston, and Babette refused to let Jeff live it down.

Click. Click, click, click.

"I mean it, Babette," Ethan repeated, still trying to hold his smile.

"That wasn't me," Babette chirped. Then she turned toward the front row and winked at Granny Gert, seated beside Janie Robinson. Gertrude's camera smashed against her eyes, and her finger clicked the photograph button an amazing number of times, given her recent complaints of arthritis.

Ethan gave up on his mission to rid the place of monotonous-sounding cameras. Instead, he focused on the waves crashing on the shore behind him, the seagulls flying overhead and the woman currently taking his breath away. She kissed her father on the cheek, then accepted Ethan's hand.

"Did you get my list?" she whispered.

"Oh yeah."

"Going to give me what I want?" she asked, while the preacher welcomed the crowd.

Ethan visualized her curly script, and the one line of her list that had caught him off guard.

Strip for me, Ethan.

With her voice barely above a whisper, Clarise repeated, "I asked if you're going to give me what I want."

Ethan could have told her that he'd simply be returning the favor—that she'd given him everything he ever wanted and more. He could have gone on and on about how she completed his life and made him whole, but instead, he gave her what she wanted. The truth . . .

"Always."

About the Author

KELLEY ST. JOHN'S previous experience as a senior writer at NASA fueled her interest in writing action-packed suspense, although she also enjoys penning steamy romances and quirky women's fiction. Since 2001, she has achieved over fifty writing awards and was elected to the Board of Directors for Romance Writers of America (RWA).

Writing has always been St. John's first love. She thrives on creating new worlds and bringing readers along for the ride. St. John follows the philosophy that in order to write about life, you have to live. Therefore, she makes it her business to enjoy life to the fullest. Traveling is one of her favorite pastimes and one she doesn't indulge in nearly enough for her tastes, especially since some of her best ideas have been sparked by weekend getaways. She loves extended car trips that involve marathon plotting sessions and swears that she can plot an entire novel in the time it takes to drive from Atlanta to Orlando.

Visit the author's Web site, www.kelleystjohn.com, to read deleted scenes and enter her beach vacation contest.

See below for a preview
of Kelley St. John's sexy first novel,

Good Girls Don't

available now in mass market.

CHAPTER 1

Digging through her briefcase, Colette Campbell snagged her cellular phone in one hand and her contact's information sheet in the other, while her sister rummaged through her green glitter-embellished duffel bag to grab a bright pink, misshaped vibrator. Both girls were notorious for bringing their work home; tonight was no exception.

"Amy, what the heck is that for?" Colette eyed the odd curve at the end of the oversized contraption. In her opinion, Amy's current employer had taken its passion line to the extreme, with the most popular products designed by her imaginative sister. But they were shooting for the next must-have sex toy. And Colette had to admit several of Amy's creations were already must-haves for her own bedroom.

Too bad they were the ones meant for singles.

"This baby will put Adventurous Accessories over the top," Amy said, grinning with unabashed pride. She made the same claim with each of her toys, though Colette chose not to point that out.

At merely twenty-two, Amy Campbell already had a mind for business. Coupled with an affinity for the intricacies of sex, which she'd obviously acquired from their mother, Amy had a hot combination for today's boudoir market. Consequently, she fully intended for one of her personally designed products to become the next Jack Rabbit.

Like practically every other female in America, Colette had watched Kim Cattrall's Samantha lose her senses over the unique vibrator on *Sex and the City*. And, like practically every other female in America, she'd wasted no time purchasing a set of talented rabbit ears of her own.

Thank God. Lord knows that battery-operated bunny helped her numerous times when Jeff hadn't got the job done. At least she had one "energize-her" in the apartment during her six months dating Mr. Perfect.

"So what does it do?" Colette asked, accustomed to Amy's tendency of bringing her sex trinkets home to show off her latest idea.

While Amy played Vanna, running a finger down the smooth length of the toy, Colette scanned her client's data sheet. My Alibi's customers were extremely specific regarding when she should make calls. In this case, the woman wanted a message left while the contact was gone. A typical request. For some reason, the lie seemed more believable when heard on an answering machine.

Colette's eyes ventured to the referral line on the bottom of the front page. "Amy?"

"Yeah?" Amy said, still grinning at the toy.

"What's up with this?" She pointed to the name scribbled across the page. "Referred by Amy Campbell?" Colette read the annotation made by the My Alibi sales associate.

Client specifically requested Colette Campbell as her sales representative.

"Oh, I can't believe I forgot to tell you," Amy said, scooting closer to Colette on the couch. She pointed to the data sheet. "That's a friend of mine. She needed a way to spend a week with her boyfriend, and I told her about My Alibi."

"You're helping your friend cheat on her husband?" Colette didn't like lying for a living, and she didn't plan to do it much longer, only until she had enough money to start her boutique. "I thought you agreed that what these people do isn't right."

"I know it isn't, but Erika isn't lying to a husband."

Colette's attention moved back to the information sheet, specifically the "Relationship to Client" line. "Her uncle?"

"She's found the love of her life, but she doesn't think her uncle will approve," Amy explained, shrugging as though this were no big deal. "She needs an alibi for a week to spend some alone time with Butch and see if he really is the one."

"Why does she have to lie to her uncle to spend a week with her boyfriend?" Colette didn't like the sound of this. What was Amy getting her into?

"He's her guardian, and he's a bit overprotective," Amy explained; then, at Colette's raised brows, she continued, "Listen. I knew you wouldn't help on your own, so I had her go through My Alibi. That way it's merely another client, right? And besides, she's my friend and needs help. You won't let me down here, will you?"

Letting Amy down was something Colette was determined not to do. And Amy knew it. Occasionally, like right now, she used it to her advantage. However, there was no way Colette would help if Erika wasn't an adult.

"You can't hire My Alibi unless you're eighteen. And if she isn't eighteen, I can't help her."

"She is eighteen. Her birthday was last month."

Sure enough, the client's date of birth on the application matched Amy's statement.

"Come on, she's an adult looking for an alibi, and she isn't lying to a husband. She simply wants to spend some time with her boyfriend. You'll help her, right? Give her a chance at true love?" Amy asked. "For me?"

Colette sighed. "All right," she conceded. "I'll help her."

Amy leaned forward and hugged her sister, while her long ponytail smothered Colette's face and made her smile.

"You're rotten, you know that, don't you?" Colette asked.

"Yep," Amy agreed, moving back to her bag and holding up the new toy. Her mission had been accomplished, so naturally, she turned her focus back to her newest product.

"Tell your friend I'll help her this one time, but I don't plan to do it again. She really shouldn't be lying to her uncle."

"Got it," Amy said, punching a finger in the air for emphasis, but her eyes never ventured from the vibrator. "Isn't it amazing?" She switched her voice to produce infomercial appeal, flicked the switch and started the thing buzzing. "This exclusive curve allows the smooth, pulsing tip to hit the G-spot precisely. Every time. And if that doesn't pique your interest, feast your eyes on this." Sounding like a late-night home-shopping host, she pushed a small button on the handle with her index finger. "Ahhh, see? The end lights up like a rainbow."

Holding the glowing contraption against her forearm, Amy let the pulsating head play against her skin while she giggled. "Cool, huh?"

Okay. Colette failed to see why illuminating like a multicolored strobe light would be of importance, particularly if you considered where those colors would be located *if* and *when* they hit the proverbial bull's-eye. But she humored Amy, nonetheless. "Yeah, sis. Real cool. If you have a spot to find."

Amy punched the switch and dropped Pinky to the couch, where it rolled like a deformed banana until lodging between the back of the sofa and the cushion. "No way. You haven't found it? *Jeff* hasn't found it? Geez, you don't know what you're missing."

Colette merely smirked. From what she could tell, Jeff did good to find his own part, much less hers. But rather than elaborate on how extremely dull those six months had been, she dialed the number listed on the My Alibi fact sheet.

"Seriously? Did he, you know, even look for it?" Amy asked, obviously bewildered at this revelation.

Did he look for it?

Hmmm. Let's think about it. Well, that'd be a definite no. Matter of fact, all he looked for, as far as Colette could tell, was his own satisfaction. Which he obtained. Every time.

And pretty dang quick, at that.

Funny thing was, Jeff looked and acted every part the ladies' man. Strutted around with his much-too-muscled chest puffed out, his politician's smile plastered on tight and every wavy hair in place. Oh, and not a single tan line on his body, thank you very much. Or thank his home-tanning bed, coupled with his ritual to make certain he stayed on each side the same number of minutes.

Colette had mistakenly believed the attention he paid to his looks stemmed from his business, rather than his mega-ego. He'd used his primary asset, his body, to promote a growing chain of health-food stores; therefore, he had to look healthy, right?

Of course, the result was quite phenomenal. Folks saw him as their goal and bought his stuff aplenty. The fact he'd tacked on a couple of Atlanta's Best Body titles didn't hurt either. Yep, he was pretty to look at, all right.

But a dud in the sack.

Heck, Colette would've bet plenty of money on his ability to please.

She'd have lost that bet.

Shoot, she'd have put money on him staying true too. Ditto for losing the wager.

"In case you've forgotten, Jeff and I have been over for two months. Matter of fact, I heard he put a ring on Emily Smith's finger last weekend. Just as well, since he was banging her the whole time we were together. Hey, who knows? Maybe he found *her* G-spot. He sure never found mine."

That sounded bitter. And she was *not* bitter. Relieved was more like it. She'd tried to make the whole commitment thing work, in spite of Jeff leaving much to be desired in the bedroom. In her bedroom, anyway. As she learned two months ago, he'd made his way through plenty of other beds during their time together.

"Maybe you should try this out. It'll find the spot." Amy picked up the translucent pink vibrator and held it to her cheek. "It's waterproof too. And you don't even need a man. Really, you should give it a trial run."

Don't need a man. Yep, that'll fit the bill.

"Maybe I should." Colette laughed. Heck, maybe a pink, rainbow, light-up G-spot finder was what she needed to get her out of this funk. Twenty-nine-and-knocking-on-thirty, she was still searching for a guy who could carry on an intelligent conversation, had at least some semblance of a career plan and—wonder of wonders—could make her toes curl as much as one of Amy's toys. She was beginning to think she might have to let go of one of the three qualities. But if anything had to fly out the window, it would *not* be curling toes.

Amy lowered the vibrator and focused on the phone perched against her sister's ear. "Hey, Colette, you dialed the number, didn't you?"

Colette's laughter lodged in her throat. She hadn't heard the answering machine pick up. But there'd definitely been a ring on the other end.

Hadn't there?

Yeah, she'd heard a ring. When had it stopped? More importantly, how much of their sisterly conversation had been recorded?

Dang.

A path of heat blazed from her throat to her face. She'd have to do major damage control at the office tomorrow for this faux pas. How do you explain leaving a message about sex toys on a customer's voice mail?

But she couldn't hang up. She'd used the cellular provided by My Alibi, and the fictitious name Amy's friend had chosen for her company would be displayed on the caller ID.

She gathered her wits. So this wouldn't be her best performance as a My Alibi representative; it'd be okay. She'd simply apologize and begin her regular spiel.

Taking a deep breath, she prepared to start the process of prevarication via the uncle's answering machine.

Then she heard a responding exhalation on the other end.

No. Way. There was *not* a living, breathing person listening to her now. Hearing her discuss G-spots, no less, when she supposedly represented a computer-graphics training company. Certainly Erika's uncle hadn't answered the phone, heard her talking and eavesdropped on that steamy little conversation with Amy. Had he?

Only one way to find out. Tossing a wary glance to her sister, she mustered up her courage. "Hello?"

"Well, hello."

THE DISH

Where authors give you the inside scoop!

♥ ♥ ♥ ♥ ♥ ♥ ♥ ♥ ♥ ♥ ♥ ♥ ♥ ♥ ♥

From the desks of
Diana Holquist and Kelley St. John

Dear Readers,

Pirates and gypsies, swords and prophecies, ruffled shirts and peasant skirts—all in present-day America! It is so cool that we get to write this letter about two books with so much in common. So gather up your eye patch, your crystal ball, and your handsome hero and settle in to learn what happens when two authors discuss their unique book pairing in this author-to-author interview.

Diana: So, Kelley, some scenes from your book *Real Women Don't Wear Size 2* (on sale now) take place at Gasparilla. What the heck is that? And what do your characters do there?

Kelley: You don't know what Gasparilla is? Where are you from?

Diana: I'm a northerner. Hey, you thought my book took place in Boston. It's Baltimore.

Kelley: B-cities. Whatever. They're *all* cold. But to answer your question, Gasparilla is a festival that takes place every year in Tampa, where prominent business-men dress up as pirates, board the Jose Gasparilla ship, and storm Tampa (even requiring the mayor to surrender the city each year). My heroine, Clarise, is a curvy lady who has no trouble helping other ladies embrace their voluptuous figures, but has never completely ventured out of her own shell. She heads to Gasparilla to find her wild side amid the adventurous pirates.

Diana: I love pirates! I mean, I love my husband, but I love *reading* about pirates. My book is full of gypsies.

Kelley: Gypsies and pirates are always getting mixed up. (Sort of like, you know, Boston and Baltimore . . .)

Diana: Exactly. Put on an eyepatch and a ruffled shirt, and what's the difference? (Oooh, my heroine would be mad if she heard me say that!) But the point is, pirates and gypsies can really set a modern woman free.

Kelley: Mmmmm . . . I certainly like a ruffled shirt. Though Seinfeld's puffy shirt didn't do a thing for me. Does your hero wear one? (A ruffled shirt, that is, not a puffy one.)

Diana: My hero is a carpenter, so he's a jeans-and-T-shirt kind of guy. But Cecelia, my heroine, is on the cover of *Make Me a Match* (on sale now) in full gypsy regalia. Although she could be a pirate, if you squinted.

Kelley: Love that cover! And your gypsy can tell the name of a person's One True Love?

Diana: Exactly. Imagine what would happen if you really did have One True Love on this earth—and a gypsy psychic could tell you his name. Of course, he might be your worst nightmare. Or maybe, like Cecelia in my book, you're already engaged to someone else and you don't want anything to do with your One True Love— or your gypsy heritage.

Kelley: Or what if you weren't sure your One True Love would appreciate your abundance of, er, curves. My heroine, Clarise, is finally going to let her curves shine for her friend/boss/fantasy, Ethan Eubanks, at Gasparilla. Did I mention Gasparilla is like Mardi Gras, but with pirates and swords? Clarise wants to set her inhibitions, and her Robinson Treasures, free. (I'll let you guess about those Robinson Treasures.) So tell me, can your gypsy *really* know Cecelia's One True Love? Or is that something I get to learn when I read your fabulous book?

Diana: What? Sorry, I was busy wondering about those Treasures . . . You know, I think I've had enough of this chatting. I've got to get reading.

Kelley: Sounds like a great idea. Judging from your feisty cover, I can tell that Cecelia is ready to have a whole lot of fun and find a whole lot of love. Her One True Love, right?

Diana: Exactly. Well, maybe. Sometimes, you know, gypsies lie.

So readers, we're giving you a taste of pirates and gypsies, shapely women and psychics, and that ideal (and sometimes, not so ideal) situation when you meet that One True Love. Read them and let us know what you think! We'd love to hear from you!

Sincerely,

Diana Holquist

Kelley St. John

MAKE ME A MATCH

REAL WOMEN DON'T WEAR SIZE 2

www.dianaholquist.com

www.kelleystjohn.com